# FALL WITH
# HONOR

# FALL WITH HONOR

## A NOVEL OF
## THE VAMPIRE EARTH

# E. E. KNIGHT

A ROC BOOK

ROC
Published by New American Library, a division of
Penguin Group (USA) Inc., 375 Hudson Street,
New York, New York 10014, USA
Penguin Group (Canada), 90 Eglinton Avenue East, Suite 700, Toronto,
Ontario M4P 2Y3, Canada (a division of Pearson Penguin Canada Inc.)
Penguin Books Ltd., 80 Strand, London WC2R 0RL, England
Penguin Ireland, 25 St. Stephen's Green, Dublin 2,
Ireland (a division of Penguin Books Ltd.)
Penguin Group (Australia), 250 Camberwell Road, Camberwell, Victoria 3124,
Australia (a division of Pearson Australia Group Pty. Ltd.)
Penguin Books India Pvt. Ltd., 11 Community Centre,
Panchsheel Park, New Delhi – 110 017, India
Penguin Group (NZ), 67 Apollo Drive, Rosedale, North Shore 0632,
New Zealand (a division of Pearson New Zealand Ltd.)
Penguin Books (South Africa) (Pty.) Ltd., 24 Sturdee Avenue,
Rosebank, Johannesburg 2196, South Africa

Penguin Books Ltd., Registered Offices:
80 Strand, London WC2R 0RL, England

First published by Roc, an imprint of New American Library,
a division of Penguin Group (USA) Inc.

First Printing, July 2008
1   3   5   7   9   10   8   6   4   2

RoC  REGISTERED TRADEMARK — MARCA REGISTRADA

LIBRARY OF CONGRESS CATALOGING-IN-PUBLICATION DATA
Knight, E. E.
Fall with honor : a novel of the Vampire Earth / E. E. Knight.
p. cm.
ISBN: 978-0-451-46210-7
1. Valentine, David (Fictitious character)—Fiction. 2. Human-alien encounters—Fiction. I. Title.
PS3611.N564F35 2008
813'.6—dc22          2008000745

Set in Granjon
Designed by Elke Sigal

Printed in the United States of America

*To the memory of Thomas Manning,*
*a fine artist and a finer friend*

*I have also remarked, fellow-soldiers, that such as are eager in the field to preserve their lives at any rate, for the most part perish wretchedly and ignominiously, while I see that such as reflect that death is to all men common and inevitable, and seek in battle only to fall with honor, more frequently, from whatever cause, arrive at old age, and live, while they live, with greater happiness.*

—XENOPHON, *ANABASIS*

# CHAPTER ONE

*F*orward Operating Base Rally, Missouri, September, the fifty-fourth year of the Kurian Order: the Show Me state has a flat bootheel stomping a corner of northeast Arkansas.

Those who pass through the region remember only a dullish stretch of Midwestern farm country running along the river, pierced by bayous and bisected by interstate. There's little to distinguish it on the surface. But beneath the good topsoil the bootheel fascinates on a geologic scale. It is home of the New Madrid fault line that gave way in the chaos of 2022, causing the Mississippi to run backward as far north as St. Louis.

The destruction that resulted from the earth writhing like a heavy sea made the region ill-omened. Everyone who could move did, to the better-preserved areas of Missouri at first, and then south or farther west once the Grogs showed up.

Then came Southern Command.

The few Kurian Lords organizing the area fell rather easily, surprised by the strength and tenacity of the guerrillas. With the Kurians gone, the area became another fought-over piece of no-man's-land between the Mississippi and the Ozark Free Territory, not as well patrolled as the Tennessee–Little Rock corridor or as danger-filled as the bushwhack country in southern Missouri. A powerful smuggler named Shrivastava set up shop around an old fireworks warehouse, running whatever he could between the Kurian Zone, Grogs, and Free Territory. He's long since retired to the older family holdings on a remote piece of Carolina coastline, but a nephew still runs the business, now under the probing noses of Southern Command forces directed by the new United Free Republics.

*Rally Base, set up just down the road as though keeping the post company, is only a couple of acres in size, including the killing ground outside the wire and blockhouses.*

*Of course the business isn't quite as profitable these days. There's no more smuggling of captive souls into the Kurian Zone or antitank rockets capable of taking out small watercraft up to the Grogs. But thanks to the soldiers at Rally Base, there's also less of a chance of a team of Reapers coming through and killing everyone who doesn't make it down the hidey-hole in time, or of Grogs looking to prove themselves in battle, killing security men and stealing livestock. Shrivastava & Family have shifted with the trade and opened a tiny brewery, soap mill, and bakery, growing rich on a few dozen lesser transactions a day rather than the bigger scores the old man saw.*

*Civilization, after a fashion, has returned.*

*The family business is well-off enough to hire hands to take care of the endless outside labor that keeps the bake stove burning and the meat locker filled.*

*One of their hands, a lean, bronze-skinned man with a thick head of black hair tied back from his sweating face, works shirtless in the dust of the firewood pile, reducing wholes to quarters with a shining ax. His lower back is a topographical map of old burns, his face is scarred from the right eye down, and there's something a bit off about his jaw. If he were talking you'd guess he'd just said something ironic.*

*But he's not wasting breath, talking to himself or his surroundings. He works with the easy, constant pace of an outdoor man who knows the optimum operating speed of his body, picking up the wholes, splitting them, and then retrieving the quarters with a precise economy of effort that would do a machine credit.*

*He moves with a hint of a limp as he retrieves another whole for the splitting stock. He casts quick glances all around as he works, and his momentary stiffening when one of the soft-stepping daughters of the house comes out to throw potato peelings in the pig meal suggests that he's a hard man to sneak up behind.*

*The slight, unconscious shift in his grip of the ax suggests that it might even be dangerous.*

†

David Valentine would always remember it all beginning the day he got his first gray hair.

Or, to be more accurate, the day he *noticed* his first gray hair. Three of them, in fact. For some reason all of them decided to erupt on his right temple. He'd used the mirror to shave that morning, as he had to go over to the fort to teach, and picked them out as he combed his hair back.

They reminded him of his father. His mother had never gone gray, but he had only a vague idea of her age when the Valentine clan died. His father had lots of them, which was natural for a man of fifty-six.

That's what Father Max had burned into the cross, anyway.

He'd chopped firewood for Father Max from the age of eleven until he joined up with the Cause at seventeen.

He split and stacked his last piece of firewood, wiped the ax clean with an oilcloth and hung it up in the toolshed.

YLPPUS YXALAG read the reversed letters running the roofline of the big trading post, bakery, diner, and repair shop. All the buildings of Galaxy Supply except the family home were painted in a durable barn red, though someone with an artist's eye had added white and green accents around the doors and barred windows, with smaller decorations depicting grape vines and cheery songbirds.

An unusually hot late September day was working up. The sun was hardly blocked at all by decades-old particles riding the upper atmosphere. Some said the sky was washing itself; others maintained the haze had swirled off to the southern hemisphere for a few years and would be back, the way it had returned in '43.

He's sweated enough to discard his shirt, both to preserve its condition—he had to teach at the base today—and keep himself cool. He used a bucket, a rag, and some of the milky Shrivastava soap to clean himself up in the outside sink before going in for his breakfast.

The two Shrivastava girls dodged nimbly around him in the back kitchen, giggling to each other with some private joke. There had to be more dodging these past few days in the baking kitchen than usual. Mr. Shrivastava had extracted an old pizza oven from an establishment up the interstate toward Cairo and was converting it to wood fire. Welding tools and tanks were interspersed with the usual bread racks.

The girls, rich black hair bound up in kerchiefs to keep the flour out, didn't give him a second look. They had teenage soldiers swaggering out their first forward duty to make eyes at daily, and Valentine was coming up on thirty-three, battered, and dragging a leg. Besides, he was hired help.

Not that it would have done him much good to be eighteen again. He'd been too shy to flirt back then. He would have just discreetly admired their caramel skin and wide, inviting eyes from the other side of the pastry case.

He had toast and eggs for breakfast, with a side of peppery okra leftover from last night's dinner. With real black tea. The family liked tea and through their trading connections had some strong blend that left a far more pleasant aftertaste than coffee.

The fresh food was why he worked for the Shrivastava clan rather than living in the civilian squats blistered off the base.

"Finished the firewood so fast?" Mrs. Shrivastava said, her quieter sister in tow, as always. Mrs. Shrivastava loved him to death, though in her case love manifested in cramming food down his throat. As soon as he cleared one plate she'd appear with another, and if he didn't dig into that with enough gusto he sometimes worried that she'd ram it in with one of the long wooden spoons she used to fill his dish. Then hold his nose until he swallowed.

"Out of timber. I'll take the mule team out tomorrow and get some more trees."

Pines and poplars had reclaimed the bootheel farmland, but the cleared ground around neighboring Rally Base meant a drag to fill the winter dry racks.

"Why not—oh, I forget. Today is one of your days at the fort."

"I should get cleaned up."

"Use the washroom with the running water. Nice to have the smell of a young man's shaving soap here," she said, frowning at her daughters.

"It is my fault Patrick would rather be a soldier than a store-keeper?" the elder of the sisters asked.

He slipped down the hall toward the full bath. "Patrick" was something of a tender spot in the family conversation. Letters from him had ceased altogether six months before. When he hired on with Shrivastava, giving an abbreviated version of his service history, the girl had quietly asked him how often men declared "missing in action" returned.

Fresh back from Kentucky, Valentine couldn't offer much hope. Especially since he'd just spent months in Kentucky seeking another missing soul.

✝

Valentine relished the heated water in the family bathroom. The rest of the help had to make do with stove-warmed water in the bunk-house. As he buttoned his shirt he searched the sink for stray hairs and soap residue. Mrs. Shrivastava might like the smell of this young man's shaving, but it would be rude to repay her graciousness with a dirty basin.

He grabbed his teaching satchel and walked over to the base, taking his time in the unseasonable heat.

"Argent, Max," the sentry at the gate identified him, stepping out from the shade of corrugated iron. Though he knew Valentine's face and alias, he still checked the ID provided by Styachowski's specialists. "Base is on alert. We've got a sidearm and carbine for you, if you don't have your own." The guard's eyes were unreadable behind his wraparound sunglasses.

"Thank you," Valentine said.

Valentine's weapons were arranged in netting hanging from the un-nailed floorboards of his bunkhouse. He visited the base as a civilian expert, and at the moment his boots and pocket knife were the only military-issue items he had.

"No drill," a sergeant who handed him a pistol belt with magazine harness said. He was heavy as a side of beef, and Valentine couldn't remember him pulling a shift in the guard hut before. "How's a model four?"

"I qualified. This serious?"

"River traffic reported. It may have landed."

Valentine had heard a largish patrol go out in the predawn but had thought nothing of it. Pizzaro was an experienced enough forward area base commander to make sure nothing left or entered his base by regular schedules.

"Message too," the sergeant added as the sentry made a notation of the gun's serial numbers. "The CO wants you to come by his office after your class."

"Can do," Valentine said, adjusting the pistol belt.

Valentine headed into the base, where windows were being filled with sandbags and extra men idled in the shade at the mortar positions, ready to get the tubes into action as soon as orders came down. The quick step of the men carrying the sandbags and the lack of joking put Valentine on edge.

He had militia today, mostly young men fresh from a year or two with Labor Regiment. Unless the boys or girls were lucky enough in their LR term to get apprenticed into a technical field, they were dumped into the militia pool and made miserable enough that joining the regulars seemed like an elevation to paradise. Some stuck out militia service for a four-, six-, or eight-year term in return for land and tools, a "stake" in some new community in land won from the Kurians.

Only six years, and the militias rotated a lot of soldiers through good vocational training. Texas had huge swaths of fallow land to fill with stakes. If the former militiamen were lucky, they never heard the words "or such time and duty as the needs of Southern Command require."

He had two classes, a basic literacy-and-science group fresh out of the bush and his "advanced" class, who was learning about Southern

Command and how it hoped to disassemble the grim Kurian Order surrounding the embattled freeholds.

Today would be his advanced group. They met in a dining hall, a wood-framed building with a roof and canvas sides, pulled up now to admit the breeze.

Valentine had drawn a misshapen pyramid of figures on his blackboard. It rather reminded him of the ranks of invading aliens he'd seen in a video game at the Outlook back in the Cascades.

He leaned against the front table.

"So that's it," he said. "There's a reason pyramids last so long: They're stable. Wide at the bottom and thin at the top."

The men and a sprinkling of women, mostly first-year recruits growing their hair back in save for a couple who went the other direction and shaved down to bald, took notes on loose paper. Because of the alert, each had his rifle on the table within reach, combat harness hanging off the back of the chair. The platoon sergeant could form them up in a few seconds.

"Bottom is the population in the Kurian Zone. Middle-level functionaries direct and take care of them. At the cream level you've got those trusted with weapons and the people watching the functionaries. Above them are the Reapers, the eyes and ears and appetites of the master Kurian at the top. What's the weak point?"

"The alien at the top."

"Physically, you're correct. If you've got your hands on him, it's about as easy to kill a Kurian as a chicken. A good stomping is all it takes. It's the getting at them that's dangerous."

Valentine turned, lifted his shirt, and showed some of the burns running his back.

"But they usually live in towers that are very hard to get into, complete with bolt holes and escape tubes that you can't fit down if you're bigger than a bobcat. They're about as easy to catch as running water."

"You got three," a second-yearer named Hoke said. "Or was it four?" Hoke had been an early doubting Thomas at his classes, wondering how a rather beat-up civilian worked up the nerve to lecture soldiers, until a lieutenant with an interest in the Hunters took the sophomore warrior aside during a break.

"But what is he: Wolf, Cat, or Bear?" Hoke had asked. Valentine's Wolf-sharp ears could pick up the conversation, but he intentionally softened his senses to avoid the rest of the conversation after the lieutenant said something about *He's dangerous, and that's enough. . . .*

"Three," Valentine said. "But the third's sort of unofficial." Then there was the one he wasn't sure of, in the sunken sub off Hispaniola.

"Getting back to my point, it's the Reapers we try to hit. Yeah, they're the most dangerous thing on two legs you're ever going to meet, but they're the connection between the Kurian and the Quislings. The Kurian feeds, gives orders, and judges, all through his pale-skinned avatar. If you can get one just after a feed or in a hole far from the Kurian avoiding daylight, you've got a chance, if you can put enough lead on target and get in with explosives. Or a well-swung ax."

"They run from sunlight, right?" a Missouri kid said.

"Sunlight doesn't hurt them one bit. It messes with the communication with its Master, though, like static. They sense us, because intelligent living beings give off something we call lifesign. They can home in on it at night. That's the whole point of those breathing exercises we've been doing at the beginning and end of each class: getting you guys trained so they might mistake you for a paddock of horses or a pack of wild pigs."

This elicited some quiet hog calls and chuckling.

Valentine felt jealous of their youthful confidence. *The first Reaper's easy. It's the second that makes you shit your pants*, went an old saw from the Wolves.

There was a time when Southern Command left killing Reapers to the Hunters. But the Lifeweavers, brothers to the otherworldly Kur but their mortal enemies who trained the Hunters, had been scattered during Solon's brief occupation of the Ozarks. Valentine was an advocate of giving more of the rank and file of Southern Command at least the basics of first avoiding and then dealing with the Reapers, and Pizzaro agreed, giving him an occupation until Highbeam could get going.

If Highbeam would ever win approval. It was one thing to raid into the Kurian Zone. Quite another to establish a new Freehold, especially one so close to the great nerve trunks of the Kurian Order.

Valentine brought himself back to the here and now of his class.

"There's another reason for going after the Reapers. A lot of times the Quislings aren't even sorry to see one offed. Sure, your die-hard churchmen will still damn you to the cleanup crew, but everyone else is walking around a little easier. On the other side of the river they don't have guns, don't have grenades, and a lot of times they aren't even allowed to have locks on their doors. If you're lucky, you'll see a couple Reapers before you muster out, at a distance, usually running away. Quislings see the Reapers all the time, poking around at night with the full authority of the KZ behind them. They've got to talk to them."

†

Valentine walked past a sandbagged observation point camouflaged to look like another water tank. A pair of soldiers had set up a twin-lensed range finder, just poking above the rim of the tank like the antennae of a lead ant checking the exit from the nest. Wires dangled from the phony tank, running to the underground PVC tube leading to the mortar pits.

The command building was two units of prefabricated housing, easily ported by trailer and then joined, its outline concealed under a mesh of netting and some young trees. A dugout stood just opposite, its door open and beckoning thanks to the alert.

He signed in with Colonel Pizzaro's admin and chitchatted over coffee until Pizzaro waved him in from the door. He had lined, leathery skin but very bright eyes that reminded Valentine of the comical little goggle-eyed walnuts the church youth groups sold as fund-raisers. A squawk box crackled in the corner. A flak jacket, combat harness, and carbine like Valentine's rested on a foldout extender on his desk.

"Let's take a walk," Pizzaro said, buckling his harness and picking up the carbine.

He led Valentine out to the two layers of perimeter wire. Most officers had a bit of military business that either irritated or obsessed them. Pizzaro's was base security. He didn't like the idea of anything leaving or coming into his station without his knowing about it. He liked to walk the wire as he talked rather than stay cooped up in his office. According to his staff, he'd been in an interrogation camp during Solon's occupation of the Ozarks, which was enough being boxed up for a lifetime.

"You want the good news or the bad?" Pizzaro asked. The shade of his slouch hat and the hard daylight dimmed his eyes somewhat.

"The good first. Otherwise it's like drinking bourbon out of a shaving mug."

Pizzaro licked his lips. "All I ever see you drink is milk or coffee. When we go off alert, stop by."

"Is that the good news? Alert called off?"

"You're messing up your ordering," Pizzaro said, checking some frayed wiring on a quartz lamp. Valentine looked at the manufacturing stamp. It had originated in Mexico City. "Let's stick to the good news. I got a courier packet. Highbeam is on—I have this from Lambert herself. I've got to punch your ticket and give you escort to the staging briefing. Even my staff doesn't know this yet, and I want to keep it that way, but this post will be Point Zero. You'll set off from here. If it wasn't for the alert, we'd already be laying plumbing for a new camp."

"Was that the good news or the bad?" Valentine asked.

"Thought you'd be pleased to hear that all that scouting you've been doing in Kentucky is about to pay off."

"I never found what I was looking for."

"Anne..."

"Ahn-Kha," Valentine supplied.

"Sorry, not much with Grog talk. Sounds like dogs snarling at each other to me."

"So what's the bad news?"

"I'm sealing the base. First recon reports are in: It's a strong Grog column out of Cairo area. It's those gangly, hunched-over ones with the pig-ugly faces. They're avoiding contact and mostly hunting and scavenging. There aren't many settlements up that way but I'm getting reports of thievery—stealing livestock and chickens and whatnot. Anything they can sneak off when no one's looking. Some folks have disappeared, but we're not sure if they've run or the Grogs got 'em."

"Doublebloods, they call themselves," Valentine said. "Odd of them to come across the river like that. They keep to themselves."

"You spent some time in Illinois. Anything else you can tell me?"

"The Illinois Guard has a lot of stations around Mount Vernon, keeping watch on the Doublebloods. I had someone in the Illinois Guard I wanted to meet."

Sergeant Heath Hopkins. *He died badly.*

"So they're neutrals."

Pizzaro had enough troubles with the big gray Grogs inhabiting the riverbanks on his side of the Mississippi, the lonely Kurian tower watching river traffic from Cairo, and the Kurians on the other side of the twisting river in Kentucky and Tennessee. Valentine wasn't that surprised he didn't know much about the Doublebloods. There were pissworthy fires closer to the colonel's feet.

Valentine dredged up his very limited experience. "More like they hate everybody. Kurians tried to make a half Grog–half human and it didn't work out. They're ill-tempered, even for Grogs, so the Kurians planted them on the borders of Southern Command, hoping they'd be trouble for us. Problem is, they all remember which direction the trucks that brought them came from, and it wasn't southwest."

"Can you savvy their lingo?"

"No more than a few phrases they use to communicate with the other Grogs. But I'd rather not walk on into the camp. This could be a man raid."

"A what?"

"They're amazons. Something amiss with their reproductive

system. Not many male embryos live to be birthed. The ratio is four or six to one or thereabouts, if the Illinois Guard has the numbers right. There're problems up and down the Doubleblood genetic line, and the only way they're sure of a live birth is with a human donor and a Doubleblood female. Inbreeding worsens the defect. They're smart enough to grab new males now and then."

"Good God."

"It's not so bad. I hear they stick two layers of bagging over your head. Insurance," Valentine said.

The colonel tapped down some wire pegging with his foot and made a note on a pocket-sized sheet of paper. Valentine wondered if it was about the Doublebloods or the wire.

"What kind of weaponry?"

"Just small arms for fighting. They hunt with bows or crossbows and slingshots. They'll carry explosives to blow open locked doors. Tell your patrols to keep their distance."

"I'd just as soon discourage raids. What kind of casualties do we have to inflict to turn them around?"

"It's not that simple. Like I said, they're ornery. If they spill blood down here, a feud will start, and a good feud can go on for years."

"They're invading us. What do they expect to happen?"

"Logic and tribal custom. Ne'er the twain shall meet."

Valentine sensed Pizzaro was wavering, so he spoke again: "Right now you're just *other*. Start skirmishing and you'll be *enemy*. Your other option is to kill every last one of them. Then they'll think the gods punished them for arrogance. But you know how hard it is to run down Grogs who've gone bush."

Pizzaro thought it over, flicking his thumb over a rusty barb in the wire. "I'd better get to the communication center, then. Anyway, this is your chance to get out, if you like. Nobody'll say anything if you show up for the Highbeam—or whatever the crap they're gonna call it—conference a week or so early. Otherwise it'll be Rally Base cooking for you for a few days until whatever business the Doublebloods want to start finishes."

Valentine couldn't see riding away from some of the kids he'd helped train in a crisis. *Or could he?* "Can you shelter the Shrivastava clan?"

"Shrivastava? Of course. But it'll take more than a bag over his head to get him hot to abandon his store and stock."

†

Trader Shrivastava may have been a civilian, but there was something of Valentine's old captain, LeHavre, in him. He had a gentle manner masking a pirate avarice but it didn't make him any less outraged at the idea of hiding behind locked gates while the Doublebloods stole from his pens and coops.

Valentine spoke to him in front of the arms room, the one part of the store back in the family quarters. Racks of rifles and pistols lined the walls, and reloading tools filled a long workbench. There was only one other exit from the room, and it led down to a tunnel to a separate basement, the family "Reaper proof" in an old underground gas tank.

"The fort? This building is tougher than it looks, young man. Both basement and attic have firing slits to cover my property."

His nine-year-old son sat behind, loading bullets from boxes into fresh new magazines. The whole family knew the story of Grandfather Durtee, who held two Reapers off with a shotgun while the rest of the clan fled to the vaultlike underground shelter. The grandfather had been the only loss that night.

"If you draw blood, they'll be back to avenge it."

"Then I will draw more blood, young man. Yes! Let them return! I welcome all at my store, provided they pay for what they take. These creatures will pay for my stock, one way or another."

Valentine wondered if it was too late to catch that transport to the conference.

Ray, the trading post's butcher, appeared, an old army flak jacket draped over a beefy arm. He accepted an old M16 from his employer. "You take the wall covering the back door, young man," Shrivastava said, and Ray nodded. The boy passed him a bag of magazines.

Shrivastava turned back to Valentine. "You taking a gun, young man, or will you stay in the Reaper-proof with the mothers and children?"

Maybe the Doublebloods would let him guide them to a bottom that contained a sizable herd of wild pigs. They could get all the side meat they wanted and carry off the young. "I'm going to go talk to the Doublebloods."

"No! Youn—David, do not waste yourself in that manner. My great-uncle went to set up a post with the Whitefangs up beyond the ridge. They ate him. I do not call you a coward. The children will be comforted—"

Whatever else Shrivastava said was lost in the rush of an idea. Was there enough daylight left to get over the ridge?

Maybe. With a fast enough pair of wheels.

†

Within an hour he'd convinced Pizzaro to loan him a driver and transport. Plus a big bag of supplies.

*Scaring off coyotes with wolves?* Pizzaro had said, liking the idea.

He arranged for a motorcycle, his best two-wheel man, fuel, survival gear, even priceless com gear. "We'll worry about the authorizations and paperwork later."

Valentine wanted to kiss him, remembering his days in the Wolves. If Southern Command had a Pizzaro at every forward post, the Wolves would spend more time raising hell on Kurian Zone backroads and less cadging for supplies.

"You're not bad back there, sir," Callaslough, his driver, said from the front of the big Harley. Harley-Davidson still produced up in Milwaukee, and this specimen had found its way into Southern Command's motor pool. Fat-tired, with a high clearance and rugged brush breaks and plenty of horsepower and hookups for attachments. It was meant to hold a sidecar, maybe even one of the dark-canopied blisters for a Reaper, or to pull a one-body medical sled.

The motorcycle jumped and blatted along the old road, now

not much more than a potholed deer trail, quickly enough under Callaslough's urging.

Valentine had tied two small staffs of pig iron to the rear backrest/ gear bar. A white flag fluttered at one, a netted bag of Texas oranges on the other. Though each man had a carbine, they'd slung them facing down and backward, further proof of peaceful intent.

Not that it would stop an ambitious young Whitefang from trying to knock them both off the bike with a single .50 caliber bullet, a thought much on Valentine's mind as they bumped up Badblood Ridge.

Valentine's active imagination felt the notched foresight of a rifle resting on his eye, wondered if some poor, horny, unmated Grog would ignore the signals for parley. The noise the bike made must be drawing Whitefang scouts like the musical ice cream wagons of the KZ lured children to the New Universal Church ice cream that had proselytizing cartoons and homilies on the wrappers.

Callaslough spotted them first as they came off Badblood, bouncing down a gravelly wash under the gaunt, nest-and-vine-draped skeletons of power pylons. A wind chime of bleached skulls alternating with femurs and tibias hung from one long arm, threaded on old wire.

A bent, loose-skinned old Whitefang stood atop a fallen hickory, his long rifle gripped in the exact center but held stiff-armed toward them. Some females watched from the other side of the log. One, younger or more daring, climbed even higher than her male guardian to get a better look. She bore a bulging harvesting bag.

Callaslough slowed the big motorcycle.

"Pull up," Valentine said. Their seating arrangement made it easy to communicate quietly, at the cost of having to smell each other's sun-baked sweat. "Point the bike so it's parallel to his rifle, not pointed into Whitefang land."

Callaslough executed a neat stop, swinging the bike's rear tire so it sent a spray of pebbles toward Whitefang territory.

"Leathery old hangball," Callaslough commented. The old Grog's testicular sack was well below his loincloth line in the heat.

"That's good for us. Foragers mean one of the tribe's bigger camps are around."

Valentine stepped off the bike. He held up with his right hand some signaling mirrors given as trade goods, tough squares of chrome on lanyards. In his left he held a selection of Texas coast oranges in a net bag. He had several boxes of matches in reserve; he'd yet to meet a Grog that didn't love to strike a match, just for the pure dazzle and power of instant fire-creation.

"Foot pass! Parley!" Valentine called, in the lingua franca of St. Louis.

The females issued chirping noises, seeing what he had to offer. The male scratched an itch under his loincloth in thought, but his eyes didn't leave the oranges.

"I think we're good," Valentine said.

The nimble female plucked at his ears, urging.

The Grog planted his gunstock, hooted, and gave an unmistakable "get over here!" sweep of his arm. He licked his lips as he did so.

"Shit. I'd almost rather be shot at," Callaslough said.

†

They arrived about an hour before sunset.

The humans walked the bike in with the help of one of the females. They wore soup cans around their necks, indicating that they'd come in peace, and offered up tokens and gifts to be allowed on White-fang lands—the "foot pass" of Grog commerce and diplomacy.

The Whitefang encampment stood in an old field with an irrigation trench on three sides and thick woods on the fourth. Water flowed in the trench. Clay pots stood upstream for drinking water, and laundry lines hung downstream. Old books hung on the bushes shielding the toilet area where the ditch drained off.

The Whitefang villagers lived in tents made of pulled-up carpeting and quilts of plastics, weatherproofed with beeswax or musky-smelling oil.

Human captives hewed wood, made charcoal, and carried water. They looked at the newcomers with pleading eyes.

Valentine avoided their gaze. *Nothing you can do about it at the moment.*

At first the tribe wanted nothing to do with Valentine and Callaslough. The young males, unblooded and untattooed, their long hair a testament to lack of wives, glared or hopped up and down in excitement, letting out little war cries. The younger females taunted by slapping their own backsides or spitting in the embassy's direction.

"Lots of unmated Groggies," Callaslough said as they walked the bike into the village. Pizzaro had sent along a man who knew something of the Grogs, but Valentine would have preferred a little less experience. Callaslough was just finding things to be nervous about, and the Grogs read body language better than words.

The chief lived in an old farmhouse, apparently. On the lower level, the walls had been mostly pulled away to admit air, but the upper rooms remained intact. Valentine wondered how many wives were crammed into the aluminum-sided seraglio.

Stripped old farm equipment stood in the center of the village, a playland-junkyard for the little Grogs. They swung and climbed and chased each other and an assortment of village dogs in and out of old harvesting tubing, control cabs, and engine housings. At the edge of the playland, a scrubbed and polished claw-foot bathtub served as a central drinking trough.

Their escort Grog pointed to a place for them to sit and went up the stone stairs to the skeleton of the house's first floor.

The chief remained huddled with his subchiefs and elders. Valentine extracted a two-pound bag from his trade goods, went to the big drinking cistern, and ripped open the packet.

An elderly female tried to stop him, hooting and slapping at his hands. Valentine ignored her and emptied the packet, full of granules that looked like sand, into the trough.

That got the attention of the elders and the chief.

Valentine mixed the water with a clay carrying pot, upending and dumping the water as it began to froth.

"What the hell's that?" Callaslough asked.

"Root beer mix."

Valentine took his canteen cup and drank. Then he refilled it and offered it to the grandmother. She sniffed suspiciously and turned her head away.

"Damn," Valentine said. He filled another cup and drank again. It wasn't very good—the mixture really needed to sit and chill to be truly tasty—but it was sweet.

The younger Grogs weren't so shy. They slurped and squealed, and their elders ran forward to pull them away. A squirmy youngster managed to break away from his mother and go back to the tub, drinking with both hands.

The chief came out on his steps to watch, eyes shaded under a heavy brow. He had huge, woolly thighs that looked like a pair of sheep standing close together in a field. One of the youngsters brought him a cup of the mixture, babbling.

The chief sniffed. He laughed and upended the mixture down his throat. He wiped his lips and laughed again.

"Good-humored guy," Callaslough ventured.

"I'm sure he'd laugh just as hard if his warriors were playing soccer with our heads."

"I am Whitefang," he barked at Valentine in the Grog trade tongue. He stamped on the old steps, hard, and Valentine heard a commotion from the upstairs.

"O Whitefang, this foot-passed stranger begs the powers of your ears and eyes and tongue."

Whitefang waved them over with a two-handed gesture that made it look like he was taking an appreciative whiff of his own flatulence.

"He didn't just cut one, did he?" Callaslough said.

"Try and look agreeable, no matter what," Valentine said as he stepped forward.

The chief bobbed and one of his subchiefs put a pillow-topped milking stool under his hindquarters, but he didn't sit until Valentine and Callaslough were both off their feet.

It took a while for the negotiations to commence. The subchiefs and elders and warriors had to arrange themselves in a semicircle around the visitors, bearing their best captured weapons, flak jackets, and helmets. The most battle scarred of all of them, both with intentional artistry and in random wound, held a massive surgical-tubing slingshot and two bandoliers of captured hand grenades.

Whitefang's dozen or so wives stood behind him, the two most heavily pregnant in front of the others, turning now and then to display swollen bellies as proof of the chief's potency. Others gripped their children by the ears to show them how their father conducted himself with strangers.

A splendid-looking teen female, almost attractive in her careless lounge, wore the white headband of an unmarried daughter as she rested against Whitefang's scarred shoulder. By the woolliness of her thighs, Valentine guessed her to be Whitefang's eldest daughter. She wore a long, modest skirt made out of old Disney bedsheets, but she managed to hike it up a little in the direction of the unblooded warriors.

Valentine heard splashes and slurps behind as the Grogs drank the root beer. A young warrior made for the tub, but his fellows held him back, grumbling and grunting.

"What do the strangers beg of Whitefang?" Whitefang asked. Valentine couldn't tell what had changed in the assembly that caused him to commence negotiations.

"Battle alliance," Valentine said.

The audience gasped or hooted.

"Battle alliance. With humans?" the veteran with the artistic battle scarring asked.

Whitefang laughed. His daughter rolled her eyes.

"Battle alliance is for against humans," a white-eyebrowed old male said.

"They insult," a younger warrior shouted from the crowd to the side. At least that's what Valentine thought he said. The youth's trade tongue was clumsy, either from emotion or lack of practice.

"Want battle!" another youth said.

Others shouted in their own tongue. Valentine thought he recognized the word for blood.

"Kill us and you will have battle with humans," Valentine said.

Whitefang laughed, finding the prospect of war as funny as the taste of root beer.

"Fuck you up," Whitefang said. In pretty fair English.

If the Whitefangs killed them, at least it would be over quick. Warrior enemies would be dispatched quickly and cleanly. The Grogs reserved torture for criminals.

"Means bad old times," Valentine said. "Come soldiers. Come artillery. Come armored car."

"Let armored car come," Whitefang laughed. He barked at his harem, and they disappeared into the basement of the chief's house. They reemerged bearing steering wheels and machine-gun turret rings, executing neat pirouettes in front of Valentine and Callaslough.

Callaslough was breathing fast, like a bull working up a charge. "Bas—"

"Easy," Valentine said.

"Humans beg help," Valentine said, loudly enough for all to hear.

That got them talking: humans begging. Whitefang slapped his callused, hairless kneecaps to silence them.

"Doublebloods attack humans," Valentine said. "Steal much. Capture many. Doublebloods worst enemy humans now."

Even more talk now, with some excited yips from the young warriors. Valentine suspected that the Doublebloods had done their share of raiding on Whitefang lands, being just across the river from southern Illinois. He suspected an old feud existed.

"Worse than Night-stalkers?" Whitefang asked, his eyes lit by the setting sun.

"Night-stalkers on other side of Great South river. Doublebloods on human side."

"Humans stop Night-stalkers," Valentine said. "Otherwise Night-stalkers raid Whitefangs."

This time Whitefang didn't laugh. The uneasy truce—not without the occasional raid and ambush—that had existed in southern Missouri between Grogs and mankind dated to the brief Kurian occupation of the Ozarks. Reapers had been loosed into Grog lands to drive them away from Solon's planned Trans-Mississippi empire. The Grogs were only too happy to see Southern Command return.

Callaslough, who'd evidently been able to follow at least some of the conversation, reached into his shirt and pulled up a pair of black Reaper teeth interlaced with his dog tags. They were only short ones from the back, but the Grogs recognized them. Callaslough held them high and rattled them.

Valentine remembered teaching Blake to clean teeth just like those, only smaller, with a brush and baking soda.

"Humans beg battle alliance," Valentine repeated. "What Doublebloods stole, Whitefangs keep. Who Doublebloods capture, Whitefangs release."

"Trophies?" Whitefang asked.

"All Whitefangs keep."

The young warriors stirred at that. Their prospective mates among the females started chattering to each other. A warrior returning home with the blood of an enemy on his blade, or even better, some skulls or scalps, could marry, having proved himself worthy of establishing a household and producing children.

Whitefang's daughter stared out into the crowd. Valentine followed her gaze to a tall, proud-looking warrior standing naked with only his weapons, splendidly lush hair hanging from his head and shoulders and upper back. He hadn't wanted to contaminate his clothing with human blood, should it come to that, evidently. He stared back at the girl.

She whispered in Whitefang's ear.

Whitefang elbowed her hard and she toppled backward. He grumbled something to the female who ran to her aid.

The chief tongued the remainders of root beer out of his cup. "Trade root beer?" he asked.

"If battle alliance is successful."

"Trade licorice?" Whitefang asked.

"Yes."

Whitefang licked his lips and the eyes under the heavy brow brightened. "Trade—*Soka-coli*?"

"All Coca-Cola same."

An entrepreneur was supposedly bottling RC down in the sugar farms near the Louisiana border. Valentine had seen some cases behind lock and key in Shrivastava's mercantile Galaxy. Whitefang wouldn't notice the difference. He hoped.

Whitefang held out his hand, and a senior wife placed a sawed-off, double-barreled shotgun in it. He extended the butt end toward Valentine.

Valentine wasn't sure what to do. He'd never observed a battle alliance; he just knew the term. But it never hurt to imitate the head honcho in any organization, human or Grog. He unslung his own carbine and held it toward Whitefang, butt end extended.

The oldster with the hand grenades cackled.

Valentine approached Whitefang, and the chief gripped the end of his gun. Valentine wrapped his fingers around the pistol grip of the shotgun.

The warriors cheered.

"Fuck Doublebloods up," Whitefang said in English, winking at Valentine. Then he laughed long and loud into the night.

†

The Mississippi, wild and untended since 2022, had carved little islands along its banks for most of its length. Within twenty-four hours of his promise of *Soka-coli* to Whitefang, Valentine was swatting mosquitoes and trying to keep from being splashed by the paddlers.

*Grogs paddle as though they were at war with the river.*

Grogs had an instinctive knack for warfare. Once they made up their minds, they did everything at the hurry-up. After a conference that lasted long into the night—most of it taken up by definitions of geographic points—Valentine sent Callaslough back to Rally Base with a written report. Whitefang called for his warriors, and Grogs loped off in every direction.

They left a substantial reserve at the camp, perhaps still fearing a human trick, and a core of veterans set off with the youngest warriors on the Doubleblood hunt.

The Grogs were proud of their weapons. They displayed their prowess to Valentine, sending steel-tipped arrows through entire trunks of trees from bows made out of truck leaf springs (Valentine couldn't even string the bow, let alone draw it, and felt very much like a sham Odysseus) or driving spears through practice dummies made of old kegs and barrels. The tall young Grog Whitefang's daughter had made eyes at had a big Grog gun and ten bullets probably donated by his entire family. The .50 caliber rounds were scarce on this patch of riverbank, and Valentine suspected they represented an investment of his whole family in the warrior's future.

He used one to shatter an old bowling pin at a distance of a kilometer, making Valentine stand within ten paces of the target to show that no tricks were involved. For a split second between the shot (Valentine saw the Grog take the recoil) and the pin's destruction, he wondered if he'd be dead before he heard the sound of the report.

With the young males gathered, their chief led them to war, leaving the old fellow with the slingshot and the hand grenades behind.

Valentine felt like a war correspondent watching them hike off in loosely grouped bunches, formed into a diamond shape if you plotted them on a map at any particular point. A poor sort of war correspondent at that, because he could get only a vague sense of their intentions. At first he feared they were just going to plunge into Southern Command's territory and make straight for the Doubleblood trail, but they proved craftier than that and took big war canoes down a stream to the Mississippi.

The Grogs watched him sit down in the canoe and unroll a

condom over the business end of his carbine. A warrior with six feet of lethal, single-shot steel-and-wood showed Valentine how he protected his piece: Valentine recognized a leathery testicular sack, undoubtedly human, closed by a tight drawstring.

The Grog had left the hairs intact, probably to help it bleed water.

Then, with a call from Whitefang, they paddled as though chased by living fire. One hundred and eightysome Grogs moving fast with the current, canoes swerving and crossing like a school of excited fish.

They reached the islands opposite Cairo by dark, and Valentine saw smaller scout canoes hook to either side of Whitefang's. Valentine's canoe waited with several others under the metal remnants of an old interstate bridge.

They spotted the pulled-up canoes and flatboats and hulled pleasure boats and houseboats floating at anchor, shielded from Southern Command by a long strip of muddy island, tree roots fighting the Mississippi for possession of the soil.

With their objective in sight, Whitefang let his Grogs rest and feed, waiting for the moon to go down. Valentine found himself dozing, resting against a big warm Grog who smelled like brackish water.

Owl hoots from Whitefang's canoe woke him. Grogs slipped into the summer-warmed water.

Most of the canoes huddled against the banks, while scouts swam, or crawled, or slithered forward, depending on the depth of water.

Valentine's Cat-sharp eyes picked out a shadowy shape, glistening wet in the darkness, climb onto a sailboat and merge with something that looked like a bundle of canvas leaning against a mast. Others of the Whitefang tribe emerged from the riverbank and stalked into the trees.

Evidently the Doublebloods hadn't counted on an attack from upriver.

A flaming arrow, looking like a bum-winged firefly as it turned tight circles along its parabolic arc into the Mississippi, announced that the scouts had done their job.

Valentine splashed ashore with the veteran Grogs carrying belt-fed machine guns and laced-together Kevlar over their broad frames. Valentine felt sorry for anyone going against this contingent. It was hard enough to get a bullet through Grog-hide around the shoulders and chest. Add Kevlar to the mix and you had something resembling a living tank.

The younger Grogs were showing each other gory trophies taken from the Doubleblood sentries.

The remaining unblooded Whitefangs prepared to win their own bloody prizes. The Grogs caked themselves with mud, dead leaves, and bracken. It would conceal them from the eyes of their enemies and be an earthy burial shroud should they die.

By dawn Doubleblood message runners showed up at the Southern Command bank. Valentine got a good look at one. She looked a little like a bloodhound, with short dark hair, lots of loose skin about the face, and a gangly, underfed look compared to the gray Grogs. But the Doublebloods could run like deer and climb like spiders—even with an arrow through her leg that one Grog shot through the brush on the riverbank like a snake.

Valentine didn't care to watch the questioning of the captured messengers, but it amounted to bringing the bigger boats around the south end of the island and setting up boarding ramps big enough for young cattle and pigs.

The Whitefangs happily followed the plan. They were setting up the inviting-looking boarding ramps (and brush blinds for snipers and archers flanking the landing) when a brown-water river patrol motored upriver and turned in to get a good look at the operation, covering the Grog boats with what looked like 20mm cannon while a squat mortar boat watched over matters from mid-river.

Valentine slipped into the water off the side of one of the Doubleblood boats, just in case the Quislings stopped to search. He felt the deep Mississippi mud, cool and gritty, around his toes. But the patrol recognized the Whitefang warrior tattooing and gave the chief some boxes of ammunition and a case of incendiary grenades in the interest of bringing a little extra misery to Southern Command and staying friendly with Whitefang's people.

The tall young warrior who'd caught Whitefang's daughter's eye was able to fill his bandolier with .50 rounds, and stick extras behind his ears, braided in his long unmated warrior's mane, and up one cavernous nostril.

The patrol sped away, not wanting to draw more attention to a Grog raid than necessary. Valentine could still hear their motors from upriver—they were making for the Ohio, seemed like—when the first of the Doublebloods arrived.

Valentine stayed in the water with his carbine, waiting in the shadows beneath the gangplank, battle harness with his ammunition wrapped around his neck and shoulders to keep it out of the water. The bullets were supposed to be water-resistant, but Valentine had an old soldier's mistrust for allowing muck and gear to mix.

A panting line of warriors loped up, waving to a couple Doubleblood bodies on the flatboat nailed to wooden staves, gruesome puppets already thick with flies. Grogs hidden behind the gunwales worked the arms with bits of cattail.

Valentine slipped the condom off his gun barrel. He'd used more of the things keeping water out of his barrel than he'd had in sexual assignations. Not that one of Southern Command's rough-and-ready prophylactics could compete with the artfully wrapped, gossamer-skinned little numbers smuggled in from Asia at great expense that he'd tried in Fran Paoli's well-appointed bedroom back in Ohio.

The advance party fell to a hail of arrows. Two in the rear who figured out what was happening and shouldered carbines to shoot back were brought down with well-placed shots. Valentine knew Grog sniper checkdowns all too well: obvious officers, then anyone giving signals of any kind, then machine gunners. Sometimes they wouldn't even use their precious bullets on ordinary soldiers.

One of the Doublebloods spun as he fell, and Valentine thought of young Nishino on Big Rock Hill.

The time and miles that yawned between made him feel as old as one of the riverbank willows.

Things went badly as the Grogs cleared away the bodies. The main body of Doublebloods were close behind their guard, driving herds of cattle, geese, and swine. Blindfolded human captives, linked by dowels and collars at the neck, staggered under yokes with more bags of loot attached or pushed wheelbarrows.

The west bank of the Mississippi went mad as the bullets began to fly, with animals fleeing every which way and the humans getting tangled, falling, dragging their fallen comrades, until they too tripped and fell hard.

More and more Doublebloods arrived, seemingly from all points west, and the arrival of their rear guard gave the Doublebloods the advantage. Now it was the Whitefangs who were pinned. The Doublebloods even managed to set up some knee mortars, raining shells on the riverbank.

Grogs hated artillery. Many of the younger warriors crept back to the water.

A crossbow bolt whispered past Valentine's ear and struck the transom of the flatboat with a loud *kunk*.

As the skirmish progressed a group of Doublebloods forced their way toward the boats, using cattle as bleeding, lowing shields, splitting the Whitefangs.

Valentine laid down a steady stream of single shots at the shapes moving in the cow dust, but the Grogs on the boats had a better plan. They cut the anchors and sent the boats nearest the bank off downstream.

Something splashed into the water near Valentine. *Grenade, mortar shell, or flung rock?* his brain wondered for a split second, waiting for an explosion.

It didn't come.

Seeing their salvation float away took the heart out of the

Doublebloods. They broke and scattered for the riverbank, abandoning their prizes.

The Doublebood rear guard stayed together, fighting as they turned north instead of south after the boats. Whitefang sent his most experienced warriors after them. Valentine emerged from the river, shimmied up a thick trunk and got a chance to observe a Grog assault from the rear, with warriors avoiding superior firepower by exploding from cover to cover in short hops.

Whitefang shook his head in disgust at the slaughter of livestock. He kicked a shrapnel-scratched youngster to his feet and set him to work hanging and dressing some swine who'd been caught in the cross fire.

Someone had tossed an incendiary grenade in his excitement and started a small brush fire. Valentine gesticulated and pointed and a few Whitefangs stamped and kicked dirt on the smoldering wood.

It gave him a chance to go to the captives. Using his utility knife, he started cutting ropes and unhooking yokes.

"Much obliged, son," a man with four days of beard croaked.

"He's a renegade. He's with these other stoops," another said. "We're just out of the frying pan and into the fire."

Valentine showed the beat-up militia tag on the shoulder of his half-wet tunic. "No, sir. This is a joint operation, of sorts. Southern Command will be along in a bit to offer assistance."

"A bit" turned out to be about fifteen minutes. Valentine marked the approaching troops flitting from tree to tree up the trail of the departing, exchanging shots with the last of the Doubleblood rear guard, a pair of sappers so occupied in shooting at the humans and keeping from getting shot themselves that they probably didn't even feel the arrows striking between their shoulder blades.

Valentine stood among the freed captives, waving one of the men's grubby yellow cotton shirt.

Luckily someone recognized him from Rally Base and waved him forward as the Grogs collected and organized their loot.

"So you're the Grog lover," a corporal said.

Valentine heard the expression with a pang. He'd had it shouted to him now and then as he rode next to Ahn-Kha on the long drive into Texas after Archangel had freed the Ozarks. It had angered him then, Ahn-Kha being worth any three of Southern Command's men. Now it just made him miss Ahn-Kha.

He'd spent months in eastern Kentucky chasing rumors. No time to think about that, or the possibilities Highbeam presented . . .

"You call me sir, Corporal," Valentine snapped. "The Whitefangs just saved Southern Command another small war."

Someone snorted.

Valentine added, "This was just a raiding party. If the Double-bloods had come across the river with a couple of their warrior regiments, Rally Base would have been scratched."

"Sorry, sir," the corporal said, smart enough not to show that he doubted Valentine.

Of course, that younger Valentine who'd watched Nishino fall might have doubted this road-worn, tired Valentine too. He had willow leaves in his hair and his boots were drifting down the Mississippi on the flatboat.

A captain came up and Valentine gladly turned the captives over to him. Southern Command and the Whitefangs watched each other over a few dozen yards.

The smell of a roasting hog brought the two groups a little closer together. Valentine filled a birch-bark platter with a cooked haunch and presented it to the Ozark boys with the compliments of Whitefang. A few soldiers cautiously traded.

"Excuse me, son. Can I buy that off you?" Valentine said as he saw a private extract a bottle of RC from his sack, smacking his lips at the scent of hot pork fat and crispy skin.

"Dunno, sir. You don't look like you got—"

"Just give it to him, dummy," a sergeant said.

A Grog veteran probably would have grabbed the younger warrior by the long hair on his shoulders and given him a shake, but Valentine recognized correction when he heard it.

"Carry it all this damn way . . . ," the private said, handing it over.

Valentine trotted across the open space and presented the bottle to Whitefang, who smacked his lips as he held up the caramel-colored water to the sky, evaluating its color.

"Not *Soka-coli*?" Whitefang said, tapping the logo with a claw.

"Try," Valentine urged. He wondered if the Whitefangs would be up for a march on Atlanta. Most of the Cokes he'd had in his life bore an Atlanta Gunworks imprint.

The Grog flipped off the cap and took a generous swig. He rolled the liquid around in his mouth and gave a rather girlish giggle. Then he swallowed.

The chief belched. Now it was his warriors' turn to laugh.

"More, yes?" Whitefang asked.

"Soon," Valentine temporized, wondering if one of the Shrivastava clan would be brave enough to open a small post in Whitefang territory.

The tall young warrior who'd made eyes with Whitefang's daughter slapped Valentine on the back and gabbled. Valentine was pretty sure he was describing a victory over the Doubleblood rear guard but caught only a word here or there. The young Grog grabbed Valentine by the hair on the back of the neck and shook him, and Valentine felt his eyeballs rattle in their sockets.

The youth opened up a wet canvas case and extracted a Doubleblood head, yammering something that could only have been "Take one, I got plenty" as he tried to hand it to Valentine.

Valentine demurred as politely as he could.

The warrior pushed the blood-caked mess on him again, making a gesture with his forearm from his waist, clenched fist at the end, that Valentine found easy to interpret.

"No, you're right, still not married," Valentine said in English as the Grog pointed at his long hair. "But I don't think a skull will help."

A little cautious trading took place between the soldiers and their usual adversaries. Southern Command offered jars of honey or wrapped pieces of taffy or can openers or clasp knives in exchange for Grog machete sheaths and wrist protectors or earrings.

Valentine facilitated where he could, using a half-gnawed pork rib as a pointer. He found himself smiling more than he had at any time since that Fourth of July gathering.

It wouldn't last, of course. Some Grog would kill a pack trader, looking for loot and a trophy to show his prospective bride's family, or a hotheaded sergeant would teach cattle-rustling Grogs a lesson in the language of the noose. Then matters would flare up and not be calmed down until the next holiday or bad-weather season.

The past was done and the future would come soon enough. If better than thirty years on Vampire Earth had taught David Stuart Valentine anything, it was to enjoy the good moments for what they were.

# CHAPTER TWO

*S*tipple Field, Arkansas, October: The skeleton of Southern Command's short-lived Air Force School crawls with fresh activity.

There was a time when Southern Command had a substantial fleet of aircraft and helicopters. Accidents and lack of spares has reduced the fleet to a few choppers and long-wearing crop dusters or air shuttles, Frankenstein flyers operating on the parts of dozens of dead ships.

Twenty years ago the airfield, tower, hangars, and office space of Stipple Field had trained younger pilots and mechanics to handle and fix Southern Command's air wing, but with so few craft left, the school only operates for two months in the winter as experienced pilots and mechanics test and give initial training to the few recruits they need.

In the summer, Stipple hosts the cadet games, where promising youngsters compete in marksmanship, riding, and athletic and academic face-offs.

The rest of the year, a few custodial workers keep the place painted, cut back, and lit.

Because the location is remote and easily guarded, low-level conferences between political and military leaders in eastern Arkansas use the facility, mostly to give each side a chance to have grievances heard and smooth over the resulting ruffled feathers over alcohol in the "Flyer's Club."

Kurian spies don't pay much attention to Stipple. Nothing important ever was decided or planned there.

Which is why Colonel "Dots" Lambert chose it as the site for the High-beam conference.

†

David Valentine hated Stipple Field's folding metal chairs. And the hangar lights turned the attendees' faces shades of blue, purple, or green, but that didn't bother him like the chairs. There was something exactly wrong about their design for his butt and lower back. Sitting in one for more than an hour made his bad leg ache and his kidneys hurt.

Most days of the Highbeam conference he was in it for six, wearing his rather ill-fitting militia uniform and a fine new pair of fatigue boots, Dallas-made no less, a present from Colonel Pizzaro to replace the ones lost to the Mississippi current—or a Grog scavenger looking for something he could fashion into knee pads.

The hateful chairs were arranged in a square in a big, cold hangar around a map drawn onto the floor in four colors of tape. White for topography, green for Southern Command's routes toward New Orleans, red for known Kurian strongholds and Quisling bases, and yellow for notations.

It was all bullshit. But well thought-out bullshit, in Valentine's opinion. Lambert had probably kept a team of officers working in odd hours planning an operation that wouldn't take place. Maybe it was part of the General Staff training Valentine had once been set to enter.

Lambert did her briefings on whiteboards, which she and her staff worked on for hours each morning and then meticulously washed each night.

The sentries for the conference, all of whom were going on the trip, had every reason to be alert. But Kurian promises of eternal life had found willing ears before. Some maintenance person might figure out a way to get a picture of the map with a micro-digital camera.

The first day of the conference had been spent mostly in social activities, as officers got to know each other and inevitable late arrivals trickled in—Southern Command's rather rickety infrastructure did well if you arrived within twenty-four hours of the time on your travel orders.

Valentine played cards the first night with a craggy Wolf captain named Moytana. Moytana sported streaks of gray in his long, ropy hair and had once served as a junior lieutenant in LeHavre's old Zulu company, Valentine learned. The Gods of Poker chose not to favor Valentine that night, but Moytana consoled the losers by buying drinks.

He also received, and smoked, a cheroot with an agreeable young staff lieutenant named Pacare. He had a golden, round face, and Valentine thought he'd make a good sun king. Pacare was a communications specialist and told Valentine about the latest mesh that was supposed to keep the juice bugs out of the wiring. Pacare did enough talking for both of them.

Valentine turned in early.

After breakfast, everyone was directed into the hangar. Forty folding chairs, ten to a side, were arranged in a square around the chalked map. Each chair had a name taped to the backrest. Each person stood in front of his or her chair; a few of the regulars stiffly "at ease." A civilian who'd sat stood up again when he realized no one else was sitting.

Everyone waited to take their cue from the general, who stood chatting with some lieutenant colonels.

General Lehman, in charge of Southern Command's eastern approaches, opened the first day of the conference. The general had a famously heavy mustache that covered most of his lips. He was affectionately known back at Rally as "The Big Dipper," as the ends of his mustache visited soups and beverages before his taste buds. The moniker might have also referred to his habit of dipping his little silver flea comb in his water glass at the end of the meal.

Valentine's name had been put in the line with support and technical staff, judging from the insignia around him. Opposite him sat Moytana and a couple of his poker-playing Wolves. A lieutenant with a scarred cheek and absent earlobes and who Valentine guessed to be a Bear waited at the far end of the row. Only a Bear would come to a conference wearing a crisp new uniform shirt with sleeves freshly snipped off. A pop-eyed civilian in a natty sportcoat that looked about two sizes too small fidgeted uncomfortably next to the Bear. The fresh sunburn and two-wheeler full of reference binders gave Valentine a guess that a quick look at his ID card confirmed—he was an expert from Miskatonic.

The row of chairs to Valentine's right held General Lehman and the big bugs; to his left, Guard regulars.

The assembly was mostly officers, with a smattering of senior sergeants and neatly dressed civilians seated with the big bugs.

The chair with the name "Lambert" taped to it stood empty, as did the one next to it with no name on it. Lambert was present; Valentine had seen her in the hangar office with some other uniforms. She was the closest thing he had to a commander in his ill-defined, ill-starred relationship with Southern Command.

Valentine also recognized one civilian to the other side of Lehman, a well-dressed fixer named Sime. At this distance Valentine couldn't tell if he still used that rich sandalwood soap or not. Valentine had last smelled it when Sime came to visit him in prison, when he was offered up as a sacrificial lamb to doubtful Kansas officials who were considering switching sides and feared reprisals. The Kansas uprising hadn't gone as well as most hoped: The Kurians brought an army all the way from Michigan across the Mississippi and Missouri rivers and smashed most of the rebellious territories before Southern Command could get there.

Sime ignored him. Valentine, skin crawling as though trying to make a discreet exit, doubted it was out of embarrassment.

Lambert and her group arrived. A man on the hard side of middle age with a loose-skinned face that reminded Valentine of a woeful hound stood next to her at the unmarked chair. He wore a plainly cut black coat, trousers, and leather shoes that made him look like either a Mennonite or a backwoods undertaker. Valentine wondered if he was a Lifeweaver, relatives to the Kurians and mankind's most powerful allies in the war against the Kurians.

"Be seated," Lehman said. Lehman tightened his words before shooting them out of his mouth in little explosions of air, making his mustache ripple like a prodded caterpillar.

Valentine's relationship to the uncomfortable metal chair began well enough. He was glad to sit. Metallic creaks echoed in the empty hangar.

Lehman remained on his feet: "We're present at a historic moment. You've been brought together for an important campaign. What we have come here to plan is no ordinary op. A new Freehold is about to be born. You will all be midwives." The general unbent a little. "Let's just hope it's a live birth.

"Some of you have heard rumors of Highbeam being a move against New Orleans. That's still what it is as far as the various people in your commands who are going to help you organize the men and material are to think. I expect you all to go to sleep every night with a Creole phrasebook next to your bed and maps of swamps and bayous piled on your desk.

"Our true objective is an area in the Appalachians. Some of you may have heard what's happening in West Virginia and eastern Kentucky. A coal miners' revolt has grown into a thriving resistance. Usually uprisings like this are stamped out in a few months, but the fellows running the show there vanish every time the Kurians think they have them trapped. They've got popular support and friends on both sides of the mountains.

"We're going to cross the Mississippi and Kentucky in reinforced brigade strength and offer assistance."

He let that sink in.

Valentine felt a momentary loss of balance. He'd been working out a route of march but had only a couple companies of Wolves and perhaps a contingent of training and technical units in mind when he presented his ideas to Lambert.

Lehman gestured to the big bugs behind him. "And that's it for me. I'm just here to sign and seal the op orders. You all are going to do the planning over the next two weeks. With forty of us I think we can get a little softball going on Wednesdays and Saturdays. I'll handle the rosters and decide who'll be playing and who'll be grilling and baking when. Unless you vote on basketball, that is. My headquarters, barring contingencies, will be located at the old motel just across the road. I've given most of my staff furlough or dispersed them for training. I'll try to get the pool filled so you can use it, if you like. Drop by if you want to sample the liquor and tobacco a general gets."

Valentine's heart warmed at that. It wasn't often you met a general who knew when to get out of the way.

Lambert took over the rest of the welcome briefing. She introduced the big bugs and allowed the other three sides of the squares to present themselves. Valentine was most interested in the first man introduced: Colonel Seng, who would be overall command of the expeditionary brigade. Seng had a flat face; indeed, he looked as though he'd spent some time using it as a battering ram, as it was heavily pocked and built around a big, pursed mouth suggesting he'd been tasting vinegar. After each introduction, Seng's chin dropped and he shifted his eyes to a blank space between his knees.

Seng had a lot to think about. A full regiment of two battalions of Guard regulars would be his responsibility, each with organic light artillery, plus a support battalion with more artillery and anti-armor—or anti-Reaper—weapons. Of course the men and gear couldn't travel without commissary, transport, and medical companies. Another smaller ad-hoc regiment included a full company of Wolves, three Bear teams under the sleeveless lieutenant, and logistics commandos—the scroungers. Seng's headquarters would have engineers, signals, and intelligence staff, and even a meteorologist and an agronomist.

Valentine hoped he had a good chief of staff.

When it came time for Valentine to introduce himself, Lambert nodded at him, giving him the go-ahead to use his real name. Valentine just stood and said: "David Valentine. Last held the rank of major, Hunters and Special Operations."

"I was wondering what a militia corporal was doing here," a civilian sitting next to Sime murmured, showing off the fact that she could read shoulder tabs and stripes. Sime didn't seem to hear her; he was busy refolding his handkerchief.

Some of the regular officers took another look at Valentine. For once, Seng didn't look down. Valentine nodded to Seng as he sat. The chair squeaked and the colonel returned his gaze to that spot between his knees.

"He's attached to my Special Operations Directory," Lambert said.

"Knew he was an SOD," someone in the regulars muttered.

Lambert moved on, beckoning to the woman next to Valentine, a captain with training and indoctrination who smelled faintly of boiled vegetables and butter.

Only one face hadn't been introduced, the person Valentine suspected was a Lifeweaver. If so, he—she—it? was an extraordinary specimen. In Valentine's limited experience they never mixed with so many humans at one time. He suspected they found all the thoughts and moods stressful, or perhaps frightening. The human imagination sometimes wandered into rather dark and nasty corners when not otherwise engaged.

"You've probably all noticed that I skipped someone," Lambert said, stepping forward again to give voice to Valentine's thoughts. "Brother Mark is an expert on the Kurian Zone. He's former New Universal Church with the rank of elector, I believe. He's serving as liaison between Southern Command and the rebels."

Valentine received his second shock of the meeting. An elector was a senior priest with voting privileges that allowed them to set Church policy—for all intents and purposes a bishop, though they were technically below bishops and the all-powerful archons. Most Quislings were expected to obey orders from the Kurians. Churchmen were trained from childhood to love doing so.

"He's also been prominent in the Kurian Order longer than I've been alive."

The sorrowful spaniel in black rose.

"I'm not sure the guerrillas rate a term like 'army' from such professionals," Brother Mark said. "May I call them partisans without offending anyone? Good. The partisan army in the Virginias–Kentucky borderland triangle isn't like the military as you understand it. It is a small cadre of leaders who go from place to place, where they temporarily swell their numbers in order to destroy a specific objective, be it a mine or a tunnel or a garrison house. With the job done the guerrillas return to their homes and remove all telltales of their participation. Still with me?"

Valentine could tell from the exchanged glances and squeaking shifts in weight the officers were uncomfortable being addressed by a churchman. Or maybe it was the patronizing tone.

"There's a potential in that part of the country for a true Freehold. With regular soldiers such as yourselves to handle external threats, the populace could organize its own defense on a county-by-county basis. I'd say the population is six-to-one in favor of the guerrillas, though they've seen enough reprisals to be chary of rising up en masse. Not the best specimens in that part of the country, either physical or mental."

He paused again to let his gaze rove over the room. He settled his stare on Captain Moytana, who had the thumb of his fist pressed to his mouth as if to keep his lips from opening.

"Yes, we all know what happened when a rising like this was attempted in Kansas. Unlike Kansas, we already have local fighters in place who've lost their fear of the Kurians. This time the rising won't take place until your forces arrive and are integrated with the locals."

Lambert spoke again: "It's not Kansas. The Kurians are holding on to their mines by their fingernails. A couple strikes on key Kurian-held centers, destruction of the local constabulary, and a few Reapers burned out of their basement lairs would greatly further the Cause in North America."

A hand went up, and Lambert nodded.

"That's awfully near Washington," a lieutenant colonel named Jolla with the big bugs said. He was perhaps the oldest man at the briefing other than General Lehman. Campaign ribbons under his name lay in neat rows like a brick wall. "They're tender about that, what with all those Church academies and colleges and such. The Kurians in New York and Philly and Pitts would unite."

"The Green Mountains are just as close," Lambert said. "There's a Freehold there. Smaller than ours, but they're managing."

"Can we count on them to take some of the heat off?" a youngish Guard major named Bloom asked.

"You won't be alone," Brother Mark said. "God sees to that."

Valentine glanced around the assembly. Some eyes were rolling, expecting a mossbacked homily.

"You'll have friends to the west," Brother Mark said. "The guerrillas are getting help from some of the legworm ranchers in Kentucky. About four years ago the Ordnance—that's the political organization north of the Ohio, for those of you unfamiliar with the area . . . as I said, the legworm ranchers have grown restive, especially since the Ordnance began conducting raids into their territory, coming after deserters and guerrillas."

Valentine, who had fled into Kentucky from the Ordnance as something between a guerrilla and a deserter, could tell the assembly didn't like their renegade churchman. The officers were keeping their faces too blank when they listened.

"Some of the troops won't like it," a Guard captain said. "That's a long way from home."

"Their forefathers went ten times as far against lesser evils," Brother Mark said.

This time General Lehman came to his rescue. "Tell 'em what the gals in Kentucky look like, brought up on milk and legworm barbecue. You know that area, Valentine."

"They're pretty enough. Tough too," Valentine said, thinking of Tikka from the Bulletproof. "All that time in the saddle. The backhill bourbon's smooth. Everybody and his cousin has a recipe. Some of the older ones will want to allot out and become whiskey barons."

"Whiskey barons," someone chuckled. "They'll like the sound of that."

†

The second day they broke into working groups. The big bugs from the one end divided the assembly into three groups: "combat," "support and liaison," and "hunter."

Valentine ended up in the support and liaison group, under the bald lieutenant colonel with the wall of campaign ribbons who'd asked the question about how the Kurians would react to a new Freehold. Valentine wondered if the question hadn't been prearranged by Lambert.

"Don't be fooled by all this," Jolla chuckled, tapping the campaign ribbons. "Just means I'm old. I don't know much more about Highbeam than you. They called me in because I know how to keep the soup pots full for an army on the march." Valentine couldn't help liking him. Some of the other officers who knew him from other campaigns called him "Jolly." Jolla told those in Valentine's team to do the same.

There were study guides to go through about Kentucky, the Virginias, and the surrounding areas. Every day Valentine lugged around two hundred or more pages of text and maps in Southern Command's battered three-ring binders, with tabs for future additions as the operational plans were developed. An artist, or maybe just a bored student, had sewn a denim cover on Valentine's binder at some point or other. Valentine smiled when he saw William Post's name as one of the intelligence staff who'd prepared background. Post was at Southern Command's general headquarters now, studying and tracking Quisling military formations and assessing their capabilities.

The appointment said a lot about his old number two, Will Post.

General headquarters wasn't a place for cushy assignments bought by politics, patronage, or a mixture of rank and bureaucratic skill. You had to be good to get an office at GHQ. Post was good.

They thumbed through the study guides until Lambert and Seng arrived. The big bugs had worked out a preliminary organizational chart before they even arrived, but gallstone surgery and the death of a major's spouse had meant a little last-minute juggling.

The pair met with Jolly first, relocating to a corner while everyone else read through their local study guides. Valentine was studying a history of the legworm ranchers—he recognized some phrasing from his own reports about the Bulletproof, one of the Kentucky clans—when Jolly told him Seng and Lambert wanted him next.

They shook hands and the triad sat down.

"Glad to meet you at last, Valentine," Seng said. His squashed-flat face was pulled down a bit at the corners, reminding Valentine of a catfish.

"Thank you, sir," Valentine said, a bit befuddled by the "at last."

"I had charge of the brigade in the Boston Mountains that was keeping Solon's boys busy while Southern Command was reorganizing in the swamps. They were getting set to roll over us when you derailed them in Little Rock."

*Why in God's name isn't this man a general?* Seng's history, prompted, came back to Valentine in a flash. He'd kept ten times his number tied down with a couple of regiments of regulars and some Wolf and Bear formations. He'd been at the Trans-Mississippi combat corps briefings.

"I should be thanking you, then," Valentine said. "They were so scared of you, they never shifted enough men to Little Rock to just roll over us. It's an honor to meet you, sir."

"If you two want to hug, I won't tell," Lambert put in. "We've got twelve more sit-downs today, Colonel."

"Terrible thought. Dots is off schedule," Seng said.

"Are you sorry you're not with the hunter or combat groups here?" Lambert asked Valentine.

"I'm just happy Highbeam is under way," Valentine said.

"I know. Ahn-Kha," Lambert said. "There's a picture of you and him up at GHQ, by the way. It's in the case with some mementos from the drive on Dallas. You guys are sleeping on the hood of a truck. He's sitting with his back against the windshield and you're pillowed on his thigh. It's rather sweet. His fur is all muddy and spiky. I recognized you by the hair."

"He was a good friend," Valentine said. If the rumors of a golden Grog leading the guerrilla army in the coal country had any truth to them, a piece of Valentine's soul knew it had to be Ahn-Kha.

"He's the one who brought in the heartroot tuber, right?" Seng said.

"It's more like a mushroom than a tuber," Valentine said. Heart-root was protein rich, with a nice balance of fats and carbohydrates. It was usually ground up and made into animal feed, or a hearty meal that could be boiled in water or baked, or a sweet paste that could be put on a biscuit, the last variant popularly called "Grog guck." "But we're putting Dots off schedule again."

"Thanks, Val," she said.

"Where's Styachowski?" Valentine asked. "I'd think she'd be in-volved in this."

Lambert's face blanked into a funereal mask. "Killed, two months ago. Plane crash in Mississippi. She was coordinating our Wolves with some guerrillas in Alabama."

"I'm sorry to hear that," Valentine said. Numb now, he would feel the shock sink in when he was alone at night, the way it always did. He was horribly used to this kind of news after a dozen years of fighting.

"That's why I try to avoid the bother of a personal life," she said. She opened the thick folder on her lap. Bookmarks with notations on it ran all around its three edges like a decorative fringe. She glanced at Seng and he spoke.

"We want you to put together a formation of company strength. You'll recruit them out of a pool of refugees at Camp Liberty. You know about Liberty?"

Valentine had heard of it. He'd even seen horse-drawn wagons full of people leaving for it. Just like Camp Freedom in the South, or Independence in the Northwest. What was the new one in north Texas called? Reliance. "That's where the rabbits picked up by Rally Base were sent."

"Rabbits" was Southern Command slang for people who made the run out of the Kurian Zone.

"Been there?"

"No."

"The commander's a good egg. He'll help you out," Lambert said. "He'll be ordered to assist, as a matter of fact."

"What has he been told?" Valentine asked.

"The bare minimum," Lambert said. "Keep using the Argent ID for now. 'Southern Command indulges war criminals' is one of the more popular Kurian propaganda points. They talked up your escape in Kansas, to show what Southern Command does with murderers. Even the *Clarion* still mentions you now and then, when they're picking at old scabs. 'Sham justice for real murder.' That sort of thing."

The *Clarion* was an antiwar paper. Most of the soldiers called it the *Clarinet*, because of the high, squealing tune its editorial page frequently played.

"What's the purpose of this company?" Valentine asked, though he was already guessing.

"We want a few locals who can speak to the folks in their own language," Lambert said. "Facilitation with trade, scouting, scavenging. Ideally, your men will later get promoted to lead squads and platoons of their own, once we're set up properly in the triangle. So think about that: One day your company could swell into a regiment."

"Officers?"

"We'll give you a lieutenant to take your place if something happens to you," Lambert said.

Lambert was a chilly little calculator at times. "Happy thought. NCOs?"

"Take your pick, though we'd rather you did it from the ready reserve. We'd hate to disturb frontline units too much. We've got some names if you feel like you're out of touch."

"I'd like to be able to offer a sergeant major star, sir."

"For a company?" Seng asked.

"You said it might grow."

"I don't see a problem with that," Lambert said. "I'll speak to the general."

"Where will we train?" Valentine asked.

"Haven't worked that out yet. It might be Rally Base, unless they decide that's too far forward. Highbeam will establish a separate depot, wherever they end up."

"I don't suppose you can tell me when we're going."

Lambert smiled. "You must be joking. But it won't be before next year. So if you want to take some time off to disappear into northern Missouri again, you can have a couple weeks once you've got your men assembled and they're training. Clear it with Seng and myself and we'll square things with the general. Just don't get yourself caught."

"Be terrible if they found out New Orleans was about to be hit," Valentine said.

"So, how does it sound?" Seng asked. "I know you've wanted a mission to aid the guerrillas in the coal country. Suit you?"

"It's back to the Kurian Zone. I like it there. I can shoot at my enemies."

"You'd like to take a shot at Sime, I bet," Lambert said.

Valentine shrugged. How did she know that? Well, not worth thinking about that. Lambert had taken an unusual interest in him. He wouldn't be surprised if she'd read the old letters from Molly Carlson, resting in some warehouse with his Cat claws and other souvenirs.

"One more thing. Do you mind being available for questions about conditions in Kentucky? I get the feeling Brother Mark isn't going over that well."

"New Church just sticks in some of these guys' throats," Seng added. "They're not swallowing what he says."

Valentine didn't like churchmen, even former ones. "My gag reflex has been acting up too."

"Speaking of swallowing, he only eats raw food. Nuts and milk and honey and stuff," Lambert said. "Gets odd looks at lunchtime and he never joins in for pizza or barbecue."

"I saw him eat a hard-boiled egg," Valentine put in.

"But you don't mind being called on for an opinion?" Seng asked.

"Not at all, sir."

"Go on to your next meeting," Seng said to Lambert. "I'll catch up in a minute."

Lambert glanced at Valentine. "It's going to be a busy ten days. We'll talk again."

"I'll look forward to that, Colonel," Valentine said.

She left and Seng shifted his chair so it faced Valentine directly.

"You were headed for staff training when they arrested you."

The shock and hurt had long since healed over. That was a different young man. "Yes."

"Sorry to hear that. I went through it, you know. I think we would have done it about the same time, right after Dallas."

"How was it?"

"Tough. Felt like I was being rotated through every unit in the command. I've got most of a footlocker filled with my texts and workbooks. I'd like to loan it to you. There's a lot of good training materials in there. I expect if Highbeam gets off the ground, it might be useful to you. Lambert wasn't kidding about that regiment. We're going to have to rely on the locals to supply most of our manpower. They'll need training from our best people."

Valentine fought down a stammer. "Thank you. I'd like that."

Seng wasn't a smiler, but his mouth relaxed. "You haven't had to decipher my handwriting yet. I know we've just met, but I'm glad you're with us on this trip. When I went over the list of names our sharp young colonel drew up and I saw yours, I remembered when we heard you'd blown up the Little Rock depot. You don't know what that meant to us, boxed up in those mountains."

Again, military formalities saved him embarrassment. "Thank you, sir."

Valentine spent the next ten days on double duty, working with the planners in his group and acting as a second opinion to Brother Mark, though he couldn't answer the questions about the guerrillas in the triangle, of course. He attended working meetings, helped write plans and orders, but mostly thought about the company he was to build. Some days he had little to do but listen and be grateful for the quiet time to get himself organized and draw up his own plans.

The officers bonded in meetings, at meals, and especially on the baseball diamond. Colonel Gage, in charge of the regulars, blew hot and cold, alternately charming and cutting. Gage's chief of staff was the rather pugnacious and compact Major Cleveland Bloom—an odd name for a woman, Valentine thought. She captained Valentine's team and went by the name Cleo on the baseball diamond, where she once pitched a shutout—not the easiest thing to do with softball. When her team was at bat she slapped each of them, man and woman, on the butt and ordered them to "get a hit." She didn't care about stolen bases, doubles, or walks—she wanted hits and more hits.

She had a similar reputation in the field as a fighter.

The Bear lieutenant, a scarred figure named Gamecock, only stayed a week and was the first to leave. "One of my team is in hospital," he said as they said good-bye at dinner. "I've got two places to fill, and there's few enough Bears about these days. I'm going to try to talk a couple out of retirement."

Valentine heartily wished him luck, thinking of his own plans after the departure date.

Gamecock hadn't been much involved in the meetings in any case. Bears didn't give a damn about planning. You put them up close to the enemy and turned them loose.

The civilians rotated in and out of the meetings unpredictably. Usually one or two were away, but never all three. Valentine began to think of them as a single organism that morphed, for they dressed and spoke remarkably alike.

One day a courier arrived bearing a package. Valentine unwrapped it in his Spartan quarters and found a basket containing a set of paper-wrapped soaps inside.

> *Glad things worked out for the best.*
> *Please accept this peace offering.*
> *Best of fortune and rewards of honor in the coming year—*
> *—S*

Valentine unwrapped one of the soaps and took a cautious sniff. Sandalwood. They even had elegant little labels written in French.

Sime had remembered that Valentine had asked for a bar during their interview while he was incarcerated in the Nut awaiting trial.

At Valentine's shower that evening he spent an extra fifteen minutes wallowing in the silky feel of Sime's gift. It lathered up at the barest kiss of water and left his skin as smooth as an infant.

He found Brother Mark silent, gloomy company during their meetings together. He was the one member of the group Valentine couldn't get a feel for one way or another. Of course, high-ranking members of the New Order were habitually standoffish, quiet, and reserved.

He sometimes wondered if Lambert just placed Brother Mark with the planning group to act as a lightning rod for discontent. In mistrusting the churchman, all the other officers grew closer together.

He grew fond of the unassuming Jolly. Valentine was looking forward to serving under him.

"Beats being called Jelly, my old playground nickname," Jolla said. "I was chunky as a kid. Don't know how I managed it—whole family was just about starving, thanks to the cold summers. At sixteen I became a letter boy and started biking around with mail, and it finally came off."

Meanwhile, Valentine's denim-covered file folder grew ever thicker as they worked out variants on the basic plan involving weather and enemy countermoves. Highbeam was taking shape, and Valentine approved. He learned there was even a network of Cats in place to wreck rail lines in Tennessee and a bridge or two across the Ohio to delay any countermoves with large formations of troops. There was only one functioning rail line through central Kentucky anyway, and it would be easy enough to disable it.

Then it was time for them to disperse. They'd meet again outside Rally Base in a gradual buildup. The regulars wouldn't arrive until the last moment. They'd marshal farther to the south to preserve the illusion of the move on New Orleans.

†

Lambert walked around the square one last time and handed each of them a folded sheet of paper the size of a small piece of stationery. Lambert's neat handwriting was a little blotchy. Obviously the ink she used to write the forty notes wasn't the best quality.

The note read:

*The code name for this operation is now Javelin. Any changes to the blue-book plan will be marked Javelin. Everyday correspondence and orders will still be marked Highbeam, as will certain messages from me designed to bring confusion to the enemy. Please ignore any Highbeam order from my office dated with an even number.*

*This message is printed on sweet rice paper. It's tasty—enjoy.*

Valentine smiled. Confusion to the enemy.

†

A week later he stood before a house well outside Russellville, Arkansas, wearing civilian clothes and carrying his Maximillian Argent identification.

The imposing brick house had a rebuilt look to it, with a newer roof and windows added to something that had probably stood vacant and deteriorating since 2022. There was paper over the upstairs windows and Valentine saw a pile of sawdust in the garage. A big garden stood out back, and melon patches flanked the house. Household herbs grew under the sills.

Valentine scanned around with his ears and heard soft clicking out back.

He walked through the nearer of the two melon patches and found Nilay Patel next to a small mountain of stacked river-smooth rocks, digging what looked like a shallow trench connecting two foxholes but judging from the roll of waterproofing might be a sizable artificial pond. Patel had put on a little weight since he'd last seen him.

"Sergeant Patel!" Valentine called.

"No need to shout. I heard you come off the road," Patel said, fiddling with some tools in a bucket.

Valentine took a closer look. There was a revolver handle in there.

Patel's bushy eyebrows shot up. "Lieutenant Valentine!"

Valentine felt pleased to be recognized. He wondered if he'd recognize himself. "How are you, Sergeant?"

"Come across the hedge, just that away. Nadi," he called to the rear screen door. "Drinks! An old comrade is here to visit."

He picked up a curve-handled cane and limped to some garden furniture with hand-sewn cushions.

Nadja Patel, whom Valentine had once met as Nadja Mallow, emerged with a tray. Though she kept her glorious head of hair, she'd aged considerably, but then Solon's takeover of the Ozarks had taken her first husband.

She turned her back on Valentine as she set down the tray. Valentine smelled spicy mustard. "I thought I might as well bring you your lunch," she said to her husband. "Would you like something . . . ummm—"

"David," Valentine supplied. "Yes, it's a good walk from Russellville."

"I like it that way," Patel said. He used his cane to help himself sit. "Ahhh. The knees. I stayed too long a Wolf," Patel said.

"You're not listed as a disable."

"If there's a crisis, I don't want to be stuck behind a wheel or a desk," Patel said, rubbing his kneecaps. "I have good days and bad ones. I've been working since morning, so this will be a bad day."

Valentine heard a clatter from the kitchen and the woman's voice, quietly swearing.

"Can I help in there?" Valentine called.

"No," Nadja called back.

"I know this is not a social call," Patel said. "She has guessed too."

"Nilay, you were the best sergeant I ever knew in the Wolves, which makes you the best I ever knew, period. I saw you listed as inactive. I would have called, but—"

"We don't have a phone," Patel said, smiling. His teeth had yellowed. "I keep a radio. For emergencies."

Nadja Patel emerged and dropped a sandwich in front of Valentine. "You're welcome," she said, before Valentine could thank her. A quartered watermelon followed.

"Now, Nadi," Patel said.

"I know what he's here for. A sandwich he's welcome to. Another husband he's not."

Valentine thought it best to keep silent.

Nadja returned to the house.

Valentine didn't touch the sandwich. "I'll leave. You two enjoy your lunch. It's a beautiful garden, by the way."

"Sit down, sir! Let me hear what you have to say. You came all this way."

"It's an op. Outside the Free Terr—Republics. I can't say any more. But your legs—"

"Are still fit to carry me. David, I've been retired just long enough to feel the grave close in. With nothing to do I've started smoking again. I should like very much to help." Patel tossed the cane he'd been using into the diggings.

"Here I thought I'd have to convince you," Valentine said, getting up and retrieving the cane. "I've got warrant papers for a star to go in the middle of the stripes. You'll be my top."

"I do not need convincing. She does. That would help."

"Don't you want to talk it over with her first?"

"For three years I have done my best to give her whatever she wants. This, I want. She is upset because she knows me. I said no once before to Captain LeHavre and came to regret it."

"He's still alive, as far as I know. He made it to the Cascades. He's fighting out there now."

"I always suspected there was more to you."

"Tell her it would raise your pension. You'd get a sergeant major's land grant too. You could sell it or add to this spread."

"Thank you, sir. Not for the land; for the chance to get back to important work."

Valentine raised his voice, hoping the woman inside was listening. "It's just for a few months' work, all in the Free Territory. Training. When we step out, you'll come back here with your rank permanently raised. I'll promote someone else into your place."

"We shall see. You say you need men trained? Not Wolves?"

"Unfortunately, no. Regulars, more or less. I'm due at Camp Liberty in six days. Is that enough time to get your affairs in order?"

"Camp Liberty? Yes, if I have the written orders."

Valentine opened his rucksack and extracted his order book. "I pre-filled out most of it. Except your . . ." He lowered his voice. "Next of kin. That kind of thing."

"I know where to submit the copies," Patel said.

"Thank you, Nilay. It'll only be a few months. I can promise her that, if you like."

"Don't. It would be better coming from me. She knows promises don't mean much where the Cause is concerned."

"I could find housing for her, you know. You wouldn't have to be separated so much."

"I think she would prefer to keep fixing this place. She's a better carpenter and painter than me anyway. When it comes to homely matters I'm fit only for ditch digging. Besides, she has a sister in Russellville. She will be better off here."

Valentine ate his sandwich, wondering if she'd spit in the mustard. They talked about old friends until it was time to leave.

Patel's eyes shone with excitement as they shook hands. Odd that Valentine was now the reluctant one. Maybe it was the faint sobbing from inside the house.

# CHAPTER THREE

*C*amp Liberty, November: The word "camp" implies a certain bucolic simplicity, but Camp Liberty is anything but. It is in fact a small town once named Stuttgart: "The Rice and Duck Capital of the World."

*A few old-timers remain in town, "making do" as the locals say with the constant influx and outflow of people picked up from the banks of the Mississippi. Everything from exhausted, half-starved families to rogue river patrol units who beached their boat and ran for it are funneled into Liberty.*

*The former Camp Liberty, which stood just south of town, headquartered at the old high school just off Route 79, was destroyed during Solon's takeover. Much of Stuttgart's housing was demolished and populace was herded into "temporaries"—prefabricated homes designed for easier concentration of a populace, a Kurian specialty. Solon had great plans for the rice-growing region, and construction materials were hauled in for apartment buildings, a New Universal Church Community Apex, even a theater. When Solon's Trans-Mississippi order collapsed, most of the residents fled the wire-bordered housing, happy to abandon the roof over their heads for wider horizons.*

*Southern Command was not about to let the construction gear, raw materials, and prefabricated housing go to waste, so Stuttgart became the new Camp Liberty and work began on a new hospital, training and orientation center, and combined primary/secondary school for children who escaped the KZ with their parents.*

*Meanwhile, their elders were put to work in the rice mills, when they weren't attending class to acclimate them to life in tougher, but freer, lands.*

*When David Valentine visited Liberty, it was the finest facility of
its kind in the Texas and Ozark Free Republics—and it was still under
construction.*

†

After checking their luggage at the station, Valentine paid for a horse
cart so he and his new sergeant major could ride through town—or
the camp, rather—saving Patel's legs from the walk.

They passed through two checkpoints—there were no wire, towers,
or searchlights, at least not visible from Main Street, as Valentine learned.
There were guards watching from a balcony or two, and more mounted
officers riding horses chatted and swapped news with the locals.

They held handkerchiefs over their faces as they passed through
construction dust. Men in dungarees with sleeves and trouser legs of
different colors were digging a foundation.

"POWs?" Patel asked.

"Doesn't look like it. I don't see a single guard," Valentine said.

"Look at all the signage," Patel said, gesturing to a general store.
A universal white stick figure pushed a wheeled basket across a plain
green background. Iconography for beds, phones, and even babies
and animals hung over other doors or were stuck into second-floor
windows. The streets, too, were color coded and marked with animal-
cracker outlines.

Valentine had visited more Kurian Zones than even an experienced soldier like Patel. He was used to signs both written and in
iconography. It hadn't registered this time for some reason.

"It's for illiterates," Valentine said. "Shopping cart for store, dollar
sign for bank, syringe for medical center . . ."

Of course in the Free Territory there wouldn't be a smiley face for
the NUC building.

They ate in a diner, killing time until Valentine's appointment
with the camp supervisor. Which was just as well, as the service was
slow to the point that Valentine got their own coffee refills.

Valentine helped the attendant at the register make change for his bill, when Valentine threw him off by paying a $12.62 tab with $13.12.

"I'm all muddled up from multiplication and division, sir," the attendant said, tucking his head in that old Kurian Zone gesture of submission. "Clean forgot my subtraction."

"Take your time," Valentine said. "I just wanted a couple of dollars to buy a paper."

"Always amazes me that they can even find their way to the Territory," Patel said once they were back on the street.

" 'West to the big river and freedom,' " Valentine said. "The underground helps some of them along."

Valentine turned a WET PAINT sign right side up as they walked down the sidewalk, and the gap-toothed painter gave them a Morse-code grin and a thumbs-up.

Liberty's administration building looked like an old town hall or possibly a courthouse. They got directions from a bright and attentive young woman in another strange dual-color outfit.

Supervisor Felshtinsky had a nice corner office with a view of the towering rice mills and a staff of three. One was arguing over the phone with someone about duck poaching and the other two were buried in paperwork.

"My name's Argent," Valentine said. "Southern Command. I've got a two o'clock appointment."

"The super is out on the grounds," an older woman said. "I can page him on the walkie-talkie."

"I'd appreciate that."

"Sorry he's out, but you never know with the trains," she said, smiling. "He's a very busy man."

The other put down his pencil and turned around and took a plastic bag off a bureau.

"Welcome to Camp Liberty. Visitor ID tags and a house key," he explained, handing the bag to Valentine. "You can use the ID tag to eat in any of the cafeterias. Your trailer's in the southeast quadrant, just behind this building. Go in through the green arch. You can see it from the south side of this building. You're lucky: As guests, you have a kitchen with a fridge and everything. We'd appreciate it if you didn't wear pistols, and you can check any other guns in at the armory. It's in this building's basement."

"Why no pistols?" Patel asked.

"Most of the folks here, they just wilt when they see someone with a gun," the older woman with the walkie-talkie said. She spoke into it again and then returned her attention to Patel. "Might as well put on a pair of lifts and a Reaper's hood."

Patel looked at Valentine and glanced heavenward.

Valentine changed the subject. "I'd asked for an index of your current residents who came out of Kentucky and Tennessee. Even the Virginias."

"And we haven't got to it yet," the man on the phone said, covering the mouthpiece. "We've got only one computer allocated to admin and only one man who knows how to work the database. Our old printer runs on curses and tears."

"Hot dog," Valentine said, letting out a deep breath. "Hammer's going to go red as a baboon's butt."

Patel's eyes widened, then he nodded. "Tell me about it."

"Who's Hammer?" the man with the key packet asked.

"My CO," Valentine said. "Ex-Bear." He tapped the scar running the side of his face for emphasis. "He'll probably be here by tomorrow to get things moving."

"You think the file cabinets will fit through that window?" Patel asked Valentine.

"Eventually," Valentine said.

"You'll have your list delivered to the trailer this evening," the man with the phone said, clicking off his call and dialing a new set of numbers.

†

They met Supervisor Felshtinsky out front. He had a tall, muscular assistant and rode in an electric golf cart.

Valentine had never seen a golf cart fitted out with a gun rack. A beautiful over/under shotgun rested in its locks, and Felshtinsky had flying ducks painted on the back of the low-riding vehicle. Its rear was filled with plastic file folders.

"You'll excuse me not standing," Felshtinsky said as he turned in his seat to shake their hands. He looked relaxed and tan in a polo shirt. "I've been on wheels since 'fifty-eight."

He had a strong grip and heavy shoulder muscles. Valentine guessed he lifted weights; you didn't get muscles like that just dragging your body around. Valentine felt humbled and apologetic, as he always did when meeting someone who'd lost a piece of themselves.

"Hop in back there. I'll give you a tour."

As they drove around to the cart's smooth, almost silent engine whine, Felshtinsky told them about his post. He was proud of his operation. He had close to four thousand people under his charge, temporary residents acclimating to the Free Territory, or permanents who'd settled around Liberty.

"We've got as many teachers here as Little Rock or Dallas," Felshtinsky said.

"How long do they stay?" Valentine asked.

"Depends. Sometimes a young couple meets up here, decides to get married and start fresh, and leaves right away. We get some not much smarter than a well-trained horse. They count on their fingers and can recite a few Church verses about flushing only once a day. Try learning to write at forty-three."

Felshtinsky explained how all the residents earned "Liberty bucks" doing training. Liberty bucks could buy them furniture and appliances for their homes or beers at the camp's bowling alley, and most of the merchants in town let them use the scrip to buy from a limited selection of toiletries and merchandise provided by Southern Command's warehouses at a discount.

They passed the first wire Valentine had seen. It was ordinary fencing, and a military policeman with a pistol stood in a guardhouse at a gate.

The tightly packed trailers inside the fence looked too numerous for a prison compound, unless the residents of Liberty were unusually lawless.

"What's that?"

"That's for Quislings. They stay there until they're cleared by Southern Command. They're worried about another big sabotage outburst, like just before Solon showed up, so they make sure."

Valentine saw one of the residents pushing a wheelbarrow with a yellow plastic water keg in it. He wore that alternate-color scheme Valentine had seen here and there.

They drove around the hospital and the ethanol plant, the rice mill and the cane fields. Arrowheads of ducks and geese flew overhead.

"Lots of waterfowl in this part of Arkansas," Felshtinsky said. "If you want to get up early and go for a duck, I've got the best blind in the county. Privileges of rank."

"Sergeant Major?" Valentine asked Patel.

"I would like that. If I could have the loan of a birding gun. What about you, sir?"

"I'll spend the morning going over the printouts. Assuming they showed up and we don't have to sic the Hammer on our host's staff."

†

Everything about the next day, save for Patel's ducks—simmered in a homemade korma sauce all afternoon in their tiny cabin oven and served over (what else?) rice—disappointed.

Their first order of business, after dressing the morning ducks, was to check out Liberty's militia training camp. The young men and women were sad specimens, mostly undersized, undertrained, and undereducated. Valentine had never seen so many hollow chests, flat feet, bad eyes, and rickety knees.

"To think these are the ones with the ability to make it out," Patel said.

They stopped by the rifle range and saw a bored Southern Command corporal watching a couple of men in the two-tone Quisling fatigues training some kids to shoot.

"Hold it tight into your shoulder," one said, patting a recruit on the back. "It's not going to hurt you, 'less you hold it like a snake that's gonna bite."

"Kur's sake, keep your damn eyes open and on target when you pull the trigger," his companion bawled.

"Let me see that gun, um . . . ," Patel said.

" 'Probation,' " the Southern Command corporal supplied. "That's what we calls 'em."

"Sergeant," Patel barked. He still didn't have his stripes with the star in the middle for his old Wolf deerskins.

"That's what we call them, Sergeant," the corporal said, stiffening.

The "probation" came to his feet smartly, took out the magazine, and opened the breech, presenting the weapon to Patel.

"Sir," he said.

Patel placed his cane against his crotch and took the rifle, checked it barrel to butt. "They take good care of their weapons."

"They're not afraid to clean them, sir."

The other probation ignored the byplay. His recruit, firing from the prone position with the gun resting on a sandbag, shot across the field. The hidden range man in the trench flagged a miss.

"Them sights is all messed up," the militia recruit complained.

The probation/trainer next to him took up the weapon, put his cheek to it, and fired from the seated position. The spotter pulled the target down and pushed it up again with a bit of red tape at the edge of the ten-ring.

"You're right. The sights are off."

"These, I like," Patel said.

†

Valentine had announcements that called an evening meeting in one of the rec centers, but the meeting wasn't as crowded as Valentine would have liked. The basketball courts in the rec center could have held a thousand people, with more in the stands, but he got only a few hundred, and many of them were women with children.

Valentine didn't see a single person in the two-tone overalls or outfits. He wasn't that surprised. A former Quisling could expect an instant death sentence if found bearing arms against the Kurians.

"You should have advertised free beer," Patel said, sotto voce.

"I'm looking for volunteers to go back into the Kurian Zone," Valentine announced. "To go back fighting. This time with an army of our people. I don't need riflemen so much as facilitators—people who know the locals and can interact with them."

Valentine saw a few at the back slip out and head for the washrooms or the exits.

"Service grants you all the benefits of OFR citizenship, pension benefits, retirement allotment, and combat service bonuses."

He was flopping. He felt the sweat running down his back. "Anyone interested, join Sergeant Major Patel here on the bleachers. We'll come around and get your information, meet, answer questions. Then we'll let you know in the next day or so if you'll be called back for a physical and a second interview."

A man with a Riceland cap laughed as the crowd dispersed. He smiled at Valentine and touched his cap. "First rule, johnny soldier, is don't volunteer for nothing. Goes same in Free Territory."

They got eleven. Valentine could tell right off that he wouldn't want three of them—way too young or far too old. They took down the details of them all anyway.

Later, over the duck and rice and a couple of beers Patel had had the foresight to buy as the day went south, Valentine looked over the "applications." They'd had to fill out the blanks for the four illiterates—well, they could write their names, but that was about it.

"Six or eight, depending on the physical," Valentine said in the dim light of the cramped trailer kitchen. "We might get another couple dozen out of the militia in training, and that's if we don't restrict it to those from Kentucky and Tennessee. Southern Command's already got the pick of the men passing through here. The ones eager to fight have already joined up."

"The only two I really liked were those Quislings on the rifle range," Patel said.

"I think those will be our first corporals," Valentine said.

"God help us," Patel said, reaching for two more beers. That was one nice thing about the prefabricated trailer home. You only had to turn around to reach the fridge.

✝

Patel was slow getting up. He'd flex his legs and then get up on one elbow. Then he'd swing his legs down and raise and lower each shoulder.

Valentine brought him some hickory coffee. Though moving coffee beans between Kurian Zone and Free Territory wasn't illegal, at least as far as the UFR was concerned—just dangerous—and "smugglers" saw to it that such luxuries were available, Valentine couldn't afford the price. The only thing stimulating about the hickory coffee was the temperature. Whoever made this mix put just enough of the real thing in to remind you what it wasn't.

"I was thinking we could try having breakfast in that probation camp," Valentine said.

"You think we will do better with the Quislings," Patel said, massaging and rotating his knees. He paused, reached for the cup, and downed half his steaming coffee—his throat must be tough as his leathers, Valentine decided—and held out the mug for a refill.

The Quislings ate in an oversized Quonset hut. Every word, every *clunk* of cup being set upon table, every scrape of knife and fork in a tray was magnified and bounced around by the curving walls as though the diners were musicians in a concert shell. Valentine tried to turn off his ears.

Valentine looked across the group—mostly men; there were far fewer women and children in this group—with something like hunger. These specimens were straighter, fleshier, longer of limb, and more alert of eye. Some wore tool belts or had hard hats dangling from nearby hooks; others read or did crosswords over the remains of their breakfast. He shifted his feet and cleared his throat.

"Could I have your attention please?" Valentine said.

He'd misjudged the volume required. His words were lost in the breakfast clatter and chatter.

"Oi!" Patel shouted. Patel's voice was like a mortar round exploding beside him. It almost blew him out of his boots. "Who wants to kill a few Kurians?"

The room quieted admirably as better than a hundred faces turned their way in interest.

†

"Sorry, but you can't have 'em," Felshtinsky said from his office wheel-chair early the next morning. He pushed the names of the probations back across his desk at Valentine and Patel, seated opposite.

"Why?" Valentine asked.

"Ex–Kurian Forces aren't allowed to just leave Liberty whenever they want. They have to be cleared by Southern Command."

"If you just need a signature, I'll take responsibility," Valentine said.

"Sorry, it's not that simple. I can't release them to you."

"What if General Lehman's HQ signs off for them?"

"It's not just Southern Command. The civilian authority has to sign off on them as well."

"Which civilian authority?" Valentine asked.

"Interstate Security Office."

Valentine knew little about the ISO, save that their field officers were called marshals. He'd once seen one come in to Rally Base to pick up two river patrol Quislings who'd gotten drunk and decided to fish from the wrong bank of the river. The marshal wore blue pants with a navy stripe down each side and had a badge, but other than that he looked like a typical hand on a horse farm.

"I don't suppose there's someone from the ISO here."

"As a matter of fact, there is. You've got a UFR/ISO district marshal just across the street at the station. He runs a one-man show. He's got an office off our regular police force. His name's Petrie and I wish you luck with him."

†

Ray Petrie had alcohol on his breath at ten thirty in the morning.

The duty sergeant at the small police station had advised them that he showed up anytime between eight and eleven, depending on how late the card games went.

You had to catch him quickly before he left for lunch, a uniformed woman struggling with a rusted padlock on an evidence cage added. So Valentine and Patel drank police-station coffee (and used the station washroom shortly thereafter; Liberty cops liked their smuggled-in beans strong) and waited for Petrie to appear.

There was already a waiting line. A couple, both in the two-tone dungarees, the woman swollen in pregnancy, waited.

"Not long now," Valentine said, looking at the mother-to-be.

"You don't know Petrie," the man said. "I was a librarian in a Youth Vanguard school. I've got a job here, filing, but our application still hasn't been approved. We don't even want to move out of town! And we met here; that's how long the wait's been."

"I meant not long for the child," Valentine said.

"It's our second," she added, closing her eyes and sighing.

Petrie came in yawning, a fleshy man with a heavy mustache and a growth of beard. He paused on the way in, a thoughtful look on his face, grabbed the edge of the duty sergeant's desk as though to keep himself from keeling over, and farted abundantly.

"Christ, Petrie," the duty sergeant said.

The marshal took a chained ring of keys and opened his side office.

"A minute," he said to them. Valentine had time to spot a dead houseplant atop a file cabinet before Petrie closed the office door behind him.

He reemerged only to go into the washroom carrying some items wrapped in a towel. He emerged again, shaved and combed.

"Just another minute," he said, nodding to them. This time the station cat managed to flash through the door.

A radio flicked on in the office. Valentine heard the keys employed again, a file cabinet open, the pop of a cork being pulled, and the marshal sit heavily. A minute passed, then the cabinet and keys sounded again.

The door opened. "C'mon in. Open for business," he said to Valentine.

"They were here first," Valentine said, gesturing to the couple.

"They can wait. They're used to it."

Petrie turned heavily away and went to his chair.

"Go ahead," Valentine said to the Quislings.

The couple went in. Petrie didn't bother greeting them. "Good news, Courage," Petrie said. Valentine watched the interaction. "Your application came back, provisionally approved."

"Provisionally?" the man and woman groaned, if not in unison, at least in harmony.

"Your list of references got misplaced somewhere between here and the office." Petrie got up and shut the door, but that didn't matter to Valentine's ears, or to Patel's for that matter.

"Believe you me, it might take a while. I could make sure they get found soon for another five hundred," Petrie said. "You want that kid born a regular citizen, right?"

Valentine flushed. Those poor people. This was how business was carried out in the Kurian Zone. Some combination of an office and a title with a bit of power, looking for his taste of sugar on the transactions crossing his desk.

He and Patel exchanged a look. Patel worked his jaw as though he wanted to spit.

"You'll have it in a week," the man called Courage said. Valentine suspected it was a first name.

"To show you two just how good I take care of you, I'll give you the provisional without waiting." Valentine heard a couple of resounding thumps on the desk as Petrie stamped paperwork. The couple left, the man holding a file folio as tightly as he did his wife.

Valentine and Patel stood up to enter, but Petrie was right behind the couple. He took his keys out and stuck them in the lock.

"Missed your chance," the marshal said. "I'm going to lunch."

Valentine extracted a bill. "I'm in a hurry. How about I buy you lunch in exchange for fifteen minutes of your valuable time."

"You got it, militia." The bill disappeared so smoothly Valentine thought Petrie an amateur magician. He held the door open and they entered his office.

The cat crouched, peering under a bookcase. Valentine suspected a mouse down there. Maybe more than one. Enough crumbs and bits of paper-wrapped sandwich littered the desk and sat in the unemptied wastebasket to feed a family of mice.

A file cabinet with PENDING stenciled on it had another overflowing box of paperwork atop it marked "priority pending."

"What can I do for a militia major and a Wolf, by the looks of it?" Petrie asked.

"I'm going to need some paperwork processed quickly. I want to do some recruiting among the probations. About a hundred."

"A hundred?" Petrie ejaculated, showing more animation than he had all morning. "Probations? You mean, let them loose?"

"No, just released to Southern Command, through me."

"That would take months."

"You want to do this the easy way or the hard way, Petrie?" Valentine asked.

Petrie tested his newly shaven chin. "Meaning what?"

"Meaning you can say 'Anything for the Cause' and get off your duff. Figure out a way to get ISO sign-off on the men I want. Pick up the phone and talk to whoever you need to talk to in order to get them cleared to join the Command."

"What's the easy way?" Petrie asked.

"That was the easy way," Valentine said.

"I'm late for lunch," Petrie said.

"He wants the hard way," Patel sighed.

Valentine stood up and opened the door for him. "Go to lunch, Petrie. Make it a big one. By the time you get back, Sergeant Major Patel and I will have sworn out a warrant for your arrest. We both heard you extort a civilian on a Southern Command base. For five hundred dollars, to be exact. In case you don't know military law, that's a very big no-no."

Petrie looked around his office as if to see where they were hiding when they overhead the conversation.

"Lose your appetite?" Valentine said. He shut the door again and turned to address Petrie.

"You might think that being OSI, you're not subject to military law, but the people you've been juicing are certainly protected by it. You'll spend at least a night in the cells, probably more, as it'll take a bit of time to get you counsel. With our sworn statements, JAG investigators will be here tomorrow. I'll tell them to be sure to bring a good accountant to see just how your paperwork balances up for this little corner of ISO. I wonder why you don't have a clerk to help you with some of these files, Petrie. Or do you? Existing only on paper, maybe? In any case, maybe the jaggers can't prosecute, but they can tie up your case in a beautiful ribbon and present it to the circuit court."

Petrie glowered for a moment, and then his lips curled into a sneer. "You think you're so smart, militia. Didn't you read the name on the door? My uncle's the lieutenant governor of Texas. I'll make a couple of phone calls and whatever stink you made will get blown right out the window. You'll get busted down to private and you'll spend the next four years pumping out porta-johns for the biodiesel plant."

"Thanks for the tidbit, Petrie. I don't follow politics, so I didn't recognize the name. But right after I talk to JAG I'll see if I can get a couple of newspapers interested. 'Recent arrest implicates Lieutenant Governor in corruption probe,' is how the *Clarion* will put it, I expect. Better yet, 'Governor's office tainted.' The papers love a good coat of taint. Be interesting to see if your uncle lifts a finger to help you. Hope you remembered to send him his birthday card."

"Two can play your game, militia," Petrie said, folding his arms. "I can fill out warrants of my own. You're threatening an ISO officer into malfeasance. Maybe they'll put us in adjoining cells."

"You're not a big fan of reason, are you, Petrie? You never should have hit me."

"I never put a hand on—"

"The nose, Patel, good and hard."

Patel made a fist and punched him hard across the bridge of his nose. White light shot through his brain, and when Valentine opened his eyes again, he tasted blood, felt it dripping.

"Patel," Valentine gasped. "Restrain the marshal. He's flipped."

Patel moved nimbly for a man of his bulk. Petrie tried to rise but Patel sat him back in his chair hard with a good shove. When he rose again, Patel spun him around and gripped him across the back of the head and his right arm.

The cat gave up on its mouse and hid.

Valentine recognized the grip; he'd been in it often enough. Patel had been the Second Wolf Regiment's premier wrestler for three years running. Valentine had once seen his new sergeant major dislocate a horse rustler's shoulder when he didn't like the tone of his answers under questioning.

Valentine turned up the radio. "Give him something to think about, Sergeant Major."

"Hel—" Petrie began to shout.

It was a tight fit, with the three of them behind Petrie's desk, Valentine keeping Petrie's mouth shut with a stiff-arm.

Petrie finally gave, his muscles turning from wood to oatmeal.

"We're going to take care of three pieces of business this morning, Petrie," Valentine said, wiping his bleeding nose and flicking the blood onto Petrie. "First, you're going to fill out a hundred releases for me with the names blank. Second, you're going to do whatever paperwork needs to be done for your central office. Patel and I both know how to write and type. We can do either to give you a hand. We'll even send out for sandwiches on my tab and have a working lunch. When I'm satisfied, we're going to write out your resignation from ISO. You can tell your uncle you got sick of rice.

"One slipup, one bit of paperwork slowed up, one questioning telegram—and you're going to jail, Petrie. I'd better see a postcard from whatever sinecure your uncle finds you. Yes?"

He removed his hand from Petrie's mouth.

"They're Quislings," Petrie said.

"That wasn't a yes. Dislocate his shoulder whenever you like, Patel."

"Who cares if they get squeezed? They've done plenty of squeezing across the river, believe you me."

"That's in the past."

"You're assaulting an ISO officer. You'll wind up—"

Valentine heard—and felt—the pop of Petrie's shoulder.

"Arrrrgh—" Petrie grunted, sagging. Patel shoved him back into his chair, his arm hanging.

"I didn't think you'd do it," Petrie said softly, his face white with pain.

"A dislocation's easy to fix," Valentine said. "Petrie! Keep your hand away from that phone. Broken fingers are a bitch while they heal."

"I could pop his jaw," Patel said, gripping either side of Petrie's head. "That'll cut his talking down to 'Ow.' "

Valentine let Petrie catch his breath.

"So, Marshal, have we reached a deeper understanding? You've got three more limbs. I don't want to have to leave you in a bathtub full of ice without any of them working, but I will."

"You can have 'em," Petrie said. "Hope one of them rolls a grenade into your tent for me. That's all the thanks you'll get from those mooks."

"You're a mean, stubborn bastard, Petrie," Valentine said. "If your uncle can't find anything for you, you're welcome to join my outfit."

# CHAPTER FOUR

*H*ighbeam Assembly Area, Arkansas, November: Just outside the city
of Jonesboro, now notable only for its hospital, which is the only one in the
northeastern corner of the state, a new camp is going up.

Southern Command believes that the best people to build a camp are
the soldiers who have to eat, sleep, and train in it. Cartload after cartload of
lumber, tenting, plumbing, and wiring arrives as the assembly area swells,
hauled from the rail terminus to the camp by ox wagons and mule teams.

A tricky autumn dumped rain and a freak snowstorm on the soldiers as
they hammered and tacked and strung. Now, with canvas roofing above their
heads at last and corduroy roads made of scrub timber and wood chips, the
rain blows out northeast and a cool, dry fall sets in, though the chill in the
midnight-to-dawn air hints at worse to come.

Valentine's company arrived after the Wolf contingent and Bear teams but
before most of the Guard forces of the expeditionary brigade. They got their
own corner of the assembly area, a little blister near the camp's drainage.

As far as the men were concerned, they were preparing for a "long
out." Lambert had planted rumors that their destination was New Orleans
or a big raid on the river patrol base at Vicksburg. Consequently the men
assumed that they'd be going in the opposite direction, perhaps to Omaha
or another try at western Kansas. One Wolf swore that it would certainly
be Omaha, as he knew for a fact that Major Valentine was familiar with
the city, as his sister had served under him on Big Rock Hill and afterward
on the drive into Texas. She knew all about him. Others bet him that it was
Kansas, as Colonel Seng had buried a lot of soldiers there and was going
back to reclaim old ground.

*Each man both hopes for and fears the coming "long out." On the return from such a campaign, promotions and awards are handed out like Archangel Day candy. Quieter, dirtier stories of the women looking for an easy out of the Kurian Zone appeal to some; others talk of strange liquors and dishes. The best of them, writing letters home or making out the public paragraphs of their wills, refer to the gratification of liberating a town or county, the fear of the residents that slowly transforms to hope, and the hard work of making individuals out of cattle.*

*David Valentine, looking at his motley assortment of Camp Liberty volunteers (ninety-two former Quislings and twelve refugees, of which nine are women) drawn up on a freshly cleared field within their winter encampment for their first morning's exercises, readies himself for the strain of once again being responsible for men's lives—including, in the words of his old Wolf captain LeHavre, "burying your mistakes."*

✝

Patel was still the only NCO. Valentine's requests had disappeared into the maw of Southern Command's digestive process. What would emerge from the other end remained to be seen.

He was lined up with the other men, ahead of the massed ranks. Valentine wore his oldest militia fatigues and the men were still in their Liberty handouts. They'd divide the men into platoons later. For now they'd eat, sleep, and exercise in a big mass.

Even in the early days of their acquaintance he was already conditioning himself to the idea that some of them, even all of them, might die in the coming operation.

Valentine had made peace with his own death. He'd seen Kurian rule in all its fear and splatter. Faced with his experiences and the mixture of revulsion and hatred they inspired, he had only one option, the only option a man who wanted to call himself a man had: risking all in a fight that would end only with his death or the Kurian Order's destruction.

Why the men under him signed up wasn't strictly his concern. Whether they fought so they could look other soldiers in the eye, to take the place of a lost relative, to get an allotment, or because they thought of battle as the ultimate blood sport made no difference regarding the orders he would give: He'd do his duty the same whether a man signed for faith or money.

Speaking of duty, his first was creating a healthy environment for his men while they trained themselves into a fighting company.

The only improvement to their ground was a length of three-inch piping and some conduit extending out of the main camp. The rest of their materials were in the supply yard.

Patel stepped out of the little "command shack," the only structure standing in their blister at the end of the camp. His cane had disappeared and he looked as spry as ever.

He walked back and forth in front of the men once. He'd inked in a star on his old stripes and done a good job of it. Valentine could hardly tell the difference.

"My name is Sergeant Major Patel. You came here as a hundred and five individuals. Southern Command's going to make an army of one out of you. One well-trained, sharp brain that's always alert. One tough Reaper-eating body. One heart that fears only God and Sergeant Major Patel. You read me, slackers?"

"Sir yes sir!" Valentine shouted. A few voices behind joined in.

Patel put his hands on his hips and faced them. "Rest of you haven't finished evolving? Communication occurs when the transmitter broadcasts and the transmittee acknowledges. Try again!"

"Sir yes sir!" they shouted.

"I don't want to hear harmony—you're not a fuckin' chorus. All at once, and louder."

"Sir yes sir!" they shouted loud enough to be heard in Jonesboro. Georgia, not Arkansas.

"After morning exercise, we're going to build you all shelters. Ladies get theirs first, because we're in Southern Command. We're blessed with natural gallantry."

Morning exercises lasted until lunch. Patel took them through his "twelve labors." Again and again, he managed to find fault with the

71

rhythm of their jumping jacks or the height of someone's buttocks during a push-up. He sent Valentine and four exhausted "slackers" off to get the meal while he finished with the rest.

There wasn't a chuck wagon available so they piled bread and beans and trays into a wheelbarrow and ate with spoons. Dessert was flaky pastry smeared with "Grog guck."

Valentine got tap detail. He turned on the spigot and filled cups and a couple of beat-up old canteens and bladders from the flow of water so the recruits had something to drink with their food.

With everyone sprawled on the cold, damp ground eating and drinking, Valentine finally got his pan full of beans. The beans tasted as though they'd once shared a tin with some ham but divorced some time back, though the molasses in the sauce was sweet and welcome.

Patel gave them thirty minutes and then roused them to get to work on the frames for the tents. Valentine was the only one to notice that Patel's breath smelled like aspirin as he bellowed. But they did manage to finish the women's tent and get a start on the showers.

That night they slept around fifty-five-gallon drum stoves burning scrap from the lumber they'd measured and cut.

The first day was nothing to the second. Everyone ached and groaned as they did the twelve labors. Some fool asked when they were going to get their uniforms and Patel showed them why they weren't yet fit to wear Southern Command issue by running across, covering in, and crawling through the noisome field where the camp's sanitary waters drained off.

"Too slow," Patel said each and every time they fell into the mud. Or crawled. Or got up. Or crossed the field. Or turned around to cross the field again.

They slept in a formidable stench that second night, thanks to the field and two (or more—the men had had a long trip on buses) days' worth of hard-sweat body odor. The next day, eating a breakfast of biscuits and greasy gravy out of wheelbarrows again, they learned all about democracy as they voted to finish the showers before the men's shelter.

Valentine liked the decision that they'd rather sleep rough and cold than dirty. Men who wanted to get clean had pride in themselves. He also liked being under Patel's orders. It got him out of Camp Highbeam meetings and working dinners that were more social than productive.

They had the floorboards laid, the sinks running, and the shower headings up when Patel stopped them and had them line up on the camp's main road to welcome three new companies of the Guards into camp.

They must have made a strange impression, hair spiky with mud, the odd multicolor dungarees of Camp Liberty filthy with a mixture of muck and sawdust.

"Better get back to wrangling them pigs, boys," one called.

"Whew! Someone's been on shit detail," another Guard soldier called as they walked in. Catcalls and jibes were part of the Command's proud tradition. The men stared off blankly into space or looked down. They didn't have the spirit to answer back.

Yet.

That was his job. And Patel's. And the rest of his NCOs', if he ever got any. To make up for the jokes, after dinner that night he told them a little more about what they would be doing in the Kurian Zone— scouting and trading for food, scrounging up replacement gear, and interacting with the local resistance.

Unfortunately for his company, he learned the next day that the second name stuck. Maybe it was their odd bubo placement in the camp's layout, but Valentine's company became known as the "shit detail" in everything but formal correspondence.

He discussed the problem the next morning with Patel in the little command shack as the men slept—clean now, thanks to the functioning showers but still in tiny field tents or bags in the cold dew—as they planned the day's training.

"What do you think of promoting from within?" Patel asked. "There are several ex-sergeants. You've even got a busted-down captain in your ranks."

"I'd like to see talent rewarded," Valentine said. "It's more of a mind-set than technical and leadership skills that I'm worried about. In the Kurian Zone, it's enough to just issue an order. Here the men like to know the whys and hows so they feel a part of something larger. I'd like to see initiative—intelligent initiative—from privates on up."

"I don't think that's possible in a few months. If you want some sergeants taught to be Southern Command sergeants, I may be able to help. Can you get me any money?"

"I can try. What are you talking about?"

"About thirty thousand dollars."

"I don't have a pension to borrow against anymore, Patel. I'll try Lambert. She might have access to a slush fund. Tell me what you have in mind."

They worked out the deal with Lambert, the general, and Southern Command in three days. When Valentine pointed out that in the long run it would be cheaper than adding more men to the "long out" with bonuses and land grants and so forth, they agreed.

Plus it would be good for the "shit detail's" morale to be led by their own.

Naturally, there were staffing orders to cancel. As luck would have it, one position filled as the order was transmitted: a heavy weapons expert named Glass, rank of corporal and with a spotty record of wanting to do things his own way, showed up at camp and reported to the command shack as everyone was eating their lunches out of wheelbarrows again.

A small man with a big pack, he looked like some kind of beetle with an oversized carapace of pack and camp gear. He also sported the world's scraggliest beard. It looked like Spanish moss Valentine had seen in Louisiana.

Valentine stood up to welcome him and Patel trailed behind.

"Very glad to see you," Valentine said, shaking Glass' hand.

"Thank you, sir," he said rather sullenly.

"Don't want this assignment, Glass? You didn't get someone twisting your arm to volunteer, I hope."

"No. Nothing like that, Major. Tell the truth, I'm glad to be back under General Lehman. Just tired from the trip."

Glass was one of those compact, wiry men in what looked to be his late twenties. Judging from his qualifications list on his Q-file, he didn't look to be the type to wear down. Valentine let it rest.

"You're early, so you get to pick the most comfortable corner in the NCO tent. It's just you and Sergeant Major Patel for now."

They sized each other up, Patel in his Wolf leathers, hand sewn and patched, Glass in his ordinary Guard cammies. Glass stared vacantly at Patel, not so much challenging his superior as transmitting indifference.

"What's the company's support weaponry?" he asked.

"It's not here yet," Valentine said. "As you can see, everything's late to arrive, even uniforms. You might as well learn early, we're the shit detail of this outfit. Eat up."

"Will that be all, sir?"

"For the moment," Valentine replied.

"I'll get myself squared away, then," Glass said. He turned for the tent with Patel's name painted on the old bit of traffic sign next to the door.

"Brittle," Patel commented. "Just hope he's not about to break."

"He's got outstanding references for his competency. Leadership's lacking. His last CO called him 'prickly.' "

"Wonder how the guys who had to share a tent with him would have put it," Patel said.

"We're not going across the river to have a harvest bonfire and sing-along," Valentine replied. "I'm willing to wait and see."

†

Valentine's company's first lieutenant finally arrived late at night as Valentine caught up on paperwork in the one-bulb shack. He tripped on the doorstep coming in, straightened, saluted, and handed Valentine his orders.

They told a curious tale in the dates and checkboxes and comments. Valentine spent sixty seconds reading through.

Lieutenant (militia) Rowan Rand was Kentucky-bred; his parents made the run for Free Territory when he was fifteen. His father disappeared one night while scouting what looked like a vacant farmhouse and he'd helped his mother and sisters the rest of the way to the Ozarks, crossing the Mississippi on barrels à la Bilbo Baggins.

"Stint in the militia, and then right into Logistics Commandos?" Valentine asked, looking up from the file.

Rand blinked back at him through glasses that the ungenerous might call Coke bottle. "Bad eyesight. Astigmatism. I'm bat-blind without my eyewear plus I don't see so well in the dark. They never put it down on my record beyond 'needs glasses.' "

Southern Command's recruiters had the sense to weigh shortcomings against strengths, almost always in favor of giving a candidate a chance to prove their mettle. "You tore through the SC Intelligence and Aptitude tests. Your test scores make mine look like an illiterate's."

"Six years in a Church academy in Columbia District," Rand said.

"Church background? I'll introduce you to Brother Mark. How'd you like it?"

"The schoolwork was fun. And there were all the outings and marches and drives, singing the happy tunes as we worked. I'm embarrassed to think about it now."

"You were eleven. How could you know?" Valentine said.

"Same for you? You kind of choked up there, sir."

"I grew up in a different church, luckily."

"I would have run on my own during summer leave if my parents hadn't decided to try."

Valentine read over the file again. "Platoon leader and then a lieutenant in the militia. Five trips into Kentucky, three into Tennessee with the LCs. No combat?"

Rand shrugged. "Logistics Commandos think that if you get into a fight, you're a screwup."

The Logistics Commandos were odd units. They went into Kurian Zones to beg, borrow, or steal items Southern Command had difficulty manufacturing or maintaining. Mostly they were made up of veteran Hunter members, Wolves and Cats primarily, but Valentine had heard that with Hunter training slowed to a trickle, more and more regulars had been doing the hazardous duty.

Valentine read to the bottom of his assignment orders. Lambert herself had placed Rand with his company. If she believed in the man, there was no need to probe further.

"Welcome to Delta Company," Valentine said. "At the moment Sergeant Major Patel is running the show, turning the men into a team. When we're on the parade ground, he's in charge."

"Yes, sir," Rand said.

"I'll introduce you to the company. You'll stick close to me for a week or so until you find your feet, then you'll take over. I'm going north into Grog country. I'll be back in a few weeks, barring catastrophe."

†

Rand sank into his duties easily enough. To Valentine's delight, he soon swam lustily. He was all knees and elbows in the field and had a tendency to trip. After a sprawl he had a way of pushing his thick glasses back up his nose that disarmed the laughers and charmed the more sympathetic.

He accepted formal command of the company from Valentine with a nod and a yessir, then took off his glasses and cleaned them with his shirttail.

Valentine had a final word with Patel as the groom from the brigade stables held his horse, a sturdy Morgan named Raccoon. A packhorse stood just behind. Valentine hung his baggage and the odds and ends he'd been collecting on the packhorse.

"Keep up the good work, Sergeant Major," he said as Patel helped fix a clip.

"Enjoy your leave, sir."

"It won't all be fun. I'm going to see if I can do a little more recruiting in Missouri."

"You don't mean . . ."

"Yes. Grogs."

The horse holder snorted. Valentine took the reins and Patel shot the groom a look and growled: "Thank you, Private."

Valentine and Patel walked toward the gate. Well, not so much a gate as a big chain with a Southern Command postal number hanging from it and blocking the camp's entrance.

"Since you got out of the Wolves, sir . . . any head injuries?"

"The Cowardly Lion says it wasn't so much a head injury as Bud ringing my wake-up bell."

"Bud? Ah, yes, my old friend who tried to climb up a tree to God. Your memory's still on target. I was going to ask who was the first governor of the Ozark Free Territory."

"Kird Q. Pelgram," Valentine said. "I think you'll have to do better."

"If a Quisling troop train pulls out of New Orleans at twelve thirty, going twenty miles an hour toward Baton Rouge, and eight hours later their support train pulls out, going forty miles an hour, when will—"

"It won't. We'll blow up the bridge at Red River so the Quislings have to fight without artillery."

"When are you going to change out of that militia rag?"

"Near the border, at one of those shifty inns that does business with the Grogs out of a basement armory."

"Speaking of uniforms," Patel said. "There's a Kentucky gal in second platoon who used to be on some big bug's staff. Ediyak—Private Ediyak now. She knows Kurian auxiliary forces from the Gulf Coast to the Lakes. She's got a design for a uniform based on their priority labor. Moleskin, they call it, almost as tough as leather, with denim shirts, both dyed down to a foggy gray."

"I've seen something like that in the KZ. Those the guys who run phone lines?"

"Yes. Flying specialists that work their communications and electrical. Always moving from place to place, so strange faces won't raise eyebrows."

"Denim's easy to get. Labor troops. I dunno about the moleskin."

"Popular with ranchers. Rand says he can find some with his old LC connections."

"If she can modify them so they're Southern Command but still look KZ, that would be ideal."

"I'll speak to her about it."

Valentine decided to jump in with both feet. "Put Rand to work getting denim and dye and sewing supplies. He might as well get his baptism of fire with Supply or put his LC background to work in the UFR. Worst-case scenario is they'll be a fresh set of civvies for our guys."

"These leathers are getting a little gamey anyway."

"How are the knees holding up?"

"I'm now a confirmed aspirin addict, sir."

Valentine extended his hand and they shook. "Give yourself a break, Patel. Let Glass take them through the twelve labors. No one's going to think worse of you if you pick the cane back up after these last weeks."

With that he rode out of camp, turning north into a November wind.

†

For six gallons of root-beer syrup he got a Whitefang guide to take him up to St. Louis, the Grog clearing a path through the brush with a year-old legworm. His guide frequently stopped his mount to scout on foot, and at these rests Valentine would feed the horses and check their trail. The only thing that picked them up was a slight cold on their ride north. Both he and his guide took turns sneezing and blowing their noses, but it was better when they came into St. Louis three days later.

He traded a captured revolver—he'd tinkered with it on the journey and modified the grip and trigger guard for Grog-sized fingers—for a foot pass and toted his bag full of toys to Blake's home.

Not that Blake lacked toys. The old Jesuit researcher, Cutcher, had been observing him constantly as he played with various puzzles, games, and toys, gauging the young Reaper's mental development.

They'd built another coop and chicken run in the side yard of the prairie-style house located high on the bluffs above the Missouri. The Owl-Eye Grogs had added a rock pile at either side of the driveway. According to the scratchings, this was a place of powerful good magic for the tribe.

He gave some bolts of cloth, seeds, and religious books to Narcisse. Along with her care of Blake, she'd started a little church for the human community in St. Louis. While the only holy spirit the human river traders took came in a square bottle, Narcisse had made it her specialty to invite human captives of the Grogs into her circle. She'd been traveling to a couple of different neighborhoods more or less strapped to a mule. Valentine would have to promote his packhorse to the carriage trade and find her a little two-wheel cart. He could acquire the kind of thing high-ranking Grog chieftain wives used to visit relatives in the complicated tribal family structure, curtained to prevent lowlier Grogs from gazing on the high and mighty.

Valentine pulled the bell rope that told Blake that it was okay to come out of his comfortable basement room.

Blake, at just under four years, was as tall as a boy on the cusp of his teens. *"papss,"* Blake hissed excitedly as he emerged. He wore an oversized jacket and jeans with the cuffs extended. Gloves dangled from his sleeves. When he'd go outside he'd add a scarf and a floppy old hat to disguise his appearance.

Wobble, Blake's little dog, picked up on the boy's excitement at having "paps" home and chased his tail in excitement.

*"night games tonight?"* Blake asked.

"Anything you like," Valentine said. "Fishing, a deer run, or I can read you stories."

Blake put up with stories only when he was very tired. He didn't like to sit and just listen or read along.

*"night games!"*

For night games Blake wore a football helmet with padding sewn in at the sides so it fit snugly on his rather narrow head.

The games took place in the old St. Louis children's museum, a warren of chutes and ladders and tunnels made out of assorted bits of industrial and artistic junk from the pre-2022 world. The Grogs used it to train young warriors. At night the Grogs loosed their young on each other, to chase and brawl.

Some of the tougher human children sometimes joined in, also suitably padded and helmeted. Blake's helmet had a mesh with eye-slits attached to the grill—Valentine once explained to another human parent that the Grogs sometimes gouged with their long fingers—and with leather gloves on it would be hard to distinguish him from any other skinny young boy.

He could even shriek like a prepubescent when the mood hit.

There were no human kids there the night he took Blake. Valentine relaxed a little. Blake sometimes liked to show off by executing a jump no human could make and sometimes when wrestling he reversed his arm joints.

The most common Grog game was for one of the less dominant males to run up and swat a tougher one and then try to get away. The Grog children clearly considered it something of a coup if they could get away from Blake; they would swing or dangle from climbing obstacles and hit him, or three would strike at once and run off in different directions. Blake took the punches and swats with good humor and pursued his attackers and threw and pinned them when he could.

The roughhousing resulted in surprisingly few injuries. Young Grogs bounced like basketballs.

Valentine had stiffened the mesh in front of Blake's chin. Blake had acquired a good deal of self-control, but no sense taking chances.

He sat, watching Blake play. When Blake disappeared into one of the ill-lit buildings filled with noise and shadow, he followed, carrying a mug of sweet tea hot from a thermos.

A second thermos waited in Valentine's pack for when Blake tired. It was filled with warm chicken blood.

†

They fished the next day, then crossed into the woods on the north side of the Missouri the night after that, going on a deer run in the early morning.

Blake didn't have his helmet this time, just a hat with earflaps.

Valentine and Blake had a unique manner of deer hunting. They'd cover their scent as best they could with deer droppings and then wait. The deer liked to forage at the edges of old roads and broken-up parking lots. When they decided a herd was close enough, Valentine tapped Blake and they took off after a deer.

Last time they'd gone on a deer run, Valentine had been able to sprint ahead of Blake, even with his stiff leg. This time Blake beat him early in their dash after the bouncing white tails.

Valentine had that moment most fathers had, much earlier in the quick-developing Blake's case, when the son outdoes the father physically. He pulled up and sheathed his knife, relegated to the role of watcher.

Sometimes the deer crisscrossed and Blake got confused. But this time he bounded onto a big young buck at the fringe. Valentine had a moment's doubt, wondering if Blake would be taken for a brief ride before he lost his grip, but he brought it down like a cougar, clawing his way onto its neck and biting.

By the time he trotted up to Blake, the deer's eyes had gone dead and sightless. Blake raised a blood-smeared smile to him.

"Clean kill, Blake. Let's dress it. Sissy will have venison for the whole winter now, or deer sausage to go with her eggs."

At noon—Blake liked to sleep through the days—Valentine settled him down for a nap. They'd return with the deer carried on a pole between them that night. He read to Blake a little from *Charlotte's Web*, but Blake seemed unimpressed by Wilbur's predicament.

*"pigs don't talk,"* Blake said. *"story is not real."*

"It's a story. In stories pigs can talk. So can spiders and rats."

Blake didn't understand why, if the pig could talk to Templeton or Charlotte A. Cavatica, it couldn't talk to Fern.

Blake would rather watch the bugs moving in the grasses and find out what they were doing. Maybe he was just scientifically minded. Valentine still found it disturbing that he couldn't summon his imagination to aid him in understanding the story.

Or empathy.

✝

Blake helped him with various repairs to the house. Valentine went into St. Louis and got kerosene and tallow for light, a big bag of rice, chicken feed, and tar for a couple of weak spots in the roof and drainspouts.

Valentine watched Blake with Narcisse. She touched Blake frequently, patting him on the head or shoulder or arm, and he smiled, but he rarely touched or returned hugs with much enthusiasm.

But then he loved to nap with his head pillowed on her lap or breast.

Once, while Blake was sleeping away the morning, Valentine asked Narcisse if she was ever afraid.

"Daveed, don't be silly. I am safer with the boy here than with a whole pack of guard dogs. He tells me when the Grogs come ten minutes before I hear them."

"No, I mean of Blake."

"He cares, in his way. He is like—he is like the cat who just takes affection on his terms. One time I fell from my wheel-stool and before I knew it he was beside me and righted it. After, I had a scrape on my arm and he got a cloth with vinegar for it."

Valentine gave voice to his doubts. "Maybe he just thought he was repairing you, the way he did the chicken wire."

"One night in August it was hot and I did not kiss him good night. He asked me why I didn't as I left, and I told him I was worried that he was getting too big for a kiss good night. He said he liked it because it made him feel warm and sleepy. He has love and caring. Do not worry for me."

Valentine let the matter rest.

†

They said their good-byes in the driveway. The garage now had a two-wheeled rig for Valentine's packhorse. Wobble sniffed at the new feed trough Valentine had built.

Narcisse had shown herself adept at driving the trap and Blake found the challenge of driving a horse fascinating. Blake approved of simple action-result loops much more than E. B. White.

Valentine had acquired the rig by pledging to a loan of trade goods at the old church office in the city. He'd pay it back through the river rats.

"No sneaking blood out of that horse, now," Valentine said to Blake.

*"no, papss,"* Blake said. Neither of the horses were happy about Blake's presence. They sidestepped and danced every time he moved. The carthorse would get used to him eventually.

"Help Sissy all you can. I may be gone for a while, so you've got to look out for her."

*"no trouble for sissy,"* Blake said. Narcisse stroked his odd tufts of hair. It looked as though someone had glued old toothbrush heads in odd patterns on his scalp. It just grew in that way. He remembered one of the Miskatonic researchers saying something about it possibly being an identifying mark.

"Go with the magic of the right hand, Daveed," Narcisse said.

He plucked her out of her wheelchair and hugged her. She'd put on a little weight since he'd met her in Haiti.

"Can't thank you enough, Sissy," Valentine said.

"I go where the most need is. Blake needs someone to teach him. My whole life, I never fit in anywhere," she said. "That is something I can teach Blake. How not to fit in right. The people here, especially the captives of the Grogs, they need me too."

Valentine knew she'd been practicing her folkloric brand of medicine with the humans. She had turned a sunny south breakfast nook into a room devoted to growing herbs. How she got exotic peppers and roots in St. Louis was a marvel. Cutcher had probably helped her build her collection.

He was proud of the victories he'd won for the Cause, but he couldn't visit Big Rock Hill again without seeing faces of Beck and Kessey, knowing where they were buried and what they looked like before they'd been cleaned and shrouded.

Narcisse was also a victory, in a way. There'd never be a plaque to commemorate her, the way there was one on the old red-brick consular residence on Big Rock. Instead of brass lettering, this victory came with a shining smile, a colorful kerchief, and arms he could feel as they embraced.

He rode away from the house on the Missouri bluffs and into a cold wind. He didn't dare think of it as home, or else he'd never have left it.

†

Valentine's Whitefang guide must have had a fine old time in St. Louis. He'd acquired two wives, one for him and one for his brother, and a legworm's worth of trade goods.

It looked like his brother was getting the ugly one. But then Valentine wasn't current on Gray One aesthetics. While he waited for his guide to arrange the departure, Valentine fended off a trade Grog trying to buy his hair.

Luckily his guide didn't mind him hanging bags of horse grain from the legworm's dry, fleshy hide. First you had to sink a cargo hook into the thing, which took some judgment, as patches of skin were constantly sloughing off. Then there was the legworm's habit of crashing through thickets. You didn't want to put your load where it might get accidentally torn off as the legworm brushed a tree.

They passed south easily enough, the tough Morgan stepping easily in the legworm's wake, nibbling at bits of trampled greenery now in easy reach. Valentine only remembered wondering how big Blake would be the next time he saw him.

His efforts at recruiting a dozen or so Whitefangs met with a stern refusal from the chief:

"In the days of my grandfather, whisperers promised much and gave little. Little thinskins all same."

"Give good guns. Give good gear. Whitefangs share camp and food and battle, become friends to thinskins," Valentine said.

The young warrior who'd led the Whitefangs in battle against the Doublebloods snarled and displayed in front of Valentine, stamping his feet and tearing up ground with a ceremonial planting hook.

"Not need thinskins' guns put up plenty good fight," he said. Valentine got a nose-full of Grog breath.

"I saw Whitefangs in battle," Valentine said. It was hard not to flinch. One good swing of that hook and his brains would be leaking out of his nose. "Would want such warriors as friends against whisperers."

The young warrior squatted and looked to his chief.

The chief fingered his necklace. Valentine saw two Reaper fangs among the odds and ends of his trophy braiding, gearshift knobs and dog tags, mostly. "Whitefangs enemies enough. Not need seek more across river," the chief said.

That seemed to settle things.

†

Back at the Highbeam assembly, Valentine found his company hard at work sewing.

He changed back into the tired old militia uniform and ordered a powdered meal as he received Rand's report. A contingent of three aged Wolves had arrived. They were already known through the company as "Patel's Shepherds." Each had taken a platoon and were putting them through tough field training.

"Recon's hard work," Rand said, taking off his glasses and cleaning them with his shirttail when the formal report ended. "They've sniffed out six stills, two basement markets, three gambling dens, and a brothel and a smokehouse that does beefsticks you won't believe. They also located a mother and two talented widowed sisters in Jonesboro who enjoy giving formal dinner parties for the handsome, brave young officers of Southern Command. Handsome and young being key to an invitation to dinner."

"In other words, they're experienced soldiers."

Valentine found his desk unusually orderly. He'd been expecting an overflowing in-basket.

"Private Ediyak, the gal with the idea for the uniforms, helped me with some of the low-priority stuff. The rest is in the locked file cabinet."

They'd set up two sewing machines in a workshop next to the command tent. Someone had found a battery-operated radio and hung it high in the tent.

†

He met Private Ediyak, a small blonde with the delicately wide-eyed look of someone brought up on KZ rations, when she had a soldier model the new uniform.

It was made out of denim the color of an foggy evening. Baggy about the legs but easily bloused into boots and knee pads. She'd layered a denim jacket over an athletic sweatshirt, and put an olive canvas utility vest over that. The vest was trimmed with yellow reflective tape.

Valentine recognized the vests. They were Labor Regiment. He used to cram sandwiches and water bottles into the big pockets for a day in the fields or on the roads. There were D rings for holding more gear on this version.

He walked around the soldier modeling the uniform. He looked like a young, fit construction worker.

"The Day-Glo tape is almost out at Supply, sir," she said. "I backed it with fabric and Velcro. Removing the reflective stuff just takes a second. Speaking of Velcro, sir, the same goes for the arm patches. If it would be possible for us to get something made that looks KZ-ish, we could swap between KZ and Southern Command as needed."

"I wondered about that, sir," Rand said. "The inspector general's office won't like flags not being sewn on. 'These colors don't run' and all that."

"The inspector general's never had to look inconspicuous in a KZ streetcar," Valentine said. "Who's the honcho there now?"

"General Martinez," Rand said. "Three Hots Martinez, the men call him."

Valentine's stomach went sour, but there was no need to pick at old scabs. He offered his hand to Ediyak.

"Good work, Ediyak. You just won yourself a promotion to corporal. You're also company clerk, if you want the job."

"Clerk, sir?" she said.

"It's a quick path up to lieutenant's bars, if you'd like to start that climb again."

She considered for a second. "I'll do it, sir."

"Good. Your first job will be to requisition whatever you need to finish these uniforms. I'll speak to someone about getting us some KZ patches." That someone being Lambert and staff. Valentine rather liked being able to dump such details off on someone who could be relied on to get it done.

"What about helmets and rain gear, sir?" Rand said.

"Typically these formations wear white or yellow hard hats, sir," Ediyak said.

Valentine's liquid dinner arrived. It tasted like a shake made out of strawberries and mud but it was fast and easy. "Let's see if we can scrounge up some civilian winter coats," he said as he sipped. "I don't ever remember seeing these guys in ponchos. As for helmets, maybe we can stuff some old hard hats with Kevlar. Get canvas covers for when we don't want the Day-Glo look."

"Patrol coming in," the company outdoor fire watch shouted.

"Patrol?" Valentine asked Rand.

"Patel's Shepherds have been taking them out, platoon at a time, on overnighters or three-dayers, sir. This should be first platoon coming back from a three-dayer."

Valentine went out to take a look.

The platoon looked dog tired and strained, rolling on their feet in the toe-in manner of footsore men as they carried sand-filled artillery shell casings instead of guns. The bearded old Wolf in charge straightened them up and they saluted as they marched past. Valentine saw some bandages across noses and a few blackened eyes.

"Sergeant, halt," he called.

"Line up for inspection," the bearded sergeant bawled. Valentine saw Corporal Glass at the other end discreetly check the line.

Valentine took a look at one of the bandages. "What happened here, Sergeant?"

"We paused at a roadside for fresh pretzel bread and beverages, sir," the old gray Wolf said. "The gentlemen owning the establishment didn't care for scrip. We convinced them otherwise."

"Anything serious?" Valentine asked. He doubted the road-stop in question would make a report. Everyone was required to take Southern Command scrip but some business owners didn't care for the exchange rates.

"One of them drew a knife, sir. The civilian in question will be working his fly with his left hand for a while. Corporal Glass has a good eye. He's quick or I might not be standing here."

"Good work, first platoon. Get some food and sleep."

†

Valentine fell back into the regime of training as the days turned grim and gray and the nights cold. They'd formalized the roster at last and had three balanced platoons. Valentine had known companies where there was a crack platoon that took the toughest jobs and two less-reliable ones to support it, but he'd rather distribute his best men where they could teach the others than rely too much on a single elite formation. The NCO slots were filled with ex-Quislings.

He gave them a brief speech about duty, as he saw it. In the KZ command flowed down, with a lurking "or else" implicit at the end of every order. While that was a fact of military life regardless of origin and uniform, Valentine would rather have those under his command following orders because they understood the stakes and consequences of failure.

Several of them turned down offers of promotion to leadership roles.

That was the big shortcoming of these men, he'd learned. They could use their equipment but not their minds. Everyone was terrified of making a bad decision, lest they be out a seat when the next round of musical chairs orchestrated by the Reapers came round. Soldiering wasn't for the dumb—not if you wanted good soldiers rather than gun-toting robots.

They held a company party at Christmas, with everyone in their smoky denim uniforms and the kind of glossy shine you could get with new boots. The base hall was being used by the Guards so Valentine spoke to the pastor of a local church and got the use of a big revival tent, complete with a deacon to open the ceremonies and offer a Christmas homily. The company made paper lanterns and fire balloons and put up a Christmas tree in front of the command shack. A distribution of quality flour, confectioner's sugar, and food coloring allowed the foodies in the company to make green- and red-iced cupcakes. With a couple of guitarists, a fiddler, and Rand, who turned out to be an accomplished hurdy-gurdy player (he claimed he was always too clumsy to dance, so he might as well play for others), they held a dance.

Valentine paid a visit to the hospital in Jonesboro to issue a general invitation to the nurses there. A handful were brave enough to show, and a few brought friends. Valentine issued strict orders not to talk about the "move south" no matter how pretty the face or how good the reason for future correspondence.

"We might as well get to know them. Some of us are going to end up seeing a lot of nurses before the operation is over," he finished.

Valentine enjoyed an opening waltz with the senior nurse chaperoning her charges—the nurse had a lot of experience dancing with a man with a stiff leg—and then settled down with Patel to watch the festivities and make sure the punch bowl wasn't spiked to over eighty proof.

The smiles on the men and the laughter of the nurses cheered him more than the music. The company had worked hard on their uniforms and decorations, and he liked seeing them show off a little.

A blat of a trumpet interrupted the music. There was some kind of stir at the door of the tent and then a group of Guards forced their way in, dragging what sounded like Marley's chains and lockboxes.

The dancing stopped and the men parted.

"We brung you a Christmas present, Major," one of the Guards said, with a rather drunken salute. "New recruits. You was looking for some Grogs."

Valentine heard a riding crop strike flesh and a "Go on." Two other Guards pulled on a chain, and Valentine smelled a zoo-like stench.

"They'll fit right in with the shit detail," someone guffawed.

A Grog sprawled for a second, then stood up. Two more were pulled in behind. But Valentine couldn't take his eyes off the foremost. She was a female gray dressed in an oversized pink tutu and fake ballet slippers.

It was the Grog he'd once known as Bee.

"Bee!" Valentine said.

"Beeee," she said back, eyes open wide and staring. She tried to slink sideways up next to him.

The room fell silent. Most of the men there had never heard Grogs do anything but ook or cry out *graaaawg* when wounded and begging for assistance.

Valentine locked his gaze on the joker who'd called them the shit detail.

"What did you call this company?" he asked.

"Errr, nothing, sir," the Guard said, red-faced and counting the number of men coming to their feet. One of Patel's Shepherds snapped his teeth at them.

Patel thumped his cane on the floor. "Boys, these visitors seem to be confused as to the location of their barrack. Escort them back."

The party dissolved into chaos. Southern Command soldiers would probably have let out their trademark foxhunt shriek as they chased the Guards back to their regimental grounds. Valentine's company let out a deeper *uhuh!*

Patel's Shepherds used the confusion to dump a couple more preserve jars of busthead into the punch.

The Guards wisely dropped the Grog chains and ran, with half the company in hot pursuit, throwing Christmas cupcakes.

The male Grogs behind Bee fell to their knees and covered their heads with their hands as men hurdled them. Bee dragged herself up to Valentine and sniffed his hand.

†

Valentine took Bee, the other two, and a plate of cupcakes over to the workshop tent. As he issued cupcakes—most Grogs had a sweet tooth— he employed his rough-and-ready Grog but her dialect made it slow going. The other two Grogs understood him well enough, after a period of suspiciousness broken by Bee's emphatic thumping of Valentine's chest, a Grog version of saying "He's a stand-up guy," evidently.

Hoffman Price, the bounty hunter Bee traveled with, was dead, evidently of some illness. He'd made it into free territory and turned Bee over to an old friend before dying during a surgery Bee didn't begin to understand. The old friend, whom Bee called White Hair, promptly dropped dead a short time after Price. White Hair's family either gave or sold Bee to a circus.

That's where she met the other two Grogs, Ford and Chevy. They'd been warriors from a tribe in Mississippi who crossed the river in some incursion and were left behind, wounded. They were captured, defanged (they pointed to the big gaps in their teeth), and bought by the D.C. Marvels Circus.

They didn't know the name of the circus—Valentine had guessed it. He'd seen posters put up around the hospital giving the dates for the circus performances at the Jonesboro fairgrounds.

According to the men, it was mostly a set of rigged carnival games and bad ginger ales sold for three bucks a bottle. A beer that was all head cost six.

In the circus Bee performed what Valentine guessed to be a comic ballet in her tutu—all Valentine got from her was "make dance, make fall, make roll." The other two took turns standing in an empty kiddie pool while spectators threw rotten onions and tomatoes at them.

He ordered a couple buckets of warm soapy water, a sponge, and towels. First thing to do was get them cleaned up. And Bee out of that ridiculous tutu.

"You want finished circus?" he asked the three.

"Yes, yes," Ford and Chevy chorused. Bee used another word of her limited English vocabulary: "Pleease."

"Like join thinskins warrior tribe?"

Bee said her version of please again; Ford and Chevy pointed to the gaps in their dental work. "Not warriors. Us finished warriors."

"Not matter with thinskins," Valentine said.

They thumped Valentine's chest. This time Valentine relaxed into it, though he couldn't help taking a tender, experimental breath afterward to see if any ribs were broken.

†

The men didn't much care for having Grogs among them. The former Quislings considered the troops who fought using Grogs the lowest of the low, hardly human themselves. Discontent filtered up through the sergeants and to Patel.

"Yes," Valentine told Patel, who seemed a little discomfited himself. "The Kurian Zone despises them. Southern Command hates them. But a uniformed Grog can cross a bridge or stand at a crossroads without anyone looking at him twice in the Kurian Zone. I'm sure you can see the use of that."

"Yes, sir."

"We're going to have to put them under someone. Any ideas?"

"Why don't we just call them the major's bodyguard?"

"That's a bit Lawrence of Arabia for me. Anyone who wants to do it gets to be a corporal, quick promotion—that is how they entice people to do it in the KZ. I'll teach whoever volunteers the language."

Glass, their heavy weapons expert, took the job. "Not so much that he likes Grogs; I just think he hates people more," Patel said. They talked over how they'd juggle the platoons once again.

A messenger interrupted them. "You won't believe what's outside, Major. It's quite a show."

Valentine peeked out one of the many cracks in the shack, and believed it. A pair of civilians stood at the gate, a rather dazzling bronzed man in a purple tailcoat and oversized yellow bow tie and a black mountain of muscle in overalls.

He'd been half expecting this. He went to the corner of the shack and took a tin plate off a bucket he'd been saving for just such an occasion. He filled his pockets.

Valentine closed the top button on his old militia tunic—he wanted the men to have their uniforms finished before they made his—and stepped out to the top step of the command shack.

"Is that him?" the man in the purple asked.

"Yes, sir," the gate escort said.

"Hello, Major," the man in the purple said, flashing whiter-than-white teeth. "D.C. Marvels is the name. Dazzling cavalcades of marvels is my game. You've heard of me?"

"Not until recently."

"Then I'd like to extend a personal invitation to the show. You're aware that soldiers are entitled to a ten percent discount at my circus; twenty percent on food and beverages? For parties of three or more, that is."

"How can I help you, Mr. Marvels?"

"There's been some sort of misunderstanding. A few of your gallant comrades rented an attraction of mine, poor benighted Grogs I've taken under my wing, saving them from river dredging or worse. They never returned, and I'm due in Mountain Home by the end of the week."

Valentine was beginning to look forward to this. "I don't see where I fit in. Were they men under my command?"

Marvels planted his feet. "Didn't say you were responsible, Major.

The soldiers in question said things got rather out of hand at your party, and they had to leave my attractions behind. Grogs can't be left in the hands of amateurs. They'll sicken and die, poor things."

"I'm afraid they've quit your circus, Mr. Marvels. They've enlisted with Southern Command."

"You're kidding, right? They're not competent. They're mine and I want them back. I'm trying to be nice here, but I'm perfectly willing to take legal action."

Valentine crossed his hands behind his back. "So am I. Get off this post."

"Corricks," Marvels said out of the side of his mouth.

The muscle inflated his chest. "Ford! Chevy! Bee! Here now!" He pulled a whistle from his pocket and the trilling filled the company tents.

Valentine felt the whistle as much as he heard it. It gave him a headache.

"Shut your man up, Marvels."

"When I see my property!"

Valentine hurled a ripe tomato at Marvels, striking him just under the yellow tie. He drew a rotten onion from his other back pocket. The whistling didn't stop until he bounced an onion off the handler's head.

The big man took a step toward him and Valentine matched his move, more than half hoping Marvels would throw a punch.

"That's assault! You've assaulted a civilian. I'll have your commission for this," Marvels said, extending his shirtfront as though it were a warrant for Valentine's arrest.

"Then I might as well enjoy myself," Valentine said, aiming an onion for his head. Marvels ducked under it.

"The gate's that way," Valentine said, throwing another tomato. This one hit Marvels square on the buttocks as he turned to run.

† 

The expected summons to Colonel Seng's office came that very afternoon, courtesy of Seng's messenger, Tiddle. Tiddle reminded Valentine of the White Rabbit, or maybe the Road Runner, always in a hurry to get somewhere. He either ran or used a light motorbike rigged with tires for cross-country driving. His hair normally looked as though he'd had a recent close encounter with a live wire.

Valentine washed up with some of his French soap and put on his best uniform. Lieutenant Colonel Jolla didn't look particularly jolly.

"That Marvels fellow just left. He's in quite a temper."

Valentine shrugged. "Is he getting his Grogs back?"

Seng's frown deepened. "No. I pointed out that the practice of chattel slavery is against the law and is in fact a hanging offense. He said I could expect a letter from his lawyer. I don't need these headaches, Valentine."

"Sorry, sir. He had two of those Grogs in what amounts to a bear-baiting pit. Customers paid to throw fruit at them."

"Says as much about some of the customers as it does about Marvels," Jolla said.

"If he starts a legal fight, it might be worth someone's while to check his payroll accounts. When I had Ahn-Kha on my rolls, I kept up-to-date with policy. They're free to hire on or quit, and you have to pay them at least convict rate. According to the Grogs, they never saw so much as a dollar."

"Still not a defense for your behavior," Seng said. "Save it for the enemy."

Valentine smiled at that. Technically he was still a condemned man under Southern Command's fugitive law, though his face had long since been removed from the "Wanted" cabinets.

"Will that be all?"

"No," Seng said. "Lambert told me you were a little unorthodox but effective. Let's work on the effective and cut down on the unorthodox. Why aren't ordinary militia uniforms good enough for your men?"

"You want us to operate in the Kurian Zone. Southern Command militia uniforms might be a bit of a giveaway."

"Still, it's odd," Jolla put in.

"It's an odd unit with an odd role," Valentine said. "Supply in enemy territory, acting as liaison with the local resistance."

Jolla brushed back nonexistent hair with his palm. "Yet from what I've seen, you're training your company like you're part of the hunter battalion."

"You don't object to fitness trials, I hope."

"We'll see what kind of men you have when the real training starts in January," Seng said. "I'll look forward to seeing what you can do."

†

The guns arrived a few days after the unpleasant meeting. It was hard not to be disappointed.

They viewed them from the back of the wagon rig, three cases of rifles and one of pistols. A trio of Uzi-style submachine guns were in with the pistols, evidently meant for the officers.

The rest were mostly militia stuff: deer rifles and shotguns and a few venerable AR-15s. In the hands of a company of veteran Wolves, it could be a deadly enough assortment, but he wondered if they'd be heavy, expensive noisemakers in the hands of some of the greener members of his company. It would make familiarization and training a nightmare.

Plus there would be supply difficulties, trying to get everything from buckshot to .358 to .30-06 to .223 into individual hands.

Patel's cane tapped behind and Valentine turned to see his sergeant major shake his head sadly as he lifted a double-barreled bird gun. "It's like telling the men they can't be trusted with anything better," he said.

Valentine thought a couple of the Remingtons might make decent sniper rifles, if they could find optics. He had at least six trained scout/snipers out of the Kurian services—they had an easier time sneaking away than most. A shotgun or two distributed to each squad would be handy for urban use. The rest, not much more than rabbit guns, would be better off in the hands of the UFR's young Camp Scouts or backwoods raccoon hunters.

There was nothing to do but hand them out.

"They've got to be kidding," one of the former Quislings in line said. Valentine recognized him as one of the men he'd seen training the militia back at Liberty.

"Mebbe these are just to carry for practice weight, like the shells," another said.

"We should take a trip over to the river patrol reserve armory between the Tennessee and the Mississippi. They don't hardly guard that. Get us some real guns."

Valentine dredged up that last man's name: Robbins—no, Rollings. "Private Rollings. What's that?"

"Sorry, sir."

"No, you're not in trouble. Come over here."

Rollings gave his pants a subtle hitch up as he approached, his sergeant falling in beside like a protective dog. "The major wants something?"

"What did you say about an armory?"

"You're not in any trouble, Rollings," his sergeant said.

Rollings kept his gaze on Valentine's feet. "River patrol armory and motor pool, sir. The old western Kentucky number four. We used to gas up there when I was with the River Road Light Artillery of the Tennessee Troop. It's a crap—err, CRP—um, that's Combined River Patrol, sir. Reserve armory and warehouse for patrol and artillery boats on the Tennessee, Ohio, and Mississippi. Creepy place. There's those flappy gargoyles quartered in town and nests of harpies in the hills up by the Ohio."

"Explain what you meant about unguarded."

The man gulped. "Not unguarded. There's usually six or seven men about. It's just that the armory's for the river patrol, so the Tennessee Troop, they don't see it as their job to garrison it. The river patrol figures that since it's inland, it's the Troop's job to secure it. Nobody wants to be stationed there, exactly, with the harpies in the hills and the gargoyles in the empty town. Not much to do but play cards and come up with better nose plugs."

Rollings had five more uncomfortable minutes as Valentine quizzed him about the roads in the area, the terrain, the location of KZ settlements. . . .

When he finished the poor private was sweating.

Valentine gripped him on the shoulder. "Thank you, Rollings. You're the kind of complainer I like."

Rollings' eyes finally came up. "How's that, sir?"

"The kind that offers a solution."

# CHAPTER FIVE

*T*he wilderness of eastern Kentucky, New Year's Eve, the Fifty-fourth Year of the Kurian Order: With the sun an orange-and-purple bruise along the western skyline, harpy country wakes up.

*There's something odd about this particular Grog territory. Bird and animal life seems more furtive, the insects tougher and more numerous—even in the winter chill big black flies drone by like thrown pebbles. The kudzu on old utility poles and lines grows thick on every sunstruck prominence in a twisted-tendril game of king of the hill that dares you to contest its ownership. Thicker stands of wood have a bat-cave smell with nothing thriving in the shade but thistle and thorn and tree-hugging fungus looking like suppurating wounds.*

*The few highways cutting through harpy lands are barely open, the vegetation kept back only by big machines clawing through the potholed roads. The devastation from the New Madrid quake has never been repaired. Whole communities are nothing but heaps of rubble with a vine-covered wall or chimney still standing.*

†

Binoculars just made the warehouse and truck yard look worse. In the dark from a distance, Valentine could see the armory was only three buildings, two of cinder block linked by a nicer brick office forming an uneven U lit at the doors by tired bulbs that looked like they wanted to surrender to the night. With the aid of the binoculars, Valentine's night eyes picked out peeling paint, the tires and blocks holding down plastic sheeting on the roofs, and the plywood nailed over the windows.

Patel and Hoboken, the youngest of Patel's Shepherds, looked at it with him.

The ad-hoc raid had come together as though it were a natural, expected event, like a birth. When Valentine proposed the operation at a scheduled meeting, he met initial resistance in the form of a frown and a shake of Colonel Seng's head, but Moytana and the Bear lieutenant Gamecock both came to assistance, claiming that their men were fretting, wanting either leave or an operation. They could have both by joining in the raid, as Hunters back from the KZ traditionally enjoyed at least a three-day pass, if not a twenty-one, in Southern Command's vernacular.

Valentine argued that the rest of the brigade might be reassured by a quick successful strike into the Kurian Zone and a return across the Mississippi, and Seng gave his approval.

Valentine turned in his written plan that very evening and started on the orders for the company the next morning.

As Rand organized transport, Valentine received an unexpected visitor. The Bear lieutenant knocked on the open door of the command shack. Dust fell from the ceiling and the spiders hunkered down in their webs.

"Morning, Major," Gamecock said. He had thick hair on the arms projecting from his sleeveless shirt, and wore the first legworm leather pants Valentine had seen since he lost his rig in Pacific Command. Most officers in Southern Command knew better than to lecture Bears on proper attire. He had an ear of roasted corn in hand and a flour sack over his shoulder. He gave Valentine a casual salute with the roasted ear as he looked around the command shack. "Okay to talk about the op?"

"In here," Valentine said. The command shack had a divider now, so Valentine enjoyed the luxury and status of a knothole-windowed office.

They went into the back room.

Gamecock finished off the roasted ear and tossed it in the wastebasket. The basket wobbled briefly. "Sorry about that, suh. Had to eat breakfast on foot this morning. This scheme of yours: You're going to be a Quisling Grog officer."

"Yes," Valentine said.

He tossed the flour sack on Valentine's table-desk. "I was going to trade this to a sorry excuse of a Guard captain for a case of Canadian scotch, but it's turning my stomach to see the guy who held at Big Rock walking around with an old single-shot militia rifle.

"Go on, suh," Gamecock said. "Got it off a Quisling lieutenant colonel with matching tooling on his belt, hat, and boots. Even dead, he looked like a show-night fag, but he knew his hardware."

Valentine extracted a gleaming submachine gun and a screw-on tube as long as the gun itself. It had odd lines; the barrel was pitched on a bias different from the frame. He picked it up and extended the handle just under the muzzle.

"That's an Atlanta buzzsaw," Gamecock said. "Model 18 Select entry model. Limited production run, elites and officers only. That cockeyed barrel's there for a purpose. The bolt's at an angle so recoil keeps the muzzle from climbing off target. Pretty accurate one handed, even on full auto. No selector switch—you can tap them out single shot with light pulls. Goin' over to full auto, you just pull the trigger all the way. She'll group under a meter at a hundred paces. That silencer there is something I rigged."

Valentine looked at the magazines—two short and four long—and the twenty- and forty-round boxes. "Nine millimeter Parabellum."

"I know—a little light for stopping a Reaper in full charge," Gamecock said. "I threw in some boxes of silverpoints. Team Fumarole's had good results with them. They don't flatten out against Reaper cloth so much."

"I don't suppose you've got any Quickwood bullets."

"We got a box of 7.62 for the whole team, suh. One lousy box. Production problems. Wish they'd tell me where the trees were. I'd make myself some friggin' stakes."

"I'll show you one personally when we get back. Assuming some farmer hasn't cut it down for tomato stakes. By the way, where's the accent from?"

"South Carolina born. First name's Scottie, suh."

"Val will do from now on, when things are less formal. Grateful to you, Scottie."

"Grateful to you, suh. My boys are ready to kill each other. Only three things will keep a Bear quiet if there's no fighting going on: sleeping, eating, and . . . well—"

"Screwing," Valentine finished. "Lieutenant Nail in the old Razors put it a little more colorfully."

"Any case, suh, we've all put on ten pounds and everyone's caught up on sack time. I got all I can do to keep the women and chickens round here safe."

†

Pizzaro at Rally Base greased the entire operation, even setting up an escort by a contingent of the "Skeeter Fleet," Southern Command's own force of low-draft vessels that were employed in riverine combat. The SF's airboats and fast motorboats weren't a match for the bigger, cannon-mounted craft of the Quisling river patrol, but they could cause enough trouble somewhere else to draw off the forces guarding one set of loops in the twisting Mississippi.

Valentine practiced entry drills with the Bears and ran short patrols with the Wolves, always taking a few of the company with him. It did a little for their confidence and it was good to see the men getting over some of their wariness when it came to the Bears. Most of the men thought Bears would just as soon kill a man as look at him, and the day might come when members of the company would have to guide a Bear team to a target.

Valentine expensed three hundred rounds training with the new gun while Bee worked on sawing off the barrels and smoothing down the stocks on the old shotguns she'd been converting to pistol grip. Valentine practiced changing magazines until he could do it without thinking about it. Then he cleaned the weapon and test fired a couple more rounds to make sure he didn't foul something up.

The Bears and most of the Wolves were employed in a strike at a collection of river patrol docks and blockhouses on Island Ten, while a short platoon of Valentine's company, escorted by a striking team of Wolves, made for the armory. The rest of his command remained at either side of the Mississippi under Rand, blowing up rubber boats and improvised rafts called "Ping-Pong ball miracles" in preparation for the trip back.

The trip across and the movement to the armory had gone off well, with the Skeeter Fleet bringing them across just before dawn on New Year's Eve, their camouflage-painted twin-outboard boats growling into the muddy Mississippi waters like dogs giving the angry warning that comes before the leap.

Valentine's picked team of twenty, Bee, and the Wolves paralleled the east-west highway heading into Mayfield, Kentucky, and then turned north into the Grog country, the Wolves out front and behind and flanking, continually restoring contact like sheepdogs with a flock.

They took advantage of a chilling rain to make good time down the road, which had deteriorated into a rutted trail. According to Rollings no one "who counted" lived up this way, in a region of low, sandy hills and scrub forest. River patrol supply trucks and Grog recruiters were all that used the roads meeting at the armory.

They rested, ate, and observed while the skies cleared and the sun went down. Valentine taped a thin commando dagger to his forearm—it never hurt to have something in reserve. After giving everyone inside a chance to get deep into REM sleep, Valentine decided the time was ripe.

He, Rollings, and Bee approached from the east down the tree-throttled road, three Wolves trailing through cover behind. Valentine carried his 18 Select in a battered leather courier pouch filled with a meaningless assortment of captured paperwork. Valentine smelled harpies on the cold wind blowing down from the northwest.

As they approached the gate, he slipped on the brass ring he'd won in Seattle. He didn't like to wear the thing.

"No Kurian towers around here, right?" he asked Rollings, nervous as he felt the warmth of the ring when it contacted his skin.

The armory had old-fashioned bars around it, linking cement columns. Valentine wondered if something more ostentatious had once stood on the other side of the fence. This was like garlanding a turd.

"No, sir. Well, none that I know about. Never went into the harpy woods, though, or met any Reapers on the river road that way. Is that what I think it is, Major?"

"Yes."

"You take it off a—"

"It's a long story."

A dog barked as they approached, a mud-splattered, hungry-looking thing that seemed to be a mix of a German shepherd and a long-haired camel. It jumped atop its shelter to better sound the alarm.

Behind its house was a line of trucks and a wrecker. The trucks looked rusted and worn, though they had hedge-cutting blades fixed below the front bumper and iron bars welded across the windshield and windows.

Valentine approached the buzz box on the post outside the gate and opened the dirty glass door covering the buttons.

"Anything here indicate there's more men here than usual?" Valentine asked.

"No, sir."

Rollings nodded and Valentine hit the button marked "call."

When Valentine didn't get a response in ten seconds, he pressed again, long and hard, the way an impatient Quisling ringwearer would when he wasn't getting service to his liking.

It took a full minute for a crackly voice to answer.

"Yes?" the voice crackled through the tarnished, oil-smeared speaker.

"This is Colonel Sanity Marks, Combat Tech Service. I've got a wiring team broken down three miles west of here and I need transport. I'll require one of your trucks and a motorcycle for at least forty-eight hours."

"Tell it to the Coastal Marines, sapper."

Valentine raised his eyebrows to Rollings.

"Is Sergeant Nelson in there?" Rollings said.

"Who wants to know?"

"Tell him it's Rollings, late of the River Road Light. This colonel is steamed, I shit you not, and he's got a brass ring and a crapped-out truck full of guys with computers and fiberoptic line."

"Someone will be out in a moment."

Valentine snapped: "I had a harpy swoop overhead not five minutes ago. Get out here before the damn thing comes back and shits on me. I hate those fucking things."

A corporal and a private appeared, looking like they'd just yanked their uniform shirts off of hangers: The shoulders were riding ridged and high.

"Sir," the corporal said. "I'm going to need to see some orders and identification."

Valentine shoved his ring fist through the bars. "I've got a broken-down truck and a wiring team that's six hours late now. Get us the hell inside."

The corporal bussed the ring with his lips. Valentine had made the obeisance often enough during his sojourn as a Coastal Marine in the Gulf. On a ring belonging to the proper wearer, it gave off a slight tingle.

"Not the Grog," the corporal protested.

If he folded once, he'd fold again. Valentine turned his gaze to the silent armsman.

"Private, you want to speed things up for me? You can have this corporal's stripes. I think by the time I've written my evaluation, he won't need them anymore."

"Sir, no disrespect, but I'll get into more trouble by not following procedures than you could ever bring down."

"I wonder. You know anything about distributed secure networks?"

"Uh—no, sir."

Which was just as well. Valentine didn't know anything about it either. The corporal silently allowed the group inside.

"Gas up two trucks. Put batteries in or whatever you have to do to get them going."

"Thought you said—"

"I'm going to listen to the engines of both," Valentine said. "I'll take the truck that sounds healthier."

Valentine didn't wait for an answer and headed toward the main office door between the two bigger buildings. Bee trailed behind.

He opened the door and wiped his feet. Two men in undershirts were lacing boots up. There was a duty desk, a mail sorter, and a long bureau with an electric coffeepot and pieces of weaponry, lighting, and com gear wearing yellow toe tags atop it beneath silvery letters reading:

**HAPPY NEW YEAR—LOOK ALIVE IN 'FIFTY-FIVE**

"Where's Sergeant Nelson?"

"Celebrating in Paducah, sir."

"They're having fireworks," the other added, gaping at Bee. She sniffed the warm, stale air. Valentine smelled a grilled cheese sandwich and coffee.

"Rollings!" Valentine called over his shoulder. He used the opportunity to scan the little office. There was a sort of wooden loft above with a water tank and boxes of supplies. He had a moment's startle—a shadow above pointed at him with an accusing finger. . . .

It turned out to be a mannequin of a nude female with a feather boa.

"Right here, Major."

Valentine thought quickly. "That's 'Colonel,' son. I'm not your old CO. You keep forgetting."

"Sorry, Colonel."

"You know any of these fellas? Who's in charge?"

"That would be me," a gruff voice came from the doorway to what looked like a residence room. A sergeant with a beer gut partially covering a pistol belt stood in the doorway. "What's the emergency, Colonel?"

"Worse than you know, Sergeant," Valentine said. He reached into his attaché and began extracting paperwork and placing it on the duty desk. He took out the gun and pointed it at the NCO.

"I'm sorry to inform you all that you're my prisoners. Rollings, that's a nice-looking .45 the sergeant has on his belt. Relieve him of it."

Bee stiffened and drew her own shotguns from her waistband. "Watch the door, Bee. Door," Valentine said.

"Turn your backs, gentlemen, and place your hands on the back of your head, fingers interlaced. Kneel."

Valentine made sure they complied, listening for other sounds of life in the dark warehouse next door. Out in the motor yard, he heard a truck turn over. "Now, if you're cooperative for the next hour or so, you'll be taken prisoner and brought back to a Southern Command base. You'll be surprised how nice the day-release POW camps are. If you give us any trouble, I'll leave you tied here for the Reapers. Decision time."

†

Valentine called the other two in. They gaped at their comrades kneeling with faces to the wall.

"What's with all this?"

That was the kind of quality manpower that pulled duty on New Year's Eve. Only after Valentine prodded the corporal with his barrel did the Quisling realize what was going on. He made them the same offer he did the others.

They cooperated.

Valentine snipped the telephone wires, hoping that if it activated a trouble alarm, there wouldn't be enough New Year's staff to investigate right away. He set Rollings to work unscrewing the station's radio from the shelf at the com desk. They did a quick sweep of the building while the Wolves watched both ends of the road, and then started looking through the armory.

The river patrol had good gear, including rocket-propelled grenades that Corporal Glass looked over and selected. Valentine found a case of four Type 3s—that had been the weapon issued to his Razors by Solon, who'd evidently had a bigger budget than the river patrol. The small arms were a little disappointing, mostly cut-down versions of the venerable M16. On the other hand, there was a plentitude of small support machine guns that could be carried or fixed to a boat mount. Most of the weapons were packed in protective lubricant—it would take hours to clean them—so the platoon would have to get back with what they brought.

They ended up filling two truck trailers with boxes of weapons and ammunition and other assorted pieces of lethality, plus as much com gear and medicines as they could find. As Valentine and Patel supervised the loading, the assigned drivers checked the tires and tested the lights and horns on their vehicles.

The men rode in the beds of the camouflaged service trucks with the prisoners secured to floor bolts. They'd even liberated some walkie-talkies so the drivers could communicate with each other. Condensed and dehydrated foodstuffs and extra gear was piled in bags hanging off the back and strapped to the hoods.

They even took the dog. Valentine didn't mind; he liked dogs. Though it was heartbreaking if you had to eat them.

As they pulled out and bumped west, witch fingers of tree branches scratched the sides of the truck.

In the dark, with the roads potholed and washed out, they couldn't go much faster than a man could trot. Patel had the Wolves lope ahead and behind, scouting and checking for pursuit.

All that marked their departure was noise, and that only briefly. A siren started up from the armory as soon as they were out of sight.

"What you figure that signifies, Major?" the man at the wheel asked.

"We'll find out soon enough," Valentine said.

Valentine shifted the machine pistol to his lap and checked the soldier's rifle and the bandolier resting on the dash. He and this version of Southern Command's single shot breechloaders were old, conflicted friends dating back to his days in the Labor Regiment. It was a fine gun, accurate with stopping power sufficient to knock a Reaper off its feet, if you didn't mind having to reload every time you fired a round.

Valentine opened the glass panel between the cabin and the back of the truck.

"Someone ask our prisoners what that noise is," Valentine said over the truck's protesting suspension.

"Alarm, sir."

"Was there someone there they didn't tell us about?"

Valentine waited a moment while Patel asked a few questions.

"Could be a gargoyle, Major. They overfly the area all the time. One might have seen the trucks leave. Could be he flew down to investigate. Gargoyles are smarter than harpies."

*They're also smart enough to guide in a few Reapers.*

Valentine opened the truck door, checking that he wouldn't be swept off, or worse, by the branches ahead. He searched the night sky.

The glare of the following truck's headlights made it difficult to see.

"Kill the lights," Valentine said to his driver, dropping back into the cab.

"Pass back to the following truck: Kill the lights," Valentine said to Patel. Patel lifted a brand-new walkie-talkie from the armory and spoke into it.

With the lights out on the rear truck, Valentine tried again, ducking under a branch that snapped and snipped as it broke along the truck's side.

A shadow hung behind the trucks, following the road. A shadow that closed in on itself, thickening as it followed their vehicles.

Harpies. Dirty, flapping—

Valentine wondered what they were carrying, apart from ugly. He wondered if the theoretical gargoyle had sent them after the trucks. They had enough cunning to know something was wrong and that they'd be rewarded for stopping the trucks.

Fixated by the shadow, Valentine started to pick out individual wings and short, skinny bowlegs. A branch slapped him out of his trance, and he ducked back into the cabin.

"Harpies," Valentine said. "Pass the word. Honk and bring the Wolves in."

He hated those snaggletoothed bastards. A sort of cold clarity took over as he stifled the urge to get one in his hands and dismember it like a well-cooked chicken.

"We could stop under thick trees, Major."

"No, that'll just give them more time to figure something out. And let them aim."

Valentine looked at the bungees holding the cargo on the roof. He detached a couple of the S hooks and fitted them on to his vest and belt. Testing his grip, he exited the cab, closed the truck door, and hooked another bungee to the bars covering the passenger window.

"Stop a sec and pass me up the gun and bandolier," Valentine said. "And try to keep to the left."

As the truck ground into motion again, Valentine now hanging on the outside with his foot on a fuel tank, he found that the side-view mirror protected him from the bigger branches. All it did for the smaller ones was bend them back to give them a little more energy for a swat.

The Wolf scouts returned and perched on the hood and front hedge cutter. At a turn Valentine saw the following truck also had Wolves atop the driver's cab.

"Pass the word: Wait until I shoot," Valentine ordered.

The shadow broke into individual forms as it neared. Valentine searched the flock for the bigger, longer-legged form of a gargoyle. The harpies darted and zigzagged as they flew; it was how their bodies kept aloft. He placed his foresight on one hurrying to get ahead of the trucks. Its course was a crazy mix of ups and downs, backs and forths. . . . But between the frantic beats of the wings you could sometimes track them on a glide—

BLAM!

Valentine had been so used to firing guns equipped with flash suppressors he'd forgotten the white-yellow photoflash. And he'd forgotten just how hard you had to press into the stock to absorb the shock.

Valentine worked the lever and ejected the little thimble of the shell casing, his shoulder smarting with the old mule kick.

Missed.

The Wolf on the hood had a combat shotgun, a sensible weapon for brush fighting. He tracked one of harpies above and fired.

Valentine heard a high, inhuman scream.

*Time to get down with the sickness.*

The sickness. The shadow half. The monster.

Valentine had a few names for it, depending on his mood. He'd learned long ago that a part of him rejoiced in the death of his enemies and his own survival. Whether it was a character flaw or some piece of strange heritage passed down from his Bear father didn't matter. The awful exhilaration he felt when he killed, triumphed, made him wonder whether he wasn't even more deserving of destruction for the good of the world, like some rabid dog.

But for now the sickness had its uses.

Valentine, remembering his early years in the Wolves, made an effort to thank those left behind at the landings and hear their accounts.

He shouldered the gun. One was diving right at the truck. Its feet rubbed together and a plastic strip fell—it had armed some kind of grenade. BLAM!

Damn cranky gun.

Maybe he put a bullet through its wing and spoiled the dive. It flapped off to the left and dropped its explosive.

It detonated, orange and loud, in a stand of brush. Valentine wondered what the birds and critters residing in the undergrowth thought.

*Don't get weird now, mate. Job at hand.*

Valentine heard canvas tearing. The men in the bed of the truck were hacking off the truck-bed cover to better employ their guns.

Valentine aimed again, but a twiggy smack in the back of the head spoiled his shot.

"Four o'clock!"

A line of harpies were coming in, bright plastic grenade tabs fluttering as they pulled the arming pins. They were flapping hard, each bat form describing a crazy knuckleball course.

"There's a good straightaway ahead, sir," yelled the driver.

"Put on some speed," Valentine said.

He fired, and the men in the trucks fired, and when the orange ball of light cleared there was only one harpy left. It dropped the stick grenade on the road and flapped hard to gain altitude, but someone in the second truck brought it down.

Their luck was in. The device didn't go off.

Another line of harpies had gotten around the front.

"Twelve high!" the Wolf hanging off the brush cutter called.

Now the small, questing branches could whack him on the cheek and bridge of Valentine's nose. A good deal more painfully, as the truck had picked up speed.

He tasted his own blood and felt something sticky on his neck, but he didn't feel anything worse than a scratch or two.

The night smelled like blood, wet leaves, and rotten eggs.

Valentine reloaded as the harpies made their run. He could see their beady eyes reflecting red in the moonlight.

One of his soldiers in misty denim, a big man with bushy sideburns, let loose with a double-barrel, dropped the gun to someone below, and took up a pump action. Valentine aimed and fired. He watched his target plunge, falling loopily as a kite with a cut string, but suspected the man resting his aiming arm on the cab hood had downed the beastie.

The others dropped their explosives. Grenades bounced all over the road. The man hanging off the brush cutter disappeared into flash and smoke, but when they emerged again from the blasts he was still there, blackened and frazzled but evidently intact.

Valentine, with the thick fuzzy head and the muffled hearing of someone who'd been a little too near a blast, saw another harpy fall, brought down by the truck behind. The flock, perhaps not liking the punishment being handed out with little to show for it, turned and gathered to the east, doing a sort of whirling corkscrew aerial conference.

"Eyes on the road," Patel bellowed at the driver.

A pushed-over tree blocked the road.

The driver braked hard, and the truck jumped to a tune of squealing brakes. The Wolf on the front, evidently uninjured but stunned by the explosion, was thrown by the sudden braking, struck the trunk of the downed tree, and went heels-over-head onto the other side of the trunk.

Valentine, more or less secured by the bungees, lost nothing but his dignity as he saw himself swinging, holding on to the bars over the passenger window.

Patel was already out of the truck, running with a first aid kit.

Valentine saw a big, wide-winged shape flapping away low. He raised his gun, aimed, and fired at the big target.

The gargoyle lurched but kept flapping.

Valentine swore. The big, soft-nosed bullet should have brought it down. His old marksmanship trainer in the Labor Regiment had promised the kick in the shoulder was nothing to what the target experienced. He'd seen a round take a softball-sized chunk of flesh out of a wild pig. He must have just clipped it on a limb.

It disappeared behind a line of trees.

Valentine looked at the roadblock.

What kind of super-gargoyle could push over a tree? Nothing short of a Reaper could. Valentine looked at the tangle of old, weatherworn roots. The tree had been downed some time ago and moved off the road. The gargoyle had simply moved it back. Still, an incredible display of strength. Their flying arms were supposed to be powerful.

Worse, the harpies were heartened by the stationary trucks. They formed a new shadow, and then an arrow, pointed straight at the delayed trucks.

"Get that tree out of the way," Valentine shouted.

The men piled out of the trucks while the other Wolf helped Patel with the injured man.

"Faster," Valentine urged. He raised himself up so he could shout to the truck behind. "Second squad, deploy. Let's keep those bastards off us."

The men, with their varmint and bird guns mixed in with the militia rifles, spread out.

Valentine fired into the flying mass without picking out a target. Hitting with the wonky old rifle was purely a matter of chance.

"Watch each other's backs—there's more coming around from eight o'clock," Valentine shouted.

The rest began to pepper the harpies with careful shots. One pair, Rutherford and DuSable, shifted position to give better covering fire to the men working on clearing the fallen log. Valentine made a note of it—the noise and confusion of gunfire short-circuited some and they forgot the bigger picture. A flier spun down; another followed intentionally, coming to its aid. Perhaps they were a mated pair.

Valentine fired three more times quickly, and then jammed the gun. The ejector had torn off the heat-softened brass rim on the casing. He grabbed the hot barrel at the other end. The ornery weapon would be more lethal as a club anyway. Then he remembered his machine pistol.

He flipped open the stock and extended the foregrip. It did group tightly, and the harpies were closing.

The prisoners in the trucks began to yell. They'd been left handcuffed inside.

The harpies swooped over the vehicles, dropping grenades and plastic arming tabs. Valentine watched a grenade bounce under the truck, realized that the same bungees that kept him secured to the passenger door were keeping him from jumping off—

All he could do was wait for it. He fired a burst at a harpy coming straight for the cab, watched with satisfaction as the bullets tore it into a blood-rain of gory pieces.

The grenade went off but didn't sound much louder than an overstuffed firecracker. Other explosions rocked the second truck.

Valentine brought down another harpy, who'd suddenly appeared from behind a tree as though he'd popped into existence just to aim a leg claw at Valentine's throat. He reloaded, but the sky had cleared. The harpies had had enough at last and the flock was keeping low.

The soldiers moved the obstacle and got on their way again.

The front truck was leaking coolant, and a couple of the mechanically minded did a bird-droppings-and-bubblegum fix that slowed the leak. They had to stop and refill with water. They'd destroy the engine before recrossing the Mississippi anyway.

It got them to the landing.

The men were in admirably high spirits. The only serious injury they'd suffered was to the Wolf from the front truck, who'd broken a wrist, hurt a knee, and taken a piece of shrapnel to his calf, though one of the prisoners had an ugly gash in his scalp and another had torn his wrist open trying to get out of his handcuffs as the trucks were bombed.

The injured Wolf rode back to the landing, scratching the dog's ears in good humor despite his injuries.

At the landing Valentine was happy to let Rand take over.

"Far shore says river watchers report clear river," the man at the radio said. "We've got the okay to cross."

A pair of the Skeeter Fleet roared downriver.

Valentine's head felt thick and the old gunsmoke smell was getting nauseating. "Get the swag loaded and the men on the boats and rafts. And—"

There it was. The cold spot on his mind, a bit of ball lightning lurking in the thick river woods, raising the hairs on the back of his head. *Reaper!*

"And, sir?" Rand asked.

"And I'm going back up the road a bit to make sure there's no pursuit."

Rand pushed the glasses back up on his nose and nodded. "Ten, fifteen minutes at most, sir."

"Patel. Hoboken."

They trotted over, Patel solemn at the tone in his voice.

"Hood," Valentine said, using Southern Command slang for a Reaper.

They took the news like experienced Wolves. Concern but not panic. Hoboken put his hand on the big parang at his waist.

It was back along the road away, somewhere at the top of the river-bank. It might just be watching, waiting for someone to trot off into the bushes to take a crap. Sure, it could wade into them and do a lot of damage, but how many dead pawns would make the Kurian control-ling it think the sacrifice worth the loss of his knight?

But who knew what might be rushing to its aid.

Valentine and the Wolves slipped off into the brush, spread out by a few meters, preventing the Reaper from taking two at once if it decided to fall on them.

"Lifesign down," Valentine said.

Reapers hunted by seeking the emotional signal given off by intel-ligent minds. The Hunters had spent a good deal of time in mental training, learning to meditate their lifesign down until it was like background radiation.

Problem was, it was hard to forget that you were on the wrong bank of the river, with your friends about to leave, and a walking death machine lurking, probably as fast and strong as all three of you put together. At night Reapers were at the height of their lifesign-sensing powers. He hoped this one was concentrating on the throng at the riverbank.

Valentine quietly removed the stiletto from his forearm. If it grabbed him, he might get it through the eye or ear or jaw as it snapped his spine or tore into him with its foot-plus long, flanged tongue.

Purely a matter of chance which man it would target, but Valentine took the middle. A smart Reaper might strike there, hoping that the others at either wing would shoot at each other in the confusion.

They took turns walking, one going forward while the other two covered, the men behind giving soft clicks of the tongue when the first man could no longer be covered.

Something was wrong—the location. . . . Valentine cast about like a dog in a swirling breeze. No, it was to the side, too high.

He froze, gave a signal for the others to keep still as well.

*Jesus, Mary, and Joseph*—

It was up a tree, resting on a flattish branch above a deadfall that gave it a good view of the river and landing. But the silhouette was all wrong—the pelvis and lower limbs were turned around, like a bird's. The limbs were thin. Valentine had seen starvation cases that looked fat compared to this Reaper's limbs. Leathery wings like a bat's extended from overlarge arms and oversized fingers, now flaccid and hanging like a child playing superhero with a sheet pinned to his back and clutched at the fists.

A backswept forehead had a little plume of stiff hair to it, like a centurion's helmet.

Valentine must have startled, misstepped. The long, backswept face turned and cocked, just like a robin listening for a worm.

The eyes, the color of a dying sun, were cold and familiar.

Valentine shouldered the 18 Select and it launched itself off the branch with a spring of its rear limbs. A short, forked tail had more webbing leading to the legs. The thing could maneuver like a duck. It turned and Valentine loosed a burst.

It disappeared into the trees. Valentine got a glimpse of elongated ostrich toes as it disappeared. He hardened his ears and heard branches snapping.

"What the blue hell was that?" Patel asked, coming forward at a crouch. He scanned the branches above, as if fearing nests filled with little chirping Reapers.

"I don't want to wait to find out. Back to the landing."

Valentine's head wanted to disappear between his shoulders, turtlelike, the whole way back. It was far too easy to imagine the avian Reaper—if it was a Reaper—reaching down and knocking his head off with one of those slender legs like a perched cat swatting at a ball of string.

The men had fun stripping and destroying the trucks. They'd even used a tree limb to winch out one of the diesels. Patel made some flatbread on a greasy skillet while the strike platoon rested and let Rand's team do their jobs filling the boats. Valentine rode back on the ricketiest-looking raft, leaning against stacks of tires and boxes filled with headlights and radio gear as he watched the old houseboat's pontoons and netted masses of Ping-Pong balls scrape and roll through the water.

He could hear firing from downriver, a *kak-kak-kash* of small cannon that reminded him of the old *Thunderbolt*'s Oerlikon. He watched signal flares fired from the friendly shore, and a boat roared by with the last of the Wolf rear guard.

The sky was already pinkening.

Some of his men gathered at the far end of the boat, watching the hostile shore recede. As Valentine watched the southern half of the mighty river in the direction of the firing, he listened in on a member of his strike platoon and a member of the landing detail talking to a rafter as they were towed back across the Mississippi:

"The major is the coolest sonofabitch under fire I've ever seen, I'm here to tell. The bat-bastards came in and he stood up on the truck, just picking them off while grenades dropped all around."

"They can't train guts into you," another agreed. "He's tough."

*Well, you can bungee yourself up so you can't run too.*

Valentine was too pleased to correct them; besides, the shaggy hound had decided to hop up on the piled tires and deploy a rasping tongue on the cuts and scrapes courtesy of the Kentucky roadside growth.

†

All in all, it was a successful operation. A sniper had killed one of Moytana's Wolves and a Bear was missing in action. He'd last been seen roaring down after a blood trail in the assault on the river patrol docks. Gamecock was hopeful he'd wander back into camp in a week or so once he sniffed out a method to get back across the river.

The worst losses had been suffered by the Skeeter Fleet: A motorboat with three men had blown up during a riverine duel with river patrol craft. Their pictures had already gone up on the memorial wall at Backwater Pete's, a bar up the Arkansas River near the Skeeter Fleet general headquarters.

That was the hateful side of the Cause. A chance conversation leading to an opportunity to hit the enemy where he wouldn't expect. And at the end of it, when the excitement was over and the ineffable, after-action halo faded, came the bill. All because he did his duty.

But his duty was also to turn this assortment of experienced soldiers (and the odd ex-sailor; he had two floaters in with his fighters) into a cohesive unit, to know which pieces functioned in what way under stress. They'd been over the river and back again together, in spirit, even if everybody hadn't crossed the Mississippi.

Now he had a team.

†

At the debriefing back at Camp Highbeam, the only person unhappy about the raid was Brother Mark. He looked strained and pale in the fluorescent lighting of the camp classroom that doubled as a conference room. He'd been out on one of his contact trips, negotiating with legworm ranchers, the resistance, and who knew what else.

"There is a plan, you know," Brother Mark said after asking questions about exactly where the fighting had taken place. "We don't need to be jamming sticks into the hornet's nest, stirring them up."

Valentine was a little dissatisfied too, when he told the story about the flying Reaper.

"Sure it wasn't just a real skinny gargoyle?" Captain Moytana asked. He'd written the letter about the dead Wolf and posted it to his folks that morning.

"I'll send a message to the Miskatonic about it," Valentine told the faces around the conference table. "I don't suppose there's a good artist somewhere in the brigade."

"One more matter," Colonel Seng said, his wide catfish face graver than usual. "The usual after-action leaves will not take place. I wish to intensify training. The whole camp is going to start route-marching exercises and war games. The orders and scheduling will be on your desks within two days."

Gamecock groaned. "My Bears expect their due."

"They're not your Bears, Lieutenant," Seng said. "They're Southern Command's. They'll get their chance at a short leave. So will all of you. This operation may begin sooner than anyone dreams."

Valentine intercepted Brother Mark as the meeting broke up. It was easy; he wasn't a popular man. Valentine didn't know if it was his fussy manner of speaking or the resentment of soldiers who had to work with a civilian's eye on them.

"Excuse me, sir," Valentine said. "Were you just with the rebels in the Virginias?"

"I can't tell you that, son."

"You've been there, though. You've told us that much."

"Yes," Brother Mark said, wary.

"Have you seen the Grog that's supposed to be with them? Leading them?"

"I don't know about leading. They definitely listen to him. He's sort of a mascot or good luck charm. They always perk up when he's around."

"What's he like?" Valentine asked.

"I suspect you know. I was briefed on your trip through Kentucky. Big. Leaner and less stooped-over than those thick-hides with the fangs. He can speak too. I've never met a Grog who can do that."

"The last time you saw him, was he well?" Valentine asked. Brother Mark should be able to answer that.

"Healthy as a horse. They call him the Uncle, by the way. I just remembered that. He's scarred, but the injuries are healed. Does that put your mind at ease?"

"You've— I'm very happy to hear that, sir. Thank you."

"Happy. I remember that. I'm jealous, son. Excuse me, I must attend to the colonel. Be true."

He turned away, hurrying to catch up to Colonel Seng, ending the conversation.

†

The brigade made practice marches interspersed with combat training. Jolla's command, including Valentine's company, was often matched against the rest of the brigade.

After one of these skirmishes, the Guard lieutenant colonel Gage sat Valentine in his command car, a beat-up old Humvee with an oversized bed and extra brackets that allowed it to double as an ambulance.

"Goddamit, Major, our boys are supposed to win. How are they supposed to build confidence when your glorified chicken wranglers burn a couple dozen of them?"

"Tell your junior officers that just because an area's been checked for mines, it doesn't mean I can't go back and replant after they've passed through," Valentine said. "My orders were to delay your march on Red Ridge."

Valentine wanted to add that if Daniels would keep his companies in closer contact, Valentine wouldn't have had time to mine their road, but that would be presumptuous.

"You could act a little more like Quislings. They always fall back in the face of superior numbers. They don't hunker down and let the first wave get past."

"I know, sir," Valentine said.

Gage cooled down. He'd obviously just been chewed on by Seng, who was pushing the brigade like a madman. "They still calling your guys the shit detail?"

"I haven't heard it in a while," Valentine said.

"Got to hand it to you, though. After the last time getting at those Grogs of yours with the auto 50s, everyone figured we hadn't run into your boys yet because they hadn't started sniping. Weren't you staff at one time?"

"Supposed to be. An old ghost caught up to me and I never made it."

"Sorry to boil up on you like that. I'm glad you'll be on our side when we march up-country."

†

As January turned to February, a big duffel bag arrived, labels and identifying inking scrawled all over it. It turned out to be all the way from Pacific Command.

Valentine read the letter in the waterproof courier pouch stitched onto the canvas:

> *Valentine,*
>
> *After many wanderings your goods surfaced and I became aware of their existence. I promptly inventoried and dispatched them to Denver, courtesy of a liaison, and I'm confident they'll make it to Southern Command before too many more months pass.*
>
> *Been seeing a lot of your friend Gide. She's got a mouth on her but she's turning into a dead shot witch of the woods. They're talking about putting me into GHQ up here and if that happens I might see about a ring for the end of those snake tattoos. She lost three toes and a chunk of buttock to a mortar round, so she's off the A-active list but is recovering nicely. She sends a kiss and wants to know if you're still musky. I won't be ungentlemanly and speculate.*
>
> *Please accept your property with my compliments and apologies for the delay. What the hell is that thick leathery material, anyway? If you've got any to spare I'd like some for a jacket.*
>
> *Yours in the Cause,*
>
> *J. LeHavre, Colonel, Pacific Command*

123

His old legworm leathers, gear, and sword had been wrapped up in a waterproof, but someone had made off with his boots either before it was turned over to LeHavre or along the road. Valentine wished their new owner's feet well.

The thief, if there had been a thief, missed a stiffened cuirass of cross-grained Reaper cloth, light and breathable and yet strong enough to stop a rifle round.

He looked at the sword. Some craftsman had put a new sharkskin grip on it—at least he thought it was sharkskin; it might have been roughed up big mouth—which was just as well as the old woven one had been getting ragged and bloodstained. He looked closer. There was a tiny little G inked just under the hilt cap next to the stitching. Now that he knew what to look for, he found a similar initial stitched just inside one of the interior side's many map pockets.

Nice to have a souvenir of his best memories of the Cascades.

Valentine noticed that she hadn't returned the old Steyr Scout. He didn't regret it—she'd probably make better use of it than he could.

†

With the company full up and the training proceeding as planned, Valentine found more time to study Seng's texts and notes from his term at the staff school. Seng was generous with his own time, translating cryptic notes if nothing else. Seng's graduation thesis, filling an entire binder, was on Winston Churchill when Britain was fighting alone during the dark years between the fall of France and Operation Barbarossa, when Germany launched her fatal attack on Soviet Russia. Valentine found the Seng thesis more interesting and readable than many of the historians he'd read in Father Max's old library.

He still felt his company lacked a certain spark of initiative that Southern Command's soldiers seemed to be born with. Or perhaps Valentine, with more experience in picked commands, was used to building a unit with a better grade of materials. Their instinct was to hand every problem up rather than improvise a solution and then report.

He took to sending out small units with simple tasks—find a backpack he'd placed in a ravine without being spotted by pickets— and then change their orders at the last moment and kill all radio communications. He and Patel would then lead a couple squads in a mock pursuit.

If they weren't bred to think on their feet, he'd train it into them.

The bright spot in the shakedown was Glass' improvement. He knew the men joked that in Ford and Chevy, Glass finally had some friends who shared his taste for mostly communicating in grunts. Glass wanted to try them out with grenade launchers or the new, ultra-light knee mortars from a Southern Command inventor.

Valentine allowed himself one luxury (other than the occasional long shower with his gift soaps): He taught Bee to shine his shoes and polish his belt buckle and name tag on his A uniform. Bee was feminine enough to like things pretty, though he occasionally had to take the woven daisy chains of wildflowers off his pack or remove the mini-bouquets peeking out the gutter at the bottom of his pistol holster. Some of the other officers in the brigade asked him how he classified her—adjutant, aide, or spouse—but Bee's elephantine grace and gentility gave her a charm that assured her a constant stream of sweets and ribbons from officers "just passing through the trader stalls and thought she'd like this."

He'd even heard the Command sergeant major, the senior NCO for the brigade, refer to her as their "big beauty." She'd come a long way in the men's opinion since her arrival in a tutu.

For relaxation he played chess with Rand. Rand won most of the time. He was such a talented, cold player that Valentine wondered if he made intentional mistakes out of curiosity to see what his CO would do when presented with an opportunity, just to give his brain a new set of data points and challenges. Rand apparently never let anyone behind the shield of his professionalism, even when they chatted after their chess games about the progress of the company.

They weren't close, but he was as fine a junior officer as Valentine could ever want.

Then came the spring storms. The camp began to buzz. As usual, the men had somehow picked up that something was about to happen and soon, days before Valentine got his orders to report to a final briefing.

†

The camp grapevine proved to be right. All future leaves were canceled, the day trips into town ended, and last-minute munitions arrived, including a small supply of Quickwood bullets.

With the gear, the important men and women who came equipped with bodyguards, advisers, secretaries, and drivers began to arrive the next day. Valentine gave the same status report for his company three times in one day.

It would have been four but General Lehman cut him off as Valentine spoke to him in the base officers' club that never really got going. The dusty chairs, old movie posters, and license plates from the states making up the UFR all looked like they wanted to be put out of their misery.

"Javelin's under step-off orders, Major. Any reason your men can't go with it?"

"No, General."

"Heard good things about you. Gage says your men have been giving him hell playing OPFOR."

"That's kind of him, General."

"Not sure I like you training Grogs though. Sniffer dogs have their purposes, but you don't want them juggling grenades." He stopped, waiting for an answer.

"Of course not, sir."

An aide appeared and handed Lehman a flimsy. Lehman excused himself, scanned it, and nodded his head yes as he handed it back.

"They'll add a bit of verisimilitude to the, what is it, technical crew your men are supposed to look like."

"That's the idea, sir."

"A good one. Yours?"

"No, one of the Liberty recruits'. She's company clerk now."

"I don't trust ex-Quislings much farther than I can throw them. They caused us a lot of trouble before. Hope it works out for you. See you at the briefing tonight, Valentine. Dismissed."

The briefing, held in the guarded mess hall and using chairs begged and borrowed from every headquarters tent in the brigade, was mercifully brief. Which was just as well; the blackout curtains killed airflow as well as light. More than a hundred bodies burned a lot of calories over a couple hours. The tent quickly became stuffy.

Lehman opened it with a few words about how javelins were used in ancient warfare to strike troops behind the front ranks. Lambert and Sime and a few new faces were there, politicians most likely. In the throng of uniformed aides and assistants stood one man in hunting gear who took a lot of notes and a few pictures. Valentine guessed he was from the *Battle Cry*, Southern Command's military newspaper.

Conspicuously absent, at least to Valentine, were Brother Mark and Moytana's senior Wolf lieutenant. Rumor had it they were already in the Kurian Zone, somewhere north of Memphis.

What combination of diplomacy and guerrilla havoc might be already under way? If Valentine had had his choice of assignments for this operation, he would have been with them as well. But support and logistics would be critical in an operation this far from Southern Command's bases.

Seng gave some final instructions for the movement to Rally Base, the terminus for the operation's communications with GHQ and what would one day, hopefully, be a routing station for troops staging trips to or back from the new Freehold on the northern Cumberland Plateau and Appalachians.

The campaign map had a few new notations. Three Cats had been dispatched to Kentucky, spaced out along their line of march. Logistics Commandos had infiltrated in behind the Cats. Valentine wondered what they'd been told about Highbeam, or Javelin, or whatever false information they'd been fed in case of capture.

Lambert look strained. But she collected her old briskness for a few words to the assembled officers.

"Yes, this operation is a risk," she said. The junior officers and senior NCOs had just found out their true destination from Colonel Seng. The news was still sinking in.

"But the coal country of Virginia, and the legworms of Kentucky, are both key to the Kurian Order. Civilization needs electricity and the people living in that civilization need protein."

For a moment Valentine thought he was back in the Cascades, where denial of resources had meant grisly strategies involving civilian bodies stacked like cordwood, while Adler carried out his war against Seattle. He envied the men around him for a moment. To them, Lambert's words were just military jargon.

"They'll hit back hard when they figure out what you're doing. But if you can win that fight, it'll put cracks in the foundation of every Kurian tower east of the Mississippi. Remember that. Remember, also, that you're not alone, even in the darkest valley of fear. The people across the Mississippi hate the Kurians just as much as we do; they just don't get a chance to do anything about it. Is Javelin Brigade up for this challenge?"

Variations of "Sir," "Yes," and fighting yips broke out in the cafeteria.

"Send 'em back to hell," General Lehman said.

With that, the meeting adjourned, though Seng somewhat killed the theatrical mood by announcing a new series of meetings starting before breakfast the next day.

†

The columns marched out of camp in a drizzle. Valentine rode, but he stopped his horse across from the gate to admire the rare sight of Southern Command forces marching in step, swinging their arms in time, rifles over their shoulders.

"Good luck in Louisiana," someone called. Valentine wondered if he was a plant or just a camp civilian employee who'd picked up the rumor that they were heading south.

The general's color guard was present for the occasion. The pipes and drum set up a merry tune. Valentine thought it might be the hoary old sports perennial "Who Let the Bears Out?"—a favorite at basketball games.

"Next stop, New Orleans, Major," Rand called to him as his company wheeled to head south down the highway. He'd been coached to say it, and it sounded forced. Whatever his other strengths, Rand couldn't dissemble.

Valentine nudged his horse forward and took his place in the column at the head of his company. Their strange un-uniforms stood out so they marched at the rear, among the wagons, trucks, cook vans, and pack animals.

"That's a nice mule, mister," a woman's voice called from the crowd as Valentine walked the Morgan on the Malden road. Valentine recognized the voice.

He searched the crowd.

"Molly!"

It was her. Valentine saw a tan, full-lipped face. Her blond hair shone even in the blustery spring gloom. She'd made an effort with her face and eyes.

He hadn't seen her in four years. The emotional rush almost unseated him from the Morgan.

They'd once been intimate—no, that wasn't fair, they'd once been lovers and passable friends. He'd met her on a long courier mission to the Great Lakes, when her family had helped an injured comrade of his. He'd extracted her family from the Kurian Zone, and Molly as well, by a near miracle after she'd been arrested for the murder of an important Illinois mouthpiece. She'd become engaged to a Guard while he was in the Wolves.

Edward stood next to her in what Valentine guessed was his only pair of long pants, judging from the state of the knees. His dark, cowlick-filled hair looked like it had waged a morning-long guerrilla war against its combing. How old was he now? Six?

He'd lost his father before he'd been born, in Consul Solon's invasion. Graf Stockard was one of thousands missing in action from the "old" Ozark Free Territory.

Valentine turned his horse and got it out of the way of the marching column. Engines blatted and wheels creaked on by. He dismounted swiftly and Molly gave him a friendly hug.

"What in the world—"

"It's a long story," she said. "We made a special trip to see you off, Edward and I."

Molly had a small cap stuck in the belt of her overcoat. Valentine lifted it and checked the insignia.

"I purchase horses for Southern Command now. Do you remember Captain Valdez from Quapaw? He got me a job as a wrangler for the equine department at Selection and Purchase. I got promoted last year." She patted the Morgan's nose. "I might even have bought your mount. It's about the right age and from Half-Day Farms."

"Raccoon's a good horse," Valentine said. "I don't understand. You found me through Logistics?"

"Oh, no. I was worried about you, after—after that business where you were . . ."

Her eyes had lines at the edges. But then she spent a lot of time outside. Up close, the blond hair looked a trifle brittle. She hadn't had an easy time of it either, raising a son on her own.

"Arrested," Valentine said, coming back to the road.

Edward seemed fascinated with the butt of Valentine's .45. His eyes hardly left it.

"I wrote a letter. I wanted to know about your trial. It took forever to get an answer. A junior secretary in civil affairs, a very nice corporal named Dots. I guess she saw it in a pile and she wrote an answer. It's those long-service corporals who are always nicest to work with, I find."

Valentine would have introduced her to Glass if he had the time. He reminded himself to add a private message to Lambert on his first report.

"I'll have to thank Corporal Dots. I—it's nice to have someone see you off."

"She sent me a quickie a week ago, saying that your unit was moving out. I wondered that she kept track of you. I bet she's got a bit of a crush on you. She said you had a very handsome file photo."

Valentine saw her eyes flit to his scar and then his jawline. "Must have been an old photo."

She hooked her cheek with her index finger and showed a missing molar. "The years haven't been kind to either of us."

"You could get that fixed."

"Thought about it. But I stick my pencil there when I'm testing horses."

"Good luck, Daddy," Edward said.

Molly grabbed him at the shoulder. "Edward! We talked about this."

Raccoon seemed to sway first one way, then another, as Valentine used the horse's neck to hold himself up. "What?" he thought he said. Maybe it was just a choked exclamation.

Edward went wide-eyed in recognition of his own wrongdoing.

"You can't break promises like that," Molly continued. She looked to her left. "Mrs. Long, can you make sure he doesn't run under a truck?"

Mrs. Long looked like she wanted to hear the rest of the conversation. "Yes'm," she said. She gave Valentine a dirty look as Molly pulled him away.

"Edward, do me a favor, watch my horse," Valentine said, passing the reins to the boy.

They dodged between trucks and made it to the other side of the road, just missing Tiddle roaring along the column on his dirt bike. A soldier with a clipboard near the gate gave Valentine a curious look but didn't move to intervene.

They got out of the way of traffic and stood under a yew.

"David—" she said, hard and quiet. "I'm so sorry about that. I've been stupid."

"Molly—it's not possible."

"Of course it's not possible. David, there's so much you don't know. About Edward's father."

Obviously there was, if Molly wasn't willing to call him her husband. . . .

"Molly, it's not my business. But how?"

"I told you, I was stupid," she repeated. "I . . . I didn't show you when you visited that time, but I've got a drawer with some pictures of you. That old scarf of yours you gave me that winter in Minnesota. Two paper clippings too, one showing you getting a decoration, or was it a promotion? It was while you were fighting in Texas. I keep the letters from you in there too. It's not like a shrine or anything. I've just always wanted you to do well with your Cause."

"I still don't see the stupid part," Valentine said.

"Edward got to the age where he got snoopy. He was poking around in the drawer and saw all the stuff they'd written about you. He said he remembered you being at our house, God knows how."

"He called me his father," Valentine said.

"Yes. I don't keep pictures of his father around the house. I thought, *What'll it hurt if I shave the truth a little?* If things had fallen together a little differently, you might have been."

Valentine, who'd calmly given orders with the gigantic shells of a massive Grog cannon called the Crocodile making the earth ripple beneath his feet, stood dumbstruck.

"Oh, it doesn't matter anymore." She wiped the corners of her eyes.

"Here," she said, passing him a packet extracted from her overcoat. "Three chamois. They're the best Texas kid I could find. I embroidered your initials into the corner. Not like my mom could do, but I did my best. You can use them for your boots or guns."

Valentine didn't know what to give her. The only piece of jewelry he owned was that brass ring acquired from Seattle. "Molly, I—"

"Sorry about Edward. I can tell him the truth."

"You know my name's under something of a cloud, officially."

"Yes. I had this reporter ask me about you, by the way. I wonder how he got my name."

"A reporter?"

"For the *Clarion*. His name's Qwait. Ever met him?"

The column had finally passed. Valentine felt the eyes of the small crowd who'd turned out in the rain focus on them. "No. It's not important. I'll leave Edward to your judgment. I'm honored, in a way." He paused. "I need to catch up to my men. I'll write you, if I get back."

"When you get back," she said. "You won in Texas. You'll do the same in Louisiana—or wherever you're really going."

Molly always was smart, or maybe just sensitive to lies.

He trotted back across the road and retrieved his horse.

"I'm sorry, Momma," Edward said.

"Edward, there's nothing for you to be sorry about. I should be saying sorry to you."

Mrs. Long stepped back, staring at him as though wishing to shorten him by at least the length of his shins.

Valentine wondered what he could leave Edward with. He opened a shirt pocket and took out his battered old compass.

"Edward, do you know what this is?" he asked.

"An officer compass."

"An officer's compass, yes. With one of these and a good map, you're never lost." He handed it to the boy and mounted.

"Thank you, Father," Edward said, wide-eyed again.

"He's got your hair," Mrs. Long said, approving for a change.

Molly tightened his girth. "You're good, Major," she said.

"Good God, man, kiss her good-bye," Mrs. Long huffed. "What's this world coming to?"

Molly blushed. Valentine had never kissed a woman from saddleback before. It wasn't as easy as it looked in the movies; he almost fell on top of her.

"Uh. Thanks," Molly squeaked.

Valentine rode on in the tangled tracks of the column, trying to catch up. He passed a member of the general's color guard dumping rainwater out of his drumhead.

Irony. That's what it was. He had a daughter in the Caribbean who thought he was an uncle, and a son in St. Louis that ninety-nine out of a hundred would insist was an abomination and demand to be destroyed. Now this tousle-haired boy was calling him Daddy. Or Father, when he remembered his manners.

*God is just, but that doesn't mean he lacks humor*, Father Max used to say.

"Amen," Valentine muttered, clicking his horse into a trot.

# CHAPTER SIX

*B*reakthrough, western Tennessee, March: Operation Javelin and Colonel (later General) Seng's march to the Virginias, later to be studied and
debated—turning point or footnote?—with good arguments on both sides,
began with a masterstroke.

The thousand-foot Kurian tower at Mississippi Point had stood for two
generations. Every now and then Southern Command would bring some
heavy artillery forward and shell it for an hour or so, just to see the light
show as mysterious rippling bands of violet rose and detonated the shells a
mile from target. The scientists from the Miskatonic attending these shows
tried to study the effect with their poor collection of instruments but always
left flummoxed.

The Kurian in that tower controlling the Mississippi between Memphis
and Paducah is called "the Goobermaker." Even the best Hunter, sneaking
into the woods around that tower, slowly becomes confused and disoriented.
The more cautious, or maybe luckier, stagger away, underwear sometimes
loaded like a sopping, sagging diaper, wondering what their name is. Most
recover their sensibilities and memory eventually.

The Miskatonic consider the Goobermaker a powerful Kurian, feudal
lord to sub-Kurians stretching from the outskirts of Nashville to Memphis
and into southwestern Kentucky. He makes claim to the river as well,
extracting tolls for water traffic, and ever more exorbitant fees in auras
for cargo cutting across his territory to the Ohio or the Tennessee when
Southern Command gets the upper hand against the gunboats of the river
patrol.

David Valentine always chuckled and dismissed his participation in the

135

*assault as being "on the bench—when I wasn't sitting in the bus with my helmet."*

†

"Are you fucking kidding me?" Glass said on his return from the ammo dump with the last boxes of brass, lead, and smokeless powder for the .50s.

" 'Are you fucking kidding me, sir,' Corporal," Valentine corrected. "You'll follow orders, just like me. No matter how ridiculous."

It was the last week of February and spring peeped through the twigs and breaks in the iron gray clouds as a bitterly cold storm blowing in from Canada exhausted itself somewhere over southern Missouri.

Their assault barge yawned before them at the end of a boarding plank. It was a Kurian transport for aura fodder, and someone had painted the inside a soothing pink. It looked like a giant mouth extending a sickly, rusted tongue held down by a twelve-foot depressor.

Valentine smelled of sandalwood. He'd treated himself to a long shower to relieve the jump-off tension.

He looked out at his company through the Halloween mask rubberbanded across his face. The soldiers looked like a bunch of burned matches, with tinfoil wrapped around their head except for eyeholes.

Glass submitted to having tinfoil wrapped around his head and spray-painted dull black. Patel helped him poke eyeholes and breathing apertures in it.

"At least it's warm," Glass muttered. His heavy-weapons Grogs already had their masks on. Some artiste in the company had formed tinfoil strands into horns on the Grogs' heads.

"Hey, Sergeant Major," a soldier called. "Shiny side out, remember? Glass's grouchy enough without getting brain bake."

"It doesn't matter," Patel said, securing Glass's headpiece with a rubber band at the forehead.

It wasn't a very good joke, but Valentine was relieved to hear it. The men smelled nervous, that sharp electric acid odor of anxiety.

136

Word had filtered up through the NCOs that some of the men were remembering what happened to Quislings caught fighting for Southern Command. The Kurians developed imaginative and painful manners of extracting auras from those guilty of such treasons.

Every Southern Command soldier knew that, if captured, they could probably expect to be shuttled to some work camp or other—they were young and fit, after all. Officers could expect a good deal of interrogation. Leading figures of the resistance, majors, colonels, and especially generals could expect a long period of wear and tear under drugs or blunter instruments before the inevitable show trial. Valentine could never find it in himself to condemn those captured in the Kurian Zone who confessed to plans ranging from blowing up hospitals to poisoning Youth Vanguard bake-sale cookies, because the confession was undoubtedly forced and false.

"We're ordered to load, sir," Preville said. Preville was a near-sighted company com tech with an old Motorola headset wired to the pack radio. He made do with some old round glass women's frames that didn't do much for his face. Valentine, through Rand, had insisted that he see a Southern Command doc and get some regulation glasses, but Preville liked how he looked in his lenses. The new ones hadn't shown up in time anyway.

Patel had overheard, so all Valentine had to do was nod.

"Load up and board! Load up and board!" Patel bellowed.

Word had it that General Lehman was watching the embarkation, going from formation to formation giving a last few words of encouragement. He hadn't made it to Valentine's group.

Odd-looking and inhuman in the painted tinfoil that obscured hair and ears, they filed into the barge.

"Enjoy, guys," Valentine said. "This'll be the easiest part of the whole trip."

With Ediyak, the company clerk, and Preville trailing behind, Valentine boarded. "Last on gets to be first on the Kurian shore," he said.

The Skeeter Fleet and Logistics Commandos who'd arranged

for the barges had chalked all sorts of helpful messages on the inside. Valentine could see two:

**THANK YOU FOR CHOOSING MUDSKIPPER CRUISE LINES WE ACCEPT RESPONSIBILITY FOR NOTHING BUT GETTING YOU OVER AND HAULING YOUR BODY BACK**

and

**TETANUS SHOTS ARE RECOMMENDED FOR ALL PASSENGERS**

When the recently constructed loading doors closed, Valentine saw another.

**NO POINT WORRYING ABOUT IT NOW**

A single overworked tug, a temporary buoy, and various lines from smaller craft working together got them across, with some help from the Mississippi current. Someone discovered that knife hilts made decent drumsticks on the barge's side, and soon there were two dueling syncopations.

Bee stamped out a pretty good 4/4 base beat as she hung on to the drooping camouflage netting hanging across the open top of the barge.

Valentine wondered what the sentries on the other side of the river made of it all. A couple of sentries would get their sergeant, who would get an officer, who would probably call in an even higher officer, who would give the alarm.

This part of the operation was secret enough that even Valentine knew only the outline. His only orders were to get in column with the rest of Jolla's command and move out to the northeast along an old highway.

They splashed ashore in darkness, fiddling and adjusting the tinfoil headdresses as they waded in the slough between two sandbars, heading for blue signal lights on the shore proper. Upstream and down there were more boats and barges landing, and the riverbank echoed with the throbbing engine of the tug, the honking cries of outraged mules, and the low, firm voices of sergeants and corporals who could manage to make their softly spoken words carry through all the noise without shouting. Valentine saw lines of craft of all descriptions waiting to vomit out men and material.

Sailors and Logistics Commandos had set up lines, and netted bags full of gear came ashore like a parade of lumpy bats swinging in the wind. Someone had hung a portable radio from a tree, where it muttered out love songs in tribute to expectant and new mothers everywhere. In between the songs were tips on prenatal health and nursing given by a woman with precise, softly hypnotic diction.

The Skeeter Fleet's ships weren't manned by pregnant women. The men liked the songs, and if the Kurians sounded some kind of civil defense alert for western Kentucky, they'd hear it over the broadcast.

"Make to route green," said Preville at the com set. "The colonel wants us to take over for the Wolf pathfinders."

Valentine relaxed a little. That was according to plan as well.

"Break open a box of green chemical lights," Valentine told Patel.

He heard a crump of artillery being fired downriver. Southern Command was supposed to be bringing a trio of big guns across. Rumor said they were Harry, Hermione, and Ron, three old 155mm behemoths. Hermione was famous for having fired the first shot of the Archangel counterattack.

Southern Command was sending them into the Kurian Zone with the same long-range blessing.

He instinctively checked the big-numeral watch looped through his top buttonholes. Oh five twenty-eight. The detail would be of interest to some historian or other. Valentine hoped it wouldn't be a New Universal Church archivist collecting notes for a paper on the suppression of the Cumberland insurgency.

Valentine formed his men into rather ragged lines, wishing he could find a high spot and see the light show. The Goobermaker's strange defense had been described to him, but he'd never seen the effect personally. All he saw was the occasional flicker of a shell heading east through breaks in the trees.

He didn't hear any counterbattery fire. One would think that the local Quislings would at least have mortars in place to harass the landing by now. Perhaps they were as wary of the Goobermaker's woods as the Wolves and Cats.

Pairs of Wolves marked the path to the old highway, looking even dumber than Valentine's company with painted tinfoil topping their weathered buckskins. A trail up from the riverbank gave over to a little road, which crossed a bridge and passed through a wood before joining the old federal route. Valentine distributed his men in corporal-led units, supervising the placement of the glow sticks himself so that they'd be visible only to those coming up from the riverbank and following the trail.

The Wolves were glad to be relieved and hurried off in the direction of the firing.

It was a strange sort of KZ. As far as Valentine could tell, the Goobermaker made no attempt to build farms or settlements. He kept the old federal highway clear enough, though as they came into town he saw brush growing out of broken windows of otherwise fine brick buildings. The town looked like a decrepit old man with untrimmed eyebrows, ear, and nostril hair.

Jolla arrived and set up temporary HQ in an old primary school. As the rest of the support battalion showed up, he distributed the units so they'd be ready to move north.

"There's quite a show, if you want to go up to the school roof, Valentine," Jolla said. He'd ripped open a big triangle from his mask so it only half-obscured his face, making him look a bit like the Phantom of the Opera. "Just follow the power cords from the mobile generator."

Easily done. Valentine left Rand at company HQ with Glass and the heavy weapons Grogs and headed into the school, Bee trailing dutifully behind. Valentine had long since given up trying to get her to do anything but watch over him. Evidently he'd replaced Hoffman Price in her life in some manner.

He followed the cords up the stairs and to the roof, where the main signals team was working. Seng's chief of staff, Nowak, was throwing orders like hand grenades. She was a rather willowy woman with baby-soft skin, though that too was obscured by tinfoil.

Valentine brought up his binoculars, focused on the torchlike flicker six or seven miles away.

The Goobermaker's turret-snail tower, topped by what looked like a broken minaret, was aflame, sending a long spiral of smoke like a question mark into the sky.

Artillery shells landed somewhere in the hills well south of the tower, looking like distant lightning in the growing dawn, big horizon-shaping flashes punctuated by smaller bursts. Someone was putting up a steel curtain between the Goobermaker's lands and Memphis.

Southern Command was apparently giving everything it had in the eastern approaches to start them off.

"They did it?" Valentine asked, astonishment making him ask self-evident questions.

"Really and truly," Nowak said. She told the person at the other end to stand by. "Chatter says they've captured a Kurian alive. It may be the old bastard himself. They've sealed him inside a glass fish tank, and a couple Cats and a Bear team are hauling ass back for the river."

"Has that ever happened before?"

"If it had, guys like us wouldn't have heard of it," Nowak said in a tone that indicated she was smiling. "Of course, they're yakking about it almost in the clear. Might be a diversion trying to sucker in a big effort to recapture him, catch the patrol under our guns."

The sun was visible.

Valentine smelled food cooking. He suspected that if they moved out again, his troops, in their uniforms designed to confuse identification, might have to lead the way again. Best see if they could be relieved and get them fed, to keep their strength up for the next lap.

Valentine organized the distribution of hot chicory coffee and sandwiches for his strung-out platoons. Jolly had a quick meeting, showing the next route that they'd take as soon as a few more companies of Guards arrived, and set the next leg of the march to begin at noon in any case. Seng wanted everyone through the Goobermaker's lands and out the other end, heading for Kentucky, as soon as possible.

A tired-looking figure in black rode into camp on a lather-streaked mule. It was Brother Mark under a thick coat of dirt and dead twigs. He dismounted stiffly, handed his mount to a groom, and tottered to the field kitchen.

Valentine found a folding camp stool and brought it to him.

"You have my profound gratitude, son," he said, seating himself. "You wouldn't know if my baggage has been unloaded?"

"You need a change of clothes?" Valentine asked. Brother Mark smelled of sweat and smoke.

"My goosedown pillow. I've been on my feet or in my saddle since . . . is it Sunday already? Since Friday morning. I feel as though I could sleep propped up against that wall over there."

"I thought only the Wolves went over before Saturday night."

"Oh, I was well ahead of them. Meetings to attend. You can remove that ridiculous tinfoil now, young man. Not that it ever provided anything but psychological comfort."

Valentine would have liked nothing better—his skin felt itchy and he had sweat in his eyes—but decided to wait for official orders.

"Meetings?" Valentine asked, since Brother Mark seemed in a mood to answer questions.

He dipped a doughnut in his coffee and ate half of it. "Yes, concerning the settlement of the estate of the late Ri-Icraktisus. I beg your understanding—the Goobermaker, you boys call her. The Goobermaker's estate."

Valentine felt the ground beneath his feet tilt. "Who attended this meeting?"

"Some of the local Kurians," Brother Mark said, pulling off his boots and socks. "He was quite unpopular with the Nashville clan, and

Memphis only just tolerated him because of his military acumen. When she switched over to female and started budding off her own clan, that was the last straw. The feel went out that Memphis was willing to withdraw her support. . . ." He rubbed a finger between his toes, sniffed, and made a face. "If I were in the old bishop's palace, after a night like that I'd take a steam with a pair of flexible fourteen-year-olds scrubbing me down. I'm reduced to cleaning my own feet. I wish I could indulge my humanist patriotism in a more comfortable manner."

"You're saying the Kurians ganged up on one of their own?" Valentine wasn't sure what he had a harder time believing: Southern Command helping other Kurians bring down the Goobermaker or Brother Mark, ostensibly a high Church renegade, meeting with other Kurians and returning alive to tell.

"Not so much ganged up as withdrew their minds from her contact, leaving her rather alone at a key moment. Once the conspiracy started, everyone wanted to join. There's an old proverb from the Silk Road: A falling camel attracts many knives."

"So the tinfoil was pointless?"

"Not pointless. Useless, maybe, but it did its job. Everyone was afraid to set foot on this side of the river near that great tower. It gave the troops confidence. I understand the Bears were quite a sight, blowing open holes in the bottom of the tower with turbans of glittering foil wrapped around their heads."

"Those Kurians are not going to be happy when we march into Kentucky," Valentine said.

"Memphis or Nashville don't give two figs about the legworm ranchers. The only ones who claim control over central Kentucky is the Ordnance up in Ohio, and they're happy to cause trouble for them. They see it as removing two turds with one flush. Is that how you say it? I'm still not used to all this colorful cracker-barrel talk you fighting men use down here."

"There's a rumor that she was captured."

"No, one of her detached buds. Developed enough to inherit much of her mind. He may prove useful."

Valentine tried to digest that. "How do you meet—"

Patel walked up, using the help of his metal-tipped hickory cane. When in front of the men, he mostly used it as a pointer or to scratch maps in the dirt.

"Colonel Jolla's called for all the staff-level officers, sir," Patel said. "The route's been changed. Moytana's Wolves have captured a motor pool and fueling station. We're to move there at once."

Brother Mark finished his coffee. "Go and line your men up neatly, Major. I think I shall despair of my pillow and just sleep on my coat for whatever length of time God and Colonel Seng allow. Oh dear, it looks like rain. As if I'm not uncomfortable enough."

†

By nightfall they were almost out of the Goobermaker's territory, camped at the captured garage that reminded Valentine of the rig yard he'd briefly seized back in his days as a Wolf lieutenant. This one had no organic labor force, however, just a few mechanics and relief drivers who took a motorbus in from Memphis every day.

Just before setting off on the hard march for the garage, Jolla had ordered the men to discard their tinfoil and officially announced the destruction of the Goobermaker's tower.

Valentine wasn't able to determine which bit of news made the men cheer harder. But he was glad to feel air on his skin again.

†

The march out of the Mississippi camp marked the last time that Valentine's company stepped in ranks and files together for weeks.

Once out of sight of the river valley, they were put to work, scattered into details and squads gathering news and sustenance, watching road crossings, finding fords or paths, siphoning gasoline and warning off wandering locals.

Two days later they crossed into Kentucky, following old Route 79. Patel and a platoon rode scout, traveling ahead or around the flanks to major intersections where they could idle beside a utility pole or beneath a bridge, quietly keeping watch. Glass and Rand stayed with the main body at company headquarters. Valentine switched between the scouts and the men riding with the Logistics Commandos gathering supplies.

Valentine was happy to quit Tennessee, mostly because it meant he wouldn't have to deal with Papa Reisling any more.

Reisling was an unpleasant individual, a former Logistics Commando who'd married and settled on the fringe of the Goobermaker's grounds north of Clarksville. He was a strange figure of a man, old yet hale, thick-haired but gray flecked with white.

He didn't like Valentine from the moment he first set eyes on him, when a local underground contact arranged a meeting. Perhaps it was due to Bee, who didn't like the look of the old Dairy Queen garbage nook where they met while Reisling's brother-in-law kept watch from the roof.

Reisling considered the entire Southern Command invasion of Kentucky—the first true offensive across the Mississippi in the history of that Freehold—a deep-seated plot to make his life difficult and bring the Reapers down on him.

"I can make a pork loin disappear, or ten pounds of flour and molasses," Reisling complained, showing Valentine a flyleaf from an old book scrawled with requirements. "But *this*. Two thousand eggs, powdered or fresh. Thirty pounds of salt. Six hundred chickens at the very least, and 'as many more as I can provide.' Fruit juice or dried fruit. Where am I supposed to get dried fruit by the goddamned barrel?"

"Nobody's going to die if you miss a few line items," Valentine said. "It's a great help to us to get anything. Every mouthful you provide means less that comes out of stores that we carry along for emergencies."

"Three weeks ago I was told to start setting aside food for a big operation. I thought it would be a company of Wolves. Got a pen of year-old pigs and two fifty-pound bags of beans the local production officer doesn't know exist. Thought I'd done my job and done it well. Then half of the goddamned Southern Command crosses over the river and stands here, mouths open like baby birds expecting me to stuff 'em."

Reisling's voice reminded Valentine of a transmission giving out, all grind and whine.

"Old tricks are usually the best," Valentine said. "Find a Church relief warehouse, loot it, and set it on fire."

"And have Church inquisitors questioning half of Clarksville? No thank you, Lieutenant."

"Major," Valentine said.

"That's why we're in the state we're in. Kids with momma's milk still on their lips throwing rank around."

It had been a while since anyone called Valentine "kid"—Brother Mark's "my son's" hardly counted; churchmen of his rank called everyone obviously beneath their age son or daughter.

"Just give us what you can. Even if it's just those yearling pigs and the beans."

"Harebrained operation you're on, Lieutenant—Major," Reisling said. "You want to fool the Kurians, you gotta go on tippy-toe. You boys are stomping into the KZ in clown shoes. They're going to slap down on you, hard."

"Just get us what you can. We'll be back tonight with a truck."

The supplies showed up, including a surprising quantity of eggs. The underground men who helped them load it said practically every family in Clarksville had given up little reserves of food they kept in case of shortages. Word had gone out that eggs were needed, and they came in straw-packed, ribboned baskets. Many of the eggs had been decorated using vinegar dyes, red and blue mostly, with gold stars stuck on.

*God bless you*, read the tiny, cursive ink letters on one.

But Reisling just stood with arms crossed in an old overcoat, watching them load.

"You'll get your food. The people here are going to pay for every bit. Mark my words."

Valentine could taste his grudge in every mouthful.

146

†

At the first camp in Kentucky, Seng had a ceremony inviting members of all the companies in his command to see him hand out commendations and medals. Most were going to the Bear and Wolf teams who destroyed the Kurian tower.

Valentine and Patel decided to send Glass and his Grogs under the supervision of Patel and Rand. Valentine wanted the rest of the brigade to get used to the sight of the Grogs, lest some nervous picket open up on them as they brought a cartload of pork back. He called Glass into the company headquarters tent.

"Send someone else, sir," Glass said. "That crap doesn't impress me."

"Glass," Patel said.

"Oh, he's free to talk," Valentine said. "You've got something against medals, Glass?"

"The right guys never get 'em, that's my problem."

Valentine felt he should reprimand Glass, but he wasn't speaking contemptuously of any particular person, just the practice in general. Valentine could hardly upbraid him for having an opinion and expressing it when asked. "Don't tell me you think that way about Colonel Seng too. He's got too many medals to wear, and probably deserves twice that."

"Only medal that means much to me is the combat badge. If you've faced fire, you've proved all you ever have to prove in my book. The valor medals look pretty, but valor's just another word for something getting screwed up. A well-run fight's where you throw so much shit on target what's left of the enemy crawls out begging you to stop."

†

As they camped in the quiet, greening hills of Kentucky the first day of April, Rand brought him the front page of the *Nashville Community Spirit* ("Giving a little good for the betterment of all" read the motto just under the rather imposing-looking font of the newspaper's logo).

Rand pointed to an article at the bottom of page one.

# MISSISSIPPI SECURE AGAIN

Guerrilla WRECKERS STRIKE OUT! A full-scale raid on rail and river routes north of Memphis ENDED WITH A WHIMPER Monday. The last elements of the bandit incursion gave up or swam for their lives as LOCAL VOLUNTEER HEROES restored ORDER AND SAFETY to north GREATER MEMPHIS.

Security spokesmen affirmed that there had been unusually DESPERATE WINTER SHORTAGES IN TRANS-MISSISSIPPI. The attack failed utterly as a heavy barrage pinned them against the river. The barrage, which ALARMED PEACE-LOVING MEMPHIS FAMILIES, lasted only long enough to organize the COUNTER-ATTACK which SWEPT TO VICTORY against the banks of the Mississippi.

This paper is one of many voices happy to see GREATER COOPERATION BETWEEN MEMPHIS AND NASHVILLE SECURITY ZONES and looks forward to further SUPPRESSION OF TERRORISM.

The paper had helpfully printed a few blurry pictures on the second page of bodies lying along the edge of a dirt road and a group of men sitting cross-legged, with arms tied behind their backs.

"Skinny Pete showed up again. That boy makes a good living," Edi-yak said, glancing at the pictures but not bothering to read the rest.

"Skinny Pete?" Valentine asked.

"That's what we used to call him. He's a little wisp of a thing from Alabama; looks like he's never had more than two mouthfuls of soup at one time in his whole life. He's always sitting there with his collar pulled up around his ears in the prisoner mock-ups, since he looks hungry as sin."

"Doesn't anyone else notice him?"

Ediyak shrugged. "I had to have it pointed out to me. It's not like you'd recognize him unless you're close. Sometimes he's grown in a scruff of beard, sometimes they shave him bald, sometimes he's in a wool watch cap. Anyway, that's his job. Go sit beneath a sign that says 'Clarksville, thirty klicks' and look like you got taken prisoner that morning."

Valentine had to chuckle. "They got the big story right. Just left out a few details."

"KZ papers don't print unpleasant facts. They disappear, like dust swept into a cement crack," Ediyak said.

"Civilizations are won and lost in such cracks," Rand observed.

†

Kentucky's hills exploded into spring colors, fireworks displays of wildflower and dogwood blossoms. Valentine took parties out to show them trees bearing wild legworms. The crawlers would stay in the branches, devouring bark, twig, and leaf alike, until they became so heavy they either snapped the branches or bent them until they were lowered gently to earth. Then they commenced grazing in their long, crooked furrows.

Valentine changed back into his legworm leathers, adding Velcro strips for Southern Command insignia. He had been dreading the Kurian reaction to their march with every step into Kentucky, waiting to see what shape the reaction would take. But the march covered miles with not much more difficulty than they'd experienced on the practice marches in northern Arkansas and the Missouri bootheel.

Every time he topped a rise, every time they took a bend, every time they broke out of forest or heavy brush and into pasture, Valentine expected to see them, campfires and tents and columns of motor vehicles. But the landscape remained as empty as it had when he followed Hoffman Price across Tennessee and into Kentucky.

Bee seemed happy to be back. When they cut legworm trails, little rises of plant growth and dirt that looked like planted furrows cut by a drunk plowing farmer, Bee urged him to follow. Some sense of hers allowed her to tell which way the legworm had gone, though unless the marks were very fresh Valentine couldn't make head from tail.

The legworm ranchers were a clannish bunch. Some sat you down and offered pie; others would chase you off with bird shot.

And that was just for a few wanderers crossing their grazing lands. Valentine wondered how they'd react to the appearance of better than two thousand Southern Command soldiers.

†

South of Bowling Green Valentine and a team of his men idled on a running pickup at dawn, keeping warm by sitting either in the cab or atop the engine-warmed hood. They'd been tasked with meeting a pair of Cats who were supposed to guide them into the legworm bluegrass.

The pickup sat beneath a power pylon. Birds, with their usual good judgment, had transformed it into a high-rise condominium.

The men passed around thermoses of sage tea and talked about legworms. Valentine told his story of a battle between two legworm clans he'd witnessed, with the gunmen on each side using their beasts as a cross between World War I entrenchments and eighteenth-century fighting sail.

Valentine left to take a leak. As he zipped up and turned from the back of the pickup, he tripped. As he fell, he noticed a binding-twine lasso attaching his ankle to the mufflerless exhaust system on the truck.

He fell face-first into spiky dandelion.

Two men jumped off the front of the truck, coming to his aid.

"You okay, Major?"

A shadow unfolded from beneath the truck. "He deserves it for splattering me with pee," Alessa Duvalier said. "I taped two grenades under your truck and pegged the pins to come out when you drove away. You clowns are lucky I recognized him."

"It got a distinctive left hook or what, sir?" one of the men laughed.

"I meant his leathers," Duvalier said.

Valentine cut himself free from the twine. "They pulled you into this operation? Gentlemen, this is Smoke, one of Southern Command's best Cats. I've covered more miles with her than any living thing."

"Thanks to you, I'm rated as one of Southern Command's expert Cats on the bluegrass," Duvalier said. "I've been working Kentucky since the fall, escorting that churchman around."

"He's cheery company."

"Never more so than when he's trying to stick a spitty finger inside you. Horny old goat." She put two fingers in her mouth and whistled, up-down-up.

Another woman, hair knife-cut high and tight into a cross between a mohawk and a mullet, rose from the ditch running along the road. She had legworm leather trousers and a poncho concealing what looked to be a military carbine. A camouflage bandanna added a festive touch to her neck.

"This is Vette, Val. She was blooded in Missouri. It's quieter there now, so Southern Command retasked her here because she was born in Bowling Green. Vette, this is Ghost. I went to Colorado and across Nebraska and Kansas with him."

Vette extended hands in fingerless gloves and gave a strong handshake. "Pleased to see you're still alive."

"If you watch him close when he walks, you'll see that he's had some near misses," Duvalier said.

"Hope you learn as much from her as I did," Valentine said.

"She's smarter than you when it comes to picking a fight," Duvalier said, running a knuckle down the scar on his cheek.

"So, what have you got for us?" Valentine asked.

"You guys have moved fast and hard. We're going to take you to sort of a feudal lord. He's got several tribes united under him."

"Including the old crew you ran with, the Bulletproof," Vette said. "I recognize the cut of your leathers."

"No other hints, Smoke?"

"You'll be relieved to know you're about to be reinforced," Duvalier said. "A third of Kentucky is mounting worm to fight."

One of the soldiers snorted. "Worm ranchers fight?"

"On our side, is what he means," another added.

Duvalier glared at the doubters. The fire in her eyes reminded Valentine of how pretty she was, when her real self peeped through the scruffy exterior.

"Six clans have come together," Duvalier said, nodding to Valentine's detail and shaking any proffered hand. "That churchman may like playing stinkfinger with the female help, but he's one hell of a diplomat. Every time things heated up, he calmed them down and got them talking again. It's as much his triumph as it is Karas'."

"Who's Karas?" Valentine asked.

Vette also shook hands all around. "He's a Bowling Green boy too. He's just what the Cause needs. A visionary."

†

The men of the brigade waited. With some fresh bread and Kentucky honey in them, they were in good spirits and chattering like meadowlarks. They lounged on a gentle hillside forming a natural amphitheater, warm in April sunshine that promised summer on the way.

During Valentine's training and time in the Bear caves of Pacific Command, he sometimes spent a few hours at night in the rec room. They had a LCD TV rigged there, and he watched old movies on disk. One Bear favorite was an old movie called *Highlander*.

While Valentine found it interesting enough, especially the sweeping images of scenery, he'd forgotten the movie until he saw Karas emerge from his vast tent. He immediately thought, *that's the Highlander!*

Karas had the same strong face, long hair, and impressive build, though the hair was stringier and the build wasn't enhanced by camera angle. He wore a big-pocketed waxed canvas coat that hung to midthigh and rather striking pants that were legworm leather on the inside and what looked like corduroy on the outside. His soft brown boots, with just a hint of felt showing at the top, made Valentine rather jealous. They looked durable and comfortable.

Followed by deputations from the six clans supporting him and by Brother Mark, who looked pleased for the first time since Valentine had known him, Karas approached an old pasture tree that had been butchered just that morning for firewood. Earlier in the morning Valentine had watched two men working a long saw cutting it off, but had wondered at why they went up the tree and sawed off limbs instead of simply felling it in the first place.

Valentine recognized the honey-colored hair of Tikka among the tribal dignitaries. She'd apparently assumed some role of importance within the Bulletproof.

Karas mounted the stump with the aid of a ladder. Valentine wondered how he'd look to the men in the pasture or on the lower slopes of the hill—a statue atop a column?

The breeze died down as if by command.

A leathery worm rider stepped forward. "Let the Kentucky Alliance take heed," he called in a formidable bass baritone. "Our chief is about to speak."

"This is a sight I've dreamed of for a long time. You all don't know how happy you've made me, marching to these quiet hills. It's been a long time since the Stars and Stripes has been carried openly, pridefully, across these hills. Let me formally welcome you as friends. A mite more valuable: as allies."

Southern Command's troops cheered that.

"Some of you went to school. I only had one teacher my whole life. A simple man. A plumbing contractor, before 2022. That man was my father. He taught me to ride. He taught me to shoot. He taught me to tell the truth.

"One day I was looking at pictures of animals of the world. I liked big cats, lions and black panthers and tigers. He told me that one tiger needed to eat as many as three hundred deer in a year. Three hundred! Of course, the tiger must eat them one at a time. No tiger kills three hundred deer at once."

The spring breeze contested the voice again, but Karas could project, though the men upwind were cupping their ears to catch his words.

"Imagine, though, if those three hundred deer could talk as we do. If they could take the tiger's tally. If they could organize against this tiger. If three hundred deer together hunted the one tiger, threw themselves against it, biting and goring and kicking, I reckon that tiger would never hunt again.

"We have one great advantage over the Kurians. Human beings naturally come together, the way water droplets find their way to pools. The Kurians like to remain individual drops.

"Divided, all we can do is crawl to the Kurians and lick their boots, begging not to be killed. Their tigers are the master of any one of us. United, we will hunt the tigers.

"I'm going to ask you to follow me east into the mountains. There we'll start the biggest tiger hunt you've ever seen. Then with the forces that are meeting there, we'll come back and start taking over town after town, county after county here in Kentucky. Can I count on the men of Arkansas, of Texas, of Oklahoma, Kansas, and Missouri? We're pledged to you, Wildcats and Gunslingers, Coonskins, Bulletproofs and Mammoths, and of course my own Perseids."

Valentine cheered along with the rest of them. If he understood it right, Javelin was now the largest operation against the Kurians since Archangel.

Lambert and Brother Mark and the rest had told them they'd have support of some of the legworm ranchers in Kentucky. He thought they meant foodstuffs and fuel; he'd never dreamed they'd be fighting at their side.

Why had they kept so much secret from the officers involved? To avoid disappointment if Karas turned out to be a windbag, full of bluster and promises? Or did Lambert feel it necessary to keep this from Southern Command's own higher-ups?

Valentine laughed at himself as Bee thumped him on the chest, not really understanding the reason for the cheering but enjoying the mood. As the men and women roared their lungs out, thrilled that Kentucky wasn't just supporting their advance but coming to their side, he was considering the possibility of informants high up in Southern Command's officer list.

After the speech ended men and women of the Alliance handed out coins of brightly polished nickel, it looked like. They bore an imposing stamp of Karas in profile. The reverse had a five-pointed star with a 10 at the center and "TEN DOLLARS" written around the edge.

"The king's coin," the boy who handed Valentine his coin said. "Lot more where these came from."

"Long live the King of Kentucky, then," Ediyak said in reply. "What do you s'pose we can buy with it?"

Valentine examined the engraving. A faint halo had been etched around the profile. "A whole lot of trouble, if this man wants us calling him king."

# CHAPTER SEVEN

*A*cross Cumberland Plateau, April: It is a land of sandstone bluffs and old coal fields, swimming holes and iron bridges, old loblolly pine plantations run amok and new deciduous forests.

Almost every kind of tree found east of the Mississippi can be found here, mixing among each other and gradually reclaiming land from the pines, each occupying land according to water requirements, with chestnuts and shortleaf pines atop the ridges and poplar, black gum, and maples in the bottoms.

For much of the early United States history, the eastern escarpment served as a barrier to the gradual migration west. The tough bluffs running the southeastern border dividing Kentucky from Virginia served as a natural choke. Cherokee and Shawnee hunted the land until passages through the Cumberland Gap were mapped out and opened. Even so, the region remained somewhat wilder than the states north and south until the exploitation of coal and timber resources made the area profitable.

The picturesque sandstone gorges once drew photographers, and protect the homes of cliff swallows and bats, but to David Valentine that spring they were a frustrating maze dotted with dead towns so decrepit they reminded him of his first operations as a Wolf in the run-wild forests of Louisiana. Negotiating ridges and valleys meant weary hours of scouting and camping as the columns wound their way east through the twisting, turning cuts, where one mile of red-shouldered hawk flight meant perhaps three up and down and back and forth.

Luckily, it is a wild region empty of Kurian holds. Kentucky always has gone its own way, even in its uneasy relationship with the Kurian Order.

*Self-reliant to what some might call a fault, they saw off the first emissaries of the New Order in the chaos of 2022 with torch and buckshot, demanding to be left alone. Neither at war with the Kurians or cooperative with their Reapers, they bring coal to the surface and legworm grubs to market to trade for the goods they need. Every time a Kurian tries to establish a tower in the Cumberland, he finds his Reapers hunted, his Quisling retainers ambushed and hanged, and the alleged rich prospect of Kentucky dissolving into a confusion of legworm tracks and ash.*

*The tribes have formed a feudal society, quarrelsome when at peace, uneasily united when threatened from outside. Every feudal society needs a king to smooth the former and lead them in the latter.*

✝

Karas' coins turned out to be only so much shiny dross when it came to bartering with other legworm tribes. Valentine's company went back to trading the crank-powered radios, rifles, and learn-to-read Bibles for butter and eggs.

But the legworm riders did offer spare worms, rigged for hauling cargo. Valentine's company received two, one to carry burdens while the other grazed in its wake, with roles switched the next day. Every third day the column rested now, to give the worms time to feed and recover. For all their size, they could be delicate if mishandled or underfed.

As they passed the more settled central part of Kentucky, the land became a patchwork of small towns and huge, clannish ranches. The towns were controlled by "badges" but rarely saw a Reaper, though Valentine heard fireside tales of bounty hunters and human traffickers who collected criminals and troublemakers.

Contacts with the underground dried up once they reached the ranch lands. Though the soldiers broke into a few locked NUC storage rooms in the dead of night, Valentine scanning for Reapers and his sharpshooters standing by with their blue-striped magazines in the rifles, they rarely returned to Javelin with full carts.

Where no small, easy game were to be had, Valentine felt it necessary to organize a hunt for larger prey.

†

"This is what's called hitting them where they ain't," Patel said to second platoon.

They were dispersed on a steep hillside overlooking a railroad cut. Valentine stood between Patel and Glass, who had the Grogs' .50 set up within a blind of machete-sculpted brush. Wolf scouts had relayed a report of a lightly guarded cargo train heading north on the Lexington track, and Valentine's company was dispatched to hit it if it looked like it contained anything useful.

Below them, an engine and ten boxcars stood on a single track in front of a blocked bridge. The engine puffed like an impatient fat man.

Valentine stood above Patel, watching one of his Kentucky recruits talking to the engineer from the cover of a stand of thick redbud. A few other members of first platoon stood, looking at the blocked bridge. Another pair of soldiers, Rutherford and DuSable, who Valentine considered his two coolest heads, stood at the back of the caboose, swapping some captured New Universal Church activity books and Lexington newspapers for cigarettes and what looked like a sheaf of mimeographed crossword puzzles with the guards in the armored caboose.

Whether the engineer wondered why some technical crew just happened to be blocking a bridge where trains were running yesterday, Valentine couldn't say. Crow, the soldier in question, was a good talker and had worked rail crew as a boy and into his early manhood.

The binoculars in Valentine's hands stayed steady on the armored caboose. Patel watched the gunner in the little bubble just behind the engine. They were woefully attentive to duty, experienced enough on the lines to know that any unexpected pause called for extra vigilance.

"Faces. In the boxcars," Patel said. "It's not cargo; it's fodder."

"Another load heading up for Cincinnati," Harmony, a Tennessean, said. "Blood money."

Valentine swiveled his glasses over a few degrees. His vision blurred for a moment as redbud intervened, and then he saw it. A pair of haunted eyes looking out through the bars, knuckles white as the prisoner hefted himself up to the airholes at the top of the car.

He did some quick math. Maybe four hundred human souls behind that puffing engine, bound for destruction.

"No point hitting it now," Glass said. "Nothing we can use."

Valentine ignored him.

"What caused you to get culled, cuz?" Harmony said as if talking to the prisoner. "Heart murmur show up on a health check? Forget to make a payoff? Screwup under the boss's eye on a bad Friday?"

A clean-cut young officer left the caboose. Another railroad guard trailed behind him wearing the harassed look of adjutants everywhere in any army. After a conference with the engineer, they approached Crow, who gestured for them to come and look at the bridge.

They walked out to the edge of the gorge, and Crow pointed to the pilings at the base of the bridge. A couple of the idling workers fiddled with the pile of shovels and picks at the edge of the road; another went back to a captured pickup with a freshly painted logo the platoon had been using, avoiding the officer.

A perfectly natural move.

Captain LeHavre always told him not to let the perfect be the enemy of the good. This would be as good an opportunity as they would get with this train.

Valentine looked again at the young officer, wondered why someone hardened by experience wasn't on this trip. Maybe he was fresh out of some New Universal Church leadership academy, telling himself that this winnowing, distasteful in the particular, helped the species in general.

*Tough luck, kid.*

"Give the strike signal," Valentine said. "Glass, have the Grogs hit the engine first, then the caboose."

Patel rose and made a noise like a startled wild turkey.

Rutherford and DuSable shoved the newspapers in their vests, reaching for the small, cylindrical grenades that hung within.

Glass made a face, but patted Ford on the shoulder and pointed at the engine. He and Chevy swung their .50 and aimed.

"Open fire," Valentine said.

The .50 chattered out its lethal *chukka-chukka-chukka* rattle. The glass of the cupola turned to spiderwebbing and blood.

Crow froze up. One good shove and he could have sent the young officer headfirst into the gorge. Valentine silently implored him to move, but he ducked down at the gunfire.

Another of Valentine's men in gray denim, a thick-armed ex-motorcycle cavalry named Salazar, raised a shovel and bashed the adjutant with it as Crow still gaped. The soldier didn't have time to make sure of the adjutant, for the lieutenant had his pistol out. The flat of the shovel caught the lieutenant under the chin, tumbling him into the gorge.

Two hammering bangs, less than a second apart, sounded from the armored caboose. Plumes of dust spouted up from the ventilators on the roof of the caboose. Rutherford and DuSable crawled like fast-moving snakes toward the front of the train, sheltering next to the wheels of the boxcars, where the men in the caboose couldn't bring their mounted weapons to bear.

The Grogs shifted their .50 to the armored caboose, emptying the rest of the box of ammunition, punching holes around the firing slits.

"Third platoon, covering positions," Valentine told signals, who spoke into his walkie-talkie, shielding the receiver with his palm. "Second platoon: Forward!" Valentine shouted over the firing.

They'd done it, and done it well, dozens of times in training. Now it was for keeps.

"Check fire," Patel roared, as a soldier paused to blast the caboose. "Check before you shoot. There are friendlies down there."

They did it well, moving all at once at a rush. Third platoon, higher on the hillside, moved forward to the prepared positions.

Valentine, half sliding down the steep hillside nearest the cut, landed and glanced at the front of the train. One of his men was already inside the engine compartment, waving off additional fire. At the bridge, there was nothing to see but Crow, kneeling beside the soldier who'd clobbered the lieutenant with the shovel, a bloody pistol in his hand.

Bee loped after him, one of her sawed-off shotguns in one hand and an assault rifle in the other, moving forward like a fencer with the assault rifle pointed at the caboose, the shotgun held up and back.

"Get Cabbage over to Crow," Valentine ordered as he approached the caboose. "He's not calling man down but I think Salazar is hurt."

Cabbage was the company medic, when he wasn't assisting the cook. Formerly a demi-doc in the KZ, he'd gotten sick of signing un-fitness certifications.

"Cover the cars until we know for sure what's inside," Valentine told Patel.

People were shouting for help from inside the boxcars. Valentine looked beneath the cars, searching for explosives. He'd heard of the Kurians sending decoy trains lined with plastic explosive and claymore mines to take out guerrillas when someone hit the kill switch. This didn't look to be that kind of train, but it was best to make sure.

No sign of strange wiring leading from the caboose.

Valentine looked through one of the bullet holes into the armored caboose, saw a twitching foot. Rutherford slunk up beside him.

"I'm going in," Valentine said.

"Let me go first, sir," Rutherford said.

Valentine noticed blood running down from his forehead, already caking into cherry flakes.

"Rutherford, you wounded?"

"It ain't mine, Major. I got some on me when DuSable and I were checking for booby traps. It was dripping out of the caboose. The cars look clear. DuSable's checking the rest forward."

He was a cool head.

Second platoon had taken up firing positions, covering the caboose and the rest of the cars up to the engine.

There was some trouble with the caboose's metal door; it was ei-ther jammed good or latched from the inside. Valentine pointed to the hinge rivets and the second platoon entry man employed a monstrous four-gauge shotgun on the door. Then Bee smashed it open with her shoulder.

Rutherford slipped in, pistol held in a Weaver stance.

Nothing but blood and body parts awaited them.

Valentine checked the radio log. The set itself was as dead as the gunners inside the caboose, but there was a notation that an unscheduled stop had happened, with approximate location, and that the message had been acknowledged by LEX.

Lexington, Valentine guessed.

†

They opened up the boxcars, giving in to the pleading and pounding from within.

"Liberators," an old man in a black coat shouted. "They're liberators."

"That's better than 'shit detail,' " Ediyak commented.

They thronged around the soldiers, some in blue and yellow and pink clothing that looked like hospital scrubs woven out of paper fiber. In some Kurian Zones, they even begrudged you the clothes on your back when selected for harvesting.

"Please, stay close to the train. Don't wander off," Valentine repeated, walking up the line to check on Salazar.

Salazar had two bullets in him, or rather through him. The Quisling adjutant had opened up on him at point-blank, and Salazar still managed to half decapitate the Quisling before Crow finally fired his pistol.

Crow looked miserable, rubbing at Salazar's blood on his hands like Lady Macbeth.

"I think he'll live, sir," Cabbage reported. "Four neat little holes, two coming in and two going out. His left lung is deflated and he may have lost a big chunk of kidney, but that's just a guess without X-rays."

"Nearest machine is probably in Nashville," someone said.

They held an improptu officers conference while second platoon distributed food from the stores in the forward-most boxcar to the "fodder."

Valentine had to snap Crow out of his misery.

"Crow, forget it. I need you in the here and now, okay?"

"Yes, sir," Crow said.

"Salazar's either going to make it or not. You poured iodoform into the wound and applied pressure. The rest is up to him and the medics. Worrying about fifteen minutes ago won't cause him to draw one breath more. Answer a few questions for me, and then you can go back to him."

Crow took a breath. "Yes, sir."

"They got off a message to Lexington. What happens if guerrillas hit a train?"

"It depends on if the train is just reported overdue or if they called in that they were being attacked," Crow said, his pupils gradually settling on the group of men around him.

"Let's assume the worst," Valentine said.

"They'll send out an armored train and motorbike and horse cavalry, backed up by at least a few companies of infantry and some light artillery in gunwagons. There's never been more than a few dozen guerrillas here. Too many Kurian-friendly legworm clans."

"How do they track the guerrillas?"

"Reapers, usually. I've seen them get off trains myself."

"Reapers mean there has to be a Kurian controlling them," Valentine said. Or the strange organization known as the Twisted Cross, but ever since the Nebraska Golden Ones smashed their facility south of Omaha, there were only a few odd units of them scattered around.

"I was told there's a Kurian in charge of rail security who goes around in an armored train," Crow said. "I never saw him though, just his Reapers."

"Brave of him to venture out," Patel put in.

"Yes," Valentine said absently. He was wondering how Gamecock's Bears would like a chance at a Kurian on the loose.

"What about the fodder?" Patel asked. "We can't take these people over ridges."

"No, we'll have to use the train," Valentine said. "We've crossed over enough old tracks this week. Is there a line we could use?"

Crow scratched his chin. "Lessee, sir. There's an old spur that heads off east at first, hooks around more south. Skirts the south end of the Boonwoods. It fed some mines that went dry. That'll get us back toward brigade maybe even a little ahead of them."

By "Boonwoods" Crow meant the Daniel Boone National Forest, according to the legworm ranchers' description of Kentucky's regions.

"Yes," Valentine said, reading the doubt on Crow's face. "What's the problem?"

"Major, it's really overgrown," Crow said. "The engine has a brush cutter on it, but we'll have to go slow, move fallen logs and whatnot ourselves. They'll catch up to us easy, especially since it's obvious where the trail is leading."

"We'll blow track at the cutoff," Valentine said.

"That'll only slow them up for an hour or so," Crow said. "Their rail gangs can do anything but build a bridge in just a few minutes."

"I don't suppose there are any bridges."

"Lots, but they'll dismount and follow. If we even get that far. Somebody might have torn up track for scrap steel or used ties to build a cabin. You never know."

"We'll risk it," Valentine said. "At the very least these people will be no worse off than they were before."

†

Valentine joined Preville up at the ridgeline at company HQ, where he talked to Seng over a scrambler. Seng didn't sound happy about it. Valentine had been assigned to conduct logistical raids, not start small-scale guerrilla warfare on the Cumberland a week before they were due in Virginia, but Seng was too good an officer not to see a chance to bag a bunch of railroad security troops more adept at flushing guerrillas out of the tall timber than facing combined arms attacks.

"I've only got a few Wolves left at HQ. Most of them are elsewhere," Seng said, his voice crackly thanks to the scrambler.

"I'll try to keep the Reapers homing in on lifesign," Valentine said.

Then he broadcast in the clear to "Allegheny HQ" that they'd intercepted the train carrying "Doctor Faustus" and he was safely on the way back. Some lonely slob, probably working the transmitter out of some shack near Mount Eagle and creating nonsensical chatter between Seng's HQ and the mythical operations' headquarters, acknowledged.

That would give the Kurian intelligence services something to chew on for a while as they examined the manifests of those shipped north as aura fodder. Hopefully some selection officer would be chopped for a screwup that existed only in Valentine's imagination.

It also might give the impression of a quick, fast-moving raid. If half the pursuit forces headed into the Kentucky hills following their foot trail, that many less would be left to pursue the train.

The toughest part of getting going again was convincing the transportees to climb back into the boxcars. Valentine didn't blame them; the Kurians hadn't bothered to provide much in the way of food or sanitary services. They refilled the cars' big yellow freshwater jugs from a handy stream, and his troops shared out what rations they had handy.

Valentine sent Rand with the carts that would have carried off whatever goodies they could have raided from the train, plus the small amount of supplies they'd bartered or scavenged on this trip, back east toward headquarters. He put Crow up front and the wounded Salazar with company headquarters in the caboose, now freed of bodies but not the sticky, coppery smell of blood despite a quick swilling-out. Cabbage already had an IV going, with Salazar as comfortable as doping could make him.

Even better, the intercom with the engine still worked.

The train bumped into motion. Bee didn't like being in the train, for whatever reason. She clapped her hand over her head and made nervous noises.

Valentine had nightmares of meeting a high-speed relief train coming south head-on and had to make plans for the abandonment of their charges. But they made Crow's turnoff, and the rocking and clattering increased as they moved down the old spur line.

The terrain around here was too hilly for good legworm ranching, but herds of sheep and goats grazed on the slopes. They passed signage for old coal mines, saw the rusting, vine-covered remains of old conveyors and towers frowning down on slag piles tufted with weeds and bracken fighting for a precarious existence on soil that had accumulated in nooks and crannies. In some places more recent strip mining scarred the hills, leaving the Kentucky ridges looking like an abandoned, opened-up cadaver on an autopsy table.

They set up watches, allowing most of his men to rest. There was little enough left to eat.

Valentine didn't think much of their guide, a rather slow man in his thirties who thought that by "guide," his duties required telling old family stories about who got married in which valley, the hunting abilities of his preacher's astonishing coon dogs, and the time Len Partridge got his index finger blown off by Old Murphy for sneak-visiting Mrs. Murphy while he was off gathering legworm egg skin. Valentine did manage to glean that the Kurians still sent trains into this region in the fall to trade for legworm meat, though it was sandwiched into a story about a wounded hawk his cousin Brady nursed back to health and trained for duck hunting.

Luckily there were only brief delays due to downed trees on the tracks. The men moved—or in one case dynamited—the trees with high-spirited enthusiasm. The audacity of a theft of an entire train had been the highlight of the march across Kentucky.

But the sinking sun set him nervously pacing the caboose until he realized he was making the rest of the occupants nervous, and he distracted himself by discussing Salazar's condition with Cabbage.

They came to a small river and stopped to check the bridge's soundness, with Valentine thanking his lucky star that he had such a diverse group of ex-Quislings in his company. He consulted his map and saw that the river arced up into the hills where Seng was headquartered. Sheep and goats and several legworms grazed in the valley.

"The bridge'll hold, sir," came the report over the intercom. "We can take a span out with dynamite and slow up the pursuit."

Not the Reapers. They'd come hot and hard with men on horses, or motorbikes, or bicycles, homing in on the crowded lifesign in the railcars—

Valentine tapped the intercom thoughtfully. "I want a conference with all officers," Valentine said. "Give the refugees fifteen minutes out of the cars."

✝

They traded the captured rifles and shotguns and boxes of ammunition with the shepherd families for a generous supply of sheep and goats. The shepherds and goatherds thought him a madman: He was willing to take kids, tough old billies, sick sheep, lamed lambs. Valentine was interested more in quantity than future breeding potential. He warned them that there'd be some angry Reapers coming up the tracks shortly, and they'd better clear out and play dumb.

Then he had his men load the animals onto the boxcars.

The toughest part was convincing Patel to leave the train with a squad of men to guide the hundreds of refugees into the hills.

"Do I have to make it an order, Sergeant Major?" Valentine asked. Valentine hated to fall back on rank.

"It'll come to a fight when they catch up to you, sir. The men will need me."

"I know the job now. I was lucky as a junior lieutenant. My captain put me with his best sergeant on my first operation in the Kurian Zone."

Patel relented and walked around to the remaining NCOs, giving tips and hurrying the loading of the livestock.

"Give 'em hell, billy goat legion," Patel said as he walked off with the crowds from the boxcars and into a hillside defile on the far side of the river. Patel wanted to put at least a ridge between the tracks and the lifesign he was giving off before nightfall.

David Valentine watched them go, silently wishing them luck.

The animals he'd purchased but couldn't fit into the train, he left behind to muddle the tracks. They'd fuzz up the Reapers' sensing abilities for a few moments, anyway. The smell of goats reminded him of his induction into the Wolves. Valentine wondered what he'd say if he could have a talk with that kid he'd been.

He thought of a young couple he'd noticed, clinging to each other in doubt as they looked back at the boxcars as Patel led them into the defile. How did they get selected for harvesting? Sterile? Passing out anti-Kurian pamphlets printed in some basement? The woman had mouthed "thank you" at him. That goat-sniffing kid would have written Father Max a long letter about those two words.

"It's worth it," Valentine muttered.

Valentine still had a few refugees: the old unable to make a long walk, the sick, and a few devoted souls who stayed behind to tend to them. He gave them a boxcar of their own just in front of the caboose.

Then they pulled across the bridge and dynamited the center span in a frosty twilight.

Valentine didn't hear any cheers as ties spun like blown dandelion tufts into the river. He had too many engineers in the attenuated company who'd sweated over the calculations and effort required to build a bridge.

The train squealed into motion again. Now the clatter of the wheels passing over points was accompanied by the bleating of goats and bawling of sheep.

Now the question was whether they'd make enough of a lifesign signal to draw the Reapers. He had what was left of his company, plus the refugees, plus whatever signal the sheep and goats would send.

He sent another message to Seng, reporting the destruction of the bridge.

"Scouts confirm you are being pursued. Two trains out of Lexington. The rear is heavily armored with engines at either end. Coming your way. Over," headquarters reported.

"A Big Boy might be managing the pursuit. Over."

"GC will attend to it," Seng's headquarters replied. "Instructions on the way. Over and out."

Valentine slowed their progress to a crawl, both to check for track obstructions and so they could easily see a messenger. He smelled roasting goat in the refugee car—with tarragon and cumin, it seemed. The resourcefulness of soldiers in feeding themselves still found ways to amaze him.

A mile later the intercom crackled. "Stopping. Rock slide."

Valentine swung off the caboose and took a look. His Cat-sharp eyes made it plain. That ended it. Piles of sulfur-colored limestone had ended the chase. This was no tree that could be sawn and rolled, or blown. The rock slide would take his entire company working with beams, chains, and the train engine to clear.

At least half a day, working in daylight.

The door in the next car opened. Valentine caught a whiff of the improvised charcoal brazier they had set up under an air vent. Glass and the Grogs were eating chunks of goat meat toasted on skewers made from bedsprings. Other members of the company dismounted from the train to take a look at the rock slide. Everyone shook their heads.

It was a tight little corner of Kentucky, Valentine decided, looking at the steep hillsides to either side, the *braaak* of complaining sheep and goats from the railcars magnified by the cut.

They'd come at least ten miles. Horsemen or cyclists would be strung out, keeping up with the Reapers. Would whoever was puppeting the Reapers risk them? Valentine wondered if there was a finders-keepers policy for the rail security Kurian.

The hills around this cut would allow his troops to set up murderous cross fire. There'd be no danger of the men hitting each other; they'd be shooting down.

There was a slight upward slope to the rail line. Valentine thought of the wild cart ride he'd taken down Little Timber hill.

"Set up company headquarters back in that rock pile," he told Ediyak and Preville. "Try to make contact with the brigade."

"Yes, sir."

Valentine felt something tickling at the back of his scalp. He decided it was his imagination, fretting at the dark and the delay, with Seng still miles away. He put some men to work making stretchers from the rickety beds in the boxcars.

He posted Glass and the two Grogs in the rocks above at the source of the fall, having him take some illumination flares. The .50 would have a nice look down the cut from that point, and they could make a quick retreat over the ridgeline.

He put Rutherford and DuSable on the other hill, just above the caboose, with a machine gun taken from one of the train's mounts. He made sure they had pistols with Quickwood magazines loaded and ready.

Valentine posted himself with the majority of the platoon around the caboose. The cupola gun in the engine could cover a quick fallback and serve as a rally point in the rock pile.

Valentine posted Crow at the coupling between the engine and the boxcars.

He walked from position to position, checking the men, checking that nagging itch at the back of his neck that was turning into a doubt, stiffening the hairs there. He told Bee to stay in the caboose. She'd be an unpleasant surprise to any Reaper who clawed his way in.

There were Reapers somewhere off to the west. Or maybe it was the Kurian, reaching out with his senses, searching for his quarry.

Valentine heard a sudden burst of voices from company headquarters. He saw a flash of messy, knife-cut hair in the dim light from the LED bulbs lighting up the radio log.

Duvalier?

He clambered up the rocks, saw Duvalier putting away her sword into the walking-staff holder. He smelled sweat, rubber, and lubricating oil on her.

Ediyak's mouth was opening and shutting like a landed fish, and Preville trembled like his heart had been jump-started.

"Sorry, guys, had to make sure. Where's your major?"

"Right here," Valentine said, stepping across a rock.

She sat down on a rock and rubbed her thighs. "Three hours on a bicycle bumping along a railroad. The things my poor body does for you."

"That's it. I'm shooting for senior rank," Preville said to Ediyak, sotto voce.

Valentine offered his canteen and Duvalier cleared her mouth out, then drank.

"I wish we could have saved you a few miles. These rocks prevented it," Valentine said.

Duvalier unwrapped a piece of dried legworm jerky and took a bite. "Seng's got half the brigade on the way. The Bears and what Wolves he has left are on their way to the bridge you dynamited, along with some of the legworm troops. Karas gave another whoop-'em-up speech and sent them off hollering. There's a big file of legworms following this track too. They're tearing a bunch of new holes in their mounts, prodding them at speed."

"Any orders for me?"

"Just to let them know if you found some good ground for an ambush."

Valentine let himself soar a little. Seng saw an opportunity to sting the Kurians good and was grasping for the rose and not minding the nettles. Even if it drew lots of troops into this part of Kentucky, he'd be across another line of mountains by the time they could organize themselves.

"Can you help me here?" Valentine asked.

"Sure. Want me to brew up some of this Kentucky hickory nut coffee? Not like those cafés in the French Quarter, but it's hot."

Valentine smiled. "Not that easy. The Reapers could be here any time. I'd really like another trained Hunter up with my men. You could jam yourself between a couple of boxcars, wait for a chance to make a move."

"Me? I'm no heroic kinda fighter, Val. When bullets start to fly, I prefer to head the other direction."

Valentine touched her on the shoulder. "I know. Just this once. Please, Ali."

She looked off down the tracks and into the Kentucky night. "No, Val. I don't like the odds. Multiple Reapers, at night?"

Duvalier at least had the sense to refuse quietly. At most, Preville and Ediyak heard her.

Valentine wondered if she'd obey a direct order. Technically, Cats bore the rank of captain, but he suspected she'd tell him to get stuffed and bring her up on charges. "All right, how about a job more in line with your tastes?"

"I hope it doesn't involve climbing back on that bike."

"No, I want you to scout out a good, covered route away from the rails and up this ridge. Take Ediyak with you and show her it. If a Reaper starts sniffing around in our rear, take care of him, or warn me."

"That's more my style," she said, fixing a button on her coat. "Want some of this bug jerky? It's not half bad. I think these guys use molasses."

Valentine stomped down his vexation with Duvalier. "Ediyak, go with Smoke here. Don't worry, she's just marking out a line of retreat. She'll keep an eye on you out in the dark."

"Two eyes," she agreed, smiling at his clerk. Ediyak was rather good-looking at that. But then the kind of Quislings who ended up in the Order's services had better access to nutrition and grew up well-formed.

A soldier trotted up.

"Sir, Red Dog is acting really weird. He's hiding under the sheep and whimpering. Harmony says they used to have a hound that acted just the same way when there were Savio—mean to say, Hoods around. He told me to get you."

Valentine still felt disquieted.

He turned to Duvalier. "You'd better make your exit now, or you won't have an option anymore."

She gestured to Ediyak. "Direction is the better part of valor," she said. Ediyak picked up her rifle and checked it.

Valentine was beginning to suspect Duvalier liked to misquote Shakespeare just to bug him. He reached into a cargo bag and extracted a flare pistol on a lanyard and a pouch of flares.

"Don't get yourself taken," she said to Valentine. "One is my limit for heroic rescues." She gave him a quick buss on the ear, standing on tiptoe to reach, kissing lightly enough that Valentine felt like Peter Pan brushed by Tink's wings.

Then the Kentucky night swallowed her.

They were right about the dog. Valentine tried to tempt him out from under the train engine, but the dog bobbed his head and whimpered, tail tucked tightly between his legs.

"I know just how you feel, ol' buddy," one of the company said.

Valentine nodded and reached, opened a Velcro flap on his canvas ammunition harness. He extracted one of the blue-taped magazines, loaded it, borrowed some camouflage gun tape, and married a regular 9mm magazine to the Quickwood bullets.

Valentine walked up to his foremost pickets. He knelt, sent them creeping back to the main line, relieved in more ways than one.

They were out there. Reapers. Valentine's heart began to hammer.

*Use it. Use the fear.*

It woke him up with a capital awake. Each insect in the Kentucky night hummed its own little tune with its wings.

Valentine saw brush move. A peaked back, like an oversized cobra hood, rose from the brush.

Valentine felt its gaze. Every fiber, every nerve ending, came alive. He felt as though he could count the blood capillaries in his fingertips and the follicles on his scalp. Individual drops of sweat could be felt on his back. He opened the front grip on the gun, put the machine pistol tight to his shoulder—

The attack came from the hillside. Valentine heard a flap—*laundry on a line.* The gun went up without Valentine willing it and the muzzle flash lit up a falling, grasping parachute of obsidian-fanged death.

The next one was up to him before he could even turn to face it.

WHAM and the gun was gone, spinning off into darkness. Valentine fell backward, rolled, came up holding his sword protectively in front, noted coldly that the Reaper he'd shot was clawing at its chest, foot-long barbed tongue extended and straining.

The unwounded Reaper advanced at a crouch, a thin sumo wrestler scuttling insectlike in its squat. The inhuman flexibility of its joints unsettled. Your brain locked up in frozen fascination, trying to identify a humanoid shape that moved like a fiddler crab.

Valentine backed up a step, opening his stance and setting the sword behind, ready to uncoil his whole body in a sweeping cut when it leaped.

It sprang, taking off like a rocket.

BLAM! BLAM!

Shotgun blasts struck it, sent it spinning away as unexpectedly as a jack-in-the-box yanked back into its box as Valentine's sword sweep cut the air where it would have been.

Bee rose from some brush clinging to the small gravel swell the tracks ran along, other shotgun now held forward while she broke open the one she'd just fired with her long, strong fingers.

Valentine heard crashing in the brush as the shot-struck Reaper ran away. Valentine's instinct was to pursue. If it was running away, it was damaged and disadvantaged. He forced himself back to his senses and his men, sheathed the unblooded sword.

"Good work, Bee," Valentine said.

"Beee!" Bee agreed.

Officers' whistles cut through the darkness somewhere down the tracks that led toward the pursuing Quislings. Valentine located the sound. It came from the middle of a trio of tall robed figures in the center of the columns. Valentine saw movement all around them in the dim light.

Someone—Glass probably—had the sense to fire an illumination flare. The firework burst high, lighting up the steep-sided cut as it wobbled down.

The railroad cut was full of troops walking their bicycles uphill in two open-order lines up either side of the tracks, carrying their rifles at the ready so that the muzzles were pointed toward their open flanks rather than at their comrades.

Valentine backed up a few steps, fired another flare with his own gun as he retreated toward his line, more to highlight himself to his men. He drew a shot and then another from scouts the Quislings had sent forward. Luckily these troops didn't have nightscopes.

"Check fire, check fire. It's the major," someone shouted.

Valentine made sure Bee was following—she was backing through the brush like a living fortification between him and the advancing troops—and came up to his men. They'd stripped the boxcars of bed frames, thin mattresses, and water barrels and improvised a breast-work, shielding it with cut brush.

"Fire on my order. Single shots only, and take your time," Valentine said. "Pass the word. Single shots only. We're guerrillas, remember. All we've got are deer rifles and bird guns. Sergeants on up, have your pistols out with Quickwood magazines in."

Valentine trotted to the other side of the tracks, passed the word to the troops opposite the cut. As he was about to climb into the caboose, Valentine heard something skip and bounce through the dirt toward the fortification.

"Grenade," he shouted, embracing gravel like it was his mother.

It blew on the far side of the breastwork. The men began to shoot back, placing careful single shots. The machine guns from the caboose opened up and drew fire in return.

Did the Reapers know they were chasing nothing but sheep and goats yet?

More whistles, and the Quislings came forward at a rush, bright flowers of shotgun blasts cutting through the brush as the assault began.

He fired another flare and saw them coming, heads bobbing as they advanced, the foremost less than twenty yards away, covering each other with bursts of fire that pinged off the caboose or thwacked into the bed-frame breastworks. If they could be turned now . . .

"Fire at will!" Valentine shouted.

Gunfire roared into the night. Grenades bloomed and died, each one exploding more softly as the ears became overwhelmed by the noise. Valentine saw figures falling or diving for cover.

A Reaper ran toward them straight up the rail line, a satchel held in each hand. The Kurian animating the Reapers must have been either desperate or determined to overwhelm them in an all-or-nothing gambit. Bee fired and missed, and then tore up its robes with her second barrel. Valentine didn't need to wonder what was in the satchels, or see the digital seconds ticking down. God, his pistol was out there somewhere—

A sergeant, Troust—though the men nicknamed him Surf, as he combed his thick blond hair into a wave on his forehead—appeared beside Valentine and rested his 9mm on a step of the caboose, firing steadily, aiming with each shot. Valentine duly noted his coolness as though already composing the report.

The Reaper stiffened, leaning oddly, and started a throw, but the blood drinker's fingers refused to release. The momentum of the satchel toppled it, and Valentine saw the astonishment in its eyes.

Valentine saw heads rise as the Quisling soldiers scrambled out of the way of what was coming.

"Down!"

Valentine covered his ears and felt the weight of Troust come down on the back of his head. The satchel charges went off in twin booms that must have echoed in Georgia, and Valentine felt the world momentarily give way.

Surf let him up, the weird underwatery feel of the explosions' concussion sapping his strength and wits. A Quisling in a torn green uniform was at the barricade, staggering as he tried to climb over, and suddenly Valentine's backup pistol was in his hand and he shot, realizing as the bullets hit that he was killing a man trying to surrender.

More bursts of fire came from the darkness down the track. The gunfire seemed wrong. Those titanic blasts should have been an operatic blast at the climax of the fight, not punctuation in the middle of a long, deadly symphony. His flare hung on a tree downslope, sputtering as its light died.

More whistles, low and muted to his outraged ears. Valentine saw wounded men being carried back.

Had to do something to break up the attack.

"Empty the caboose," he told Troust. "Fall back to the rock pile as soon as the cars start moving."

Valentine crept along the tracks, sheltering from the wild high bullets in the wheels, Bee trailing him like a gigantic dog. He opened each boxcar door about halfway. A goat jumped out. The other livestock looked stupidly at him, jumping and quivering at each shot.

He climbed into the engineer's cab, told the soldier there to start the train backward, and hurried to the back door.

He found Crow still posted, moving the barrel of his rifle at every sound.

"I want you to uncouple as soon as the cars have a little momentum."

"While the cars are moving?" Crow asked.

"Yes."

The cars bumped into motion, their squeals curiously innocent after the noise of combat. Valentine gauged the train's speed.

"Now, Crow. Release!" Valentine shouted down from the engine.

Crow waited until the tension came off the coupling, then pulled it. Pressure cables for the car brakes hissed as the valves closed.

Valentine extended a hand and helped pull him back into the engine as the man working the controls applied the brakes. The rest of the cars pulled away, picking up speed on the slope.

"You did well, there," Valentine told Crow as the latter wiped his greasy hands on a rag.

The sheep and goats didn't like the motion and began to leap from the train. First a few goats, and then the sheep, all in a rush. Some went head over heels as they came off in a mass, a waterfall of wool and tufted hair. The goats' instinct was to head for high ground, and the more nimble goats made the escape up the hillside first. The sheep stuck together in bawling clumps.

Crow slipped and Valentine lunged, catching his arm. Crow's toes skipped on the tracks, sending up pebbles and dust. The train wasn't moving that fast, but the engine's tonnage could maim or kill even at a crawl. Valentine hoisted him into the engine compartment as the gunner opened up on some unknown target. Tracers zipped off into the darkness, zipping like hornets with meteor tails toward an enemy.

"Back up toward the rock pile," Valentine told the engineer, who applied brakes and sent the engine in the other direction. The gun overhead chattered again and Valentine heard casings clink into the canvas bags that prevented the spent shells from rolling around underfoot in the control cabin. Then, to the men at either side, he yelled, "Fall back! Fall back up the tracks."

Bullets rattled off the engine in reply. But the men began to move, NCOs tapping their charges on the shoulder and gesturing.

Valentine watched the spectacle of confused sheep and goats caught in a cross fire. Even experienced soldiers would hesitate to just gun down animals—there wasn't a man among them who didn't sympathize with the poor dumb brutes with little control over their fate, for the obvious reason that soldiers occasionally felt like sheep in that way—and Valentine's company used the confusion to scuttle back behind the rocks blocking the railroad cut.

The rocks were comforting in their thickness and sharp edging. There was good cover for shooting all along the fall; a crenellated wall on a medieval castle wouldn't have been more heartening.

The engineer and Crow leaped for the rocks, jumped over, and took cover, Crow leaving his rifle behind in his panic, the idiot. Valentine picked it up.

He tapped the gunner's leg. "C'mon. Leave it."

The gunner ignored him, emptied the weapon's box, and stood dumbly for a moment, as though waiting for someone to reload the weapon. Then he turned and looked down at Valentine with confused eyes. There was blood running down his face from a wound on his scalp.

"Out, back to the rocks," Valentine shouted, slapping him hard on the ankle.

The gunner finally left the cupola, slithered like a snake out of the battle seat and stirrups, and jumped out.

Valentine reversed the gears on the train one more time, clamped the pedal of the deadman's switch shut with a heavy wrench left for that purpose, and sent the engine puffing back down the tracks after the freewheeling boxcars, more to open the field of fire from the rock pile than anything. He paused in the doorway, suddenly tender about jumping, and leaped so that he landed on his good leg. He scrambled back toward the rock slide as sheep bleated in alarm at the engine picking up speed through their midst.

Valentine wished he'd thought to set some explosives in case a hero tried to jump into the cab to stop the engine before it collided with the boxcars.

The Quisling rail soldiers came up the cut one more time, but Glass and Rutherford and DuSable poured fire down the cut as the rest of the company took positions in the rock pile. More sheep and goats fell than men, but the return fire was inaccurate in the dark. Mortar shells began to explode on the hillside. The fire corrected, and a shell dropped into the rocks. Valentine heard a scream and he saw Cabbage run forward toward the blast, the big medical pouch bouncing on his hip.

Valentine drew his sword. The Reapers would come now, with the whole company listening to the sound of a man screaming his life out. Or they'd kill the men high on the hillside and then come tumbling down the grade like jumping spiders.

But he didn't feel them. The only cold on the back of his scalp was from the chill of the Kentucky spring night.

"They're coming! Brigade's coming," he heard Ediyak shriek from somewhere above.

Valentine felt a lump in his throat. He heard horse hooves and a motor from somewhere up the cut. The mortars shifted fire, sending a few rounds exploding back along the ridge, and then went silent.

Valentine saw a wave of soldiers pour over the ridgeline to his right, taking up positions to fire down on the railway Quislings. Every yard the enemy had fought for now meant a yard they'd have to fall back under fire from support weapons on the hillside. Valentine saw hands go up or men stand with rifles held over their heads, hurrying toward the rock slide to surrender.

His company ran forward to group the prisoners and relieve them of their weapons. Valentine saw one officer carrying the machine pistol he'd lost; he recognized the colored tape holding the magazines together.

Harmony relieved the prisoner of his souvenir.

Valentine felt dazed, half awake, with the smell of gunfire and smoke and livestock and sweat in his nostrils. The weird elation that settled on a man when he starts to believe he'd survived, won, picked him up and floated him back toward the foremost troops to report.

Seng, frowning, sat in the passenger seat of his Humvee, issuing orders into a headset.

"You caused me at least two days' delay, Major," he said in response to Valentine's salute. "More likely three."

"Yes, sir," Valentine said, wondering if he was in for a dressing down.

"I'll take it," Seng said. "Gamecock's Bears and the legworm outriders are hitting the support train now, and the Wolves are raising hell with some artillery tubes at the crossing they set up where you destroyed that bridge. A captured prisoner says their Kurian Lord's in a panic, disappeared into some secret area of his command car."

One of Valentine's company trotted up and presented him with his recovered gun. It now bore a nice set of scratches on the barrel just behind the foresight, a souvenir of the Reaper's power.

Valentine begged off from the questions and congratulations to check on the wounded. Which reminded him: "I've got wounded, sir. Can we set up a field hospital here?"

"Of course. This ridge is good defensive ground. I'll establish brigade HQ here until all our, ahem, stray sheep and goats are rounded up."

The fight already had a name—Billy Goat Cut. Valentine heard one of his corporals relaying the details to a Guard sergeant deploying his men for a sweep of the battlefield to look for enemy wounded or hiding.

Duvalier wandered out of the hills with Ediyak trailing behind, his clerk looking like she'd just been through the longest night of her life. Duvalier carried a Reaper skull by its thin black hair.

"Found him lurking on the ridge, all dazed and confused," she said, sticking the skull on a rail grade marker with a wet squelch that sounded like a melon being opened. "I thought I'd solve his problem for him."

Just like a Cat. She did everything but leave it on the back step.

"Don't mess with that," a corporal warned a curious Guard. "You'll seize up and die if you get some of that black gunk in you."

"It's safe once it's dried," Duvalier said, rubbing some on her index finger and making a motion toward her mouth. Valentine slapped her hand down.

"Cut it out, Ali. What's the matter with you?"

"I wonder sometimes," she said.

†

Valentine's holding action was just one-third of the story. The Bears, Wolves, and assorted legworm-mounted troops had fallen on the support trains like hyenas on a pair of sick cattle.

Gamecock had found a piece of tentacle that looked like it came from a Kurian in the wreckage. It was already sealed in a specimen jar for eventual delivery to the Miskatonic.

Of course, there was no way to identify the remains positively. Valentine imagined the Kurians weren't above sticking some unimportant former rival or inconvenient relative in an aquarium marked "In case of emergency, break glass," so to speak, should a body ever need to be left behind while the Kurian stuffed itself up a hollow tree somewhere, or in the rear engine that managed to decouple and escape at full speed.

Moytana's Wolves had their own triumph, tearing up the artillery support hurrying toward the railroad cut. They were already working on chain harnesses so the legworms could haul the tubes up and down Kentucky's hills.

Seng was wrong about the delay. It took four days to get everyone organized, the refugees and the two men too shot up to move to a local brand.

Miraculously, Valentine had no one killed in the fight; his only losses were wounded—and the jibes from the rest of the expedition.

†

They crossed the Big Sandy into West Virginia. Special Executive Karas commemorated the occasion by having his legworm riders offer a banquet.

They sacrificed an egged-out legworm to feed the troops. For all their size, legworms didn't offer much in the way of edibles. The tenderest pieces were the clawlike legs themselves. They reminded Valentine of the shellfish he'd eaten in New Orleans and the Caribbean. The farther away you traveled from the legs, the worse they tasted. The riders assured him younger legworms were both tenderer and tastier, as were unfertilized eggs—"Kentucky caviar."

Legworm flesh barbecue was something of an acquired taste and depended greatly on the quality of the barbecue sauce. Southern Command's soldiery invited or shanghaied into attending chewed manfully.

Valentine ate his deep-fried with a lot of cider vinegar.

They put Karas' chair on another stump, this one only a foot off the ground at the high end of the picnic field's slope, but it still gave him a commanding view and a sort of dais from which to command his legworm-riding knights-errant.

Seng tapped Valentine on the shoulder. "Major, our ally heard about Billy Goat Cut. He wants to see you."

Gamecock and Moytana were there as well, along with a Guard captain whose command had taken a whole platoon of railway security troops prisoner. A small crowd of legworm riders and soldiers had gathered to watch events, while sneaky dogs, including Valentine's company mutt, raided unattended plates. Valentine saw Duvalier's freckled eyes in the crowd. She had a broke-brim felt hat pulled down almost to her knees and looked lost in her ratty old overcoat.

The leaders of the assorted clans of the Kentucky Alliance arranged themselves behind Karas. His handsome face smiled down at them.

Valentine saw Tikka again, standing next to her adoptive brother, Zak. Zak had a welt at the corner of his eye, but then it was a rare day when there wasn't a good fistfight in the Alliance camp. Kentucky men fought the way New Universal Churchmen golfed, as both a recreation and a social ritual.

"The major first," Karas said. "Congratulations on your brilliant fight."

"Brilliant" wasn't the word Valentine would have chosen. Brilliant commanders bagged their enemy with a minimum of shooting back.

Karas stood up. "A presentation is in order, I think. Bravery must be rewarded, just as treason must be punished."

"Bow," Tikka urged in a whisper that somehow carried.

Valentine wanted to tell her that the only time a Southern Command officer bowed was as sort of a preamble before asking a lady for a dance (Captain LeHavre used to say that it gave you a last chance to make sure your shoelaces were tied), but decided to cooperate in the interest of keeping the new allies happy.

"I dub you a knight of the New Kentucky Homeland," Karas said as he looped the medallion over Valentine's head. Valentine noticed that Karas' hands smelled like a cheap Kurian Zone aftershave called Ultimate, strong enough to mask a hard day's body odor in an emergency. Valentine liked Karas a little better. No one with royal pretensions would walk around smelling like a blend of gasoline and window cleaner.

Valentine straightened again.

"Kentucky thanks you, son of both Southern Command and our own Bulletproof."

Kind words, but Valentine hoped he wasn't using the word Kentucky the way the Kurian in the Pacific Northwest used to be called Seattle.

While Moytana, Gamecock, and the Guard captain got their ribbons and medals, Valentine examined his decoration.

It looked like a piece of old horse show ribbon with a brassy circle at the end. Valentine looked closely at the medal. It was an old commemorative quarter glued facedown on a disk of brass—the Kentucky state design, rather nicked and scratched, but as clean and polished as elbow grease could make it.

Karas must be some kind of coin enthusiast. That or he was a student of the little common details that built a culture and a community.

Zak gave Valentine a discreet wave. His sister winked and moistened her lips.

†

The rest of the march had its share of difficulties. Valentine lost two soldiers of his company, whether through desertion or simple loss he never learned—they took bicycles into a town that allegedly had a good, safe market and never returned.

Seng was moving too hard to the northeast for Valentine to delay in searching for them. He led a detail in civilian clothes into town but could learn nothing.

Bee slept outside his tent like a dog. Duvalier brought home grisly trophies now and then—Quisling scouts, an unfortunate pimp who tried to drug her at a trans-Appalachian inn, a Reaper who'd lost a foot to a bear trap.

Word of Red Dog's Reaper-sensing powers spread, and Seng attached him to brigade headquarters as scouting and detection gear. The dog went out with Wolf patrols and nighttime picket checks. Red Dog's cheery enjoyment of his excursions rubbed off as they neared their goals.

There certainly were pleasures to the march. Valentine loved the vistas of this piece of country. The old, round, wooded mountains had a tumbledown beauty, and seemed to keep secret histories in the silent manner of aging former belles.

Valentine visited the Bulletproof camp and learned some of the ins and outs of the Kentucky Alliance. All the clans were powerful organizations, powerful enough so the Kurians kept watch on them and sometimes started feuds to prevent any one from getting too powerful. At least that's what Zak thought, expressing his opinion over some well-diluted bourbon at one evening's camp.

After a final pause that allowed Brother Mark and a pair of Cats to attend a meeting with the guerrillas and the underground, they marched to a map reference point and made camp on a defensible hillside. It was well watered, with a nasty rock pile to the north on one flank and a swamp to the south. Below, just visible between two lesser hills, was the town of Utrecht, seemingly chosen for its misty, mountain environs and the echoes of history in its name.

The representatives of the guerrilla army guarding the town seemed woefully undermanned, tattered but well-armed. The legworm ranchers mixed with them more freely than the Southern Command troops.

With Bee leading the cart horses and Ediyak sitting beside with the company fund, Valentine took a barter cart down into the valley and saw a better ordered group of men, perhaps in reinforced regiment strength, camped on another hill to the northeast of town. Thinking that this was the partisan army proper, he turned the cart onto a road skirting town and toward their pickets, and received yet another surprise when he saw tattered flags identifying the men as belonging to Vermont and New Hampshire.

"Who the hell?"

"I'll be damned. Those are the Green Mountain Boys," Ediyak said. "Jeebus, all that's missing is a complement of Kee-bec Libertay for us to have every Freehold east of the Mississippi represented here."

Valentine waved hello to a corporal's guard watching the road but the soldiers just stared at him, waiting for orders from their superiors.

They were good-looking men, wearing woodland camouflage, boots, leather gaiters, and a good selection of Kevlar. Most had 4x combat sights on their assault rifles. On closer examination Valentine saw what were probably masked gun emplacements on the hillside, and a headlog or two peeped out from covering brush at the edge of open hillside pasture. Anything short of a divisional assault on this hill, with armored car support, would be torn to bits.

Their tents weren't laid out in an organized fashion, but in little groupings that made their gently sloping hillside look like it had sprouted a case of green ringworm. Camouflage netting covered some tenting and mortar pits; others were open for the world to see.

"Dots, you magnificent bitch," Valentine found himself saying. *Good God, how did all this come about?* She'd played her cards very close to the chest.

His vision had come true—and then some. He'd imagined leading some Wolves and technicians to the aid of the guerrillas. Lambert had taken that idea and turned it into something for the history books.

It made him clammy just to think about it.

Valentine turned back into town. It was a rather old-fashioned main-street type of town, and every third building seemed to be named after somebody or other, nineteenth-century achievement emblazoned in Romanic letters in stone ready to bear witness to their greatness until wind and rain wore down even their gravestones.

The civilians either were keeping indoors, were terrified, or had fled the gathering of forces. Valentine saw Southern Command uniforms mixing with the timber camouflage of the Green Mountain Boys, guerrillas in patched riding coats and legworm leathers, all meeting and talking and buying each other drinks. A trio of milk-shouldered girls in halter tops, plump and tempting, called out to the soldiers from the expansive porch of an old Victorian mansion just off the town square. Valentine wondered if some entrepreneur had followed a regiment on the march and set up shop, or if it was a local establishment operating discreetly under Kurian eyes and now enjoying a quick gold rush of uniforms.

Bee whooped excitedly. Valentine saw a tower of faun-furred muscle, back to him, moving through the crowd in the middle of a complement of men with foxtail-trimmed ponchos hanging from their shoulders. Valentine felt his throat swell. He whipped the cart horses, hard, and caught up to the short column.

"Yo! Old Horse," Valentine called to the Grog's back. It ignored him, perhaps not hearing him in the noisy street. "Hey, Uncle!" Valentine yelled.

The men in back turned, and so did the Grog.

It had a long scar running up its face and a fang missing. An eyelid drooped lazily; the other glared at him, keen and suspicious.

It wasn't Ahn-Kha.

# CHAPTER EIGHT

*T*he Allegheny Alliance, West Virginia, June: The campaign surrounding
the great union in the Alleghenies near the town of Utrecht is one more men
claimed to be at than ever were. Or if not themselves in person, a brother, a
cousin, an uncle or aunt—laid down like a trump card when veterans get
together to talk about their experiences in the Liberation. (Only writers of
lurid exploitative novels title the fight against the Kurian Order the "Vampire Wars.")

It's safe to say that Utrecht, West Virginia, had never seen such a feast,
even during holidays during the platinum age pre-2022. The town square
had a smaller square of groaning white-clothed banquet tables set up
within. The old pedestal in front of the courthouse that had once contained
a memorial to First World War veterans (replaced by a statue of a Reaper
holding a human baby up so it could look up at the stars, and happily sawn
off at the ankles the week before when the "guerrilla army" occupied the
town) had a new set of stairs, as well as a platform and loudspeaker system
for speechmaking. Most said Special Executive Karas had been working on
a stemwinder for months, looking forward to this moment.

For David Valentine, out of thousands readying themselves for a party
of special magnificence, the night held little promise.

†

David Valentine drove the cart back into company headquarters, fighting tears. All around the people were putting up colorful bunting (red,
white, and blue or yellow being the colors of choice, but some folks
were making do with tinsel and other old Christmas decorations).

Blueberries were in season, and Bee happily scooped out an entire pie Ediyak purchased for her. Ediyak was whistling Southern Command marching tunes, rather off-key. Every storefront had fresh baked goods for sale, and around the back door bottles and flasks and mason jars of liquor were being passed out in exchange for everything from gold or silver coin to overcoats, old eyeglasses, and boots.

Southern Command's officers and NCOs spoiled not a few prospective evenings by checking packs and ammunition pouches of those traveling to and from town.

Valentine pulled himself together enough to institute a liquor search of his own when he returned, and three bottles were emptied into the thirsty Allegheny dirt and Patel had new miscreants for latrine and garbage duty. Though he'd laid out his best uniform for the banquet, the prospect of a feast had lost all its luster and he decided not to attend. He checked in at headquarters and swapped purchases he'd made in town for twenty-four duty-free hours after the banquet. He wanted quiet and solitude.

Jolly was left in command of the camp. He said he'd heard enough speeches about Kurian tactics of fear never conquering the human spirit in his life. But he almost ordered Valentine to go.

"If anyone deserves a good feed, it's you, Valentine," he said. "You've kept us in fresh eggs and vegetables for three months."

Moytana saved him from being ordered to attend by appearing. His Wolf patrols were routed or posted, and this bit of Virginia was at peace, though they had intercepted some high-ranking Quislings scuttling north with a couple wagons of clothing and valuables, and Moytana needed orders.

Valentine, hearing that the brigade was still attending to basics despite the festival, went to the commissary and got a sandwich. He found a comfortable stump and watched the partiers depart. Seng led the way with several other officers, some with hardy wives and husbands who'd come along for the march, plus select NCOs and regular soldiers—the wounded or those deserving of special consideration. Music echoed up from the Kentucky hills.

He finished his sandwich. Tasteless, despite the fresh vegetables and mayonnaise.

Duvalier waited for him in his tent. She was reclining in his hammock, her boots off and her bony feet greasy with something that smelled of lanolin and mint. "What's got you down?" she asked, dropping a Kurian newspaper bearing a headline about a rail accident in Kentucky.

"I was in town," Valentine said. He decided to tell her. Talking might ease the heartache. Ahn-Kha's loss was real, fresh and raw again like a stripped scab. "I saw a Golden One. Thought it was Ahn-Kha. It wasn't."

She sat up. "That bites. I—I can't believe it. I heard the stories about him organizing the partisans."

"Ahn-Kha's not the only Grog who could organize a revolt. This one wasn't as well-spoken. I got about three words out of him," Valentine said. "He's probably wary of strange uniforms."

"This is still a big deal, Val. You helped make it happen. I remember you laboring over reports about Kentucky, when we wintered. You had a stack of papers the size of—well, you remember."

Valentine didn't say anything, willing her to be as miserable as he was.

"In a way, it's still Ahn-Kha's victory. You decided Southern Command could march across Kentucky, what with the Kurians few and far between in the legworm ranch country."

"I know."

"Look, I should just say it: I was an ass to you back then. You were killing yourself looking for Ahn-Kha. I thought you were wasting your time, tried to slap you out of it. Plus we fought about that baby Reaper. Is it doing well? Did you tame it—er, him?"

"Blake's well enough. Growing fast. I don't think anyone but Narcisse could have brought him up."

"Want to talk about Ahn-Kha some more?"

"No," Valentine said. He hated the celebration he was missing. It felt like a dance on the Golden One's grave.

"I've got a bottle," she said, patting one pocket on her long coat. "Want a drink?"

"I ordered everyone in camp searched," Valentine growled.

"If they can't locate someone, it's a lot harder to search them," Duvalier said. "You've got some good guys here, but they're not that good."

He could stand her company. She'd known Ahn-Kha almost as long as he had. "Pour it out. I don't want liquor in the camp. We'll arrange passes soon so people can go into town if they want to get drunk."

"I'll do no such thing. There's no swiping liquor. I had to buy that with some of Karas' funny money."

"Strange that they took his coin. Or did you offer a little personal bonus to get the booze?"

"Fuck off. I've blown a few sentries to get over a bridge or through a fence, but I'm no whore." She angrily shoved the bottle back into the coat.

Valentine retrieved his ten-dollar piece from his pocket. It was crude, and it had nothing more than the word of some jumped-up legworm rancher behind it. Maybe the citizens of Utrecht were swept up by patriotic fervor.

"I sometimes think we fight just to keep from falling in love," Duvalier said.

Valentine almost dropped the coin.

She rolled on her side, not the easiest thing to do in a hammock. "So, you going to dance with me at the glam-up? I'll get dressed. Ediyak has a civilian skirt and a top she said she'd loan me." She gripped the edge of the hammock and put her delicate chin over the edge, smiling like the Cheshire cat after a three-canary meal.

"I volunteered to stay in camp," Valentine said, shaking his head. "Speaking of which, my four hours starts soon."

"I'm not a fan of parties either. But I did go to the trouble of swiping some new underwear. Cute knit stuff, like lace from a fancy doily."

"Ali, these people are patriots," Valentine said. "It's not some KZ three-dollar store."

"I guess so. They're making a very patriotic profit on fresh bread and pies for the soldiers who liberated them."

*In worthless coin*, Valentine thought. Something about that was bothering him.

"Do me a favor. Stick close, okay? I want to talk to you when I get off."

"That sounds kinda perverted for sterling Major Valentine," she said.

†

With the tent next to empty, his duty time at brigade headquarters crawled. So he spent it roving. He walked the posts, checked the firewood and water supply, saw to it that no one had dug the latrines so they drained toward the food preparation area. The reserve supply dumps were still being built and a mini-backhoe was still at work digging magazines for their small supply of artillery.

Seng had chosen the spot for their new base well. Utrecht stood on the heel of a short mountain range, at a crossroads that would allow a shift northeast up either side of a mountain ridge, or to the southwest, and there were further cuts east and west, old roads and disused rail lines that were in poor shape but better than hacking one's way through woody mountains. At the last officers' meeting, Seng had stated that the first order of business would be a new survey of the area; Seng wanted to know every cow path and bike trail.

Valentine's company would probably be put to work improving old roads or creating connecting trails.

Valentine thought he saw the shape of the coming campaign. He guessed Seng hoped to imitate Jackson's Valley Campaign from the American Civil War near Winchester just on the other side of the Appalachians, as a matter of fact, popping in and out of mountain passes and sliding up and down roads to catch the Kurian forces unawares.

Even now Valentine saw some dozens of legworms being driven

into a brushy area south of town, on the other side of a twisting, turning stream where he saw some old, collapsed roofs. Ever since the linkup with Karas's group of rebel tribes, Seng had his regulars learning to handle the creatures. Legworms didn't need much more width than a jeep, and they never got stuck in mud or hung up on a rock. He watched them feed their way into the tangle of bush and young trees. They'd soon have it grazed down into open country, potential pasture or field. Legworms were better than a Bush Hog.

Some of the goats he'd purchased back on the Cumberland Plateau had made the long trip. Valentine paused to scratch one. A few of the men were already developing a taste for goat milk. He wondered if they had anyone with cheesemaking experience in the brigade.

The wind was blowing sound away from the torchlit town, but every now and then when the wind died he thought he caught words punctuated by music.

†

At the end of his duty he made a brief report to Jolla, who was dozing in a chair in his office near the headquarters tent. He turned the duty over to Nowak and left, walking past Brother Mark's tent. Valentine's ears heard soft snores from within. The old churchman had pushed himself hard, riding ahead with parties of Wolves, setting up meetings and last-minute details for the unification.

He wondered why he wasn't at the party. Brother Mark, from what he could tell, led a rather Spartan existence. Maybe he didn't like parties.

Duvalier waited in his tent. The soft, comforting aroma of a woman in the canvas-enclosed air was more welcoming than the thermos of coffee she opened on his return.

Instead of some dripping trophy, she'd brought two big slices of cherry cobbler. She smelled faintly of sandalwood too.

"You snuck a little whiskey into this," Valentine said, trying the coffee.

"Just a tetch, as they say here. I think we deserve a celebration too."

Valentine sipped the coffee, thinking of Malita in Jamaica. The coffee had been real there. Had the emotional connection been fake? What was real and what was wishful thinking—on both their parts— in this little hillside tent?

Duvalier leaned on the tent pole, sipping hers.

"You used to joke all the time about sexing me up. I think you're the only man who crossed the whole state of Kansas with a hard-on."

"Twenty-three will do that to you. My balls did my thinking for me whenever you seemed approachable. You used to say, what was it—"

"Dream on, Valentine," they said in unison. They both giggled.

She kissed him, softly, on the lips. Looking up into his eyes, she smiled. "There's a grand alliance forming down there, helped along with liquor and barbecue. I think tonight's a night for dreams coming true."

It was so tempting. He could forget everything, thrusting into her. He could find oblivion in satisfying lust the way some men lost themselves in drink, or at the green gaming tables, or in swirling clouds of narcotics. So tempting. No more thoughts of Ahn-Kha's face, those curious townies peering at him from behind quilted curtains, the apparently bottomless supply of alcohol . . .

Valentine put his hands on her, tickled the back of her neck. "But we'd—"

The *krump* of an explosion interrupted him. The distant *pop-pop-pop* of small arms fire followed.

Duvalier's brow furrowed. "I hope that's fireworks."

Valentine grabbed his pistol belt and sword and poked his head out of the tent. No comforting bursts of fireworks filled the mountain valley, but there were red flares firing in the air above the Green Mountain Boys' encampment. He couldn't see the town, but the torchlight glow in the sky over it was almost gone.

"I've got to get to headquarters," he said.

"I know," she said. "Where do you want me?"

"If any of your fellow Cats are in camp, round them up and report to Moytana's headquarters."

The corner of her mouth turned up. "It was a nice moment, while it lasted."

"It was," Valentine agreed. He trotted a few feet over to company HQ as the brigade bugle sounded officers' call.

Rand was already up and Patel came into their two-pole headquarters tent carrying his boots and his rifle. Red Dog was running around, excited in the commotion but not looking at all frightened. That gave Valentine some comfort.

"I'm going to brigade," Valentine said. "Preville, come along in case I need a messenger. I've no news, other than that something's wrong. Assemble the men with full field kit and three days' rations. Make sure the reserve dehydrated food and ammunition reserves are handy. Get a meal into the men if there's anything hot handy."

They nodded. Patel just kept putting on his boots. Preville patted back some rather straggly hair over his ears that made him look more than ever like a revolutionary intellectual.

Valentine could rely on them. He hurried to brigade headquarters, saw Duvalier's head bobbing off toward the Hunters' collection of tents within the larger encampment. Lights died out all over camp, and she vanished as a lantern was extinguished. He tried to let the red hair take his regrets with it.

He beat Moytana into the headquarters by fifteen seconds. Others trickled in, way, way too many junior officers who missed the celebration thanks to privileges of rank. Nowak was speaking to someone over a field phone.

Major Bloom stood behind, looking like a pit bull waiting for the release. From her position, Valentine guessed she was the temporary senior for the Guards.

Jolla's balding head glistened. He kept wiping it with a handkerchief. "There's been some kind of disturbance in town. We don't know anything more than that."

"Observers report the firing is dying down. There's still some torchlight and lanterns in the town square, but the rest of the lights in town are out," Nowak reported.

"Are ... are the lines to the Green Mountain contingent and Karas', er, headquarters functioning?"

"Not strung yet," Nowak said. "We're in radio contact with the Green Mountain troops. They're asking us what's happening in town, since we've got a better view. They got a walkie-talkie distress signal, it seems." She spoke with the flat monotone of someone operating on autopilot.

More officers arrived and Jolla silenced the babble.

"Defensive stance," Jolla said. "Let's get the men to their positions for now. Where's Colonel—oh, at the party, of course."

Valentine dispatched Preville to pass the word to Rand, met Moytana's eyes, and jerked his chin toward Jolla. As everyone filed out to get their men to battle positions, some of which were only half-completed, they were joined by Bloom and Nowak.

"Your Wolves haven't reported enemy formations?" Valentine said.

"No, Major," Moytana said. "Only thing out of the ordinary they reported was a lot of activity at an old mine north of here. Military-style trucks and command cars. Locals said it had been shut down for years and just reopened and was being garrisoned. Said it was because the guerrillas had wrecked a couple of other more productive mines and they had to reopen. Seng's got us keeping an eye on it, and a Cat is taking a closer look."

"You could hide a lot of men in a coal mine," Jolla said.

"Maybe the 'Green Mountain Boys' aren't really Green Mountain Boys," Bloom said.

"No, they're real enough," Nowak said. "Lambert and Seng were expecting them. We've had progress reports."

"Perhaps we should shift camp, Colonel," Valentine said. "Move closer to Karas' bunch and the Green Mountain Boys. Right now we can't support each other."

"In the dark?" Jolla asked.

"Old Wolf trick, sir," Moytana said. "If somebody's marked out our positions for artillery, might be better if they wasted their shells on empty space."

"I took a look at their positions this morning," Valentine added. "They've got a good high hill to their backs."

"I think the enemy would be firing on us already if they had our position," Jolla said. "We don't even know what's happened in town yet."

"We may soon, Colonel," Nowak said, ear to the field phone again. "Pickets are reporting Private Dool is coming in. He ran all the way from town. Says there's been a massacre."

"No one else?"

"Just Dool, sir. He said they took away his rifle and his pants."

"His *pants*? Get him up here," Jolla said.

Valentine had the uncomfortable sensation that Dool's missing pants was just the first oddly heavy raindrop in a storm to come. He could almost feel trouble gathering, like the heavy air in front of piled up thunderclouds. Like an animal, he wanted to get away or underneath something.

Dool showed up soon enough, shoeless and footsore, a blanket wrapped around his waist. Dool was a Guard regular who'd been wounded by a grenade in the cleanup action after the fight at Billy Goat Cut. He looked distraught. He still had his uniform shirt, though a blood splatter ran up the front to his shoulder like a rust-colored bandolier.

Jolla said, "Just give it to me, Dool. Don't worry about military form."

"Killed them all, sir. Colonel Seng and the rest, Roscoe next to me—they're all dead. They told me to tell you. Said that someone was to come into town to hear terms at dawn. They told me to tell you."

"They?"

"The fellers with the squared-off black beards."

"Like this," Moytana said, passing his hand just under his chin.

"Yessir, yes, Cap'n, that's just it."

"What's this, Moytana?" Jolla demanded.

Moytana cleared a frog from his throat. "It's the Moondagger Corps. Or elements of it. They all wear beards like that." Moytana's face went as gray as the washed-out ropes in his hair.

Valentine knew the name. Oddly enough he'd heard it from Duvalier when they were discussing recent events in Kansas. They were some kind of special shock troops used to quell uprisings and had caused the '72 operation in Kansas to fall apart before it even got going.

"Never mind that," Jolla said. "Tell us what happened. Take your time."

Dool hitched the blanket around his legs a little tighter. "It was a fine dinner, sir. Officers from the Green Mountain troops were across the square from us, and the legworm guys were around the statue and on our left. Guerrilla troops too, only now I think they wasn't guerrillas but turncoats. Like Texas and Okie redhands, only worse.

"Then King Karas, he gets up and starts one of those fine speeches of his."

A siren started up, interrupting him.

"Engine noise reported overhead. One plane," Nowak reported from the field phones.

*A second drop. How long until they start to fall, hard?*

"Is the HQ dugout done yet?" Jolla asked.

"It's just a hole at the moment, sir," Nowak said.

"We'll adjourn there."

The hole was only half dug. There weren't any floorboards even. They squelched uncomfortably into the mud. It was deep enough so they could sit with heads below ground level. Nowak stayed at the headquarters tent.

Some squatted. Valentine's bad leg ached if he did that for more than a minute or two, so he settled uncomfortably into the mud.

"Go on with your story," Bloom said to Dool.

"Here, sir?"

"Little else to do," Jolla said.

*Except get the camp moving. Forward, back, just somewhere other than where the Kurians expected them to be.* Valentine could hear the engine noise growing—a single prop, by the sound of it.

Observation planes. The herald of coming trouble.

Moytana was gnawing on the back of his hand again.

"Where did I leave off?" Dool asked.

"Karas's speech," Jolla said. "Do they really call him King Karas?"

"King of the Cumberland, some of those legworm fellers say, sir. It was a real good speech, I thought. Real good. He was just going on about mankind saying 'enough,' and there was this bright blue flash from the podium and he was just gone. Like lightning struck him, only there wasn't no bolt.

"Then the town square just sort of exploded, sir." Dool thought for a moment, as though trying to describe it. "Like a minefield wired to go off or something. Anyway, they blew up like mines. One went off right under the colonel's chair. I've always had decent reflexes, otherwise that grenade I tossed from the squad at the rail line would have been the end of me. Gunfire then, a real sweeping fire, and they started cutting down everyone. Women with serving trays and beer mugs—everyone. Only now that I think back on it, the guerrilla leaders clustered around the podium, they weren't blown up or shot; they were sort of clear from it in this little cement area with benches and a fountain. I think they all jumped in that old fountain. Wish we could have put a shell into it. The top half of the colonel was still sitting in his chair, tipped over, like. You know, like when you're at the beach and the kids half bury you in the sand, only it was real. I tried to drag Roscoe into some bushes but he was dead."

He paused for a moment. Valentine looked away while Dool wiped his eyes.

"All clear," Nowak called down into the hole.

Valentine noticed that the engine noise had died. They picked themselves up and returned to the headquarters tent.

Gamecock was there in full battle array, a big-handled bowie knife strapped to one thigh and a pistol on the other. Black paste was smeared on the exposed skin of his face and each bare arm. He had his hair gathered tightly in a food-service net.

"The whole Bear team's ready to go into that town, suh," Gamecock said. "I got twenty-two Bears already halfway up. We'll get the colonel back safe."

"Too late for that," Jolla replied. "I'm afraid he was killed in an ambush."

"Treachery, you mean," Bloom said.

"Then we'll pay them a visit to even the score," Gamecock said. "Just say the word."

Jolla tapped his hand against his thigh. "No, they're probably fortifying the town now."

"Sir, they told me to tell you what I saw," Dool said. "There wasn't anything like an army in town that I saw, just maybe a company of these bearded guys and the guerrilla turncoats."

Dool spoke up again. "The ones that surrendered, they took the prisoners and chopped their heads off. That big gold Grog was taking off heads with this thing like a branch trimmer. I thought I was gonna get chopped but it turned out I was the only one left from the brigade. Colonel Gage drew his pistol and was shooting back and they gunned him down, and a sniper got Lieutenant Nawai while he was wrestling with a redhand for his gun."

"And they told you we'd hear their terms in the morning," Jolla said. "I think we should wait."

"Wait?" Valentine said, unable to believe his ears.

"Way I see it, the fight's started," Gamecock said. "I think we can guess what their terms will be."

"Javelin's almost four hundred miles from Southern Command," Jolla said. "The locals were supposed to support us, and now we've found that they're hostile. How long can this expedition survive without the support of the locals?"

Gamecock sat down in a folding chair, took out his big bowie knife, and started sharpening it on a tiny whetstone.

Frustrated, Valentine felt like he was playing a chess game where his opponent was allowed to take three moves for his one. They'd be checkmated in short order.

"Longer than it'll last if we wait on what the Kurians have dreamed up," Valentine said.

"Javelin was named right, that's for sure," Jolla said. "Thrown over the front rank of shields at the enemy. If it hits, great. If it misses, the thrower doesn't expect to get it back. 'Sorry, General Lehman, we missed.' "

Bloom and Moytana exchanged glances. They both looked to Valentine. What were they expecting, a Fletcher Christian moment? Valentine wondered just what was said about him in Southern Command mess halls.

Valentine didn't want to think that Javelin's acting CO had his nerves shattered. Maybe he'd recover in the light of day.

Except by the light of day it would be too late.

"I'm willing to wait and hear what their terms are," Jolla said. "They may allow us to just quit and go home."

"Why would they do that?" Bloom said. "We're at the disadvantage now."

"Perhaps their real target was Karas. Kurian regulars are good enough when suppressing a revolt by farmers with pitchforks and rabbit guns. They're not as successful against trained troops. Except for in extraordinary circumstances, like Solon's takeover."

"All the more reason to pitch into them," Valentine said.

Jolla wiped his head again. "I'll go and see what they have to say. Bloom, this is a little unorthodox, but I'm promoting you to command of the Guards with a brevet for colonel. Radio to Lehman's headquarters for confirmation and orders about how to proceed. Do you think we can get a signal through, Nowak?"

"So the radio silence order—"

"I think the Kurians know we're here now," Jolla said.

Nowak's face went red. Jolla shouldn't have snapped at her. Anyone might ask a dumb question under these circumstances.

"Thank you for your confidence, sir," Bloom said.

*Nice of you, Cleo, changing the subject.*

"You know the regiment and commanded them when Gage was away. If something happens to me, you're the best regular . . ."

*Of what's left*, Valentine silently added the unspoken words.

Valentine didn't know Southern Command military law well enough to know whether a colonel commanding could promote someone to colonel in the field, and frankly didn't care.

Nowak put down the handset.

"Colonel, I don't think you should go," she said, her face still emotionless. "Let me get their terms."

"They might pull one of their tricks," Jolla said.

"All the more reason for me to go," she said.

"Oh, Dool," Jolla said. "Why did they take your pants? I can see your shoes."

Dool tugged at an ear. "What's that, sir?"

"Your pants."

"I plain dumb forgot! They said to tell the brigade commander, 'Caught with your pants down.' I thought they were nuts. He was laying there dead in the town square. I guess they meant you to get it."

Jolla stood up. "Those were their words?"

"Yeah, caught with your pants down. I was to remind you."

"That mean something, sir?" Moytana said.

"It must just be a coincidence," Jolla said. "It's an old joke, goes back to my days at the war college. A dumb stunt I pulled."

"Has it come up recently?" Valentine asked.

"I . . . we were telling stories over cigars. Right after that fight at the railroad cut. Colonel Seng, myself, Gage was there, Karas, a few of the leaders from the legworm clans."

"I remember, sir," Nowak said. "The story about six-ass ambush. Five got away."

"And one didn't," Jolla said. "Forever branded as the one who couldn't get his pants up and tripped on his own belt."

"I wonder if there's a spy in our ranks?" Bloom asked.

"Dumb spy, to give himself away with a detail like that," Moytana said.

Or did the Kurians want everyone looking over their shoulder? Valentine wondered. They were better at sowing dissension than fighting.

†

The meeting broke up and Jolla ordered Valentine to check the defensive perimeter of the camp. Everyone was nervous, so he took the precaution of using the field phones to let the next post know he was on the way as he left each post.

He was checking the west side of camp when he saw a group of men. It looked like some sort of struggle. One had lit a red signal flare and held it high so the troops knew not to fire.

Valentine trotted up to the mob. They were mostly regulars from the Guard regiment.

"Stop, hold there!"

"Who says?" someone in the mob called.

"Shut it, you, it's Major Valentine," a corporal said. "Sir, we caught our spy."

The mob parted and two men dragged another forward, one holding each arm. He already had a noose around his neck. The man was folded like a clasp knife, coughing, clearly gut-punched—or kicked.

They raised his face, using his scant hair as a handle. It was Brother Mark.

"He was dressed all in black. Sneaking off."

"He always dresses in black," Valentine said. "Let him go; give him some air."

"He's the spy for sure," someone called, and the group growled approval.

Valentine wondered how word of "a spy" in camp had spread so quickly. Soldiers had their own communications grapevines, especially for bad news.

"God help me," Brother Mark gasped.

"Let's hope so," Valentine said. "Who arrested him?"

At the word "arrest" the mob stiffened a little. Valentine had used it intentionally, hoping that a whiff of juridical procedure would bring the men back to their senses.

Brother Mark groaned and sucked air.

"I guess it was me, Major. Corporal Timothy Kemper, Bravo Company, first battalion. Pickets under my command caught him sneaking out of camp."

The man in question came to his knees, grabbed Valentine by the sleeve.

"The pickets didn't 'catch' me," Brother Mark almost wept. "I hailed them and requested a guide to get me to Karas' encampment. For God's sake, tell him the facts, Corporal."

Valentine wondered if crying on bended knee got you off the hook in the Kurian Zone. Tears wetting his uniform coat cuff just left him feeling embarrassed for both of them.

"Stop that," Valentine said, backing away. "Karas is dead."

"I'd heard there was some kind of treachery in town. I thought I should see to our allies. I'm sure they're as frightened as we are."

The men growled at that again. For a man of the cloth and a diplomat, Brother Mark wasn't very good at communicating with ordinary soldiers.

"Who told you to do that?" Valentine asked.

"I thought it was my duty," he said, reclaiming some of his spaniel-eyed dignity.

"Your duty?" Valentine said, almost amused.

"My higher calling to unite—"

"Save it. You should have checked with someone and had orders issued."

"I've never had to ask permission to come and go, son." With the noose now loose around his neck, he rose to his feet, dusting off the plain black moleskin.

"Major," Valentine reminded him.

"I'm not sure where I fit in to your hierarchy."

"Under the circumstances it would have been wiser to get permission and an escort. Corporal, return to your pickets." Valentine picked out two men who made the mistake of standing a little apart from the others. "You two, come with me as an escort. I'll take our churchman to headquarters and see what he has to say. Consider yourself confined to camp for now, Brother."

"I must be allowed to visit the other camps. We must hang together, or as Franklin said, we shall all surely hang separately."

Valentine saw no point in engaging the churchman in a debate. They were already wasting time. Wasting words would just add insult to injury.

He took him up to the headquarters tent. Jolla had pushed two tables together and spread out a map of western Kentucky. He had the mission book, a set of standing orders that covered several contingencies, including loss of the commander and abandonment by the legworm clans.

Nowak was gone. Another officer was handling the communications desk—if a folding-leg table covered by a tangle of wires connecting assorted rugged electronics boxes could be called a desk—but if anything, headquarters was busier than in the first shock of the alert. Complaints and problems were coming in from all points of the compass. It was just as well that they weren't under attack, Valentine thought. The artillery spotters couldn't communicate with the mortar pits, two companies were trying to occupy the same defilade, leaving a whole eighth of the perimeter unguarded . . .

Valentine ignored the assorted kerfuffles and explained what he'd seen, and stopped. He let Brother Mark do the rest of the talking. Jolla apologized for the men being on edge.

"But you must give me orders to contact our allies, it seems," Brother Mark said.

Jolla scrawled something on his order pad and signed it.

"Do you think it's wise to just let him wander around, under the circumstances?" Valentine asked.

"I wouldn't be wandering," Brother Mark said.

"You're right, Valentine, and you just named your own poison. Go with him. They tell me the Reaper hasn't been built that can sneak up on you."

"Yes, sir," Valentine said, fighting a battle with his face.

"Besides, someone in uniform should be representing Javelin. Tell them that I've informed Southern Command of the situation and I'm waiting for orders. Until then I'm free to act as I see fit."

*That'll reassure a bunch of nervous Kentucky wormriders.*

Valentine had heard rumors as a junior officer that the Kurians could befuddle key men through some sort of mental evil third eye, but had never attributed to mysticism what could be explained by stupidity. Jolla's sudden plunge into routine and procedure, when circumstances called for anything but, made him reconsider his old attitudes.

"You're a sharp instrument of good in His hands, my son," Brother Mark said. "Thank you for getting the noose off me. Those poor anxious men were rather letting their passions run wild on them."

Valentine decided he wanted the far blunter instrument of Bee along, just in case, so he delayed Brother Mark for five more minutes. He took Ediyak as well. Beauty sometimes calmed better than brawn. He grabbed some legworm jerky and peanuts and took an extra canteen. If the real fireworks began, they might be forced to flee in the wrong direction.

As they set out, Brother Mark graced them with only a single aphorism: "Let's be about God's work this night of fear and doubt." Then he stalked off toward the legworm campsites, taking long, measured strides, for all the world like a hero in one of DeMille's old biblical videos they liked to show on washed-out old 1080 screens in church basements on community night.

Valentine almost liked him. He couldn't say whether the renegade churchman was crazy, a true believer, or simply the kind of man who always stepped forward when necessity called.

He took care moving—God knows what might be prowling in the dark—with first Bee scouting while he made sure nothing was following him, and then swapping with the Grog.

The legworm clans didn't even have anything that could be called a camp. They'd gathered their legworms together into five big clumps, feeding them branches cut and dragged from the woods, with a few more grazing at the borders of their camps. Their sentries and picket positions were two-man pairs who lay behind clumps and lines of legworm droppings, the fresh deposits notched with little sandbags the size of small pistols supporting deer rifles. Behind the spotter/sniper positions more men stood ready to mount their legworms.

Valentine had seen the mobile breastworks that legworms provided in action before. The riders planted hooks and straps in the fleshy, nerveless sides of their mounts and hung off the living walls, employing their guns against an opponent, using tactics that combined First World War trench warfare with wooden ship actions from Nelson's day.

The legworm clans were quick to blame Southern Command for not properly securing the town. Valentine conceded the point. The Wolves had checked it out, and then the Guards conducted a more thorough search, but whatever soldiers had been posted at key buildings and crossroads were missing along with the rest of the celebrants.

"I told Spex Karas this whole affair would go wrong," the dispatcher of the Coonskins said. He glared at Valentine through his one good eye. The other was a milky wreck. "The Free Territories egg us into fighting with the Kurians. We're for it now. For it deep."

"It's not this young man's fault," Brother Mark said.

Valentine thought of correcting him. He'd urged Southern Command to explore an alliance with some of the legworm clans and support the guerrillas in the Alleghenies.

"Careful, Coonskin," a low female voice said. "He's Bulletproof. Might just challenge you to a duel."

Tikka forced her way to the front of the throng. "Welcome back, reiner. My life gets interesting whenever you show up."

"Hello, Tikka. Where's Zak?"

Valentine heard startled breaths. She replied in a monotone, "He was at the party."

"I'm sorry to hear that," Valentine said.

She thanked him quietly, looked around at the assembly. "I'm able to speak in my brother's place, with my dispatcher's authority. The Bulletproof won't quit. Won't throw down their guns. Won't run."

"I stand for the Alliance too," another called. Cheers broke out.

But they sounded half-hearted.

By the pinkening dawn, they were at the camp of the Green Mountain Boys and Valentine was growing tired. The New England troops took the precaution of blindfolding the party before letting them into camp. Bee didn't appreciate being blindfolded, so Ediyak offered to wait with her outside the lines.

The Green Mountain Boys still had their senior officer, General Constance, who'd begged off the party because of a broken ankle. He looked like Santa Claus without the beard, sitting with his leg extended.

"Thought we had a bit too much of an easy time getting here," Constance said. "Thing is, if a trap's been sprung, where are the jaws?"

"Have you decided on a course of action?"

The cheery, red-cheeked face frowned. "If I had, I'd be a fool to tell you now, wouldn't I?"

"I don't blame you for not trusting us," Valentine said. "We're all wondering what's going to go wrong next."

"They've got a twist on us, that's for damn sure," Constance said. "Masterful, suckering us out like this. Masterful. They've set us up. Now I'm wondering how they're going to knock us down."

With that unsettling thought, Brother Mark got a promise from Constance not to act without first consulting Javelin's headquarters.

Under blindfold again, they were led back to the pickets. But Valentine knew the sound of a camp being packed up when he heard it.

Full daylight washed them as they returned to camp. Valentine looked around at the hills and mountains of West Virginia, black in the morning glare. The only sounds of fighting were from birds, battling and defending in contests of song and chirp as squirrel-tail grass waved in the wind. How long before the shells started falling?

The Kurians usually came off the worse in a stand-up fight. But this was above and beyond, even for their standard of deviousness.

He checked Brother Mark back in, gave Nowak's adjutant a report of his estimation of the situation in the Kentucky and New England camps, and returned to his company. After passing along what little news he had, he entered his tent and slept. Bee sat upright at the foot of his bed facing the tenthole, snoring.

†

Valentine's first captain in the Wolves, LeHavre, once told him a story of a Kurian trick, where they emptied a town and filled it up again with Quisling specialists who pretended to be ordinary civilians. The Kurians had done something similar here, on a much larger scale, involving even the partisans and the underground. Or perhaps used agents posing as them.

Valentine dreamed that he was in that town, walking down the center of the main street, frozen statues on sidewalks and in doorways and shopwindows watching him, their heads slowly turning, turning past the point their necks would snap, turning full around like turrets.

"What brings you here, missionary?" one of the reversed heads asked.

Valentine woke to find Ediyak shaking his shoulder. "Some kind of emissary from the Kurians, sir. Thought you might like to see it."

"Is Nowak back?"

"I don't know, sir."

His platoon just coming off guard detail was skipping a chance for both breakfast and sleep to catch a glimpse of the Kurians' mouthpiece.

When Valentine got a look at him, all he could think was that D.C. Marvels had an evil twin. The mouthpiece rode in a jointed-arm contraption on the back of a Lincoln green double-axle flatbed wrecker, modified for high ground clearance. Loudspeakers like Mickey Mouse ears projected from either side of the truck cab, and a huge silver serving cover, big enough to keep a turkey warm, rested over the hood ornament.

What really caught the eye was the contraption mounted on the flatbed. Valentine thought it looked a little like a stick-insect version of a backhoe, suspending a leather wing chair where the toothy shovel should be. Gearing and compressors appropriate for a carnival ride muttered and hissed at the base.

Valentine marked an insignia on the truck, a crescent moon with a dagger thrust through it, rather reminiscent of the old hammer and sickle of the Soviet Union.

"That's an old camera crane, I think," Rand said, wiping his glasses and resettling them on his nose. "Big one."

The mouthpiece himself wore a plain broadcloth suit over a white shirt and a red bow tie, though the suit had apparently been tailored to fit a pair of football shoulder pads beneath. He wore a red-trimmed white sash covered in neatly arranged brass and silver buttons, with a few dazzling diamond studs here and there. Jewels glued into the skin sparkled at the outer edge of each almond-shaped eye. Close-cropped curly hair had been dyed white, fading down his sideburns to two points at either side of a sharply trimmed beard.

He flicked a whiter-than-white lace hankerchief idly back and forth, his hand moving in the dutiful measured gestures of a royal wave. With his right he worked the crane and the chair, rising and dipping first to one side of the flatbed, and then sweeping around the front to the other side.

"I am the Last Chance," the mouthpiece said. Valentine noticed a tiny wire descending from a loop around his ear to the side of his mouth. It must have been a microphone of some kind, because the mouthpiece's words boomed from the speakers, startling the assembled soldiers. "For credentials I present only the mark of my obedience and the tally of my offspring."

He lifted his beard. A silver bar, widened and rounded at each end in the manner of a Q-tip, pierced the skin at the front of his neck just above his Adam's apple. Then he made a sweeping gesture with brass-ringed fingers at the sash.

"The holy balance represents the duality of existence. Life and death. Good and evil. Order and chaos. Mercy and cruelty. Wisdom is knowing when to apply each and in what measure and Grace how to accept each in submission to the will of the gods, who see horizons beyond the vision of human eyes."

He gave his speech in the measured, rehearsed manner of a catechism. Valentine wondered how long it had been since the mouthpiece had thought about those words.

Valentine found Moytana standing next to him. "Silver buttons are children who entered Kur's service; gold are children who had children of their own who took up the dagger. The cubic zirconium means someone who died in the Moondaggers."

"Lot of kids."

"Tell you about it later," Moytana said.

"He doesn't look old enough to have brought up that many soldiers."

"They start fighting at thirteen or fourteen, whenever the balls drop," Moytana said as the mouthpiece blatted something about the kindness of the gods giving them a last chance.

"Who in this assembly of the disobedient is in authority to speak to me?"

He spoke in a stern but kind tone through the speakers, with a hint of suppressed anger, making Valentine feel like a third grader caught putting a frog in the teacher's pencil drawer.

"That would be me," Colonel Jolla said, stepping forward.

"I wonder. You have the face of one who has lost a bet. You look like—what is the phrase you swamp-trotting crackers use?—you look like the 'bottom of the barrel.' And not a good barrel at that."

"Where's Captain Nowak? Why hasn't she returned with your terms?" Jolla asked.

As the mouthpiece dipped, Valentine noticed a golden-handled curved blade with an ivory sheath resting in his lap.

"Oh, but she has."

He worked the joystick and swept his chair around the front of the truck, removing the silver serving cover. Nowak's head was spiked, literally on a platter, her insignia, sidearm, personal effects, and identification arranged around her head like a garnish.

"She chose not to let her womb be a nursery of my greatness. As in her arrogance she took the counsel of her head rather than that of her body's blessed womanly nature, we took the liberty of ridding her of its burden."

He swung his chair around, turned the winged leather. Valentine saw gold leaf painted on the exposed wood at the front and tiny Moondagger symbols painted precisely on the nailhead trim. The mouthpiece fixed his eye on Ediyak.

"I trust others will not be so foolish."

"You killed a soldier under a flag of truce?" Jolla said.

The mouthpiece laughed. "What new folly must I expect from men who would have women do their fighting? I made her an honorable proposal of motherhood. Let that be a lesson to you. Do not send women to speak in a man's place again. Besides, she is not dead, just free of the body whose duty she refused in the first place. Tell them, sexless one."

Valentine saw him press a button next to his joystick. Nowak's eyes opened.

"I live," Nowak's head said. "If you want to call it that." Valentine noticed her voice came through the speakers. Clearly Nowak's, though the words sounded forced.

Some of the soldiers backed away. The more ghoulish craned their necks to get a better view.

Nowak's eyes rolled this way and that. "Well, hello, Jolly. You look intact this morning."

Valentine searched for the mechanics of the trickery. You needed lungs, a windpipe, to speak. A head couldn't just talk. This was some bit illusion by a Kurian or one of their agents.

He just wished real-looking blood wasn't slipping out of the corner of Nowak's mouth as she spoke.

"Tell them our terms," the mouthpiece said. "You must remember.

I whispered them to you often enough on the ride up as you rode in my lap. First, obedience—"

The eyes in the severed head blinked. "First, obedience to the order to lay down your arms and a solemn pledge to never resist the gods again," Nowak said. "Second, a selection of hostages, one taking the place of ten in assurance of future good conduct. Third, a return to the squalor of our bandit dens on the other side of the Mississippi, taking only from the countryside such as needed to sustain the retreat."

Her voice broke. "This is your only alternative to horrors and torments everlasting. The grave that gives no rest is my fate, for my willfulness," Nowak's head said, bloody tears running from the corners of her eyes.

*The Kurian Order always provided plenty of evidence for your eyes. After a lifetime spent trusting your senses . . .*

"You men may save your families by giving up your arms." A faint, low drumming carried up from the town. Must be some massive drums to make that deep a noise. "Women, shield your children from Kur's wrath by offering up your bodies to our commanders."

Valentine wondered at that. Was the mouthpiece so used to giving his last-chance speech that he failed to notice he was in a camp full of soldiers?

"Listen to him!" Nowak shrieked.

"You've got a long drive ahead of you, prance, if you want my boy," Cleo Bloom called from the back of the crowd. "He's six hundred miles away."

The chair rose and spun toward the sound. The mouthpiece fixed her with a baleful eye. "No matter. We'll simply take one from a town between here and Kantuck. We will let the mother know the willfulness, the arrogance, the insolence that demanded his sacrifice."

"Twisting tongue of the evil one, begone!" a commanding voice said in a timbre that matched the amplified speakers. Every head turned, and Brother Mark stepped forward.

Brother Mark stared at the head on the front of the hood and Nowak's features fell still and dead, the eyes dry and empty.

The chair descended again, sweeping forward just a little. The men next to Brother Mark retreated to avoid being knocked over. The two stared at each other, the mouthpiece's hand on the hilt of his dagger. Valentine sidestepped to get nearer to Brother Mark.

"Don't let this one fill your ears with pieties," the mouthpiece said. "He's expecting you to die for a cause. Futility shaped and polished to a brightness that blinds you to the waste. Honor. Duty. Country. How many millions in the old days marched to their doom with such platitudes in their ears? Wasted potential. It is for each man to add value to his life. Don't let wastrels spend the currency of your days."

The crane elevated him to its maximum extension.

"Our divine Prophet's Moondagger is still sheathed," the mouthpiece boomed through the speakers. The drums in town sounded in time to his pauses. "Do not tempt him to draw it, for it cannot be put away again until every throat in this camp is cut."

"We're volunteers," Valentine said. "We've all seen how lives are counted when Kur is the banker."

The crane lowered the mouthpiece.

Valentine stood, arms dangling, relaxed. He opened and closed his right fist, warming his fingers.

"Your face will be remembered. You'll regret those words, over and over and over again, tormented in the living hells."

"Can I borrow that?" Valentine asked. He whipped out his hand, raked the mouthpiece under the chin, came away with the silver pin—and a good deal of bushy black beard.

"Outrage!" the mouthpiece sputtered, eyes wide with shock. Blood dripped onto his white shirt.

Valentine, keeping clear of the extended crane arm, cleaned his ears with the silver pin and tossed it back into the Last Chance's lap, where it clattered against the curved dagger.

"Thanks," Valentine said.

"You'll writhe on a bridge of hooks. You'll roast, slowly, with skin coated in oils of—"

"Is that part of the living hells tour, or do I have to pay extra?" Valentine said. He called over the shoulder at the brigade: "That's how it always is, right? They hook you in with the price of the package tour, but all the worthwhile sights are extra."

The soldiers laughed.

"Here's my moon. Where's your dagger?" someone shouted from the back of the mob. Because of the crowd, Valentine couldn't see what was on display.

"You have until dusk to decide," the mouthpiece said, pulling his chair back toward the truck. The drumming started again.

The mouthpiece's flatbed rumbled to life. It backed up, turned, and rocked down toward the picket line. Some stealthy Southern Command hooligans had hung a sheet off the back of the flatbed, with

**ASS BANDIT—PUCKER UP!**

written on it in big block capitals.

The rest of the assembly laughed the Last Chance out of their camp.

Had this Last Chance ever ridden off to the sound of raucous laughter? Valentine doubted it.

Outside of the color guards and bands, no officer had ever quite succeeded in getting any two Southern Command soldiers to look alike in dress and hair, even for formal parades. They etched names of sweethearts in their rifles, sewed beads and hung tufted fishing lures in the caps, dipped points of their pigtails in tar, and stuck knives and tools in distinctly nonregulation snakeskin sheaths. But David Valentine had never been more grateful for their mulish contrariness.

# CHAPTER NINE

*D*ecision: *One of the vexations with writing histories concerning the Kurians and their intentions is the lack of records as to their thoughts and plans. In previous wars, there were government archives, speeches, even laws and commands that offer some insight into enemy intentions. Debriefings of the captured and memoirs written after passions had cooled also offer particular, if limited, insights.*

*The Kurians left nothing like that.*

*At best, we have the guesses from those under them. Church archons, generals, civil administrators. Sometimes the order of events give some clue as to priorities.*

*For example, in the Appalachian Catastrophe in the summer of '77, some argue that the Green Mountain Boys (itself a misnomer, as many of their numbers were made up of formations active in upstate New York and even western Pennsylvania) were the real target of the ruse, for they were the Moondaggers' main concern. Others say they were attacked first because they had the shortest trip home.*

*Assorted lies, threats, promises, and deals from the Kurians are equally unreliable, for whether they were kept or canceled depended very much on the character of the individual Kurian lord and what sort of situation he found himself in when bargaining with his friends and enemies.*

*The reader, alas, is left to draw his own conclusion from events as experienced by the human side in the struggle. So were commanders in the field in that fateful summer.*

†

The brigade HQ tent had an unusual number of soldiers buzzing around with the busyness of bees in a flower garden. They'd found something to do in its immediate vicinity, camouflaging lack of purpose with energy. Valentine told a couple of sergeants to find something to keep them busy.

The only idler seemed to be Red Dog, snoring after an anxious night at the fringes of the camp, whining whenever he was brought to the defensive positions facing Utrecht.

Bloom opened the meeting with her usual blunt style.

"Hit them hard now," Bloom said. "Can't let them just draw blood. We're in as good a shape as we'll ever be."

Valentine checked the corners and under the tables. If there was ever a good time for a Kurian agent to plant a bomb, now would be it. Some captains and Duvalier would be running the brigade.

"The same could be said of the legworm clans and the Green Mountain Boys," Brother Mark said. He looked exhausted from his efforts against the Last Chance and spent most of the conference with his eyes closed, rubbing his temples.

"What are your thoughts, Valentine?" Jolla asked.

"I wonder if they sprang their trap too early. Were I arranging a trick like this, I'd have these hills filled with my army. We'd be listening to the man in the whirly chair with one eye on the hostiles."

"Reliable troops have always been the Kurians' Achilles' heel," Brother Mark added. "They have their elite cadres and the Grogs, but they've had problems with mutinous formations unless they're carefully controlled and properly motivated. Church archives are full of it. In more ways than one."

Jolla turned a clipboard, showed them two pages of taped-together flimsies. "Southern Command has confirmed your promotion to colonel, Bloom. Congratulations. We should have a toast. Carillo, won't you bring in some glasses?"

"How about a rain check, sir," Bloom said. "Let's get the men moving before they have too much time to think about how far they are from home and family."

Jolla ignored her. "GHQ also promoted Colonel Seng to general in recognition of his achievement."

Carillo slipped in with a bottle of real black-labeled Jim Beam and a stack of thumb-high leaded glass vessels.

"Seng arranged for six barrels of very good bourbon for the men. The connection from the distillery gave us a few cases as a bonus. Came with a card, signed 'a patriot.' I wonder if he's sweating whether he left fingerprints on it. Pour everyone a neat, would you, Carillo?"

The meeting was taking on a dreamlike quality. Valentine knew the bourbon was real enough; one of his platoons had met the distillery smugglers.

"Gratifying as gratis liquor is," Brother Mark said, "shouldn't you be writing orders by now?"

"Keep out of solemn military traditions, Brother," Jolla said. "I'm still waiting to hear what the Green Mountain Boys intend to do."

"They intend to leave unless we *do* something," Valentine said tightly.

"I've made up my mind about that. First, the toast."

Valentine accepted his glass and pushed his hair back with his left while he tipped most of the liquor out with right, feeling a little like a cheap stage musician. He covered the glass with his fingers.

Jolla stood. "First, to the memory of General Seng. May his example inspire future generations of officers."

*It's sure not inspiring the present generation*, Valentine thought. *Seng wouldn't want us drinking to his memory. If he were still running the brigade, we'd be arguing with the Green Mountain Boys over whose rope would be used to hang the ringleaders of the ambush in town.*

"Now, I've come to a decision. After consulting with Southern Command and a careful assessment, I've decided our position here in West Virginia is untenable. Remaining here would seem to assure our destruction."

That got their interest. The shifting and note taking ceased from everyone but Jolla's military secretary.

"We were misinformed—note that I say misinformed, not misled,

Brother Mark—as to the support we would receive from the local populace. We've found plans drawn up against us. The enemy executed a masterful ruse and struck just as we were busy congratulating ourselves on our own cleverness."

The word "masterful" poked at Valentine. He'd just heard it—where? He needed to think.

Jolla didn't give him time. "My one hope now is that the Kurians will allow us to leave quietly. God knows, the Kurians prefer carefully controlled bloodshed. They don't like battles any more than we do."

"Sir," Bloom protested.

Jolla held up his hand.

"I've made up my mind. Now there's just a matter of choosing a route and an order of march. We'll need a strong fore guard and an even more capable rear guard if this operation is to succeed."

"There's no doubt that the guerrillas exist," Brother Mark said. "I've seen the reports of the damage they've done. For all we know, they're trying to reach us at this moment."

Jolla frowned. "In view of the situation we find ourselves in, perhaps you should leave retrieving the situation to the professionals. I'm sure we'll need your diplomatic expertise on the way home. Perhaps you could turn your thoughts to that."

Brother Mark returned to his chair and put his head down. Valentine saw his lips moving.

Valentine wondered at Jolla's manner. Did men in the midst of some kind of mental breakdown acquire a new vocabulary? The cadence and pronunciation were right, but the words seemed unusually fussy and chosen, as though they'd been preprinted. But the personality, the attitude, was Jolla! Gage would probably have slapped Brother Mark down hard. Seng would have turned a frowning fish stare on him until he withdrew his objection and apologized for intruding onto military matters. Jolla was the same polite, go-along-and-get-along self.

Valentine heard two flies turning pirouettes over a tub that held some dirty plates and utensils from the headquarters breakfast. An opportunistic spider was already at work on a web.

*How far do your strands extend, Kurian?*

"Now, Colonel Bloom will assume command of the regulars and be second in command in the event something happens to me. Valentine, I need a new chief of staff. Can your lieutenant take over your company?"

Valentine turned cold. He could just see the headlines in the *Clarion. Scraping the Barrel Bottom: Disgraced, Condemned Officer Organized Humiliating Retreat in Appalachian Disaster*.

"Rand's a good man, sir. As to me being the new chief . . . perhaps someone already from the headquarters would do better."

Jolla fingered the buttons of his field jacket. "In an hour like this, you're—you're saying no?"

"May we speak for a moment privately, sir?"

Jolla nodded. They both angled for a corner of the tent and spoke with their backs to the rest of the assembly. Valentine heard whispering behind.

"Sir, I don't have anything like the training. I've done my share of reading, but I haven't led military forces since Archangel. I'm a lieutenant who found himself with a major's cluster. Until Seng gave me his texts, most of the training and experience I had above the platoon level was leading Quisling formations, after a manner."

"You never struck me as the kind to crayfish when responsibility comes your way, Major. Of course, if you really believe you're not up to the job, I'll select someone else. If I didn't think you were the best man for the job, I wouldn't have selected you."

"Thank you for your confidence, sir. But . . ." Valentine grasped for the right words but they got lost somewhere between his brain and his larynx.

"I'll add a 'but' of my own. But, well, I need you right now, Valentine. The men like me well enough, but we need another Seng, God rest him, and I don't think liking me's enough. They need to believe in something. I've never been all faith and vision like Karas, or brilliant like Seng."

"Quiet plodders have won their share of wars, sir," Valentine offered.

"This war's over before it even got going. Turns out the Kurians have been one step ahead of us the whole time. The troops need to believe we'll get them out of this.

"Chief of staff isn't easy, I know," Jolla continued. "You'll be running your legs off. I've been in the service about as long as you've been alive, Valentine. I've watched the men when you're around. They look at you and then they talk. You wouldn't believe some of the stories floating around about you. They bring ideas and complaints to you. There aren't many in Southern Command—at least good ones—who can boast of that. Then there's that business with your nose, that tingle. Even if it's just luck, well, luck counts for something in life. Thirty years service proved that to me too."

Valentine's throat tightened. "Very well, sir. Then, as chief of staff, I'd like to propose taking one good crack at these Moondaggers before we leave."

"No. I'm certain we're outnumbered. Even a win could doom us. I want to keep the brigade intact. Let's save their lives for future use."

"As chief of staff, I'd like permission to coordinate our departure with the Green Mountain command and the legworm riders."

"Granted. Hope you don't mind working from Nowak's cubby. Now, let's get back to the meeting."

Valentine tried to pay attention to the rest—the empty congratulations for himself and Bloom, the anxious silence from Brother Mark, who stared and stared and stared at Jolla as if he were studying some strange species of animal.

But all he could think about was how Jolla could be so certain that they were outnumbered.

†

Valentine broke the news quickly to Rand. Rand suggested some kind of farewell dinner was in order; Valentine left the details to him.

"Don't think I'm not going to keep riding your backs," he told the NCOs who gathered as the news spread.

"Congratulations," Patel said.

"More like condolences," Glass said. "He's been given command of the *Titanic* ten minutes after the iceberg."

"I don't want any of you to worry," Valentine said, hopping up into the bed of one of the company supply wagons. "Javelin's not about to surrender to the Kurians or anyone else. We're going back under our own terms, and God help anyone who gets in our way."

They cheered that. Spin, they used to call it. The idea of fighting their way back appealed a lot more than being chased out of the Appalachians with their tails between their legs.

Valentine waved Patel over.

"If you want a little garnish around your star," Valentine said, "I can appoint a new command sergeant major for the brigade. You'd be at the top of my list. Less hiking and more riding."

Patel smiled but shook his head. "Douglas is doing a good job, filling in for poor Reygarth. In any case, I am stuck shepherding a promising but raw lieutenant again."

"I'm sorry I got you into this, Nilay."

"You did not get me into anything. I had little to do at home but read the newspapers and remember. It is good to be out of the rocking chair and in country. This is my life; that was just waiting. You know, my knees have not felt so good in years."

"You're a hell of a wrestler, Patel, but you can't lie for crap. You always blink when you're lying."

"You could have told me this, sir, before I lost six months' pay in poker games back in LeHavre's company."

"Here's my last company command: You ride on the company legworm. That's an order. Hear that, Rand?"

"Yes, Major," Rand said.

"Rand's my witness."

He slept for an hour, and then summoned Brother Mark. "I think we need to pay a call on the Kentucky Alliance. It would be safer for us if we left as a group, or at least traveled parallel paths so we could support each other in case the Kurians have a follow-up trick. Not much we can do for the Green Mountain Boys, but Southern Command and the Kentucky Alliance can stick together."

"Your caution does you credit, but are you sure we can't change the colonel's mind? He strikes me as a man suffering from a shock. In a day or two he may be amenable."

Valentine shook his head. "I have my orders to follow. We're turning around and heading back. I've got to figure out how best to put that into effect."

"Seems to me the great flaw in your formidable, pyramidal military machine is that it depends too much on the trained monkey working the controls."

"As a civilian, you're allowed to express that opinion."

"Tell me what you think, Valentine. That's one of the reasons that I headed south when I left the Church. Your Southern Command sounded more like a band of brothers united by common cause."

"Colonel Jolla's orders will be followed, and that's that. Southern Command's got a bunch of handy, rarely used regulations just in case you try to interfere with his command. Most of them involve a noose."

"Don't you have a noose around your neck too, Major?"

"Just get yourself ready to visit the Alliance again."

†

At the Alliance camp, they found a rather more informal debate proceeding in a sort of corral formed by tied-down legworms. Riders sat on their animals, or hung off the sides, or gathered in little lounging groups in the center of the circle, each clustering close to their own clan.

"He told us all we had to do was go home! Matches my wants, so what are we waiting for?" a Wildcat asked.

"He also told us to throw down our long guns, Geckie," a man in a sagging, shapeless cloth hat yelled back. "I don't trust a man who makes me being unarmed part of the deal."

223

"You calling me a coward?" the one called Geckie yelled back over the heads.

"No, but it's mighty interesting that that's the first word that popped into your head, isn't it?"

"I don't care if you're head rider or dispatcher. You're challenged to a duel at your convenience, Gunslinger." Cheers and claps and whistles broke out, along with a few boos.

"Right now's pretty convenient to me. Fists until one man goes down."

"So much for the alliance," Brother Mark said.

"That Last Chance fellow said we could go. Who needs Virginia anyway?" a rider from the Wildcats shouted to general approval.

"West Virginia," someone corrected.

"You lousy bunch of cowards," Tikka told the Bulletproof and anyone else listening. She stepped into the center of a hostile circle. "You call yourselves men—more than that, Bulletproof men? I've never heard of such a bunch of sunshine strikers. Sure, when it looks easy you all want a piece of the fight. But when the fight comes to you, it's hook up and run. You wormcast. No, not even wormcast. The wildflowers grow prettier on wormcast. You're more like slag from one of the mines around here: dull, cold, and useful as dry dirt."

"You're the Bulletproof and the Bulletproof is you," a grizzled rider with the Coonskins responded.

"Not anymore," the new leader of the Mammoths said. "We're still the Alliance. We've had enough of their edicts and requisitions and demands. We've thrown in with the Cause and we'll finish with it or be finished."

✝

In the end, they split into three parts.

The Green Mountain Boys headed north, hard and fast in a sprint toward friendly territory, leaving their heavy gear and a good deal of their supply train behind.

The Kentucky Alliance was the first to visit the abandoned camp and cleaned it out of the choicest gear like the first family back to the house of a deceased relative after the funeral.

The Perseids gave up outright. Bereft of Karas, they groped like lost children for a solution. Valentine watched them march and ride toward Utrecht and hoped the Kurians meant their promise not to harm any who gave up, for their sake.

The rest of the Kentucky Alliance turned for home in four separate columns. Valentine rode his Morgan hard from column to column, with Bee loping behind, and assured them that Southern Command's forces would come to the aid of any who were attacked, but the leadership looked doubtful.

And so the bright and shining dream of a new Freehold left for Kentucky. Though a bristling rear guard scouted for Moondagger troops who had yet to appear, Valentine couldn't help feeling they were abandoning the Virginias with their tails tucked between their legs, running from shadows.

# CHAPTER TEN

*Withdrawal: Directing a successful retreat can be as difficult as an advance.*

*Eastern Kentucky offers some advantages to Javelin and its legworm-riding allies. Mountain passes could be easily held against greater numbers—though this could be worked to their disadvantage as well, if the Moondaggers could slip around behind them. The mountains also serve as screens, and the clouds frequently trapped by the peaks hide them from aerial observation.*

*As Napoleon learned on his way back from Moscow, the most problematic of all is the threat a retreat poses to morale. A beaten army, like an often-whipped horse, lacks the dash and spirit needed to fight a successful battle. Any setback or check threatens a collapse of discipline and a rout. Understandably, the soldiers become shy of risk.*

*Worse, they come to see every mile of land as an enemy between them and their goal. Food, clothing, and shelter can be obtained at rifle point from the locals. Friction, any mechanic can tell you, is an enemy to speed and smooth function.*

*Worst of all, they might see the slower-moving elements as hindrances to the all-important goal of getting home. A retreating army will dissolve like sugar spread in the rain, lost to desertion and despair.*

†

Valentine's earliest woe as chief of staff was handling the Kentucky Alliance. He couldn't order, he could only suggest. He had to ask for riders to watch their flanks, to take their mounts up mountains, to go

226

ahead and seize passes and rickety old railroad bridges the vehicles could bump across.

At meetings with the company commanders, he forced himself to bluster and threaten regarding treatment of the locals, up to and including hangings for crimes of violence. If the collection of captains and lieutenants thought him a tyrant, drunk on newfound power, so much the better. He'd be the bad guy, the glowering, uncompromising stickler for regs, if it would keep the soldiers from doing anything to turn the populace against his side.

And he made it clear that responsibility would flow uphill for once.

†

They found a sample of Moondagger mercy the third morning out, planted right along the road they were using to retreat out of West Virginia.

They came to a clearing of freshly cut trees, with bits and pieces of broken guns smashed over the stumps. A black and gray mound with a charnel-house reek sat in a circle of heat-hardened ground.

Tikka, riding with a few Bulletproof at the head of the column, identified the bodies as belonging to the Mammoth clan, God knew how. The unarmed men had been thrown into wooden cages and burned. From the burned heads and arms forcing their way between the charred bars, Valentine guessed they'd still been alive when the fires had been set.

Looking at the clenched teeth behind burned away lips, Valentine would have rather gone to the Reapers.

Valentine put his old company to work clearing the bodies and burying them in the loose soil of the grown-over slag heap of a mine in a mountain's pocket just off the road.

"Sorry, men," he said, a handkerchief tied around his face to keep him from breathing ash that might be wood, clothing, or human flesh. "The brigade can't march through this."

Brother Mark rode up on muleback to have a look and say a few words over the departed. "This is their method, men," he told the parties at work moving the bodies. "They talk you into giving up your guns, and without your gun what's to stop them from taking whatever they want? Resistance is a guarantee of dignity and an honorable death."

"Come down here and help pick up these charcoal briquettes that used to be hands and feet," a man said to his coworker. "We can have a nice little talk about dignity."

"Enough of that, there," Patel barked.

Company scouts caught up with a disheveled trio, hobbling bootless up the road toward Kentucky. Glass sent Ford galumphing back to request Valentine's help with them.

They made a pathetic sight. One's eyes were bandaged, as were one's ears, and the third had dried blood caked on his chin.

"We are the blind, deaf, and dumb," the blinded man said. Valentine saw a light band on his finger where a wedding band had been. The Moondaggers certainly weren't above a little theft. "Testament to ... er—"

The tongueless man tugged on the blinded one's sleeve and said, "Ebbatren ob ah'oolisheh."

"Yes, testament to the foolishness of those who deny the evidence of their senses as to the supremacy of the Ever-living Gods. The Moondaggers did this for the good of others we might meet."

"You were with the Mammoth?" Valentine asked.

The tongueless man gave a groan, and took the deaf man's hand and squeezed it.

"There are only two kinds of people," the deaf man said loudly. "The graced and the fallen. We are warning to the fallen."

"Cutting them up's not enough," Glass said to a Wolf scout. "Had to take their shoes too. Cruel I understand, but that's just mean."

*The Moondaggers probably wanted to make sure we caught up to them*, Valentine thought, just as the Wolf voiced the same sentiment.

"Webb ub uss," the tongueless man said.

"Let us pass," the blinded one said. "We've said our words. Let us pass."

"First tell me what happened," Valentine said.

"Did you not see?" the blind man asked, his voice cracking.

Ediyak wrote something on a sheet of paper and handed it to the deaf man. He read it and looked at Valentine.

"We surrendered. We followed every instruction. They made us cut down trees and smash our guns on the stumps. Then they bound us in a line, and that's when they started working on the cages," the deaf man said, loudly and a little off key. "They laughed as the fires started. I can still hear the laughter."

"Why did they pick you three?" Valentine added on to the end of Ediyak's note.

The deaf man took it and read. "We were chosen because we all knew the Kurian catechism."

"What's that?" Tikka asked. "I never had much to do with the Church."

Brother Mark cleared his throat.

"Who are they?

      The wise old gods of our childhood.

"Where are they from?

      Kur, the Interworld Tree's branch of Wisdom.

"When did they come?

      In our darkest hour.

"Why did they come?

      To guide mankind.

"How may we thank them?

      With diligent obedience."

Brother Mark had tears in his eyes when he was done. He turned away.

"Your church gives orders for this kind of thing?" Tikka asked.

"Former church, daughter. Former. This most terrible sect of a misguided faith isn't spoken of much in the marble halls," he said. "But I fear they find them useful at times."

"Tikka, can you spare a rider to get these men home?" Valentine asked.

"I'll have to check with the veep," she said. "But the Mammoth have been friendly to us most of the time."

One more body turned up. A young woman from the Mammoth, stripped of her leathers and wearing a plain smock, dead from what was probably a self-inflicted wound to the abdomen. She'd gutted herself with one of the curved knives of the Moondaggers.

"Whoever lost his knife didn't want it back," someone observed.

Valentine wanted another talk with the Last Chance. Might be fun to chain one end of him to his flatbed and use his crane to yank pieces of him off.

"Try not to let it get to you, men," he said as the company reformed after disposing of the bodies. He sent word to headquarters that the brigade could move up the road again. "They did this to put a scare into you."

"Hope we get a chance to get scary on them," DuSable said, wiping ash from his forearms with a wet rag.

"Amen, Sab," Rutherford added.

"Remember the Cause," Valentine said. "We're the good guys. You're better than that."

DuSable straightened a little.

*You're better than that, Sab*, Valentine thought. He wondered how long he could keep the angry monster inside bottled up and channeled into duty.

†

Brother Mark, with the lower ranks dismissed from the officers' meeting, sat down wearily.

"I tried three different clans. They're terrified of helping us. Won't even take guns. The Kurians are promising destruction to anyone who gives us so much as a rotten egg."

"It's the reputation of the Moondaggers," Moytana said.

"Maybe we can tarnish it," Valentine said.

"The clans can get away with not resisting us. Claim they don't have guns and so forth," Brother Mark said. "But trade? Never. The

Moondaggers are promising to obliterate right down to the infants any clan who helps us. All legworm stock is to go to whichever clan reveals their 'treachery.' They're filling wells with dead dogs and cats as we approach."

"A little boiling will take care of that," a Guard captain said. "It's food I'm worried about. I believe we've got rations for the rest of the week. Then we're eating grass like the horses."

"Two weeks on short. That's not enough to get us home. At least not intact," Bloom said. She sounded beaten.

"So that's it, then," Valentine said. "We can't go on. Not without food."

Brother Mark shook his head. "That's what they count on, my son. Despair. A victory comes so much easier when you are the one defeating yourself."

"An army marches on its stomach," Moytana said. "What do you propose to fill my men's bellies with?"

"They must march on hope."

"That's not much butter to put on a long slice of bread," Moytana observed.

†

The next day they woke to harassing gunfire from far-off batteries of the Moondaggers. The shots weren't being observed; they were falling wide by a half mile or more and not being corrected. But it unnerved the men, made them jumpy and scattered the way a coming thunderstorm puts rabbits underground.

Valentine gave orders to put a reserve on alert and hurried to the headquarters to find a medical truck parked there and his staff silent and nervous. Even Red Dog panted and crisscrossed from man to man, seeking reassurance.

"Colonel Jolla's dead, sir," the staff agronomist reported.

"Who can tell me what happened?"

"It's like this, sir," Tiddle, the headquarters courier, said. "I had the communications duty. Colonel Jolla came up to the rig and looked at the latest communications. Everyone was talking about the worm riders quitting on us.

"Well, sir, he didn't say much. Just stared—didn't seem to be reading the communiqués at all. Colonel Bloom arrived with a report about some civilian bodies we found. She was just telling him that they were trying to bring us food. Oh, Colonel Jolla wasn't really paying attention to what she was saying. He just sort of nodded. Looked like his mind was elsewhere, like he was having a phone conversation or something."

Tiddle looked miserable, the White Rabbit stilled for once. Valentine saw a bagged bundle resting in the back of the truck.

"Well, then we heard some artillery fire in the distance, the usual calling cards from the Moondaggers to let us know they're back there, and Colonel Jolla just sort of went white. He reached for his service pistol and started to bring it up to his head. Bloom grabbed for it and they started wrestling. She said, 'For God's sake, help me,' and then we heard the shot. We were moving toward Colonel Jolla but he was too fast for us. He put the barrel in his mouth and pulled the trigger. Awful mess, sir—" Tiddle pointed at the front fender of the jeep, and Valentine saw caked blood in the crevices.

"How's Colonel Bloom?" Valentine asked, calming Red Dog and himself by flapping the dog's ears.

"Shaken up. She's in command now."

Valentine sought out Bloom. The usually quick and decisive Bloom seemed suddenly doubtful, but it might be the flecks of blood still on her cuff and shoulder. Red Dog approached her cautiously, sniffing.

"We could try taking a crack at the Moondaggers, sir," Valentine suggested. "We might get the confidence of the worm clans back if we prove ourselves against them."

For a moment her eyes flared.

"Hmmmm. I don't know, Valentine. Southern Command doesn't want another Kansas on their hands, you know. I'm under orders to keep the brigade intact."

They'd continue the retreat.

†

Two days later Brother Mark returned from the Kentucky Alliance camp.

"They're quitting on us," he said. "That Last Chance arranged a secret meeting with some of their leadership. Wildcats are packing up. Some of the Gunslingers are leaving, going to start a new clan. Even the Bulletproof and Mammoth are hedging their bets, sending some riders back to reinforce their main camp. All we have left are the attenuated what's left of those two and the Coonskins."

He reached into his battered courier bag, brought up a black-labeled bottle. "They gave me a farewell gift. Were it were hemlock."

"You've done your best," Valentine said, waving the others off. He sat Brother Mark down in the chair farthest from the communications desk, and the rest of the headquarters officers gave them a wide berth. Being the CO's chief of staff offered a few privileges.

Brother Mark looked thoughtful, took a pull at the bourbon.

"They always start you off easy. After I took my first vows, they put me in a little schoolhouse, helping the Youth Vanguard with their reading, writing, and 'rithmetic. Cozy. And they had a full priest there for all the tough questions. If someone asked where their grandfather went, all I'd have to say is 'Let's go talk to our guide.' Then sit quietly while the full priest talked about sacrifice for the greater good.

"Then they moved me to the hospital. I'd just taken my second set of vows. Passed all my examinations with flying colors, by the way. Dead-even emotional resonance when presented with disturbing imagery."

Valentine didn't know what that was but didn't want to change the old churchman's loquacious mood. He'd only seen the church from the outside.

"Did hospital service change your opinions?"

"No, it took me a long time to wake up. Nightmares shouldn't be allowed to pose as dreams."

"I ran into one of those about a year ago," Valentine said. He still felt conflicted about the course he'd chosen in the Cascades. Valentine was not a believer in the revolutionary's morality, where the result justified the means. Could he have come up with a better way to get rid of Adler's bloody direction of Pacific Command?

Brother Mark broke in on his thoughts. "Again, they made it so easy. At the hospital I had a nice little office, and each patient went through a rubric while their medical needs were being evaluated. Took into account age, physical condition, skill set, community activism, and responsibility . . . and of course how involved the treatment might be and prognosis for recovery to full useful life. Above a certain score and they were treated. Below a certain score and they found themselves on the drop list."

He whispered the last two words, as though they were something shameful.

"Drop list," he continued. "Sounds innocuous, right? It meant they crossed over into the hands of the Reapers, of course. In a lot of cases the really sick people stayed at home or had quacks treat them, so we always talked to the school-agers about reporting any adults they knew who were sick. Spread of contagion and so on.

"There were scores in between the drop list and treatment. In those cases I consulted higher authority. I'd call the local senior guide and we'd talk it over. Sometimes I'd visit them. Later I found out my guide would phone the family and ask them to come into his office for a consultation. He'd tell their families that serious decisions had to be made about a loved one, and by the way, the residential hall is practically falling apart on the east side and everyone knows clergy aren't paid salaries . . .

"After a year there my senior guide started having me make decisions myself and then explaining them to him. I must have been good at it. He only overruled me once, in the case of a nephew of a brass ring who had cerebral palsy. They'd found some sinecure for him, and I suspect old Rusty had a big bag of money drop between his ankles under the table. With practice it got easier. I was able to tell myself it was for the good of the species. All the usual *Guidon* false analogies and circular arguments when it's not engaging in outright devil's advocacy. You wouldn't believe—or maybe you would. But I was destined for greater things."

"So when did you start to question your *Guidon*?"

"It might have been the time I went to the basement. There was an incinerator down there for medical waste and so on, and I was responsible for destroying certain records. Lost records are the bureaucrat's best friend when trouble pays a call, Valentine, and don't you forget it if you ever rise to a desk.

"Now usually I just dumped the files down the chute, but it was after normal office hours and for some reason I thought the incinerator might not be burning since we were on a winter fuel savings drive. I went down to check. The basement had its own cargo lift, otherwise you had to take the stairs, and there were two doors out of the lift. The first set, by the buttons, went to the incinerator. I'd always heard that only people who were dropped went out the back doors.

"I took the lift down to the basement because they were painting in the stairs and the fumes bothered me—we'd hit the natal goal for the year, and the doctors and nurses from the delivery ward were having all their faces painted on the landings—and I heard a sound from the other side of the back door as my exit opened. It was like . . . like a sander, a belt sander or one of those ones with the little round pads. I heard screaming."

"We'd always been told, you see, that everything was done to make death painless and worry-free, right down to the use of drugs to relax the person designated for recycling. I still hear that whirring noise and the screams, right to this day, like someone made a tape of it.

"I went to the incinerator and burned the old records and took the stairs back up. Though it almost choked me."

Valentine asked Ediyak to see if she could scare up some food, worried what the ten fingers of bourbon consumption would do to Brother Mark's nerve-worn system.

"You're a good boy, Valentine."

"Where did they send you after the hospital?"

"Education in Washington, DC, seat of the New Universal Church. The Vatican, Medina, Jerusalem, and the River Ganges all wrapped up around one green mall. Ever seen it? No, I suppose you haven't."

"No."

"Well, all the Church upper education schools and monuments are there. 'For the service of mankind,' they all say. Yes, each and every one of them. Sometimes in letters six feet high in marble.

"My six years there reaffirmed my faith in mankind's future. I took lots of classes on old wars, intolerance, racism, studied how mankind had been in a downward spiral and that the so-called Age of Reason led to anything but. I could recite the four controls *Homo sapiens* needed and wrote long essays on the correctly actualized person.

"Oh, and I had my great moment of fame, when I acted in an atrocity film. I got to play both a local priest bemoaning the slaughter of an entire town and a colonel who admitted giving orders to your terror operatives to poison water supplies feeding hospitals and schools. Different films, of course."

"Of course."

"I wondered if anyone would recognize me. Of course I had a full beard and an eyepatch when I was playing the captured colonel.

"They assured me my script was based on actual documentation. The problem was the colonel's testimony sounded quite similar to a film I'd seen three times as a Youth Vanguard. They always began and ended with an 'authenticated documentation' seal and statement. Of course, my films bore one too. I had to wonder. Since we were filming fake documentaries allegedly based on real documentation, I naturally began to have doubts about the veracity of the real documentation. Had it been based on the documentation in that film I saw sixteen years before? I wondered whether my transcribed testimony based on the real documentation might serve as further documentation for another film. Do you follow?"

"You lost me two documentations ago."

"Sorry." He took another drink.

Ediyak arrived with some flatbread sandwiches and a shredded-meat stew that didn't commend itself to close analysis.

†

They camped the next night with Valentine's usual caution, flanked by the legworm clan encampments, Coonskins to the south and the rest of the Alliance to the north, in a hummock between two higher hills. The hills sloped off to the west like unevenly cooked soufflés, and were situated above a good supply of firewood and water in an old crossroads town. His scavengers dug up a supply of wire in town. Old copper wire had any number of uses in a military camp, mostly in quick repairs. The only interesting feature was an almost paintless church with a steeple that served as a cramped observation post. Otherwise it was no different than any of their other half-dozen camps in the hills of central Kentucky.

Distant gunfire, a sound like sheets slowly torn under a comforter, woke him. He had his boots on by the time the camp siren went off.

The sound brought moisture to his palms and dried his mouth.

Only two events warranted that alarming wail: Reapers in the camp or a surprise attack.

The wail brought the camp together like drizzle turning into pools on a waterproof tarp. Individual drops of soldiers sought their nearest comrades and corporals with the same molecular cohesion of water. The fire teams called to the nearest sergeant or officer as captains passed word and gave orders.

Valentine needed to travel only forty feet or so to headquarters, Bee appearing like a genie summoned by the siren. He forced himself to go at a brisk walk, buckling on his combat harness. The first flares burst to the south as he did so, turning the twigs and leaves of the young trees on the slope into a lattice.

Bloom, who slept just off the headquarters tent, barked orders to a succession of couriers and confused junior officers.

"Legworms coming through the pickets to the south. They'll be on top of us in a few minutes," she said.

"Already over the south ridge," a corporal at a radio receiver reported.

"I'll take a look," Valentine said. He spotted Tiddle, the lieutenant with the motorbike.

"Your bike gassed up?"

"Yes, sir, always."

"Get to the Alliance. Tell them the Coonskins have turned on us. They're not, repeat, not to come into the camp. They'll get shot at."

"What about some kind of marking, so we can tell the difference?" Rand asked. He'd been hovering, waiting for orders for his company.

Valentine gritted his teeth. He should have thought of that.

"Good thinking, Rand," Valentine said. "Have them drape a couple of sheets over the side of their legworms, anything we can make out in bad light," Valentine told Tiddle.

"How do you know the others haven't turned too?" a Guard lieutenant asked. He looked like he should be leading a high school football team rather than a company. "You've got a direct line to the Bulletproof?" he asked.

"He's got a line on that Alliance girl," Bloom said. "I'd reel her in, if I was you."

A few chuckles lightened the mood.

"Save it for the mess hall. There's no shooting to the north, is there?" Valentine said.

Tiddle ignored the byplay and Valentine heard the blat of the motorbike starting up.

"I'm heading for the OP," Bloom said, slipping a pack of playing cards into the webbing on her helmet. According to mess hall gossip, her father, a soldier himself, had given her the pack to aid passing the time, but she'd never broken the box's seal. Her eyes looked luminous in the shadow of the brim.

He barked at the communications team to set up a backup for communicating with the camp observation post, and then turned to Gamecock.

"Form your Bears into two-man hunter-killer groups. Give them explosives—a couple of sticks of dynamite will do. Have them keep to cover until a legworm comes near. Try to get the bang under the things. They're sensitive there."

"I've heard that. The middle, right?"

"The nerve ganglia's there. But if they can't get near enough to be precise, just under the thing will do. They'll reverse themselves."

Valentine braced the camp for impact. He relocated headquarters to the old graveyard behind the church, where there was a good wall and tree cover.

Artillery shells began to fall, hitting the motor and camp stores and the camp's former headquarters with deadly accuracy.

Of course the Coonskins wouldn't turn on their own—they'd coordinated it with the Moondaggers. Someone in the Coonskins had given the Moondagger spotters a nice little map of camp. Valentine wondered how the brand rank and file felt about the switch in allegiance. Sure, the leadership might decide to bet on the winning team, but what threats would have to be used on the men to turn their guns against erstwhile comrades?

Valentine climbed to the church steeple, so narrow it used a ladder instead of stairs. Bats had taken up residence in the bottom half, hawks higher up.

He felt a little like the proverbial candlestick maker trying to wedge into a shower stall with the butcher and baker. Bloom and her communications tech had a tight enough squeeze in the tiny cupola.

"Valentine, if a shell hits here now, it'll be a triple grave."

"Had to take a quick glimpse," Valentine said.

Bloom slapped him hard on the shoulder. "Moondagger troops are advancing behind the legworm screen."

Valentine watched the lines of crisscrossing legworms. The Kentuckians fought their worms differently than the Grogs of Missouri, who hurried to close from behind shields. He'd seen a Kentucky legworm battle before. The riflemen and gunners hooked themselves to one side of their worms and protected the beasts with old mattresses and sacks full of chopped-up tires on the other. Legworms were notoriously resistant to bullets, but machine-gun fire had been known to travel right through a worm and hit the man on the other side.

A new wrinkle had been added this time—classical siege warfare. The legworms zigzagged forward, acting like the old gabions and fascines that sheltered approaching troops and guns. Valentine could see companies of Moondaggers behind the worms, following the mobile walls as they moved down the night-blue slope toward the camp.

Muzzle flashes sparked on the worms' backs. The legworm riders were shooting, sure enough, but the fire wasn't what Valentine would call intense. More like casual target practice.

"Put some air-fused shells on the other side of those worms," Bloom said. "Slow those troops."

"South line wants permission to fire," the communications tech said.

"No," Valentine said. "Hold fire. Hold fire. Wait for the Moondaggers, sir. There's no artillery on our defensive line, sir. If the riders have spotted it, they're not telling the Moondaggers," Valentine said. "I think a lot of those riders are just play-shooting."

"If that's how you want to play it," Bloom said. "Don't fire till we see the whites of their eyes, eh?"

"They're almost on top of the Bear teams," the communications tech reported.

"And here comes the Alliance," Valentine said, looking north. The Bulletproof worms looked like fingers wearing thick green rings thanks to the tenting banding them.

"Pass the word not to shoot at legworms with the bands. They're Alliance," Bloom said. The communications officer complied.

"Go to the south wall, there, Valentine. Get a hit on 'em," Bloom said.

"Yes, sir."

"Where are those mortars?" Bloom barked.

Valentine hurried back down the patched-up ladder. He went forward, Bee gamboling like an excited dog. He checked his gun and magazines.

Mortar shells whistled overhead. Valentine hurried toward the flashes.

Bee looked at a sentry and Valentine identified himself to the nervous chain of command to the forward posts. Rifle fire crackled overhead.

"They're on top of us. Are we pulling back, or what?" an understandably nervous captain asked.

"The legworms are just cover for the Moondaggers," Valentine said. "They're making the real assault. Don't let your positions show themselves until you can do some real damage."

Gunfire erupted off to the right. Someone wasn't listening to orders or had been knocked out of the communications loop.

Valentine crept up to a stream cut that sheltered the captain's headquarters and took a look at the southern line. The men were sheltered behind low mounds of old legworm trails, patterns crisscrossing as though braided by a drunk, creating little gaps like very shallow foxholes. Atop hummocks of fertilized soil, brush grew like an irregular hedge. The other side had a good view of gently sloped pasture ground and the oncoming parallels of legworms.

A yellow explosion flared under one of the legworms. Gamecock's Bears struck.

Valentine looked to the east. The Alliance seemed to inch forward across the hillside, turning yellow in the rising light of the dawn, still kilometers away but coming hard. This was about to get messy.

Valentine heard another *bang!* of dynamite going off. A legworm, cut in two, hunched off in opposite directions.

"This is it. They're coming!" the captain said.

The lines of Coonskin legworms parted, crackling rifle fire still popping away atop the mounts, but the bullets were flying off toward the church and camp, not at the line of men pressed flat behind the bushy legworm trail.

Valentine took in the loose wall of men coming forward, more tightly packed than Southern Command would ever group an assault. Were they being herded forward? Valentine's night-sharp eyes made out a few anguished faces.

The Coonskin legworms angled off to the sides, retreating. The Moondaggers were revealed.

"Let 'em have it, Captain," Valentine said. "This is it."

"Open fire. Open fire!" the captain called. "Defensive grenades."

Gunfire broke out all along the line, sounding like a sudden heavy rain striking a tin roof. Screams sounded from the ranks of the Moondagger assaulting column.

Valentine saw a field pack radio antenna, an officer crouching next to it on the slope.

"Bee," Valentine said, pointing. "That one."

Bee swung her hockey stick of a rifle around and dropped him. Good shooting, that. Uphill fire took a good eye.

Rand reported in. Bloom had sent Valentine's old company up to support the line with Glass' machine guns.

Valentine issued orders for them to create a fallback line at the stream cut as though on autopilot. His mind was on the assault. The first lines fell under withering fire, hardly shooting back, and a second wave, better dispersed and disciplined, came forward.

Grenades exploded, deeper thuds that transmitted faintly through the ground.

The Moondaggers broke through and it was rifle butts and pistols along the line. Valentine realized he'd put his gun to his shoulder without thinking about it and fired burst after burst into the second wave, knocking them back like target cans. He ducked and slid along the stream cut as he reloaded.

Bee grunted and the hair atop her head parted. Valentine saw white skull. She ignored it and kept shooting.

"Medic," Valentine called.

Bear teams at the assault's flanks, like tiny tornadoes at the sidelines, bit off pieces of the Moondaggers that Valentine's line chewed up.

The Moondaggers fell back, tripping over their own dead as they backed away, shooting and reloading.

"Keep the heat on!" the captain called.

"Send back to Bloom: Repulsed. For now," Valentine ordered.

A medic was wrapping up Bee's head. He gave Valentine a thumbs-up. "Good thing this old girl doesn't set much store by hairstyle. She's gonna have a funny part."

"You all right, Bee?" Valentine asked.

In response she handed him four shell casings. Her tally, evidently. The ever-observant Bee was picking up habits from Duvalier.

Valentine sent Rand's company forward to fill the gaps in the line, just in case. He went up, keeping at a crouch behind the brush as he moved along the line. Snipers were trading shots across the battlefield as what was left of the Moondaggers' second and third waves retreated back across the south hill.

"We killed enough of 'em," a soldier said, looking at the carpet of dead from the first wave; the second wave wounded were still being hunted up from the brush.

"Yes," Valentine said. "Old men. Kids. Women even. The Moondaggers put some cannon fodder up front, and when the gamble didn't pay they kept the rest of their chips back. Those two don't even have guns. They gave them baseball bats with a railroad spike through the top."

"Those shits," a Southern Command soldier said. Another picked up one of the bats and examined it.

"Let's get a couple of their chips. To the ridgeline, men. Send back to Bloom: Have her put everything she's got on the other side of that ridge—that's where their real strength is."

Valentine felt a Reaper up on the ridgeline. It was probably assigning blame for the failure even now.

New gunfire erupted in the distance to the east as the Moondaggers and Coonskins attacked. The lines of legworms looked like fighting snakes, spread out on the hillside.

He sent word back to Bloom, asking for permission to attack. She gave it, enthusiastically. It was good to have Cleo Bloom in charge. She'd recovered some of her old spirit.

"We've busted up their face. Let's kick 'em in the ass," a sergeant called as the orders passed to advance.

Southern Command's soldiers went forward with their yips and barks like foxhounds on a hot scent. Gamecock saw what was happening and sent his Bears forward, flushing the snipers like rabbits.

Mortars fell on the other side of the hill, their flashes dimmer in the growing light. Valentine saw wild worms running off to the east, and the Bulletproof harrying the Coonskins. Hard luck for the Coonskins. Their halfhearted cover for the assault had aided in the repulse as much as the Southern Command's grenades and mortar shells.

Valentine looked behind. Bloom had better than half the camp moving up the hill.

They met strong fire on the ridge as the sun appeared, but the Bulletproof turned from their rout of the Coonskins to the east and put a fleshy curtain of gunfire against the Moondagger flank.

Valentine's assault expended the last of their grenades, pitching them over the hilltop. They captured two big 155mm guns which were being brought forward to complete the camp's destruction, complete with communications gear and a substantial reserve of ammunition.

Southern Command's forces secured the crest line, guns, and few prisoners who didn't blow themselves up with grenades and planted themselves. On that glorious reverse slope where the Coonskins had been camped, picked out for its suitable field of fire, they found the Moondaggers in disarray and falling back.

Valentine watched machine-gun tracer prod their retreat, leaving bodies like heaps of dropped laundry on the slope. Moondagger trucks, crammed with men hanging off the side, pulled off to the south.

If only they'd had real cannon instead of light mortars. The Moondaggers would have been destroyed instead of just bloodied. Valentine did what he could with what he had, sending shells chasing after the retreat, dropping them at choke points in the road.

Moytana's Wolves would give them a nip or two to remind them that they were beaten and running.

It wasn't a catastrophe for the Moondaggers. But it was enough. Valentine felt the odd, light, post-battle aura. He'd survived again, and better, won.

Seng's expeditionary brigade had fought its first real battle and emerged victorious.

They buried their dead, slung their wounded in yolk hammocks hanging off the side of the legworms, and pressed on. This time with lighter step and more aggressive patrols, half-empty bellies or no. It was still a retreat, but a retreat from victory, with honor restored.

# CHAPTER ELEVEN

*C*risis, *August: Javelin's support slowly dribbles away as it passes through east-central Kentucky. The Alliance clans shift their families and herds away from the area of Southern Command's column as though they carry bubonic plague. The Mammoth depart to settle a private score with the Coonskins.*

*Only the Gunslingers and the attenuated Bulletproof remain at a reasonable level of strength, the Gunslingers grudging the Kurians the loss of their dispatcher at the ambush in Utrecht, and the Bulletproof through the force of Tikka's personality and a twinkling affinity for Valentine as a member of Southern Command.*

*The Moondaggers reappear, reinforced after their successful destruction of the Green Mountain expedition in Pennsylvania, this time in a motorized column, hovering just at the edge of the column's last rear guard's vision.*

†

Valentine asked for, and received, permission to spend the day with the Wolves following the Moondaggers on their flanking march. Bloom had granted it halfheartedly, all the usual humor drained from her voice. Valentine wondered whether it was the strain of command—or was the strange lassitude that infected Jolla consuming Javelin's new commander?

It felt like old times, with the odd addition of Bee's constant, protective shadow and a couple of legworms carrying the Wolves' spare gear, provisions, and camping equipment. Moving hard from point to point, one platoon resting and eating while a second went ahead, the

tiny company headquarters shifted according to the terrain and movements of the enemy, small groups of wary scouts disappearing like
careful deer into stands of timber and ravines.

All that had changed was the strain Valentine felt trying to keep
up with them. He considered himself in decent enough shape, but a
day with the Wolves made him feel like a recruit fresh out of Labor
Regiment fell-running again.

Moytana himself was watching over the enemy whenever possible,
a careful woodsman observing a family of grizzlies, knowing that if he
made a mistake at the wrong moment, he'd be killed, partitioned, and
digested within an hour by the beasts.

The Moondagger column resembled a great black snake winding
through the valley. Or floodwaters from a burst dam, moving slug-
gishly but implacably forward. He could just hear high wailing cries
answered by guttural shouts, so precise a responsorial chorus that it resembled some piece of industrial machinery, stamping away staccato.

Flocks of crows circled above. Valentine wondered if they were
trained in some way, or just used to battlefield feasts.

The performance did its job. Valentine felt intimidated.

Valentine tried to make out the "scales" of the snake. All he could
think was that the army was marching holding old riot shields over
their heads.

"Umbrellas," Moytana said. "Or parasols. Whatever you want to
call them. They've got a little fitting in their backpack frame for the
handle."

"What's that they're—I don't want to call it singing—chanting?"

"That one's got some highfalutin name like the 'Hour of the Divine Unleashing.' Means they're going to chop us into stewing sized
pieces, in so many words."

Valentine saw some scouts on motorbikes pull to the top of a hill
flanking the column. They pointed binoculars and spotting scopes at
Valentine's hilltop. Valentine waited for a few companies to break off
from the column to chase them off, but the Moondaggers stayed in
step and song.

"They don't seem to mind our presence."

"They want us impressed. That's part of why they're chanting."

"You've heard that tune before."

"Yes. A small city called Ripening, in Kansas. Old maps call it Olathe."

"What went wrong in Kansas?"

"Everything. The operation made sense in theory. As we approached, the resistance was supposed to rise up and cause trouble. Cut communication lines, take the local higher-ups prisoner, blow up trucks and jeeps and all that.

"Problem was, it was kind of like Southern Command and the resistance set up a line of dominoes. Once the first couple tipped, it started a chain reaction. Sounds of fighting in Farming Collective Six gets the guys in Farming Collective Five next door all excited, and they dig up their guns and start shooting, which gets the guys at Four who've been sharpening their set of knives the idea that relief is just over the hill. So they start cutting throats. And so on and so on.

"Early on, seemed like we were succeeding beyond anyone's hopes. Wolves were tearing through Kansas knocking the hell out of the Kansas formations trying to get organized to meet us. Kurians were abandoning their towers in panic, leaving stacks of dead retainers behind.

"The way I understand it, the Kurians launched a counterattack out of the north, just a few Nebraska and Kansas and Iowa regulars. Typical Kurian ordering, from what I hear, futile attacks or defenses with rounds of executions in exchange for failure. Reapers started popping up along our line of advance, picking off the odd courier and signals post. That was enough to put the scare into a couple of our generals and they turned north or froze and right-wheeled, trying to establish a line with the poor Kansans under the impression that we were still coming hard west.

"Well, the Kurians must have got wind of our operation ahead of time. Maybe they even had, whaddya call 'em, agents o' provocation riling the Kansans up to get the resistance out in the open. They had these Moondagger fellows all ready to go in Nebraska, two full divisions plus assorted support troops like armored cars and artillery trains. Kansans started calling them the Black Death."

"I never saw anything like the Moondaggers when I crossed Nebraska."

"Oh, they're not from there. I guess they headquarter near Detroit with a couple of posts in northern Michigan, watching the Canadian border. Sort of a province of the Ordnance. That's one of the better-run—"

"I know the Ordnance. I've been into Ohio."

"They moved them fast, took them through the Dakotas on that spur they built to go around Omaha. At least that's what that Cat Smoke told me. She's the one who urged us to get to Olathe before it was too late."

Valentine didn't say anything. He let the words come.

"But once the Moondaggers started moving, they moved fast. On good roads they travel in these big tractor trailers made out of old stock cars stacked like cordwood. I've seen them riding on old pickups and delivery vans and busses, clinging like ticks to the outside and on the roof. They only do their marching when they're near the enemy, and then they pray and holler like that."

Moytana gestured at the winding snake.

"First they send an embassy of men from another town they've cut up, so the right accent and clothing and set of expressions is passing on all the gory details. I'm told their lives depend on getting the rebels to give up without a fight. Then they send in guys like our Last Chance to negotiate, get men to throw down their guns and quit, sneak off, whatever—then they make them prove their loyalty to the Kurians. Arm them with spears and one-shot rifles or have them carry banners in their front ranks so neighbor has to shoot neighbor."

He gulped. "Once they go into a town, well, they gut the place pretty bad. There are always a few Kurians in the rear, adding little tricks and whatnot, scaring the defenders. Outside of Olathe a rainstorm worked up and the Kurians somehow made it look like blood. I don't care who you are, Valentine—that'll rattle you, seeing blood run off the roof and pool in the streets. The Kurians get their pick of auras. The Moondaggers get their pick of women."

"You mentioned that before."

"Yeah, everyone from NCO on up in the Moondaggers has his little harem. Flocks, they call them. The gals are the flocks and they're the buggering shepherds jamming the gals' feet into their boots so they can't kick.

"That's the big thing in that outfit, breeding. A guy with a big flock, he's more likely to get promoted. They get decorated for the number of kids they've sired.

"Trick's getting started. You haul as many women as you can control home with you and start churning out babies. Seems the favorite age to grab is about nine to twelve. They don't eat as much, can't put up a fight, and they got all their breedin' years ahead of them."

"So making babies is like counting coup. What happens to the progeny?"

"Starting about five to eight they test them. I'm told one gets chosen to look after household when 'Dad' is away—almost always a boy. Toughest of the kids go into the Moondaggers, smartest go into the Church, the rest go off to labor training or get traded somewheres."

"Who controls the 'flock' while they're off fighting?"

"Dunno. Reapers, I suppose. Maybe the Church brainwashes some of the gals."

"You couldn't stop it in Olathe."

"No, it was just me and a squad of Wolves. We went through town after they pulled out. Found lots of bodies. And about a million crows eating the bits and pieces left in the streets. Moondaggers always like to chop a few up and stuff them back into their clothes the wrong way around, feet sticking out of shirtsleeves and heads where a foot should be. *For it is the blessed man who obeys the Gods and knows his place, for they are Wise; the man who claims for his head the mantle of godhood is as foolish as one who walks upon his hands and eats with his feet.*

"They left three men alive. One with his eyes burned out, one with his ears scrambled with a screwdriver, and one with his tongue ripped out. Just like that trio from the Mammoths. They did a story on them in the *Free Flags*. Pretty sad picture to put on the front page. Did you see it? About a year and a half ago."

"I was out west at the time."

"Whole bunch of young women barricaded themselves into one of the New Universal Church buildings and killed themselves with rat poison. I found a note: *One kind of freedom or another*. Girl looked about fourteen. That Smoke, she cried a good bit. Wasn't a total loss. We found some kids their parents stuffed up a chimney. Poor little things. I saw pretty much the same story in three other towns. Now they're here."

Valentine, feeling impotent in the face of the river of men snaking south two miles away, picked up a dry branch and snapped it. "Now they're here."

"Yeah. I know what's coming too. They'll just harry us, tire us out, get us used to running away from them. They'll terrorize anyone who even thinks about helping us. Then when we're starved and exhausted, they'll strike. Least they won't get too many candidates for their flocks out of our gals. Southern Command's shoot back."

"That's just one division there. Where do you suppose the other two are?"

"We never marked more than two in Kansas. The other's probably harrying what's left of the Green Mountain Boys."

"How did you find all that out?"

"We picked off one or two stragglers. Some just didn't talk, recited prayers the whole time or killed themselves with grenades at the last second. Some of the NCOs wear these big vests filled with explosives and ball bearings. They'll pretend to be dead and jump up and try to take a few with them. Smoke went and found a boy in Moondagger uniform and took him prisoner. Couldn't have been more than eleven; his only job was to beat a drum after the prayer singer spoke. He stayed tough for about ten minutes and then broke down and started crying when she sorta mothered him. Heard most of it from him."

Valentine had a hard time picturing Duvalier mothering anything but her assortment of grudges. But then she was a Cat, and it was her job to get information.

They left the hilltop, mounted legworms, and conformed to the line of the Moondaggers' march. Scouts found a new wooded ridge with a good view of the highway and they repeated the process for another hour. Moytana took a break and started on a letter. Valentine watched the marchers and the opposing scouts. All Valentine could think was that the Moondaggers were experts at their particular brand of harshness. He wondered how long they could operate somewhere like Kentucky without—

"Sir, scouts have met up with a party of locals," a Wolf reported. "Armed. They saw us riding. One of them asked for you by name and rank, Major Valentine."

"Locals?"

"Hard to tell if they're Kentuckian or Virginian. Mountain folk. Careful, sir. I don't like the look of them."

Valentine put a sergeant at the spotting scope and Moytana abandoned his letter. They snaked down the slope to a rock-strewn clearing and Valentine saw five men in black vests waiting around a small spring-fed pond, boiling water. Valentine carried his gun loosely, as though meeting a neighbor while deer hunting.

Valentine approached. The strangers were lean, haggard men with close-cropped beards and camouflaged strips of cloth tying the hair out of their eyes. They had an assortment of 5.56 carbines with homemade flash suppressors and scopes.

Valentine didn't recognize any faces.

What he at first took to be a pile of littered rocks shifted at his approach.

A mass of straw canvas sitting with its back to him rose. It looked like a fat, disproportioned scarecrow made out of odds and ends of Reaper cloth, twigs, twine, netting, and tusklike teeth. A leather cap straight out of a World War One aviator photo topped the ensemble, complete with Coke-bottle goggles on surgical-tubing straps, though there were holes cut in the hat to allow bat-wing ears to project and move this way and that freely.

A face that was mostly sharp teeth yawned and grinned as a tiny tongue licked its lips in anticipation. The muddy apparition carried a strange stovepipe weapon that looked like a recoilless rifle crossed with a bazooka.

Bee let out a sound that was half turkey gobble, half cougar scream.

*What?* Valentine thought, feeling his knees go weak.

The mountain of odds and ends spoke. "Well, my David. What kind of fix do you have yourself in this time?"

†

When Valentine could see again, blinking the tears out of his eyes, he looked around at the two groups of men, Wolves and Appalachian guerrillas, both eyeing the astonishing sight of a man with Southern Command militia major clusters pinned on to a suit of legworm leathers crying his eyes out against the mud-matted hair of a Grog's chest.

"Our general ain't as bad as he smells," one of the guerrillas told a Wolf. "Talks a midge funny, but by 'n' by your'n gets used to it."

Ahn-Kha and Bee exchanged pats, scratches, and ear-cleanings as he and Valentine spoke.

"Did Hoffman Price turn up again?"

Bee turned miserable at the name and muttered into her palm, thumping her chest and pulling at the corners of her eyes.

Ahn-Kha made more sense of it than Valentine could, though he caught the words for "death," "lost," and "slave" in the brief story.

"I'm sorry to hear of his passing, my David. It seems to have worked out for Bee. You're her, um, liberator and dignity restorer. As far as she's concerned, you hung her lucky moon in the sky."

"I can't tell whether she's a bodyguard or governess. She's always about yanking me out of my boots at the sound of gunfire."

"Proving that she has more sense than you."

"Can I hear your story?" Valentine asked.

"Oh, it is a long tale, and only the end matters. I managed to get myself put in command of the Black Flags. I still wonder at it."

Valentine still couldn't resist asking. "Your injuries?"

"Healed, more or less. Though I urinate frequently. I use your old trick of dusting with pepper or peeing into baking soda, otherwise the dogs would probably catch on."

"What happened to the pursuit?"

"They thought they caught a dumb Grog driver. I was sold to a mine operator. There matters turned dark in more ways than the coal face. I did not care for their treatment of someone who was kind to me and began a vedette."

"Vendetta, I think you mean."

"Vendetta. Of course. My one-hand war grew."

"What are your numbers now?"

"I will not tell you exactly," Ahn-Kha said. "Not with all these ears around. The Kurians believe our army to number ten thousand or more. But they have multiplied when they should have divided."

"I don't suppose I can count on you at my side this time?"

"These men deserve my presence. I began their war, and I will see it through. This is a strange land, my David. Victory and defeat all depend on a few score of powerful, clannish families who run things in this part of the country. Everyone knows and is related to one or more of these families. It makes my head hurt to keep track of it all. For now, they endure the Kurians as best as they can, though there are one or two families who relish their high placement overmuch. But the others, if they believe that we will win, they will place their support with us."

They talked quietly for a while. Ahn-Kha was waging a canny war against these powerful Quisling families. His partisan "army" had the reputation it had simply because it didn't exist as a permanent body. Ahn-Kha would arrive near a town and his small body of men would gather a few second cousins and brothers-in-law, Ahn-Kha would issue arms and explosives, and they'd strike and then fragment again as the Golden One relocated to another spot.

Sometimes when they struck and killed some officer in the Quis-

ling armed forces with a connection to one of the more powerful col-
laborators, they dressed him in the guerrilla vests and left him buried
nearby where search dogs were sure to find him. This led to reprisals
and mistrust between the Quislings, and the rickety Kurian Order in
the coal country of the Appalachians was coming apart.

The Moondaggers, on their arrival, had destroyed a trio of the
Quisling families under suspicion, creating bad feeling among the rest.
If they were to be treated as guerrillas, they might as well join the resis-
tance and hit back.

"You wouldn't be interested in a trip back to the Ozarks, would
you? I've felt like a one-armed man since we parted."

"And I a Golden One missing the ugly half of his face. But my
men need me. Though I started a revolt more by accident than inten-
tion, I must see it through."

"Forget I asked."

"Can I be of assistance otherwise, my David? In this last year my
small body of men have become very, very good at quick, destructive
strikes. Shall I bring down bridges in the path of your enemy?"

"It's the trailing end I'd like attacked. Do you think you can bust
up their supply lines? I want the Moondaggers forced to live off the
land as much as possible."

"It will not be difficult to find men to do that. They have carried
off a number of daughters already. As I said, everyone here knows
everyone by blood or marriage or religious fellowship."

Valentine felt an excited tingle run up his spine. Ahn-Kha usually
underpromised and overdelivered. Ahn-Kha would tweak the tiger by
the tail, and if the tiger was stupid enough to turn, it would find itself
harried by a foxy old Grog up and down these wooded mountains.

"I can't tell you what this means to me, old horse."

"I have the easy end, my David. Kicking a bull in the balls isn't
terribly difficult when someone else is grappling with the horns."

"They may deal harshly with the locals."

"They will find the people in this part of the country have short
fuses and long memories, if they do so."

Ahn-Kha always was as handy with an epigram as he was with a rifle. Speaking of which—

"What in the world is that thing?" Valentine asked. "A shoulder-fired coal furnace?"

"My individual 75mm," Ahn-Kha said. "Almost the only artillery in our possession. Some clever chap in my command rigs artillery shells so they go off like rockets."

"You're kidding."

Ahn-Kha's ears made a gesture like a traffic cop waving him to the left. "Kidding? It is more dangerous than it looks. That is why I have the goggles. You are lucky you haven't seen me after firing it. My hair becomes rather singed."

†

They shared a simple camp meal of legworm jerky and corn mush. Valentine didn't even have any sweets to offer Ahn-Kha. If it had been in his power to do so, he'd have run all the way back to St. Louis to get some of Sissy's banana bread or molasses cookies.

If he could fantasize about running all the way, he could fantasize about bananas being available in the Grog markets.

"Sorry we don't have any molasses," Valentine said. "We're a long way from home."

Ahn-Kha extracted a small plastic jar of honey shaped like a bear, tiny in his massive fist, and squirted some onto each man's corn mash.

He quizzed Ahn-Kha on the capabilities of his guerrillas and their operations, soaking up his friend's opinions and experiences like a sponge. Ahn-Kha was doing his best to make coal extracted from these mountains as expensive in repair and garrisoning as possible.

As the Golden One told a story about the destruction of a rail tunnel, a report came in that the Moondagger column was turning again, this time north. They might have finally turned toward Javelin. They'd have to relocate again to keep it under observation.

They bolted the rest of the meal and washed their pannikins in the spring. Ahn-Kha wrapped up his jar of honey and stuck it back in a vast pouch on his harness that smelled like wild onions. Valentine gave him a collection of Grog guck scavenged from the men with promises to replace it with chocolate bars from the medical stores.

Valentine would always remember that tiny plastic honey reservoir, and the way Ahn-Kha licked his fingers after sharing it out. Would there ever be a world again where people cared about the shape of a container?

He hoped so.

When they parted he shook the slightly sticky hand again, felt it engulf his own. Fingers that could snap his femur closed gently around his hand.

"Good luck, my David. We will meet again in happier circumstances."

"You said something like that before."

"And I was right. Give my regards to Mr. Post and Malita Carrasca. And our smoldering red firebug."

The staggering weight of all that had happened since they'd last said good-bye left him speechless. Ahn-Kha didn't even know about Blake.

"I trust your judgment on that one, old horse."

"Major, we have to leave. Now, sir," Moytana said.

So much for the fleeting pleasures of lukewarm corn mash sweetened by a tincture of honey. Valentine considered requesting that "Resting in peace—subject to the requirements of the service" be emblazoned on his grave marker.

Ahn-Kha's ears flicked up. "I'll give you a little more warning next time so you can receive me properly." He pulled his leather cap a little tighter on his head and picked up his stovepipe contraption. "After all, as you can see, I am a distinguished general."

"I'll bake a cake," Valentine said.

"Heartroot would do. See if you can't get me a few eyeroots, would you?"

"Good luck, my old friend. I can't tell you how good it is to see you again," Valentine said.

"When matters are settled in these mountains, you will see me again. Chance is not yet done playing with us."

With that, he turned and loped rather heavily off to the east into the woods, his men running to keep up. Valentine wondered what another brigade, three thousand strong or more, of Golden Ones could accomplish if led by his old friend.

†

The column had turned for Javelin. They were mounting a small force on armored trucks. Valentine wondered what the urgency was and requested that they make contact with base.

"Javelin's hung up at a bridge crossing. I can't get a warning through—there's some kind of jamming," the com tech reported.

"Moytana, try to delay those vehicles. Avoid a fight if you can. Block the road with trees at some gap."

"I'll see what I can do, sir. Looks like they're taking several routes, though."

The Moondagger column had turned into a hydra. One head crawled up a ridge, trying to get to the next valley over. A second was turning northeast, perhaps to get around behind Javelin.

"Send your fastest messenger back to headquarters with a warning. I think we can guess their route well enough. I'll follow as best as I can."

"Yes, sir," Moytana said, calling for his runner.

A boy of sixteen or seventeen—so it seemed to Valentine— answered the call. He carried an assault rifle that made him look even more like a child playing at war. It was a good old Atlanta Gunworks Type 3.

"Here, I'll carry that back to brigade for you, son," Valentine said, wanting the gun's angry bark.

Valentine took a slightly different path on the long road back than the boy. He angled off to the west, to see what that column marching across the ridge intended to do.

There was plenty of daylight left. If the Moondaggers were daylight fighters, it was all the better. His men would worry more about inflicting damage on the enemy and less about what might be lurking in the woods.

He topped another rise, puffing. No one was there to see him take a knee and dig around for a handkerchief to wipe off the summer sweat. His pits and crotch stuck and chafed. Legworm leather breathed well, but there were limits to any material.

The westmost column looked to have found the road they were looking for. It wasn't in good shape at all, a broken surface with fully grown trees erupting from parts of the pavement. Of course men traveling on foot without heavy weapons could easily find a path. It looked as though the deer had already made one.

He checked his bearings and picked a target on the next ridge north in the direction of headquarters.

Valentine ran down the opposite side of his ridge from the column, firing first his machine pistol, then the deeper bark of the Type 3. Every now and then he broke up the sound with a longer burst.

The phantom firefight might just turn the Moondaggers aside from their path to investigate. How well they could track and read shell casings was anyone's guess.

What counted at this point was delay.

✝

Valentine came to the Turkey Neck bridge, approaching along the eastern bank, and found chaos.

The river ran beneath deep, sculpted banks—Valentine guessed they were a flood prevention measure. Bluffs to the south frowned down on the slight river bend.

The old metal-frame highway bridge had been dynamited, quite incompetently, resulting in no more than the loss of some road bed and a few piles of paving. Bloom had sensibly sent several companies across to secure the far bank. But light mortar shells were now falling at the rate of one a minute all around the bridge area, keeping crews from covering the damage with timber and iron.

Legworms might be able to get across, but not trucks, vehicles, and horse- and mule-drawn carts. The brigade could cross, even through this shell fire, but would leave the supply train behind.

Valentine did his best not to anticipate the shells as he found headquarters, placed in a defile about a quarter mile from the east bank.

"Well?" he asked the first lieutenant he saw, ready to give someone a few choice words. Why wasn't anyone shooting back with the light artillery?

"Thank God you're here, sir. We've been under aimed artillery fire, sir. Cap—Colonel Bloom's wounded!"

"What's being done about those mortars?"

"They're trying to find a route north around the downed bridge. We're supposed to be set to move."

"On whose orders?"

"Not sure. You can countermand, sir."

"Why would I do that?"

"I think you're in command now, sir."

†

If he was in command, he might as well take charge. Valentine walked over to the headquarters vehicle, a Hummer bristling with antennae like some kind of rust-streaked insect.

Valentine studied a notated ordnance map. Pins marked the positions of his various companies. His jack-of-all-trades former Quislings were up waiting to assist the engineers in repairing the bridge.

He checked the bluff where the Moondaggers—if they were Moondaggers, and not troops out of Lexington or God knew where else—had set up their pieces. It was about a mile and a half south of the bridge.

"Set up an observer post, or better, two, to call in fire on those enemy mortars, if they can be effective. I'm going to the hospital."

He issued orders for defense of the temporary camp. He directed their tiny supply of anti-armor gear to the road that would most likely see the armored cars, and gave orders for everyone to be ready to move as soon as the bridge team could go to work. As soon as Moytana arrived, he was to take charge of the rear guard.

Then Valentine grabbed a spare satchel of signals gear, made sure one of the brigade's few headsets and a flare pistol rested in the holster within, and left.

†

The visit to the hospital was brief. It was the only tent the brigade had set up, mostly because of the big red cross on it. The only other casualty was what was left of a soldier who had a shell go off practically under him. The Moondaggers were dropping most of their shells on the bridge, either trying to keep the rest of the brigade from getting across or in the hopes of a lucky series of shots downing it for good.

Colonel Bloom seemed likely to live, at least long enough for the damage sustained by her pancreas to kill her. She sat up in bed, giving orders.

After hearing the medical report, he sent a messenger for Gamecock.

"Valentine, thank God you're here," she said, pushing away a nurse. "Silence those mortars, fix the bridge, and get the brigade across. These cutters want to sedate me and open me up. Don't let them stick anything in me until the brigade's safe."

"I think you should do what the doctors ask. I'll take care of the brigade. We'll wriggle out of this fix. The Moondaggers seem to be trying again."

"Yes, I heard the Wolf's report. Right before the world flipped over on me."

"Sorry about that, sir."

She looked like she was trying to smile. "Couldn't be helped. Don't worry about me. Go do your duty."

"If you'll let them get that shrapnel out."

She nodded. Then she opened one eye. "Oh, Valentine?"

"Yes, Colonel?"

"Get a hit."

He smiled. The old Bloom was back. "Their infield's in. I think I can poke one through."

Valentine found the doctor he'd first talked to.

"Have you ever tried transfusions from a Bear?" Valentine asked.

"I've read about some amazing results. But I believe it must be done quickly, while there's still living tissue and nerve impulses."

Gamecock arrived, breathless from a run across the bridge. His Bears were sheltering on the opposite side.

"What's Bloom's blood type?" Valentine said.

"O positive, suh," the doctor said. "Fairly common."

"Gamecock, get your Bears' blood type," Valentine said.

"I've kept up with the research too, Major," Gamecock said. "You might say I have needle-in experience. I spent a week at Hope of the Free hospital, passing blood to critical cases. They bled me white and kept trying to refill my veins with orange drink."

"I need an—no, make it two—two Bears with either O positive or O negative blood. Right away. Doctor, give Colonel Bloom a transfusion as soon as one can be arranged. Then a second in twelve hours. Is that clear?"

"If the Bears are willing, I am. I've heard stories about injecting one and getting your jaw rewired in return. I want willing and, more important, calm subjects."

"I'll watch over them myself, suh," Gamecock said.

"I'm going to need you for a few hours, Lieutenant," Valentine said. "We're going after those mortars."

"Did you take a look at that bluff, sir? It's a steep one. I'd hate to waste Bears taking it."

"The Moondaggers will have to prove they know how to hold off a Bear assault. I still think they don't know what to do about someone who fights back."

"It's still a steep hill. It'll look a lot steeper with bullets coming down."

"I know a way to get up it."

†

Valentine got a report from the artillery spotters. The height of the bluff made it impossible to accurately spot fire, so Valentine told them to save their fireworks.

"Infantry strength?"

"All we can see is perhaps platoon strength on this side. They're right at the top."

"Right at the top?"

"Yes, sir. I don't think they can see jack at the base of that hill."

They really didn't know how to fight. Or they just liked the view. No matter, Valentine had to take advantage of the error quickly, before a more experienced Moondagger arrived and corrected the matter.

The hardest part was getting one of the Bulletproof to agree to ride the legworm.

"Up that?" Swill, the Bulletproof veep in charge of their contingent, said. "If the footing's poor, you could roll a worm right over on you, especially if men are hanging on it in fighting order."

"I'll take mine up that hill," Tikka said, stepping forward. "I'm the best trick rider in the clan."

"There's trick riding and there's getting shot at. You don't know enough about the other," Swill said. "I'm not risking our senior veep's sister."

"So you told me. You're afraid to take your worms across under this shell fire. Watch this."

They did watch as she hurried to her worm grazing in some brush farther downstream. Digging her hook into its hide and using the spurs on the inner ankle of her boot, she mounted her worm and prodded it toward the bridge.

Swill ran in front of her worm and tried to divert it, looking a little like a rabbit trying to stop a bus. The worm nosed him aside, off his feet, and Swill threw off his hat in frustration.

"Watch those shells!" Swill yelled. "It'll rear back if one comes too close!" He turned back on Valentine. "The exec told me to keep her

E. E. KNIGHT

from doing anything stupid. Lookit me now. I'm going to have to go back and admit I couldn't keep a rein on one little female."

"Not the size of the dog in the fight, it's the fight in the dog," a handsome Guard sergeant detailed to the Bulletproof said. He rubbed his jaw ruefully. "That gal has her own mind about things."

Valentine sent a field-radio message to Gamecock to move his Bears toward the bluff, and then trotted up and joined his company, waiting for their chance to fix the bridge. They had all the tools and materials resting in the ditch next to the road.

"How's the shell fire, Rand?"

"Poor, if they're trying to kill us. I think they're just trying to keep us off that bridge. The fire's slackening, so I think they're running out of shells. Excuse me, sir, but is that worm rider crazy?"

"Feisty, more like," Valentine said, watching the legworm glide up the road on its multitude of black, clawlike legs, ripples running the length of its thirty-yard body as it covered ground. "Someone suggested she couldn't handle her worm."

Valentine watched Tikka fiddle with the gear on her saddle. She extracted another pole with a sharp hook, this one with a curve to the shaft.

"What's that for?"

"Legworms aren't very sensitive anywhere but the underside. She gives it a poke now and then to keep it moving."

Tikka aimed her mount straight for the hole. A shell landed near her and the legworm froze for a second. She goaded it forward again.

When it came to the hole in the pavement, she gripped the reins in her teeth, used one pole to goad her beast forward, and swung the other under what might be called its snout. It was where the food went in, anyway.

She poked it good at the front and it reared up, twisting this way and that. Tikka clung as another shell whistled down. It must have dropped straight through the hole in the pavement, because it exploded in the water beneath the bridge.

264

Tikka clung, shifted the forward pole down the legworm's belly, and then poked it again. It reared up, and she released the painful spur. It came down again, a good thirty legs on the other side of the hole. The legs over the gap twitched uncertainly, like the shifting fingers of sea anemones Valentine had seen in the Jamaican reefs.

"I didn't know they could do that," Rand said.

"I expect they can't, usually."

Tikka hurried her worm forward, a living bridge over the hole in the pavement. As she passed across, the beast's rear dropped into the hole, but with the rest of it pulling, it got its tail up and out.

Valentine checked his pack of signal gear again. How long until the Moondaggers got here?

"Preville, you've just been attached to headquarters," Valentine said. "You get to come on an assault with the Bears. Bring your radio."

"Er—yes, sir," Preville said, blinking.

"Red, then blue if we clear the hill. Understand?"

"Red, then blue," Rand repeated. "Got it, sir."

"Every minute counts. The opposition is on its way."

"They picked a good time to turn on us."

"I'm not so sure they picked it. The Kurians have long tendrils."

Valentine slapped his lieutenant on the shoulder and then ran up the extreme right of the bridge, Preville trailing, trying to run while folded in half. Another shell fell into the water. Valentine marked the glimmer of fish bellies bobbing in the current.

Someone downstream would collect a bounty of dead sunfish.

Tikka rested her mount on the other side, letting it graze in a thicket. Valentine watched brush and bramble and clumps of sod disappear into its muscular lipped throat. Valentine waved the Bears forward.

They came, three groups of four, in the variegated mix of Reaper cloth, Kevlar, and studded leather the Bears seemed to favor. Valentine even saw a shimmer of a chain mail dickey over one Bear's throat and upper chest. Their weapons were no more uniform than their attire. Belt-fed machine guns in leather swivel slings, deadly little SMGs, grenade launchers, assault shotguns, an old M14 tricked out with a custom stock and a sniper scope . . . never mind the profusion of blades, bayonets, and meathooks taped or clipped onto boots, thighs, forearms, and backs. Most of Gamecock's team favored facial hair of some kind. All wore a little silver spur around their neck—a team marker, Valentine guessed.

The Moondaggers, used to slaughtering rebellious farming collectives armed with stones and pitchforks, were in for a surprise.

"We're riding to the bluff. Can your worm hold them all?"

"It's young and strong," Tikka said. "As long as we're not riding all day."

Tikka unrolled a length of newbie netting from the back of her saddle, where it served as a lounger while coiled up. Gamecock's dozen picked Bears climbed uncertainly onto the creature.

"I've blown a few of these up but never ridden one," a Bear with a shaved, tattooed scalp said.

Another, who'd somehow stretched, teased, or sculpted his ears into almost feral points, wiggled his legs experimentally as he gripped the netting. "Not bad. Ride's smooth, like a boat. You could sleep while traveling."

"We do," Tikka said.

She kept them in the trees, keeping leafy cover over their heads whenever possible as they approached the bluff. The hills closed in between them and the riverbank. Then, suddenly, the steep slope was before them.

Valentine dismounted, carefully went forward, waiting for the sniper's bullet or the machine-gun burst. Every twig and leaf seemed to stand out against the blue Kentucky sky.

Nothing.

The Moondaggers had erred. Or at least he hoped they had. They'd put all their troops at the top of the hill, rather than on what was referred to as the "military crest," the line of the hill where most of the slope could be covered by gunfire. Even experienced troops had made the mistake before.

He trotted back to the head of the worm and tapped Tikka on her spiked boot.

"Still think you can get it up?"

Tikka winked. "I'm five and oh, Blackie. Wanna be six?"

"This isn't the time—"

She laughed. "I don't quit that easy. If I get you all up so you can cork those guns, you going to finally give me a taste?"

*Just get it over with.* "A three-course dinner."

"With dessert," she added.

"I think that's included in the price."

"Sir, how am I supposed to go red when an episode of *Noonside Passions* is running at the other end of the fuckin' worm?" a Bear named Chieftain asked Gamecock.

They started up the hill, sidewinding on the long worm. Tikka found some kind of path, probably an old bike or hiking trail. The worm tilted.

A shot rang out.

"You all better side-ride—it's going to get nasty here," Tikka called.

"Can you keep the worm upright?" Valentine asked.

"Do ticks tip a hound dog? Grab netting."

The Bears slipped down the side of the worm facing downslope. Valentine heard bullets thwack into the worm, and Tikka shifted her riding stance, clinging on to the saddle and fleshy worm hide like a spider on a wall. Somehow she managed to work the reins and goad.

The mortars fired again, blindly, sending their shells down to explode at the base of the hill.

Valentine heard shouts from above, cries in a strange warbling language.

"Drop off now. They'll keep shooting at the worm," Valentine told Gamecock, seeing a cluster of rocks trapping fallen branches and logs.

The Bears scrambled for cover. Preville pulled out his field radio.

"Whenever you're ready, Lieutenant," Valentine said.

Gamecock took out a little torch and heated his knife. "Uh, sir, if I'm not mistaken, you're the brigade commander now. I don't think it's your place to be at the forefront of a hill assault. Let me and the Bears—"

"There's a good view from that bluff. The Moondaggers are on their way, and I need to assess the situation."

"Red up, red up," Gamecock cried.

Each of Gamecock's Bears seemed to have their own method of bringing the hurt, and with it the willed transformation into fighting madness that made the Bears the killing machines they were. One punched a rock, another stamped his feet, others cut themselves in the forearm or ear or back of the neck. A Bear, perhaps more infection-minded than most, made a tiny cut across his nose and dabbed iodine from a bottle on it.

Valentine heard fire following the worm.

"Time to fuck them up," the one with the iodine rasped, wincing.

Gamecock pressed the hot knife under his armpit, clamped down on it hard.

Preville looked around, gaping. Valentine knew what his com tech was thinking: *If this is what they do to themselves, what the hell's in store for the enemy?*

If Valentine wanted pain, all he had to do was think of his mother, on the kitchen floor, the smell of stewing tomatoes, what was left of his sister lying broken against the fireplace . . .

Heart pounding, a cold clarity came over him. The next minutes would be either him or them. Doubts vanished. Everything was reduced to binary at its most simple level, a bit flip, a one or a zero. Life or oblivion.

Three . . . two . . . one . . .

"Smoke 'em up," Gamecock yelled.

A Bear from each four-man group pulled the pins on big, cyclindrical grenades. The senior nodded and they all threw toward where they heard orders being shouted.

Valentine smelled burning cellulose. The smoke grenades belched out their contents. There was a stiff breeze on the heights and the smoke wouldn't last long. Gamecock put two fingers into his mouth and whistled.

"Action up! Action up!"

The Bears exploded out of the cover like shrapnel from a shell burst, save that each piece homed in on the target line with lethal intent.

Valentine followed them through the smoke. Gamecock kept toward the left, where more of the hill and therefore more unknown opponents potentially lay, so Valentine went around the right, trying to keep up with the barking mad Bear with the clipped ears.

White eyes with a thick bushy beard appeared from the growth to the right—a Moondagger opening a tangle of branches with his rifle butt. Valentine swung his machine pistol around and gave one quick, firm squeeze of the trigger and the man fell sideways into the supporting growth, held up by a hammock of small branches and vines. He heard a shout from behind the man, a yapping, unfamiliar word, and fired blindly at the noise.

He followed the sound of bursting small arms fire up the hill.

The four-man groups divided into twos, covering each other as they went up the hill in open order and they vanished into the smoke.

"Target in sight. Grenades!" Gamecock's disembodied voice sounded through the smoke.

Bullets sang through the trees, tapping off down into the thicker timber, followed by the tight crash of grenades going off uphill. Valentine felt the heat of one on his left cheek as it passed.

Then he was through the smoke. A wide, bright green mortar tube sat, a bloody, bearded man fallen against the arms of the bipod, looking like a dead roach in the arms of a praying mantis. Just beyond, a severed head lay next to what had been its body.

A brief flurry of gunfire turned to cries and screams as the Bears did what they did best: close quarters fighting. Only it was closer to murder.

The Bear with the cuts on his nose was perhaps the most impressive of all. He grapevined through the position with only his .45 gripped carefully like a teacup, his body following the foresight like it was a scouting dog. Valentine saw him drop three Moondaggers spraying bullets from assault rifles held at their hips in the time it would take Valentine to clap his hands.

Valentine saw Moondaggers fall, blown left and right by shotgun blasts or gunfire. The men on the other side of the slope saw the slaughter and ran from their positions and into the thickest timber they could find while their officers fired guns in the air, trying to stem the panic.

By the time Valentine realized the top of the hill and the mortar positions were theirs, the Bears were already over the hill and chasing what was left of the Moondagger infantry and mortar crew down the gentler reverse slope. Gamecock recalled his team and sent them to the right to check out the rest of the hilltop. The Bear with the old M14 knelt against a moss-sided rock, squeezing off shots as he squinted through the scope.

A bullet came back and he sank down, reloading. He rolled to his right, fired three times, and then rolled back behind the rock. No shots came back this time.

Some bit of sanity recalled him to duty. Valentine posted Preville by the mortars and followed a path north, finding himself atop a limestone cliff with a good view of the river valley and the treetops they'd advanced under. He withdrew into cover and fired first the red flare and then the blue, but as the first went off he saw work was already started on the bridge. Rand had put the engineers to work as soon as he heard firing from the bluff top, figuring the mortar crews would have better things to do with Bears roaring up through the woods.

Valentine hurried back up to Preville and reestablished contact with headquarters. They connected him with Moytana, who reported the destruction of two armored cars. He'd delayed the center column, forcing them to come off the road and deploy, before retiring and leaving a screen of scouts who were giving enemy position reports as they fell back. The center column wouldn't reach the bridge for hours yet.

The long day would be over soon.

Valentine looked around at the dead being arranged by a couple of Bears in a neat row under the trees, their faces covered and arms and legs placed tightly together. Most of them had jet black hair and copper skin. Valentine recognized again the old game he'd seen so many other places—Santo Domingo, Jamaica, New Orleans, Chicago: elevate an ethnic minority to a position of authority, where their position and status depended on the continued rule of the Kurians above. More often than not, the more-visible middlemen took the blame for the misdeeds of those at the top.

Valentine counted heads. All the Bears were upright, including the four keeping watch to the south and west.

"Not even any wounds? Your command's not even scratched, it seems."

"Not exactly unscratched, Major," Gamecock said. "You left something behind, sir. Left ear. Lobe's gone."

Valentine reached up, grabbed air where the bottom of his ear should be.

"You could take up painting French countryside cafés," a better-read Bear laughed.

"Doberman can fix up your ears so they match," Silvertip said, pointing to the Bear with the docked ears.

"Want me to go look for it, sir?" Preville asked, perhaps desperate to get away from the combat-hyped Bears.

"You, with the iodine. Spare a little."

"Absolutely, Major," the bear said, exhibiting what was perhaps the deepest voice Valentine had ever heard in Southern Command.

"What's your name?"

"Redbone," the Bear said.

"Thanks, Redbone. Good shooting with that pistol. You don't give lessons, do you?"

"I can make time."

†

271

Valentine could turn the hill over to the Guard infantry now. With a few platoons posted on the bluff and some more companies spread out in those woods, the flanking column could bust itself to pieces in this manner, and every moment his forces on the west side of the river would grow stronger as men, vehicles, and legworms crossed, platoon by platoon.

With the brigade across and flanks well secured by river and limestone cut, the men could afford to relax and swap tales of skirmishes against Moondagger scouts. The Moondagger columns, discovering that Javelin had escaped the bridge choke point, skulked off for the sidelines like footballers who'd just given up a fumble.

The Wolves were coming in with reports that they'd turned tail.

"A mob. That's all they are," someone ventured.

"Like most bullies, they're toughest against people who can't fight back," Valentine said. "What happened to the third column?"

"Don't rightly know, sir," Moytana said. "Some of the scouts thought they heard explosions a mile or two to the east. The column turned toward them, then reversed itself, then turned back again east before it swung around south to where they were when we were first watching them. That's all they saw before it got dark."

The work of Ahn-Kha, perhaps, with ambushes or miscellaneous sounds of destruction getting the Moondaggers marching in a circle, chasing the noises of their own troop movements.

Valentine wondered what would have happened back at Utrecht if they'd united with the Green Mountain Boys. The Moondaggers had come to oversee a surrender, not wage a war. If only Jolla hadn't felt overwhelmed by the responsibility of command.

He'd leave the might-have-beens to the historians and armchair strategists. He had to check on his commanding officer.

†

For two days the column crept southeast as Bloom recovered from her taste of Bear blood. The doctors complained that it made her even more restive than usual.

The Moondaggers hovered in the distance, keeping in between the brigade and Lexington. Valentine wondered what sort of orders and threats were passing between various Kurians, high Church officials, and the Moondagger headquarters in Michigan. Bloom was soon up to half days in her jeep after one more Bear-blood transfusion.

Valentine, now that she was on his mental horizon, suddenly saw Tikka everywhere: giving orders to her fellow Bulletproof, cadging for strips of leather to effect repairs on tack and harness, giving advice to the cooks on the best way to quick-smoke legworm meat.

Perhaps it was just his libido, but she always seemed to be reaching, squatting, climbing, or bending over, the muscles of her backside tight in jeans and legworm-leather chaps.

She caught him coming out of the wash tent after dinner and revealed a glass flask tucked in her summer cotton shirt snuggled up next to a creamy breast.

Valentine had seen hundreds of liquor advertisements while paging through the tattered ruins of old magazines, but for all the tales of subliminal depictions of fornication in ice cubes, he'd rarely so wanted to reach for a cork in his life.

"I came here to collect on a promise," she said, taking the kerchief out of her hair and letting the caramel-colored curls tumble into a waterfall splashing against her shoulders. "Or are you going to Cin-Cin me out of my reward?"

*What the hell.* He should do something to celebrate his brief command of the brigade. Tikka seemed like five and a half feet of uncomplicated lust. He'd just have to make sure to use a condom for something other than keeping rain out of his gun barrel.

"Do you want to be seen walking into my tent, or will you sneak in under cover of darkness?"

"Let's go to mine. It's more secluded. I'm picketed to make sure the dumb things don't blunder into the stream."

"I'll change so I can blend in."

He buttoned his shirt and threw his uniform coat over his arm and went to his tent. While he put on his leathers, she refilled her pistol belt from the company supply.

"What in the world did you do to your rig?" she asked. "All your hooks and catches are gone."

"My maiden aunt Dolly was always complaining about the chips to her furniture. Kept snagging doilies at headquarters too."

She licked her lips. "I think I can tell when you're joking now."

"Good."

They walked through the knee-high grasses to the legworm camp, a little below the Southern Command encampment and closer to the stream. They wound through grazing legworms. On the hill opposite the stream, two riders sat on a mount back-to-back, keeping watch.

She beckoned him into her tent. Some tack odds and ends sat in a chest that opened out into shelves, and various ponchos and bandannas hung on a grate-like folding clothes tree. Her bed was a net-and-frame double with a rather battered-looking down mattress. It looked too rickety to support both of them.

"You should have taken better care of your leathers," she said, disrobing with a matter-of-factness that made Valentine remember a girl he'd once known in Little Rock. "You know, it's supposed to be the mark of a real well-suited pair of riders if they can do it without any punctures or lacerations. Kind of a good omen for their future together."

She had muscular buttocks and legs, good shoulders and a sleek, feline back. Her breasts, high and small and capped by determined, thumblike nipples, gave the tiniest of bobs as she danced out of her leathers. Their full firmness made her waist look even narrower by comparison.

"I could put some barbed wire around my nethers."

"Don't you dare," she said, coming forward and into his arms.

Her kiss was as wanting, hungry, and open as a baby bird's mouth. It had been so long since he'd had a woman press against him like this, her arms tight on his shoulder blades, he'd almost forgotten the delightful feel of breasts crushed against his chest, or a round hip just where his hand could fall as he tested the curves.

He lifted her easily and she laughed, pulling at his ears. She still had

274

the day's sweat lingering between her breasts. It smelled like salt and sun and that powerful, caressing scent that women carried like a secret weapon for infighting. One of her heels pressed against the small of his back; the other rubbed the back of his leg. His pants seemed insufferably confining. They worked together to get him out of them.

She dropped to her knees, employed her mouth, but he hardly needed encouragement.

"Now. Hurry. God, I'm so fucking horny!" she said.

They didn't even bother disturbing the bed. The tamped-down grass was cool and smooth inside the tent's shade, and there was less chance of breaking it as she bucked and gasped under his thrusts.

After, she played with his hair. "God, that was good. I even forgot about Zak while you were doing that Morse code with your tongue. Why didn't we do this four years ago?"

"I had someone else then. Or I thought I did."

"That redhead? She could be pretty if she tried. And cut back on the attitude."

Valentine let her be wrong. He didn't want to talk about Malita and his daughter. In the rather formal, most recent letter, she'd been described as half monkey, half jaguar, climbing trees as easily as most kids walked.

Valentine felt strangely uncomfortable at the mention of Duvalier.

"We could try making up for lost time," he said, changing the subject. He reached for her.

†

So began a love affair carried out as discreetly as could be managed in a camp full of soldiers. Luckily Kentucky was full of glades, quiet hillsides, and swimming holes. Valentine had a tough time being spared from his duties, shorthanded as the headquarters was with their losses and Bloom still needing a long night of uninterrupted sleep. They had a magnificent yet lazy, four-hour afternoon fuck when Valentine had a midnight to four/eight to noon watch.

Once she tried to use her mouth on him as he was supervising the empty headquarters tent—empty save for one sleepy radio operator with his back to them—and he had to send her back to the Bulletproof camp.

Good thing too, because Duvalier came in soon after. She extended her tongue at Tikka, disappearing into the dark in a disappointed flounce.

"That Reaper the Wolves thought they saw turned out to be a scarecrow," she said. "Some clever clod rigged it to a little track so the wind blew it around his cornfield."

She looked at his trousers. "You trying to win a blue or something?"

Valentine, embarrassed, finished zipping up.

"Odd that we haven't had more trouble with Reapers."

"They keep away from big bodies of men, at least if they're alert. Too many guns. Plus, I don't think the legworm ranchers like Reapers poking around in their grazing lands."

"Any problems between the Moondaggers and the ranchers?"

"I went into Berea right after they left and played camp follower. They left the townies alone. Of course, the Kentucks hid their girls and showed their guns."

"*Si vis pacem, para bellum,*" Valentine said.

"No, these guys favor buckshot and thirty-oughts," Duvalier said. "Does the Atlanta Gunworks make the Sea-biscuit mace-'em? I never heard of it."

†

After his duty, he retired to his tent. He heard someone tap outside.

Probably Tikka, wanting to finish what she started in the headquarters tent. He rose and was surprised to see Lieutenant Tiddle standing there, looking freshly shaved and combed.

"What is it, Tiddle?"

"Can we talk, sir? Like, off the record?"

"Come in."

Tiddle rubbed his nose, looking like he was desperate to jump on his motorbike and disappear in a fountain of dust. "Major Valentine, that story you heard about the Colonel and Colonel Jolla ain't quite what happened."

"Excuse me?"

"We lied to you, sir. We sort of agreed about it. There was a struggle over a gun, sure, but it was Colonel Bloom's. When the shells started falling and Colonel Jolla was just standing there and started talking about surrendering while watching it like it was a rainstorm and not doing anything, she took command. He put his hand on his pistol and told her she was guilty of mutiny. The next thing we knew, they were fighting. Then we heard the gun.

"She was the one who put the barrel under Jolly's chin. Awful sight. We took another bullet out of Jolly's gun and put it in Bloom's."

"Why are you changing your story?"

"I—we all agreed, as we were treating Colonel Bloom, that whatever their fight was about, Colonel Jolla wasn't right in the head, ever since we lost the colonel. I remembered that story they taught in school about how the president wasn't giving any orders in 2022 and then he shot himself, and we decided that something like that was happening with Jolly."

Valentine decided Tiddle bore watching, in more ways than one.

"I'm still not sure why you're changing the story."

"Will this cause trouble for his family with line-of-duty death and all that?"

"No. Let's leave it be," Valentine said. "Conscience clear now?"

"The lie's been bothering me, sir." He sighed, and his face relaxed into the more agreeable expression Valentine had seen here and there around the brigade.

In Southern Command, if a court found that a soldier had been killed while in the commission of a crime under either military or civilian laws, their death benefits were forfeit.

"Don't worry, Tiddle. You did the right thing. Both times."

"How can it be right both times?"

"Good question. Why don't you think about it for a while?"

Valentine decided to forget everything Tiddle had told him, if possible. Whatever Bloom had or hadn't done, survival was their main concern now.

"Sir, if you don't mind me saying, there's one more thing that's worried me."

Trust established, Tiddle seemed intent on unburdening himself entirely. Valentine wondered if he was going to hear about Tiddle's loss of virginity to a cousin.

"Colonel Bloom, sir. She's been kind of distracted lately. Just like Colonel Jolla at the end. Absent, only half listening."

Valentine bit off a "Are you sure?" Stupid question. He had to act.

"I'll talk to her. Thanks for expressing your doubts, Tiddle."

"Whatever's going on, nip it in the bud now, would you, sir? I don't want to be known as the com officer who's had two commanders shoot theirselves."

†

"I'm not sure we should be in such a hurry to leave," Valentine said, trying to wash down a hunk of legworm jerky and sawdust at the next route-planning meeting.

"How's that now?" Bloom asked.

"After their last try, the Moondaggers seem content to just nudge us along. They haven't made any real attempt to cut us off or even engage. Maybe they're licking their wounds from the last fight."

"Time is on their side, then."

"Not necessarily," Valentine said. "They're used to getting their way, and they're used to shoving around civilians when they don't. The legworm clans, they're not poor Kansas farm collective workers who don't know a rifle from a hoe. These boys can ride and shoot and they don't back down."

"They backed down easily enough back at the union," a Guard captain said.

"Now they're on their own land, though. I remember how startled I was, seeing Quisling uniforms walking around in Little Rock. Made me kind of mad. Felt more like a violation. I'm hoping the legworm ranchers will feel the same way," Valentine said.

"So what of it? They get jacked and take out a few Moondaggers in return. Does that help us?" Bloom asked.

"It gives the Moondaggers a new set of worries," Brother Mark said.

"The Moondaggers will respond the only way they know how. It could grow into a full-scale revolt. There could be advantages to that. Like better supply for us," Valentine said.

Moytana shook his head. "And disadvantages. There's a big garrison in Lexington and another in Frankfort. Right now they seem content to sit and not make waves."

"And the Ordnance, just over the Ohio," someone else added. "They've got a professional army. A lot of Solon's best troops came from there. If the Kurians there think Kentucky is up for grabs, they might make a move."

"We came across the Mississippi to establish a new Freehold," Valentine said, giving the table a rap. "I'd still like to do it. But I want it to be the ranchers' idea, not ours."

"Too risky, Valentine," Bloom said. "Javelin's low on everything."

"We win a battle and we might get more local support," Valentine said. "Right now they're just obeying the Moondaggers because they've seen that we aren't doing anything about them."

Bloom glowered. "Pipe down, Valentine. You're dancing toward a line marked 'insubordination.' "

"Sorry, sir," Valentine said, using the soothing tone that always worked with his old Quisling captain on the *Thunderbolt*.

The rest of the meeting passed with Valentine deep in thought.

He buttonholed Brother Mark as they left to get some dinner and look over the nighttime pickets.

"Is it possible that—that a Kurian agent is manipulating her? Sowing doubt, fear?"

Brother Mark's gaze looked even more droopy. He nibbled at a turnip. "The Kurians and their agents may play with your senses, just as the Lifeweavers do. I suppose you've . . . ahem . . . experienced . . ."

"The night I got this," Valentine said, rubbing the side of his face where his jaw hadn't healed right. "Speaking of night, it always seems like she's at her most timid then. Dawn comes up and she's almost her old self."

"Sunlight interferes with their abilities. If it is someone manipulating her, it would be like no agent I've ever heard of. That would put him—or her—on par with a Kurian."

"Then a Kurian—"

"No, they have to see, hear, smell—feel your aura, even, to be the devil whispering in your ear. Though I suppose they could work it through a proxy. Relay their mind through another, just as a Reaper becomes the Kurian when the Kurian is manipulating it."

"I haven't seen anyone touching her. She likes to pat you and slap you, locker room stuff, but that's never when she's making decisions. It's an 'at ease' thing with her to let you know you can relax."

"She's never slapped me," Brother Mark said in a tone that suggested he might enjoy the experience.

*Churchmen. You never know.*

"Anyway, I can't remember anyone going out of their way to make contact with her," Valentine said.

"Physical contact isn't necessary, you know."

Valentine straightened. "But you said—"

"An aura projects up to, oh, nine feet from the body. You didn't know that?"

"No."

"I saw it on a scanner once, during my education. An aura shows up on certain kinds of electrical detection equipment. It looked a little like the northern lights—ever seen them?"

"Yes, as a boy."

"It's an odd thing. A man missing his arm will still have the aura of his arm. It just looks more like a flipper. He can even move it around, to an extent, by working the muscles that used to work his arm. They could turn up the sensitivity of the equipment and show just how far an aura extends. Fascinating stuff. It's one of the reasons I don't eat cooked food. There's more aura residue clinging to uncooked vegetables."

"You don't say," Valentine said, wondering how to get the Brother back to the subject at hand. "Thank you for continuing my education."

"You weren't wrong—of course the connection is a good deal clearer when there's physical contact."

"How often would the Kurian have to make contact?"

"All I can do is guess. Different Kurians have developed different skills."

"Guesswork, then."

"Every few days. It's like a— Do you know what hypnosis is?"

"I saw a hypnotist once in Wisconsin. He was doing it for entertainment."

"It's like a hypnotic suggestion. Much of it depends on the will of the subject. With a strong-willed individual, I expect there'd have to be contact every day or two."

"Can you detect the connection?"

"Possibly. But I don't think our good commander would appreciate me hovering around her at headquarters, feeling the staff up until the hooded hours. I'd rather not have another noose put around my neck." He tugged at his collar, as if he could still feel the rope's abrasive coil.

"No sense wasting time," Valentine said. "Come to the headquarters tent for that glop that's passing for coffee. I need to talk to you about visiting the legworm clans anyway. Perhaps you can help with the snack table."

Luckily Valentine could lose himself in the detail of his position and his appetite's arousal as the food trays came in. As the nighttime activity commenced, his collection of officers gave Moondagger position reports from the Wolves and a Cat who'd single-handedly dispatched a three-man patrol, keeping one alive for interrogation. Clean bit of work, that. Valentine would talk that up with the companies as he passed through them on the march. Nervous pickets liked to hear that the other side suffered its own devils in the dark.

Bloom listened rather absently. She only spoke once.

"Send that prisoner back to the Moondaggers. Tell them if they'll leave us alone, we'll leave them alone."

A less Bloom-like order Valentine could hardly imagine. She earned her rank during Archangel by taking her company forward, hammering in the morning, hammering in the evening, hammering at suppertime (as the old song went) against Solon's forces at Arkansas Post to cut off the river.

Then there were more mundane announcements such as the discovery of leaking propane tanks in the mobile generator reserve—he'd put his old company on finding more—and the field kitchen was running short of cooking oil and barbecue sauce.

Legworm meat needed lots of barbecue sauce to make it palatable.

Valentine wondered if his opposite number in the Moondaggers was listening to his own briefing, worried over just what had happened to that three-man patrol and dealing with a shortage of hydrogen fuel cells for the command cars.

Brother Mark made himself useful. After giving his briefing regarding their allies' dwindling enthusiasm, he went about the room with a coffee pot, touching distracted officers and staff and asking for refills. Now and then he shrugged at Valentine or shook his head.

Valentine passed close and noticed that Brother Mark was sweating from the effort.

Tiddle took some catching, but Brother Mark finally managed to corner him and point out that his cuff and elbow were both frayed— Tiddle had spilled his bike with his trick riding. Valentine held his breath—he liked Tiddle.

Brother Mark sighed and shook his head.

"Perhaps it is someone not on the staff," he whispered, patting Red Dog's head as they passed. "Good God," he said, shocked.

"What?" Valentine asked, but he knew.

Brother Mark led him out of the tent. "It's the dog."

"How?"

"I don't know. Perhaps they've made some alteration to the animal, modified its brain. It seems a normal enough dog."

"It's the perfect spy," Valentine said. "It can't give anything away. Dogs won't break under duress and talk."

"You're wrong there, Valentine. I got a flash of something. A little of the Kurian's mind. I broke it off. I've had enough of *that* to last me more than a lifetime."

"How do we break the dog's hold on her?"

"A strong endorphin response. Alarm, maybe. An orgasm might be perfect."

Valentine could just picture Duvalier's reaction to that bit of line-of-duty cocksmanship. She'd herniate herself laughing.

"Regulations," Valentine said.

"You'll have to come up with something. Perhaps just explaining it to her, so she was conscious of it—"

"If there's some kind of connection between her mind and the Kurian, I'd like to use it, not break it. Play with the dog a little, see if you can get anything."

Brother Mark made himself ridiculous for a few minutes with Red Dog, wrestling and hugging it. Red Dog enjoyed himself and so did the churchman. Those passing in and out of the headquarters tent shrugged.

He returned to Valentine dusty and dirty. Valentine gave orders for Red Dog to be taken around to the sentries for the usual midnight Reaper check.

"What did you get?"

"A sensation. Cool and moist air. A glimpse or two through its eyes. The Kurian is high, over a small town on some kind of aerial tower. Fine view of these Kentucky hills. One odd thing about the town: There are train tracks running right down the center of town along the street. Shops and buildings to either side. Quite odd."

Valentine checked with the Wolves and had word back in ten minutes. There was a town to the north called La Grange that had train tracks running straight through town. Wolves on foot could be there before dawn if they pushed hard.

He had Gamecock alert his Bears.

"Can you just order an operation like this, even as chief of staff?" Brother Mark asked.

"No, I need Bloom's assent."

"I hope you get it."

"I will. I just have to get her back into the fight, somehow."

†

Valentine presented his plans for an attempt to bag the Kurian. He didn't know if the mind manipulating the dog was also directing the Moondaggers, but any chance to take out an aura-hungry appetite would be a blow for humanity.

Bloom listened impassively. "I don't think we should risk it."

Valentine slapped her. Hard.

"What in—"

"That's no way for a leader to talk. Especially not the Cleo Bloom who spearheaded Archangel."

"See here, Mister," she said, bristling.

Valentine's hand became a blur. The slap carried like a gunshot.

"I'm putting you under arrest for assault."

"You've lost your nerve, Bloom. Showing the whites of your eyes. And your teeth. All you need is a gingham dress and we'd have a minstrel show."

She gasped, swung for his jaw. Valentine took the blow. If anything, he was grateful for it.

"You couldn't do Morse code with a tap like that," Valentine said, tasting blood. "Try again, you alley ho."

"Mother*fucker*," she said, falling on him. They went down and it was a dirt fight of knees and elbows. He covered his face with a forearm as she rained blows down on either side of his head, right-left right-left right-left.

"Woo! Officers fightin'," someone called.

Cleo Bloom stood up, her eyes bright and alive. "Jesus Lord," she panted. "Jesus Lord."

"Feel better, Colonel?" Valentine asked.

Later, they talked about it in the dispensary as a nurse put cold towels on Valentine's bruises and dabbed his cuts with iodine.

"I figured pressure must have been building up in you some-where," Valentine said.

"I don't remember feeling any kind of presence," she said. "I just had all these doubts all of a sudden. I thought it was because it was the first time I was in command."

"I'm sure that helped," Valentine said. "The Kurians know what they're doing. They attack when someone is most vulnerable. It's how they fight. No need to beat us if we beat ourselves."

"Boy, when it came out, it was like a firehose. I feel better than I have for weeks. I remember you were saying something about an operation?"

"We found the Kurian's temporary hideout. Dumb luck, really. It's in a unique-looking town, as seen from above. Of course there's a big radio mast, so it makes sense that he would be there."

"And we're waiting for what, exactly?"

"Your orders."

"Given. Let's get this brigade of ours back into the war."

"I'd like permission to accompany the Bears."

"No, I'll send that Duvalier. She's very good, and she knows the country. Besides, I need you here. I was looking at the map, and there's a nice notch in the ridge ahead. We could use a rest from moving, and I think with some flank security we could mess with the pursuit. The thought scared me before, but now I want to take a crack at them. They're so used to us running after brief holding actions, we might catch them strung out."

†

Valentine passed a busy, sleepless night. While Gamecock and Duvalier, guided by a trio of Wolves, headed for La Grange, Bloom turned the brigade and launched an exploratory attack on Moondagger reconnaissance following them up the road.

Then Javelin took a much-needed rest while waiting for the Bears to return. Scavenging parties found green apples and early squash to eat. The fall's first bounty was coming in.

The hours dragged as Valentine experienced the doubts of a man who'd rather be on the job himself than sending others into danger. He gnawed on an apple core, reducing it by tiny shavings, waiting for the parties' return. Bee sensed his mood and tried to comb out his hair and pick ticks.

They came in at dusk, one Bear short and Duvalier limping on a twisted ankle.

Gamecock, thick with smoke and dirt, gave a brief report, with Silvertip standing silently behind. Silvertip looked like he'd spent the morning wrestling mountain lions.

"Town had a Moondagger garrison, but they were living it up in the roadhouse at the edge of town," he said. "Sure enough, there was a little Kurian blister on the antenna, made out of whatever crap they use as tenting. They'd camouflaged it like an eagle nest."

Valentine had heard of some kind of specially trained bug that excreted Kurian cocoon.

"No Reapers?"

"The Cat took one jumping from a roof. She gave us the all-clear even with her bum foot. I sent the Bears right for the antenna with demo gear. There were some sentries but we disposed of them with flash-bangs and blades."

Valentine wished he could have been there. Or better yet, peering into the Kurian's eye cluster when it saw the Bears hurrying up.

"Did you blow the nest?"

"Yes, but it ran before then. Went sliding down one of the support wires or whatever you call 'em, suh," Gamecock said. "Gutsy little shit."

"You saw it?"

"No, Silvertip did. A Reaper hauled outta town like he was carrying hot coals. Silvertip managed to trip him up."

Silvertip. Big, brave Bear, that. "Very commendable," Valentine said, wondering if he sounded pompous.

"I don't train my Bears for dumb. Reaper running for the line like that? He looped a satchel charge on him. Of course, the thing animating the Reaper had us on his mind so he didn't notice. It dropped onto the Reaper's head and shoulders—looked like an umbrella collapsing on him."

"Looked back at me with all them eyes," Silvertip said.

"I don't think they're all eyes."

Silvertip shrugged. "Well, anyway, it was watching me take pot shots, carried like a baby with tentacles, when the charge blew. Reaper's head went straight up like a rocket."

"Best stick I ever saw, suh," Gamecock said.

"What happened after that?" Valentine asked.

"We knocked off three more Reapers pretty easy—sprayed fire into their shins and then took them out with explosives. The Moondaggers started tracking us on the way back, but the Wolves got a twist on them. Those boys are cruel but they sure don't know much about fighting."

†

All that remained was the decision about Red Dog. Valentine had him returned to his old company for a last meal together. He explained the situation and asked for a volunteer to shoot the poor hound.

"The whole brigade likes Red Dog, sir," Rand said. "Not the mutt's fault he's a Kurian spy."

"It's just a dog," Valentine said. "I'll kill it myself." He'd had to kill dogs before. Even gut them and stew them.

Glass stood up. "That Kurian's dead, right? Whatever connection he had is gone."

"Maybe the Miskatonic would want to study it," Rand said.

"It's too much of a risk," Valentine said. "One of you might fall asleep petting him and wake up kissing a fused grenade."

"I'll take the chance, sir," Glass said. "Like the lieutenant said, the Miskatonic should have a look at him. I'm stubborn and Ford and Chevy, well, I don't know that even a Kurian could make them much more confused unless there are bullets flying, food to be eaten, or a she-Grog around."

"What about you?"

"What, sir, 'n have me lose faith in the Cause? That train long since departed. Besides, I'd like to have a word or two with one of those Kurian sucks."

Valentine looked at Red Dog, utterly uncognizant of his peril but evidently just as happy to be with the old company as parked outside headquarters with the engineering gear.

"I guess one more ex-Quisling won't hurt. And I don't know how Glass's attitude can get much worse."

The men whistled and hooted and tossed scraps to the dog.

# CHAPTER TWELVE

*he Banks of the Green River, September: The fortunes of Javelin are at their lowest ebb. Help from the legworm ranchers has all but dried up. Only the underground dares to make contact, informing Southern Command's forces where they've hidden supplies.*

*The trickle of foodstuffs, plus the usual resourcefulness of soldiers to find food even on the march, allows Javelin to stay together in body.*

*Its soul is another matter.*

*The Moondaggers have stepped up their harassment. They shift south and west faster than the brigade can move, herding the column north when it wants to go south.*

*It's too dangerous to send out patrols. Only the Wolves and Cats leave the column. Even Valentine's company keeps close, scavenging such towns and camps as they temporarily occupy. Even Vette, who grew up in Kentucky, was lost near Campbellsville.*

*The men are bearded, dirty, tired. Their rope may not have run out yet, but the tattered end is in view. Much of their artillery marks the line of retreat along the Cumberland Parkway, destroyed and abandoned as ammunition ran out. Wounded, sick, and injured are either hidden with the underground or carried along. The engineers, with their usual flair for improvisation, have rigged the legworms with yokes that allow them to carry wounded swinging from hammocks, a smoother ride for the injured than the ambulance trucks.*

*They're far from home, far from sound, and far from those dreams of becoming ranchers and whiskey barons. It's all they can do to keep moving, keep securing bridges and hill gaps, and keep the rear guard supplied in its endless leapfrogs while delaying the Moondaggers behind and at the flanks.*

†

The Moondaggers may have begun the campaign as little more than a well-organized mob of killers, but they learned quickly under hard lessons.

Either that, or more experienced formations and commanders were sent to reinforce the division harrying Javelin. It seemed each day they grew more and more aggressive, bringing their route of march closer and closer to the brigade, sending small units to harass the flanks and rear.

The ranchers remained quiescent all around. If anything, it became harder to beg food from the brands. They either fled the brigade's approach or were found to be garrisoned by the Moondaggers. Scouts and the Cats heard a good deal of complaining about the Moondaggers helping themselves to supplies and paying with New Universal Church *Guidons* personally blessed by the Archon of Detroit. Or long harangues from missionaries asking for warriors willing to fight in the Gods' Holy Struggle.

"Holy Struggle to keep from taking him for a drag behind my worm," Duvalier reported an outrider from the Gunslinger clan grumbling. "He started talking about how my wife could be thrice blessed by faith, submission, and pregnancy."

They fought three skirmishes, and each time were forced to retreat by the Moondaggers bringing up reinforcements by truck. They dug in triple lines of entrenchments on good ground to move a little more north, until their line of march was north-northwest. The roads they needed to take came under long-range artillery fire, and the bridges and fords they wanted to use were mined or destroyed.

Then came the day when the scouts returned from the outskirts of Bowling Green with a special one-sheet newspaper speaking of a pitched battle in Pennsylvania. "Wreckers" (Kurian propagandists were growing tired of the word "terrorist"; with years of use it was losing its punch, so they were increasingly substituting "wreck-ers" when they discussed the Cause) out of New England had been soundly beaten. Over a thousand captured and the rest scattered in a panicked flight north. It was dreadfully specific in its maps and photographs.

"I don't suppose any of your old Church buddies are in these pic-tures," Valentine said to Brother Mark.

They went on emergency short rations that day. The legworm clans had stuck a wetted finger in the air and knew which way the wind was blowing. Even the Bulletproof began to suffer desertions. What was worse, sometimes they took their worms with them.

Valentine's company became a productive set of food thieves. They learned to filch from the edges of far fields, creeping in and digging up carrots and sweet potatoes and wrenching off a husk of corn here and there.

†

Valentine sat in the headquarters tent, eyes closed, listening to a news broadcast from Louisville. They were interviewing an author who'd just completed a new study on drug use among youth in the old United States. The main news had to do with a record harvest in the Dakotas, where farmers had overfulfilled their goals by sixteen percent. Locally all they reported was the opening of a new facility for freeze-drying legworm quarters.

He'd started listening because one of the communications techs re-ported hearing a blurb that train service between Nashville, Louisville, Lexington, and Knoxville had been suspended due to flooding. Militia units were being called up and deployed to save communities from the rising floodwaters.

The fall weather had been the one thing that had been kind to the brigade in their trip across Kentucky. Such an obvious lie gave Valen-tine hope that the legworm riders were attacking the lines.

They hadn't repeated the announcement.

Then Duvalier was tapping him on the shoulder.

"You know your plan to have the legworm ranchers fight the Moondaggers?"

"It's more of a hope than a plan," Valentine admitted.

"Well, maybe the Kurians are waiting for the same thing to happen to us. Or their generals, high Church people, whatever. A lot of them believe their own propaganda. They probably think we're stealing everything that isn't nailed down on this march. When we're not doing that, we're chopping down trees so we can stomp the baby worms."

"How did you come by this?"

"I sat in on a Church question night. Ever been to one of those?"

"I don't think so."

"They're pretty interesting. You write down questions and a priest picks them out of a box and answers them."

"That's a foolproof system," Valentine said.

"The questions smacked of being preselected. Right after a question about our column was another one asking what was being done about it. You haven't killed a bunch of Strongbows, have you?"

"No. We've been out of their territory for days. I don't think we even talked to any."

"Well, the Church is blaming it on you. Also some kidnappings in Glasgow."

"We never even saw the town. The Moondaggers had it occupied before we even got there. The kidnappings—they wouldn't be young women, by any chance?"

"Yes. They're kinda worked up about it."

Worked up. What would it take to push them beyond worked up?

He got an idea. An ugly, hurtful idea.

*Are you a doer or a shirker, Valentine? What's the price of your honor? Is it worth more than the survival of your comrades?*

✝

Within an hour he was where the medical staff had un-hammocked the patients and unburdened their worms.

Valentine looked at the three fresh bodies, good Southern Command men who'd traded in all their tomorrows for the Cause, hating himself. They gave up their lives for their comrades in the brigade. Would they object to their bodies being of further use?

"Doctor, I'm afraid I'll have to ask you for the use of three bodies."

"What do you have in mind, Major?"

"Nothing you want to know about, Doctor. They'll be treated respectfully, don't worry."

†

The Moondagger patrol never had a chance.

Reports from the legworm liaison said they were being supplied by the Green River clan.

Valentine chose the spot for the ambush well. He used legworm pasture along the most open stretch of road he could find, just east of a crossroads where other patrols might see and investigate smoke from three directions. A collapsed barn and an intact aluminum chicken coop stood opposite his position, off the road by about fifty yards.

His company, armed with the weapons meant for trade, backed up by Glass' pair with their machine guns, lay under piles of brush taken from legworm deposits, using the tiny hummocks of the snakelike legworm trails to rest their rifles.

With one squad left guarding his escape and evasion trail, he set up three parallel kill zones, anchoring their flanks with the .50s.

Once the men were in position, barrels down and hidden, he and Rand hurried around, laying brush across the groups of prone men.

The three-truck, one-car patrol was heading east, which struck him as strange. Better for him. They were coming off the rise six miles to the southeast, a good place to observe a long stretch of the Green River Valley.

They had a single antiaircraft cannon as armament mounted in the bed of a heavy-duty pickup. Just behind the cannon truck, the rest of the men rode in the beds of the armored double-axle trucks. Old mattresses and spare tires hung from aluminum skirting as improvised armor.

Valentine waited to detonate the mine until the cannon truck was over the old soda can that served as a marker. The mine, simple TNT under gravel in the potholed road, luckily went off right under one of the wheels and sprang the truck onto its side.

His men held their fire while the other vehicles turned off the road, facing the buildings at an angle. As the men dismounted to the side facing Valentine's line, he gave the order to fire.

"Antenna!" Valentine shouted.

The platoon fired on the command car. Valentine saw blood splatter the windows as the glass cracked and fell.

The .50 calibers completed the execution begun by rifle fire. The Grogs employed their guns like tripod-mounted rifles, firing single, precise shots, sniping over open sights.

Valentine went forward with his machine pistol, leading a maneuver team with Patel offering support fire. A shielded machine gun sprang up from the bed of the foremost of the trucks, almost like a jack-in-the-box as it unfolded, the gunner cocking it smoothly. Valentine fell sideways, shooting as he fell. The gunner made the mistake of swinging his weapon to shoot back, exposing himself to the riflemen.

Valentine watched invisible hands tug at the gunner's clothes and the gunner went down, shooting in the air as he fell. Through the gap under the truck Valentine saw two figures running for the old, half-collapsed barn. He took careful aim and planted bursts in one back and then the other.

The firing died down to single shots as the platoons made sure from a distance that the enemy was down. Valentine waved Rutherford and DuSable forward. They put their autoloading shotguns to their shoulders and stepped out. They took turns covering each other as they checked the cabins of the vehicles.

Valentine heard a shotgun blast, turned around.

"Thought he moved," DuSable explained.

"This one's wounded bad," Rutherford said.

Valentine nodded. He had to finish the job. They couldn't leave wounded behind who could tell stories.

Rutherford said, "Sorry, bro," and fired.

"Give up, give up," another bearded man shouted, holding his hands up as DuSable approached him.

DuSable ordered him to the ground. "Take him prisoner," Valentine said.

He had a sort of a long scarf about his neck. Valentine thought he might have been in the gun truck. He looked dazed but could walk. He wouldn't slow them up. Headquarters could figure out what to do with him.

"We're clear to this end, sir," Rutherford called, firing one more blast at a wet coughing sound.

"The easy part's over," Valentine said.

"I admire your definition of hard, sir," DuSable said, reloading his shotgun.

While scouts watched the road, the men worked in pairs, loading bodies into one truck. Then they backed it into the barn.

Valentine nodded to Patel. They both drew their knives and went to work.

Meanwhile Glass brought forward the dead bodies they had taken out of camp, now clad in legworm leather vests and soft boots such as the locals favored, and had the Grogs dig shallow graves for them near the road. They had assorted hooks and chains looped or stuffed in their pockets.

They hung some of the Moondagger bodies upside down from the rafters and cut their throats, letting the last of the blood run onto the barn floor. Then Valentine started cutting off beards.

He'd mutilated bodies before for effect in Santo Domingo. Then he'd only been risking his soul.

From what he understood of the Moondaggers, their retribution would be swift and merciless.

Valentine could picture the local reprisals easily enough. Moytana's description of their tactics had plenty of historical precedent. People herded into old church buildings and burned. Executions against town square walls worthy of Goya.

Who bore the responsibility? The agent provocateur or the troops? The Moondaggers would claim that if there had been no attack, there would be no reprisal.

Valentine took off another beard. Easier than skinning rabbits. No legs to deal with, just a long circular cut of the knife from one corner of the mouth, down the throat, and then back up to the other corner of the mouth. The bodies were still warm and he could smell their dried sweat. The cloying aroma of death wouldn't begin to rise for some hours yet.

For now they smelled like blood and diapers.

Rand was at the door of the barn, blocking the daylight coming through the gap between the truck and the post. "Sir, there's a radio in the command car that's still working."

Valentine stepped over to another body. "Put Preville on it. Have him listen to chatter and see if they know about the ambush."

Rand kept his eyes well above Valentine's waistline and the flashing knife.

"Will do, sir." Mercifully, he left without saying anything more.

Valentine's sense of honor wasn't taken word for word from the Southern Command *Officer's Epitome*. It was instead like a jigsaw collage from three or four different puzzles, all half-formed but recognizable pictures. Some came from his parents, others from Father Max, more from his training, a few from his experiences in the Kurian Zone.

Of course he'd done despicable things in the past. He'd bled men who had no more of a chance of fighting back than bound pigs, Twisted Cross lying in their tanks in a basement in Omaha. He'd tortured. He'd acted as judge, jury, and executioner over Mary Carlson's killers. He'd helped the overlord Kurian in Seattle wipe out Adler and his staff.

Each time one bit of his conscience or another had plucked at him, he'd burned with regret later thinking back on what he'd done, but necessity compelled and partially excused him.

But this time all of the jigsaw pieces agreed. This setup of the Green River clan stripped him of whatever scarecrow of his honor had remained.

He'd decided that the brigade's survival required a sacrifice. Of his honor. More important, of some members of the Green River clan. Wide-eyed children would be fed into war's furnace as a result of a ploy that couldn't even promise victory.

Or was it really for the brigade? *Do you need to be proven right this badly, David Stuart Valentine? Tip over the first domino in what you hope will be a series of massacres followed by ambush followed by another massacre, until these beautiful green hills run with blood?*

He'd have to shave with his eyes shut from now on.

"Maybe they were right about that shit detail stuff," a woman outside the barn said. Valentine made an effort not to place the voice to a face.

"I think I've gone crazy, Patel."

His sergeant major tossed a length of strong nylon binding cord over a still-sound rafter and hoisted a corpse by its ankles. Rigor was just beginning to set in.

"You remember Lugger, from LeHavre's old company?"

"Yes."

Patel fixed the other end of the line to the bare-beam wall. "She was on the Kansas operation. She saw what the Moondaggers did there— entire towns herded out into athletic fields and machine-gunned. She was on a scout and came into one of those ghost towns after. Saw Kurian cameras viding the bodies as guys posing as Southern Command POWs confessed to the killings. Sometimes they took out towns that weren't even in the fight—just did it to make a point."

"And?"

"These guys earned their killing. This," he said, looping a running hitch around another set of ankles, "is just interest on their deposit."

"What about the Green River clan?"

"David, worrying now will not alter the future. We must wait and see what happens."

Red Dog took the opportunity to relieve himself on a Moondagger tire.

Patel added, "The Moondaggers might wonder about a couple of large-caliber holes in their trucks and where a gang of legworm ranchers got a wireless detonator. Maybe we'll get lucky and they will see through this charade. They might stop dancing around, herding us, and try to settle things in one fight. I would very much like to see these bastards attack into overlapping fields of fire and proper artillery spotting."

"I don't think we'd win that," Valentine said.

"Perhaps not. But it would make a lot of people in Kansas feel better, knowing how many we took with us."

Valentine liked the picture Patel was painting. He wiped his knife on a Moondagger uniform and sawed off another beard.

"I wonder if they have the heart for it," Patel continued, hoisting the next body. "Despite all their shrieks and prayers and bluster. Is it all an act? They are at their most bloodthirsty when striking the defenseless. And do not forget, the legworm clans around here know how to fight and will not be as easily herded as populations brought up at the Kurian teat—"

"Major," a corporal called, not even poking his head inside the barn. "Preville's got some com traffic he wants you to listen to."

"Patel, can you finish up here?" *That's it, make it sound like a bit of carpentry.*

"Yes, sir."

Valentine left the half-collapsed abattoir gladly. The revolutionary's morality clung to his back, a heavier burden than any he'd ever carried while training with the Wolves.

The command car smelled like stale cigar smoke and blood. It had a side that opened up, rather like the hot-dog trucks Valentine had seen in Chicago, turning the paneling of the vehicle into a table and a sheltering overhang where the radio operator could sit out of the rain.

The radio had a bullet hole in it but somehow still functioned.

"Are they on their way here?" Valentine asked.

"Not sure, sir." He plugged in an extra headset and handed it to Valentine.

"I don't know some of the reports; they're in another language. All I speak is bad English and worse Spanish. But they're also communicating in English. I think that's their headquarters, here—"

"Group Q," a crackly voice said. "What is the status of the reprisal against the Mammoth?"

"Gods be praised, we are hitting them, brother," a clearer voice reported back. "There is much shooting. Q-4 is in their camp now. Sniper fire has delayed them dynamiting the remaining livestock."

Valentine smiled. Legworms took a lot of killing. He wondered if the Moondaggers knew just how long-lived a Kentucky feud could be.

"Is that you, Rafe?"

"No, brother, he has been wounded. Even the boys here can hit a target at two hundred meters. They vanish into the woods and hills and the trackers do not return."

"Where's that signal coming from?" Valentine asked, not familiar with this style of radio. "Is this Group Q in the Green River lands?"

"No, sir. Due north, a little northeast toward Frankfort. I'd say it's coming from the other side of our column. This is the channel the radio was on," Preville said, punching a button.

"Patrol L-6. L-6, you are overdue at Zulu," a clearer voice said. "Report, please. Patrol L-6, report, please. We are listening on alternative frequency Rook."

Valentine looked at the dashboard of the command car. A card with L-6 written on it stood in a holder.

"Guess they didn't get off a report after all," Valentine said.

They listened for a few more minutes. They heard complaints about blown-up bridges and roads filled with cut-down trees. A mobile fueling station had been blown up.

Kentucky, it seemed, had finally had enough of the Moondaggers.

"I want to talk to the prisoner," Valentine said.

The prisoner had a scuffed look about him. His eyes widened as he saw Valentine approach. Valentine looked down. His uniform was something of a mess.

Valentine cleaned his blade off on the man's shoulder.

"I'm not going to hurt you," Valentine said. "All I want is a news report."

"News report?" the Moondagger said.

"Yes. You know, like on the television. You've watched television."

"Allchannel," the Moondagger said.

Valentine smiled, remembering the logo from Xanadu. "Yes, allchannel. It's the Curfew News. Give me the highlights from Kentucky."

Realization of what Valentine wanted broke over his face like a dawn. He raised his chin.

"The worm herders. They fight with us. Our Supreme, he says to give a lesson, but from that lesson we must give five more lessons, and then fifty. So now we must call in many more re-erforcings. Much fighting everywhere—here one day, there another. I am diligent, I am peaceable, I follow orders only."

Valentine tried to get more out of him: places, clans, the nature of these "re-erforcings," but he was just a youth taught little more than to follow orders, line up to eat, obey his faith, and of course shoot.

"Let's get him back to headquarters. Give him a little food and water. He looks like he could use it."

"I pass my test," the prisoner said.

"Come again?" Valentine asked.

"The Gods, always they test us. Both with blessings and misfortunes. Either can lead you from the righteous path."

"On that, we're agreed," Valentine said.

"I was afraid that you would kill me and I would not be taken to higher glory by the angels of mercy. I still have a chance to make something of my death."

Valentine felt like slapping some sense into the hopeful, young brown eyes. *A little understanding, please, David*, he heard Father Max's voice say, sounding just as he had when Valentine complained as a sixteen-year-old about his first and second year students' haphazard efforts with their literacy homework. What would he have become, had he been raised on Church propaganda as though it were mother's milk?

He left the prisoner and his disquieting thoughts, and plunged into planning a route back to the brigade.

✝

With the column under way again, Valentine sought out Brother Mark.

"Is confession a specialty of yours?" he asked.

Brother Mark took a deep breath. "It's not a part of my official dogma, no. But I believe in unburdening oneself."

Valentine sat. "There's a demon in me. It keeps looking for chances to get out. This damn war keeps arranging itself so I don't have much choice but to free it. I just came back from a little ambush in Green River clan territory. I did . . . appalling things."

"You want to talk sins, my son? You will have to live lifetimes to catch up to my tally."

"Killing wounded?"

"Oh, much worse. I believe I told you some of my early schooling and work at the hospital? Of course. After my advanced schooling they posted me to Boston. I did well there. Married, had three kids. All were brought up by their nannies with expectations of entering the Church in my footsteps. Poor little dears. There was a fourth, but my Archon suggested I offer her up. Parenting effectiveness coefficients for age distribution and all that. Middle children sometimes grow up wild in large families."

"I'm sorry. So you left after that?" Valentine asked.

"Oh, no. No, I gave her up gladly and took Caring out to dinner on the wharf to celebrate afterward. My bishop sent us a bottle of French champagne. Delicious stuff. I became a senior regional guide for the Northeast. The Church keeps us very busy there. There are a lot of qualified people employed in New York or Philadelphia, Montreal and Boston, and down to Washington. High tech, communications, research, education, public affairs—the cradle of the best and the brightest. They require a lot of coddling and emotional and intellectual substantiation. You can't just say 'that's the way it must be; Kur has decided' to those people. You have to argue the facts. Or get some new facts.

"So I became an elector. Myself and the council of bishops helped set regional, and sometimes interregional, Church policy. How old could an infant be before it could no longer be offered up for recycling? What was the youngest a girl could be and have a reasonable expectation of surviving childbirth? We listened to scientists and doctors, debated whether a practicing homosexual was a threat to the community even if he or she produced offspring. High Church Policy, it was called, to distinguish ourselves from the lower Church orders who spent their days giving dental hygiene lectures and searching Youth Vanguard backpacks for condoms. My glory days.

"They taught me a few mental tricks. Most of it involved planting suggestions in children to prove reincarnation, giving them knowledge they couldn't possibly have obtained otherwise. In an emergency I was taught how to induce hysterical amnesia. That's why amnesia is such a popular plot device on *Noonside Passions*, by the way. We've found it useful for rearranging the backgrounds of people who've engaged in activities that are better off forgotten.

"Better off forgotten," he repeated, taking another drink. "Then I lost my wife."

"I'm sorry."

"I was too. Caring was a wonderful woman. Never a stray thought or an idle moment. Her one fault was vanity. After the third child she put on weight that was very hard to get off. She wanted a leadership position in the local Youth Vanguard so she could travel on her own, and you had to look fit and trim and poster-perfect. She didn't want more pregnancies and of course you wouldn't catch me using black-market condoms, so she went to some butcher and got herself fixed.

"Of course matters went wrong and she had to be checked into a real hospital. Age and the source of her injuries . . . well, the rubric put her down for immediate drop. The hospital priest had more doubts about her case than I did. I signed her end cycle warrant myself. If there was any part of me that knew it was wrong, it stayed silent. I am almost jealous of you. You have a conscience which you can trust to give you pangs. Doubts. Recriminations. I've no such angel on my shoulder."

"Did you regret it later, then?"

"I'm not even sure I do now. She was so conventional, I'm sure she was happy to be useful in death. No, I didn't come to regret it. Not even after Constance, my middle daughter, killed herself rather than marry that officer. It was the strangest thing. I was at a rail station. A brass ring's mother had been put on a train, and he had enough weight to argue it with the archon, and he sent me, because as an elector and a regional guide I had enough weight to get someone taken off a train and the nearest porter who didn't genuflect promptly enough put on."

He took another drink.

"The next car had a group of people being put on. They had to know. There was one girl in a wheelchair. She must have been sixteen or seventeen. When you get to be my age, youth and strength take on their own sort of beauty, Valentine. She had so much of it she almost shone. I wonder what put her in that wheelchair. The lie that day was that they were going to work on factory fishing ships, but I think most of them knew what the railcars meant. This girl was laughing and joking with the others.

"Just an ordinary girl, mind you. Beautiful in her way. I looked at her tight chin and bright eyes, saw her laugh with those white teeth as she spun her chair to the person behind—she had a green sweater on—and I thought, what a waste. *What a waste*. Suddenly all the justifications, all the proverbs from the *Guidon*, it's like they turned to ash, dried up and illegible, at least to my mind.

"If only I'd learned her name. I want to write an article about her.

Something. I want her to exist somewhere other than my memory. But if I give her a name—well, that just seems wrong. Any suggestions for what to call her?"

"Gabrielle Cho."

"That has a certain ring to it. Certainly, my boy. Someone special to you?"

"She was."

"Very well. She'll become a part of our documentation. We'll try to tell the truth as best as we can for a change."

"So a girl in a wheelchair you didn't know made you give up . . ."

"Twenty-eight years in the Church. What's counted as a good lifetime now."

"How did you make it out?"

"From that point on it wasn't hard to plan my escape. I had travel cards, staff, and best of all, I was in no hurry. I could choose my moment." He straightened his back, jamming a hand hard against his lower spine. Valentine didn't need his Wolf-ears to hear the creaks and cracks.

"How do you perform, what do you call them, powers?" Valentine asked. "Like at the Mississippi crossing, or when you connected with the Kurian through Red Dog?"

"It's not the easiest thing to explain. You've got to remember, everything you see, smell, touch, it all gets passed into your brain. You can't see certain wavelengths, hear certain sounds, because your brain has no coding information. Much of it is simply planting new coding information into the target's brain. Of course the Kurians—and the Lifeweavers—can do the same thing. Every day, when they have to appear to us. It comes so natural to them they don't have to think about it any more than we do breathing."

Valentine nodded.

"As for me, it gives me a terrific headache. I hope your Cabbage fellow has some aspirin to spare."

Valentine watched Brother Mark totter off, wondering that the aging body didn't give in to despair.

# CHAPTER THIRTEEN

*T*he banks of the Ohio, October, the fifty-fifth year of the Kurian Order:
*The long retreat ended somewhere southeast of Evansville.*

*The events of the first week of October 2077 are still a matter of dispute
among historians. Clever shift or desperate flight? The Moondaggers jug-
gled their forces with the energy and ferocity for which they were famous,
cutting off each sidle by the spent Javelin brigade, shifting troops down the
Ohio or up the Tennessee until the retreat ground to a halt near a small
heartland city that seemed to grow more by virtue of nothing else within an
easy distance than any particular advantage of situation or resource.*

*The Moondaggers accomplished all this even with their supply lines
snipped and chewed, responding with harshness that to this day leads to a
fall blood-moon being called a "Dagger's moon" all across Kentucky.*

*In a last gambit, the column turned almost due north, hoping the
Moondaggers would not expect a movement toward Illinois. But the ploy
failed and the Moondaggers found the brigade trapped on the south bank of
the Ohio. Both sides dug in and prepared for the inevitable.*

*The camp is not well-ordered. Sandwiched in a fold of ground hiding
them from both eyes in Evansville and the Kentucky hills, the only advantage to the position is that both flanks are more-or-less guarded by the river,
and the rear is a long stretch of muddy ground pointed like an extended
tongue toward Evansville between the loops of the Ohio.*

*A pair of the city's dairy farms are now under occupation. One serves
as headquarters and the other as a field hospital. The previous night the
brigade was lucky enough to catch a barge heading upriver. A quick canoe
raid by the Wolves later, the barge's engine was in their possession, along*

*with the cargo. The raiders were hoping for corn and meat; instead they found a load of sorghum, sugar, and coffee.*

*So the morning camp now smells of fresh coffee, well-sweetened and creamy, thanks to the dairy cows. The chance to get the brigade across in the dark and confusion of their arrival evaporated as Evansville's tiny brown-water navy took up positions and shot up the tug. So the men went through the tiresome task of building breastworks and digging ditches. Each man wondering if the long chase is done, if this is the last entrenchment.*

*Not enough are in any condition to care.*

†

The men joked that they weren't in the last ditch, simply because the last ditch was full of muddy Ohio river water and collapsed every time they tried to deepen it.

This bit of river had one advantage, however. The Kurians who ran Evansville evidently feared attack from their neighbors up the Ohio or across the river in Kentucky, for the river loops in front of the city and the waterfront were a network of mines, obstacles, booms, and floating guard platforms that constantly shifted place. Only Evansville pilots knew the route that would take watercraft safely through the maze.

According to Valentine's Kentucky scouts, this was the one stretch of river where they wouldn't encounter artillery boats and patrol craft. The Kurians of Evansville clung tenaciously to their ownership of these river bends, squeezing every advantage they could from their control of the loops by exacting small tolls for passage up to the Ordnance or down to the Mississippi.

He thought it might just be possible to slip across the river and disappear into the woods and hills and swamps of poorly controlled southern Illinois, where at least he and the Moondaggers would be met by equally hostile Grogs in the form of the Doublebloods. But Evansville's flotilla of tiny gunboats and the news that more craft of the river patrol waited on the far bank downriver stifled that hope.

Touring the defensive positions with Colonel Bloom, exhausted and bloodless in the passenger seat of her command car and able to do little more than nod, he found himself giving in to despair. Their situation grew worse, practically by the hour.

The Moondaggers had reinforced their left, ready to defend his most likely breakout alley, and the Wolves reported sounds of troops being gathered for a knockout blow from the right.

A boxer's stance, poking him from the left as the right readied to lash out.

†

Valentine was woken from a sleep that wasn't amounting to much and requested to report to the command tent.

He entered, still buttoning his uniform coat thrown over his legworm leathers.

Several Guard officers had already gathered, and more were coming. Tikka and another grizzled legworm rider were taking turns slicing hunks of cheese with a knife and alternating bites of the cheese and hard biscuit.

All eyes were on a boy of thirteen or fourteen, stripped down to his underwear, who stood drinking a steaming beverage and shivering, with blankets wrapped around his bony shoulders and feet.

"Thought you'd like to hear this kid's story," Rand said. "We pulled him out of the river when we were setting fish traps."

"Pulled nothing," the boy said. "I swam the whole way."

"Story time," someone guffawed.

"When are you boys comin'?" the wet and muddy boy asked. He'd slicked his body with Vaseline or something similar to ease the swim.

"Coming?" Bloom asked.

"You're with the liberation, right? Underground says that all of Kentucky's rising. We're listening on the AM radio. Some of us made crystal sets. They took the transmitter at Bowling Green and are talking about all those Moondagger throats that got cut at their supply depot south of Frankfort."

"How do we know you're telling the truth?" Duvalier said.

The boy looked shocked, as if his long swim across the river should be proof enough.

"There's street fighting in Evansville. Some of the OPs came over to our side. Hit the downtown armory. We burned a representative when it ran into the mayor's city house. They're looking for its bones now."

"You say Kentucky is rising?"

"Of course. We thought you were part of that."

Valentine felt hope, real hope, for the first time since the catastrophe at Utrecht.

"Are we part of it?" Valentine asked Bloom.

"If we're not, we sure as hell will be by dawn," Bloom said.

"What else can you tell us?" Valentine asked the boy.

His eyes were so bright and white in the gloom of the headquarters tent, Valentine was almost hypnotized as the boy looked around. "Except for the river guard, there's not much in the way of troops in town, just some riot police holding the Kur Pinnacle. They called up most everyone they could trust from the area into the militia and sent them across the river. Hospitals in Frankfort and Lexington and Louisville are bursting with wounded. The Ordnance is mobilizing; they're skeered legworms'll be crossing the Ohio and into their state. My chief says to tell you that he's got boats and a couple of old barges. We can rig lines from the bridge and get you across if your guns can clear the river."

He was an intelligent youth. Valentine could see why they sent him.

"What's your name, kid?"

"Jones, H. T. Youth Vanguard, but I'm only in it for the sports trips. Quit now, I hope. Vanguard service is just a rotten apple, shiny on the outside."

Bloom studied the brigade's defensive positions on her map. A few of the companies had been bled down to little more than platoons. A careful assessment of the mortar readiness status sheet would bring either tears or laughter. "Valentine, can we get one more fight out of the brigade, do you think?"

"I'll ask them," Valentine said.

Duvalier shook her head. "It's another gaslighting. This greasy little squirt's eyeing up a brass ring."

"Hey," the boy said, but Valentine held up his hand.

Bloom thought it over.

"Valentine, take your old company and go across the river and offer assistance. If we can catch a break in the city, safely tuck away our wounded. We can make that dash into Illinois and get to the mighty Miss."

"Define assistance, sir." Valentine hated to sound like he was crabbing out from under orders. "If it's to be combat to clear the city, I'd like a Bear team at least. If they're holed up in the manner this boy describes, I'll need demolition gear too."

"Just get over there and make an assessment. Use your judgment. We've got those two big guns we captured. Might as well use them for something other than blind fire on crossroads behind us."

✝

They came across in the dead of night in an unlit barge, downriver, and marched through a muddy, overgrown tangle of long-dead industry on the riverbank to the west side of town.

Evansville itself burned and rattled with the occasional pop of gunfire.

Bodies hung from the streetlamps. One torn-frocked churchman still clutched his *Guidon* in the grip of rigor mortis as he twirled in the fall breeze.

He made contact with the local resistance, a trio of a butcher, a teacher, and the man who ran the main telephone office. All introduced themselves first as belonging to the Evansville Resistance Lodge.

What was left of the Kurian Order, with their few troops pulled out to fill gaps in the Moondagger lines and their populace burning and score settling, had retreated to the bowl-like bulk of the civic center.

The resistance had power, water—Valentine even passed a hospital with big, spray-painted triage signs for illiterates bringing in wounded. Barrows full of farm produce crept along the sidewalks, distributing food to small patrols and sentry teams. Charcoal-fueled pickups brought in gear—scavenged or improvised weapons. There were workshops fixing up firefighting equipment with bullet shields so that an assault might advance under cover of water sprayed into windows.

Parts of the city might be burning, but Evansville appeared to be functioning with a good deal more organization and energy than he'd expected. He met men who worked in machine shops and fertilizer plants.

Fertilizer plants could be converted to the manufacture of high explosives. How long would it take some of Evansville's workshops to convert to the production of mortar shells?

"We cut off their water and juice," the telephone office manager named Jones said. "Of course, I think they got a reserve. Some kind of emergency plan is in effect. A cop prisoner told us they had three days of water. That's how long they're supposed to be able to hold out in an emergency until help arrives from Indianapolis or Louisville."

"Who's left in there?" Valentine asked as Rand set up the fire control observation station and tested radio communications.

"Middle-management types who were in the militia," Jones said. "Local law enforcement. The Youth Vanguard Paramilitary Auxiliary. Go ahead, blow them out of there. Won't nobody miss them."

He got the nod from Rand.

Valentine had shells from the guns march up Main Street toward the civic center. The last one impacted just inside the barricade. He'd made his point.

Valentine examined the civic center and the pathetic assortment of cars piled up on the sidewalks around it, along with dropped bundles and half-unpacked trunks. Entire families had retreated to the security of the big building. In panic or by design, the Evansville Quislings had assembled a barricade out of the civilian and order-enforcement vehicles, stringing barbed wire through broken windows and between fenders.

Dead bodies hung here and there on the wire. Black birds shamelessly feasted on the detritus of desperate valor.

He couldn't blow the remaining Quislings out without killing their kids with them.

He couldn't drop 155mm shells on a bunch of kids and fill the approaches to the civic center with a mixture of dead civilians and his company.

That left talking.

One of the mob behind him sneezed and wiped his nose with a onionskin page from a New Universal Church *Guidon*.

Valentine heard a metallic *clang!* A string of men emerged antlike from a utility hole mid-street and made a dash for the civic center. Gunfire swept the street. Poor shooting—they only got one. The others made it to the safety of the barbed wire and vehicle necklace around the building.

He lay, groaning.

"Cease fire! Cease fire!" Valentine shouted, hoping that energy would take the place of training and military discipline. The gunfire died down.

"Go on and get him," Valentine shouted at the civic center. "Nobody's shooting. Just let us get to our people too."

"Really?" a voice from the dark maw of the main doors called.

"Absolutely, positively really," Valentine shouted back, feeling a little giddy at the absurdity of the question.

They dragged their man out of the street and the Evansville mob got their own. Some resistance men, pinned down beneath a school bus, took the opportunity to return to their own lines.

"Rand, I'm trusting you to keep things from getting out of hand. If someone takes a pot shot at me, I don't want a sniper duel. We'll be back to trading machine-gun fire in no time."

He unsheathed his sword and gave the blade to Rand. "If they drop me, give this to Smoke."

E. E. KNIGHT

"Let me go, sir," Patel said.

"You're too slow a target. And Rand, it would be a tragedy if someone put a bullet through your double helping of brains. Colonel Bloom gave her orders to me."

Valentine walked out into the center of the street under a white flag tied to his sword scabbard.

"Could I speak to whoever's in charge in there? I represent the United Free Republics, Kentucky Military Assistance Expedition."

Valentine had been wondering what to call the forces across the river; the improvised name sprang from his lips without involving his brain, evidently.

They answered with a shot. The bullet whizzed by close enough for Valentine to hear it with his right ear and not his left. He was either lucky or the sniper was a bad shot. He forced himself to remain erect.

"Who shot?" a voice yelled from the darkness. "Tell that dumbshit to cut it out. He's got a white flag."

"Killing me won't give you another day of water and power in there," Valentine shouted, advancing toward the barricade. "It'll just start the fighting again. Don't see that's gotten you much so far, and there's artillery being set up across the river. How many shells is it going to take to collapse that big roof?"

Valentine wondered if there'd be an instant's realization of his folly if the marksman decided to put the next one between his eyes. Would that be better than having part of his face torn off, or a bullet through the neck?

The street hit him in the back hard and Valentine felt an ache in his chest. He never heard the shot.

Valentine felt busted ribs, burned a finger in the hot bullet embedded in the woven Reaper cloth on his vest.

It felt like someone had performed exploratory surgery with a jackhammer on his chest. Valentine felt content to lie in the street for a moment, holding up the white flag like a dead man with a lily. He let his Wolf hearing play along the other side of the barricade.

312

"Quit firing. I'll shoot the next man who fires."

"That's treason talk, Vole," another answered. "Kill-or-die order, remember?"

"The man who gave that order quit on us two days ago, you've noticed."

Valentine rolled to his feet.

"I'm trying to save lives, here," he called. He tasted blood.

The next shot went between his legs, but he made it to the cover of the bus barricading the main entrance. Barbed wire hung off it like bunting.

"I'm right here if anyone wants to chat." It hurt like fire to shout. "Does that kill-or-die order apply to your kids? Maybe we can get them out of there, at least."

A bullet punched through the far side of the bus. Valentine slid to put the engine block between himself and the sniper.

The bus window above him broke and fell in shards. Luckily it was safety stuff. Valentine heard more shooting, a deeper blast of a shotgun.

"We got the gunman, Terry," Valentine heard.

Valentine looked through the rear doors of the bus. Someone had cut a hole in the other side, offering egress through the barricade. He lurched in, marked a claymore mine sitting under the driver's seat, and decided that maybe entering the bus wasn't such a good idea after all.

He sat on the bus's entry step.

"I'm still ready to talk."

"We're sending a party out to talk under a white flag."

Valentine looked at the advertisements running along the roof edge of the bus. Church fertility treatments, infant formula, exhortations to join the Youth Vanguard, warnings against black market deals ("Profit to the enemy, Poverty for your friends"), and invites for the sick and halt to enjoy a refreshing sojurn to the Carolinas and the "best medical care east of the Mississippi." A photo of a smiling silver-haired couple in beach wear lounging in chaises under an umbrella, he with a cast on his leg, her with a cannula and IV hanging from a mount shaped like a flamingo, had a buxom nurse serving what looked like tropical drinks.

Visitors to Evansville were invited to see the Eternal Flame at Affirmation Park and add their names to the Wall of Hope for a small NUC donation.

The Kurian Order in microcosm.

Valentine heard movement from the other side of the bus. A trio of men, two in law-enforcement blue and one with a clean coat thrown over dirty collar and tie, entered one at a time. A cop went forward, yanked a wire from the mine, removed the detonator with a pocket screwdriver, and tucked the inert explosive under his arm. He had a huge nose that made his eyes look small and swinish in comparison. Valentine noticed numerous breaks in the greasy proboscis, a beak of scar tissue and whiskey veins.

"What do you have in mind, Rebel Rick?" the other cop said.

"Name's Valentine, major, Southern Command," Valentine said, learning to breathe with half his chest. He'd heal from this. He always healed, but always came back only to 90 percent. He wondered how many 10 percents he'd lost over the years.

"Cloth from a robe. That's why he's still alive," the man with the tie muttered to the other cop.

"I'm Vole, senior captain, Evansville Security and Enforcement," Big Nose said. "Emergency Militia Leader Albano, Temporary Mayor Bell."

"I was clerk of Resource Allocation," Bell said. "I never carried a gun or signed a retirement warrant my whole life."

"No separate deals!" Vole barked. "What's your offer?"

"No more fighting between you guys and the resistance," Valentine said. "That's my deal. Come out without your guns. I'll put any dependents under supervision of Southern Command personnel. They'll come to no harm."

"What about us?" Vole asked.

"That's up to you and the Indiana boys."

Albano purpled but instead of turning on Valentine, he elbowed

Vole. "I say we hang him, just like they did with Sewbish. No more flags of truce—just delays the inevitable."

Vole ignored him. "Understand, Valenwhatever, we've got nothing to lose and orders to kill any rebel we can get our hands on."

"A hard rain's going to fall here, just a couple more days," Albano added. "A hard rain."

"I'm sick of that weather report, Albano," Bell said. "Where's that relief column out of Indy? Tommorow, tomorrow, always tomorrow."

"Shut up, you two," Vole said.

Bell ignored him. "Lindgren said the Moondaggers asked for it to cross the river into Kentucky to secure their lines for the retreat out of Kentucky. We're bloodpiped. Let's refugee north to Indy. Even if a new guide comes, he'll have his own people. Better to start at the bottom rung somewhere else than get caught up in a reorg here."

"You willing to let us just walk out of here?" Vole asked Valentine.

"I'm sure that could be arranged," Valentine said. "If you turn over your weapons and gear intact. I'll try to make the local resistance see the advantage of getting their hands on your guns. But are you sure of the reception you'll get in Indianapolis or wherever you end up? You might be surplus to requirements. Someone's got to take a fall for a debacle in a city the size of Evansville. Might just be you all."

He let that sink in.

"Seems to me you men have two alternatives. Stay here and fight it out, waiting for help that's not coming, or surrender yourselves to your fellow Hoosiers."

"Six of one . . . ," Albano said.

Valentine coughed up a little more blood. "Fight or die, they told you. Take 'em up on it. Fight them for a change."

They blinked at him like sunstruck owls.

"Rengade and get picked off on some Reaper's manhunt?" Vole said. "Or get a stake pounded up my ass by a vengeance team? Painful way to go."

"I'm wearing what's left of one of those Reapers you're so scared of," Valentine said. He might be called a liar. Valentine looked at it as shaving the truth. "Join the fight against the Kurians. I lead a bunch of fighting men that's nothing but former Order. I can always use more men. You might get killed, but if you fall, you'll fall on the right side and you won't get recycled into pig feed. Once you've proven in combat, you're a new man, so to speak. We'll give you a new identity if you like."

Valentine was exceeding his orders and knew it. But if it would spare a mutual slaughter—

Valentine noticed that both sides had advanced on the bus, scraps of white tied to tips of rifles or held aloft at the end of bits of pipe fashioned into spiked clubs, trying to hear what was transpiring inside.

The resistance was more numerous, the Kurian Order forces better armed, facing each other across abandoned vehicles and curlicue tangles of razor wire. . . .

The Quislings looked a rough lot. Of course there would be the bullies, the cowards, and the lickspittles—the Kurian Order attracted such—but he had a tough, experienced bunch of officers now. They'd keep them in line.

The battered, big-nosed leader looked at Valentine with suspicious eyes.

"Trust comes hard, I know. I spent time under the Kurians myself. Don't they always garland their deals with a bunch of roses? What did they tell you before you joined Enforcement? Quick path to a cushy office and a luxury card? Any of that come true? I'm telling you you'll have it hard, but you'll be able to look yourselves in the mirror. No more bundling neighbors off into collection vans."

Valentine had no more words in him. He caught his breath, waited. The three exchanged looks.

"I want all this written up on paper with some signatures," Vole said. "And I want us to keep all our light weapons and sidearms. It's got to say that too. Every man gets a choice: join you, surrender, or walk out."

"Save us the effort of finding guns for you," Valentine said.

†

Valentine left a platoon of his company under Ediyak and Patel to organize the surrendered Quislings and returned across the river in a small boat, heartened. A barge would follow, laden with food, mostly preserved legworm meat rations marked "WHAM!—hi protein" in cheery yellow lettering. The barge would bring the wounded back, where the Evansville hospital could give them a bed and rest at last.

"That Last Chance feller paid us another call while you were across the river," Tiddle told him outside the headquarters tent as Valentine scraped riverbank mud from his boots. "Said he was giving us one more chance to give up before turning us into charcoal briquettes."

He called a staff conference and gave the good news to Bloom, trying to stay awake and alert. When it was done, he felt as tired as Bloom looked. She tilted her head back and closed her eyes. "We can get home."

He took a breath. Decisions like these were always easy, when, as Churchill said, honor and events both pointed in the same direction. "Hell with that. We've got a secure base in this country and they don't. Let's go on the offensive."

"With the brigade worn to pieces?" Bloom asked, looking as though Valentine had reopened her incisions.

"Now's our best shot, Colonel. If we can buy some peace and quiet to get things organized to support us in Evansville, we can cut river traffic on the Ohio and give some real help to the uprising in Kentucky."

"What happened to going home?" a Guard captain asked.

"Every time we've had a chance to run, we've run, and where's it got us? Javelin ends with a whimper as the men pile onto barges and motorboats under shell fire. If Javelin's going to die, I want it to die hard, trying to do what it was designed for: to establish a new Freehold. If we can take the Moondagger main body with us, Kentucky has a chance. We've got the technical people, even if they've lost a lot of their gear on the retreat. We've got the Wolves and Bears, even Smoke and a Cat or two."

"I wouldn't want to be up against this brigade," Gamecock said.

"Fingers around the enemy's throat and teeth locked on hide," Bloom said. "God grant me the strength to get out of this chair one more time. Valentine, will you help me draw up a plan for your clutch hit?"

"In this situation it'll be a simple one, sir," Valentine said. It was hard to say which emotion dominated, relief that they were turning at bay like a wounded lion, or anxiety over this last throw of the dice.

"If you do this, what's left of the Kentucky Alliance will be with you," Brother Mark said. "Believe it or not, we've still got riders from all the five tribes. Most are either Bulletproof or Gunslingers. Tikka's worked out some kind of command structure. Bitter-enders all. They want their ton of flesh from the Moondaggers."

*I shot a javelin into the air, it fell to earth, I knew not where. . . .*

Valentine kept the doggerel to himself. They could hardly move any more, so they might as well fight. Where Javelin finally landed would—must!—be remembered. One way or another.

Javelin's camp was buzzing with rumor.

"I've got a message from Colonel Bloom, men," Valentine said, breaking in on breakfast. The men sat on their sleeping mats in neat rows, eating. He nodded to the commissary boy, and some of the kitchen boys brought out fresh hot coffee.

A few heads turned. Some in groups at the back kept eating. Others held out mugs for more coffee.

He climbed up onto the roof of cranky Old Comanche, the sole remaining truck. "We crossed the Mississippi to help the locals create a new Freehold," Valentine said.

"I don't know how you feel about it, but we came here to do a job. We ran hard across Kentucky on the way there, and then fought our way back. Our trail is marked by graves—some of ours, lots of theirs.

"Headquarters just received some startling news. Evansville's been taken by the local resistance. They've got barges full of grain, pork, medical supplies—everything we're short of. They're short of training and guns.

"On this side of the river Kentucky's as sick of the Moondaggers as we are. The legworm clans between Bowling Green and the Appalachians are fighting, hard. Not raiding, not burning a few bridges to give them some negotiating leverage with the Kurians. They're in it for keeps."

They stopped eating the keyed tins of legworm meat marked WHAM. That was something.

"The reason the city there fell that is that most of their militia's been impressed by the Moondaggers. What's left is willing to come over to the Cause.

"You've had some hard fights. You all know you've given it to the Moondaggers even harder. They're filling out those positions opposite with militia ordered to kill or die. Their division isn't even able to hold an entire line at our front."

A few of the men stood up, as though trying to see through the hill toward the enemy positions. That was something else.

"I think we can guess what they mean to do. Hold our beat-down brigade here until they can reestablish their lines of communication and supply, keeping their fingers crossed that we'll surrender. It's been three days. The Wolves keep hearing activity on the other side of their hills—why haven't they attacked? Last Chance told us that we'll die tomorrow. Let's shut him up for good. They're the ones worried about how much worse it'll get tomorrow, not us.

"I know what you're thinking: You've heard this story before. A populace rising, all we have to do is go help them, midwives to a new Freehold. I'm telling you what I've heard from the resistance. Maybe it's wrong, maybe it's lies, maybe they're trying to get us out of our ditches and into the open.

"Let's take them up on it. Put their money where Last Chance's mouth is. I wonder how often, in the history of the Moondaggers, they've been on the receiving end of an assault. Bears in the spearhead,

Wolves snapping at their flanks, and a real assault by trained men coming in behind mortar fire.

"And a Cat opening up that asshole in the swinging chair," Duvalier said, suddenly beside him. "If you boys will loan me a couple of claymores from the front of your positions, I'll see if I can't plant a couple around the Moondaggers' headquarters."

"Whar's a little thing like you gonna hide claymores?" Rollings called. He'd come up with some lovely new boots, probably taken from a Moondagger officer.

Duvalier opened her coat, flasher style, showing her improvised harness with clips and holsters and knife sheaths, but the men whistled at what was under her tattered old T-shirt.

Valentine spoke again. "I've told you what I know. Maybe they're setting us up for another sucker punch, with everything, including the bodies hanging from lampposts in Evansville, a sham. Fine. I'm tired of running anyway. But I don't think it's another trick. I've got a feeling this is the day. This is the day when the tide turns. I'm asking you all to turn and fight with me. Our retreat's over." He considered his words to the Quislings across the river, decided they could be improved on. "From now on, it's forward. If we fall, we'll fall with honor."

Valentine stifled a few cheers before it became general by holding out his hands.

"Quiet, Javelin Brigade. Let's not do anything to spoil the surprise."

†

During the day they came under some distracting shellfire. They were 120mm mortars, Valentine knew, having become intimately familiar with the sound of mortar calibers on Big Rock Hill. If anything, it helped settle Valentine's mind. An army baiting them to attack by feigning weakness wouldn't waste resources on random harassing fire.

Duvalier made a quick scout of the enemy right that night. Valentine heard her report in the new assault headquarters, far forward, masquerading as an artillery observation post. They were close enough forward to draw sniper fire, so they had to keep their heads behind logs and brush.

"That greased-up kid is right about one thing. There's nothing but some nervous farmers and shopkeepers in front of you here, stiffened by Moondagger units behind. They pulled the best of them back to help with the disorder in their rear."

"How do you know that?" a lieutenant asked.

"I was close enough to taste splatter when one of them took a piss. I was able to pick up a couple of conversations."

Valentine could smell blood on her. "That's not all you did."

She wetted her lips. "They had a big machine gun backing up their line with a couple of our Moondagger friends manning it. Don't know if it was there to keep the men up front from running or not, but the loader was asleep and the gunner was jacking off. Couldn't resist a target of opportunity."

Valentine communicated her report, leaving out the story about the dead onanist, over the field phone. Bloom decided to put into effect the assault they'd begun planning after dismissing the boy for a meal and a return swim. They'd leave a skeleton line on the right opposite the Moondaggers and gather for the last effort on the left.

Duvalier shoved some legworm jerky in her mouth and had a cup of real coffee. "I'll take those claymores now, if you've got them," she said.

"Going to be a hero at last?" Valentine asked.

"No. I just like the odds. Their sentry positions out there are about as much use as a screen door in a flood. I'll plant the claymores in their headquarters dugout and wait for a full house. Just hope your guns don't drop a shell on me."

Valentine chuckled. "No ammo reserve. It'll be the shortest barrage in history."

She disappeared and he walked the positions, anxious. Especially after an illumination flare fired. Maybe Duvalier flushed a deer or threw a rock to get the Quisling militia looking in the wrong direction for her final wiggle through the lines.

He inspected the Bears. Gamecock had them in three circles. Chieftain already had his warpaint on. Silvertip was tightening the spiked leather dogskin gloves he liked to wear in a fight.

The Wolves had already left, half of Moytana's under his lieutenant's command to reinforce the right—just in case—and the other half to move along the riverbank and see if they could slip around between the Ohio and the Quisling positions on the left. Valentine authorized Moytana to start the action. The rest of Javelin would follow them in, with Gamecock's Bears leading the way.

Valentine's company was at the forefront. They'd creep forward and provide covering fire for the Bears.

"Thanks for the chance, sir," Rand said, squinting. One of the lenses of his glasses had been blown out and he'd filled the pane with a bandage. It was easier than keeping one eye closed all the time. "I won't let you down."

"Another dirty job," Valentine said to the men as they filed up.

Valentine gaped at Glass. His uniform was carefully pressed and he had a barbershop shave. More important, Ford and Chevy had fresh belts for the .50s.

"Where did you find .50 ammo?"

"That little redhead of yours dropped a couple of boxes off after her last scout. She's stronger than she looks."

"Nice of her."

"She said I was to kiss you when the attack started, sir."

"I see you shaved for it."

"Turns out Chevy here was some kind of trained servant for an officer. I started shaving and he got all excited, so I let him do it. Wasn't much of a beard anyway."

"Someone might mistake you for a soldier and shoot at you," Valentine said.

"Just want this war to be over one way or another. If we're hitting the Moondaggers with not much more than guts and bayonets, I thought I might as well look nice, just in case. And it won't end until we quit playing defense and start digging these ticks out of our hide. I caught a little of that speech of yours. I've heard the same before. Hope you mean it."

"I do," Valentine said. "But I'm just one major."

"With a death sentence, I heard. Stuff like that happens to a lot of the good officers. Cocker, who organized Archangel. We lost Seng in Virginia."

"Think there's a reason for that, Glass?"

He shrugged. "Troublesome animals in a herd get culled first. That's all I'm saying. Watch yourself, sir."

Ford and Chevy started blowing air through their cheeks because they were falling behind the other men. Red Dog gamboled, too excited, or stupid, to tell a battle was in progress.

"Take care of them, Glass," Valentine said.

Patel brought up the rear, walking with the help of his cane again. He nodded to Valentine, as though too busy to pause and chat.

Valentine trotted over to him. "I thought I left you safe over on the other side of the river."

"A lieutenant with a full company of Guard walking wounded is helping in Evansville now. They said there was to be a battle. This is my place."

"Not with those knees, Sergeant Major." Valentine said.

"Cool night," Patel said. "Fall's well on the way now. They're always bad when the weather turns."

"Don't go forward with the rest. I want the company on our flank, just in case the Moondaggers launch a counterattack from their positions." Valentine had written the same to Rand, but he'd seen young officers get carried away with excitement before. "Find some good ground where you can hold them up."

"Yes, sir."

"That's all, except be careful."

"When am I not careful?"

"When you're throwing yourself on top of Reapers, for a start," Valentine said.

Patel shrugged, his eternal half smile on.

"Thanks, my friend," Valentine said. "For all you've done on this trip."

"Just doing what I always do," Patel said. "Seeing to it that young soldiers get to be old soldiers."

†

Moytana must have found a good target of opportunity, because Valentine, manning the forward post, heard firing from the riverbank. Well behind the titular Quisling line.

Valentine picked up the field phone.

"General Seng. Repeat. General Seng," he told command.

Valentine made a note of the time: 4:16.

Within a minute the brigade's last few shells came crashing down on the Quisling positions. He wondered if that militia had ever faced artillery fire before. Valentine remembered his first hard barrage on that hill overlooking the Arkansas and Little Rock. It made one frightfully aware of just how hard the enemy was trying to kill you, felt almost like a personal grudge.

Whistles sounded all along the brigade's right as the fire slackened—not by design but by lack of ammunition.

Valentine heard the bark of Ford and Chevy's .50s and watched Javelin go forward, Bears in the lead, the dirt and dust of the artillery falling on them like snow as three hard-fighting wedges pierced the militia positions.

He felt for the Quislings. Indiana stockholders who wanted more land for their herds, men who wanted to own a trucking company, boys told by their Church officiates that militia service was the path to security for their parents and siblings, a good mark for the family record. Rousted out of their beds, told to put on uniforms they wore six weeks a year, picking up unwieldy bolt-action rifles fit more for intimidating a mob than turning back Gamecock's raging Bears.

The odds and ends of the Kentucky Alliance urged their mobile fortifications into action. Just the sight of charging worms might be enough to send most of the Quislings running: They resembled a yellow avalanche moving uncannily uphill.

Valentine saw Tikka in their midst, expertly hanging off the side of her mount and using her saddle as a rifle rest. Their affair still sparked and sputtered along, though they were both too dirty, tired, and hungry to do much but quickly rut and depart like wary rabbits in fox country. Valentine wasn't sure he could even put a name to what they had, but it was something as natural as the fall Kentucky rain, and just as cleansing.

He thought of the artistic swell of her buttocks. Mad thought, with shells and bullets flying in at least three directions.

Bloom's command car bounced forward.

The Moondagger batteries joined the fray, but only a few shells fell, still heavies, hard to adjust to meet a fast-moving attack. Hopefully the tubes would be in the brigade's hands within a few hours. In the hands of trained spotters, they'd be handy against river traffic, especially if they had some white phosphorous shells that could be set to air burst.

The first reports began to come back to headquarters. The militia had simply dissolved into little groups of men lying on their faces, spread-eagle in surrender. There were reports of the Moondaggers doing as much damage to the Quisling militia as Javelin. The Wolves were finding trails blocked with bodies, shot by their alleged allies as they retreated.

It was Glass' kind of operation. No heroism required.

Valentine looked around the forward command post.

"That's a nice-looking province there," he said, pointing to some ground occupied by his company where they had a good view of the Moondagger positions. "Let's move forward. Signals, get ready to lay a new line. We're shifting operations forward."

He found Rand looking a little frazzled. "How's your first battle going?"

"It's a little more exciting than I'd like, sir," Rand said.

A wailing cry broke out from a shallow between the small hill of the observation post and the beginnings of Kentucky's rollers in the distance. A wave of Moondaggers poured up in a counterattack from the center. The phrase "gleam of bayonets" crossed Valentine's mental transom. The warrior poets were right—it is an unsettling sight when they're pointed at you.

Glass' machine guns cut into them but the Moondaggers ignored their losses, firing back wildly. They fell onto the outer edges of his platoon, fighting with curved dagger and rifle butt as grenades killed friend and foe alike. Bee was suddenly beside him, emptying her shotguns to deadly effect.

Then they were at the edge of the command post. Bee grabbed two bayoneted rifles thrust at her—Valentine heard her grunt as she seized the hot barrels—and poked the bearded men back, knocking them down like an angry mother snatching up dangerous toys. She reversed one rifle to have the long bayonet ready and used the other as a club to knock Moondaggers off their feet, sticking them like beetles on Styrofoam.

Rand fell without a cry, a bullet not caring that it cavitated one of the best brains Valentine had ever met.

Valentine, grenades bracketing him and vaguely bothered by the stickiness of Rand's blood on his face, did his best to cover Bee and Glass' gunners with his submachine gun. He reloaded, and only after emptying the gun again did he notice that he'd just wasted a full magazine of Quickwood bullets. Stupid!

Then a company of Guard engineers came forward, firing their light carbines, and it was over. Wounded Moondaggers, still lashing at their enemies with their knives, were shot and shot again until they quit crawling.

Bee poked at a loose flap of skin ragged from a bullet hole in her thigh like a child investigating a tick.

Valentine told Bee to put Rand in the shade of a beat-up medical pickup and get her wounds looked at, had Patel pull the company back together and see about ammunition supply, and then sent a bare report of the repulsed counterattack back to Bloom.

Javelin Headquarters was on the move to the old Moondagger positions.

"Sir, radio report coming in from the Wolves," Preville relayed. "The Moondaggers are running. Running! They're quitting and running hard up the highway to Bowling Green. Their legworm supports are going with them."

A lieutenant checked their large-scale map. "They keep heading down that highway, and they'll be getting into Mammoth country."

"Wonder what the Mammoth thought about the little catechism from those men the 'Daggers sliced up," Valentine said. "I wouldn't want to have my truck break down there."

"Wouldn't surprise me if they built a wooden cage or two," Patel said. "It's the end for them."

"Not the end," Valentine said. "Not even the beginning of the end." As Churchill might have put it, it was just the end of the beginning.

With the Moondaggers broken across Kentucky and perhaps beaten at last, a fatal crack in the foundation of the Kurian Order had been opened. Like any fault in a structure's foundation, it might not be easily seen or the danger recognized at first. But that first crack would allow more to appear, branching out until the whole edifice crumbled.

Even such an awful pyramid as Valentine had spoken of back at Rally Base could be undermined and brought down, in time.

Valentine hoped he'd live to see the fall.